About the Authors

Cara Colter shares [...]
Columbia, Canada, w[...]
one small Pomeraniar[...]
to hear from readers, a[...]
and contact her throug[...]

Susan Meier spent most of her twenties thinking she was a job-hopper – until she began to write and realised everything that had come before was only research! One of eleven children, with twenty-four nieces and nephews and three kids of her own, Susan lives in Western Pennsylvania with her wonderful husband, Mike, her children, and two over-fed, well-cuddled cats, Sophie and Fluffy. You can visit Susan's website at www.susanmeier.com

Born and raised in a small Vancouver Island town, **Laurel Greer** picked up her pen to write Julie Garwood fanfiction during secondary school English class. She hasn't put it down since. Ever committed to the proper placement of the Canadian 'eh,' she loves to write books with snapping sexual tension and second chances. She lives outside Vancouver with her law-talking husband and two daughters. At least half her diet is made up of tea. Find her at www.laurelgreer.com

Unexpected Surprises

Unexpected Surprises:
Secrets and Surprises

CARA COLTER

SUSAN MEIER

LAUREL GREER

MILLS & BOON

First Published in Great Britain 2022
By Mills & Boon, an imprint of HarperCollins*Publishers,* Ltd
1 London Bridge Street, London, SE1 9GF

www.harpercollins.co.uk

HarperCollins*Publishers*
1st Floor, Watermarque Building,
Ringsend Road, Dublin 4, Ireland

ISBN: 978-0-263-30437-4

MIX
Paper from
responsible sources
FSC **C007454**
FSC
www.fsc.org

THE PREGNANCY SECRET

CARA COLTER

To my friend and mentor, Joan Fitzpatrick, whose wisdom and compassion have guided and inspired me for three decades.

CHAPTER ONE

A BLOCK AWAY from a destination he had no desire to reach, it pierced Kade Brennan's distracted mind that something was wrong.

Very wrong.

There were no sirens, but the strobes of the blue and red bar lights on top of half a dozen police cruisers were pulsing strenuously. It was jarringly at odds with the crystal clear morning light that filtered, a suffused lime green, through the unfurling spring leaves of the huge cottonwoods that lined the shores of the Bow River.

Now, above the sounds of a river bloated with spring runoff, above the sounds of the cheerful chirping of birds, above the sounds of the morning rush of traffic, Kade could hear the distinctive static of emergency frequency radios. A robotic female voice was calling a code he did not understand. It looked as if there was an ambulance in that cluster of emergency vehicles.

Kade broke into a run, dodging traffic as he cut across the early-morning crush of cars on Memorial Drive to the residential street on the other side.

It was one of those postcard-pretty Calgary blocks that looked as if nothing bad could ever happen on it. It was an older neighborhood of arts and crafts–style houses, many of them now turned into thriving cottage businesses. Nestled under the huge canopies of mature trees, Kade noted, were an art-supply store, an organic bakery, an antiques shop and a shoe store.

This neighborhood was made even more desirable by the fact it was connected to downtown Calgary by the Peace Bridge, a pedestrian-only walkway over the river that Kade had just crossed.

Except at this moment the postcard-pretty street that looked as if nothing bad could ever happen on it was completely choked with police cars. People walking to work had stopped and were milling about.

Kade, shouldering through them, caught bits of conversation.

"What happened?"

"No idea, but from the police presence, it must be bad."

"A murder, maybe?" The speaker could not hide the little treble of excitement at having his morning walk to work interrupted in such a thrilling fashion.

Kade shot him a dark look and shoved his way, with even more urgency, to the front of the milling crowd, scanning the addresses on the cottagey houses and businesses until he found the right one. He moved toward it.

"Sir?" A uniformed man was suddenly in front of him, blocking his path. "You can't go any farther."

Kade ignored him, and found a hand on his arm.

Kade shook off the hand impatiently. "I'm looking for my wife." Technically, that was true. For a little while longer anyway.

"Kade," Jessica had said last night over the phone, "we need to discuss the divorce." He hadn't seen her for more than a year. She'd given him the address on this street, and he'd walked over from his downtown condo, annoyed at what his reluctance about meeting her was saying about him.

All this was certainly way too complicated to try to explain to the fresh-faced young policeman blocking his way.

"Her name is Jessica Brennan." Kade saw, immediately, in the young policeman's face that somehow all these police cars had something to do with her.

No, something in him screamed silently, a wolf howl of pure pain, *no*.

It was exactly the same silent scream he had stifled inside himself when he'd heard the word *divorce*. What did it mean, he'd asked himself as he hung up his phone, that she wanted the divorce finalized?

Last night, lying awake, Kade had convinced himself that it could only be good for both of them to move on.

But from his reaction to this, to the fact all these police cars had something to do with her, he knew the lie he had told himself—that he didn't care—was monstrous in proportion.

"She's okay, I think. There's been a break-in. I understand she was injured, but it's non-life-threatening."

Jessica injured in a break-in? Kade barely registered the non-life-threatening part. He felt a surge of helpless fury.

"She's okay," the young cop repeated. "Go that way."

It was upsetting to Kade that his momentary panic and rage had shown in his face, made him an open book to the cop, who had read his distress and tried to reassure.

He took a second to school himself so that he would not be as transparent to Jessica. He looked up the walk he was being directed to. Twin white lilacs in full and fragrant bloom guarded each side of a trellised gate. The house beyond the gate was the house Jessica had always wanted.

It was a cute character cottage, pale green, like the fresh colors of spring all around it. But it wasn't her home. A sign hung over the shadowed shelter of an inviting porch.

Baby Boomer, and in smaller letters, Your Place for All Things Baby.

Jessica had given him only the house number. She hadn't said a word about *that*.

And he knew exactly why. Because, for a moment, that familiar anger was there, overriding even the knife of panic that had begun to ease when the young cop had said she was okay. *Hell's bells, did she never give up?*

Or was the anger because the house, her new business and that phone call last night were evidence that she was ready to move on?

It was not as if, Kade told himself sternly, he wasn't ready to move on. In fact, he already had. He was just completely satisfied with the way things were. His company, Oilfield Supplies, had reached dizzying heights over the past year. Without the complication of a troubled relationship, he had been able to focus his attention intensely on business. The payoffs had been huge. He was a man who enjoyed success. Divorce did not fit with his picture of himself.

Divorce.

It was going to force him to face his own failure instead of ignore it. Or maybe not. Maybe these days you just signed a piece of paper and it was done. Over.

Could something like that ever be over? Not really.

He knew that from trying to bury himself in work for the past year.

If it was over, why did he still wear his ring? He had talked himself into believing it was to protect himself from the interest of the many women he encountered. Not personally. He had no personal life. But professionally he met beautiful, sophisticated, *interested* women every day. He did not need those kinds of complications.

He was aware, suddenly, he did not want Jessica to see he was still wearing that ring that bound him to her, so he took it off and slipped it in his pocket.

Taking a deep, fortifying breath, a warrior needing the opponent—when had Jessica become the opponent?—not to know he had a single doubt or fear, Kade took the wide steps, freshly painted the color of rich dairy cream, two at a time.

In startling and violent contrast to the sweet charm of the house, the glass had been smashed out of the squares of paned glass in the door. The door hung open, the catch that should have held it closed dangling uselessly.

Inside that door Kade skidded to a halt, aware of glass crackling under his feet. His eyes adjusted to the dimness as he burst out of the bright morning light. He had entered into a world more terrifying to him than an inhabited bear den.

The space was terrifying because of what was in it. It was the world he and Jessica had tried so hard to have and could not. It was a world of softness and light and dreamy hopes.

The stacks of tiny baby things made other memories crowd around Kade, of crying, and arguing, and a desperate sense of having come up against something he could not make right. Ever.

He sucked in another warrior's breath. There was a cluster of people across the room. He caught a glimpse of wheat-colored hair at the center of it and forced himself not to bolt over there.

He would not let her see what this—her injury, this building full of baby things—did to him.

Unfortunately, if he was not quite ready to see her, he had to take a moment to gather himself, and that forced him to look around.

The interior dividing walls within the house had been torn down to make one large room. What remained for walls were painted a shade of pale green one muted tone removed from that of the exterior of the house. The large space was connected by the expanse of old hardwood, rich with patina, and yet rugs and bookcases had been used to artfully divide the open area into four spaces.

Each was unique, and each so obviously represented a nursery.

One was a fantasy in pink: the crib was all done in pink flowered bedding, with pink-striped sheets and a fluffy pink elephant sprawled at the center. A polka-dot pink dress that looked like doll clothes was laid out on a change table. The letters *g-i-r-l* were suspended by invisible threads from the ceiling. A rocking chair, with pillows that matched the bedding, sat at right angles to the crib.

The next space was a composition in shades of pale blue. The crib and its bedding, again, were the main focus, but the eye was drawn to the vignette of boyish things that surrounded it. There were toy trains and tractors and trucks displayed on the shelves of a bookcase. Miniature overalls and an equally miniature ball cap hung on an antique coatrack beside it. A pair of impossibly small work boots hung from their laces off the same rack.

Next was one all done in lacy white, like a wedding dress, a basket on the floor overflowing with white stuffies: lambs and polar bears and little white dogs. The final display had two cribs, implying twins, and a shade of yellow as pale as baby duck down repeated in the bedding and lamp shades and teeny outfits.

Kade stood, sucking air into his chest, taking it all in and fighting the unmanly desire to cut and run.

How could Jessica do this? Work every day with the thing that had caused her, and him—and them—such unbelievable heartache? He felt all that anger with Jessica solidifying inside his chest. *Now* he was ready to face her.

He narrowed his eyes and looked to the cluster of people. They were at the very back of the old house, behind a counter with an old-fashioned cash register perched on it. Feeling as if his masculinity and size could damage the spaces, he passed through them quickly, holding his breath and being careful not to touch anything. Kade edged his way to the back of the room, inserting a firmness into his step that he did not feel.

It was unnecessary, because she didn't open her eyes as Kade arrived at the back of the store. Jessica was strapped to a wheeled gurney. Her eyes were tightly shut. A uniformed medic was leaning over her, splinting her right arm below her shoved-up sleeve. Two police officers, a man and a woman, stood by, notepads out.

Seeing Jessica would have been, at any time, like taking a punch to the stomach. But seeing her like this was unbearable.

It reminded him of the hardest lesson his marriage

had taught him: even though it was his deepest desire, he had been unable to protect her.

Studying her now, without her awareness, Kade could see subtle changes in her. She looked oddly grown-up in a buttoned-up white blouse and a gray pencil skirt. Her slender feet were encased in a pair of very practical and very plain flat pumps. She looked professional, and yet oddly dowdy, like that British nanny on television. Her look, if it could be called that, filled him with a certain sense of relief.

Jessica was obviously not out to capture a man.

But she looked so serious, not that he expected her to be upbeat, given the circumstances. She looked every inch the pragmatic businesswoman she had evidently become, rather than the artist she had always been. He was pretty sure the only day he'd ever seen Jessica out of jeans was the day they'd gotten married.

Her hair was the same color, untouched by dye, wheat ripening in a field, but had been bobbed off short, in a way that made her features seem elegant and chiseled and mature rather than gamine and friendly and girlish. Or maybe it was because she had lost weight that her features, especially her cheekbones, seemed to be in such sharp relief. She had on not a drop of makeup. Again, Kade felt a completely unwanted niggle of relief. She was obviously not making the least effort to play up her natural beauty.

Despite the fact she looked both the same and different, despite the fact she looked pale and bruised and despite the fact she was dressed in a way that suggested she did not like drawing attention to herself, Jessica did what she had always done, even though he tried to steel himself against reacting to her.

From the first moment he had seen her laughter-filled face on campus, he had been captivated. She had been sitting with friends at an outdoor picnic area. She had looked his way just as he was crossing a huge expanse of lawn, late for class.

His heart had done then exactly what it did now. It had stood still. And he had never made that class. Instead, he had crossed the lawn to her and to his destiny.

Jessica—then Clark—hadn't been beautiful in the traditional way. A little powder had not done anything to hide her freckles, which had already been darkening from the sun. Her glossy hair, sun streaked, had been spilling out of a clip at the back of her head. She'd been supercasual in a pink T-shirt and jean shorts with frayed cuffs. Her toenails had been painted to match her shirt.

But it was her eyes that had captivated him: as green as a leprechaun's and sparkling with just as much mischief. She had, if he recalled correctly, and he was sure he was, been wearing just a hint of makeup that day, shadow around her eyes that made them the deep, inviting green of a mountain pond. Her smile had been so compelling, warm, engaging, full of energy, infused with a force of life.

But two years of marriage had stripped her of all of that effervescent joy. And he could see, from the downturned line around her mouth, it had not returned. Kade welcomed the iciness he felt settle around his heart.

He had not been enough for her.

Still, even with that thought like an acid inside him, he could not stop himself from moving closer to her.

He was shocked that he wanted to kiss her forehead, to brush the hair back from the smoothness of her brow. Instead, he laid his palm over her slender forearm, so aware his hand could encircle it completely. He saw that she was no longer wearing her rings.

"Are you okay?" The hardness Kade inserted in his voice was deliberate. There was no sense anyone knowing the panic he had felt, just for a moment, when he had thought of a world without Jessica. Especially not Jessica herself.

Jessica's eyes flew open. They were huge and familiar pools of liquid green, surrounded by lashes so thick they looked as if they had been rolled in chocolate cake batter. She had always had the most gorgeous eyes, and even her understated look now could not hide that. Unbidden, he thought of Jessica's eyes fastened on him, as she had walked down the aisle toward him… He shook off the memory, annoyed with himself, annoyed by how quickly he had gone *there*.

Now her beautiful eyes had the shadows of sorrow mixed with their light. Still, for one unguarded moment, the look in her eyes when she saw it was him made Kade wish he was the man she had thought he was. For one unguarded moment, he wished he was a man who had an ounce of hope left in him.

CHAPTER TWO

WARINESS TOOK THE place of what had flared so briefly in Jessica's eyes when she had seen it was him, Kade. A guard equal to the one he knew to be in his own gaze went up in hers.

"What are you doing here?" Jessica asked him, her brow knit downward.

What was he doing here? She had asked him to come.

"Did she hit her head?" Kade asked the ambulance attendant.

Jessica's frown deepened. "No, I did not hit my head."

"Possibly," the medic said.

"What are you doing here?" Jessica demanded again. It was a tone he remembered too well, the faintest anger hissing below the surface of her words, like a snake waiting to strike.

"You asked me to come," Kade reminded her. "To discuss—" He looked at the crowd around them, and could not bring himself to finish the sentence.

"Oh!" She looked contrite. "Now I remember. We were meeting to discuss…" Her voice drifted away, and then she sighed. "Sorry, Kade, I truly forgot you were coming." Apparently she hadn't lain awake last night contemplating the *d-i-v-o-r-c-e*.

"It's been a crazy morning," she said, as if it needed clarification.

"So I can see," he said. Jessica. Master of the understatement.

"Who are you?" the woman police officer asked.

"I'm her husband." Well, *technically*, he still was.

Kade was only inches from Jessica, but he was so aware that the small physical distance between them was nothing compared with the emotional one. It could not be crossed. That was what hissed right below the surface of her voice. There was a minefield of memory between them, and to try to negotiate it felt as if it would be risking having them both being blown to smithereens.

"I think her arm is fractured or broken," the medic said to Kade, and then returned his attention to Jessica. "We're going to transport you. They'll do X-rays at the hospital. I'm going to call ahead so they'll be ready for you in the emergency department."

"Which hospital?" Kade asked.

"You don't need to come," Jessica said, and there was *that* tone again, her apology apparently forgotten. She glared at Kade in warning when he frowned at her.

She was right. He did not *need* to go with her. And he could not have stopped himself if he tried.

"Nonetheless," he said, "I'd be more at ease making sure you were okay."

"No."

Kade knew that tone: she had made up her mind and there would be no getting her to change it.

No matter how stupidly unreasonable she was being.

"I thought he was your husband," the woman police officer said, confused.

"You don't need to come to the hospital," Jessica said.

She tried to fold her arms over her chest. The splint on her right arm made it awkward enough that after three attempts she gave up. She glared at her arm accusingly, and when that brought her no relief, she switched her glare to him.

To what he could tell was her chagrin, he accomplished what she had not been able to. He folded his arms firmly over his chest.

Battle stations.

What did this mean that he was insisting on accompanying Jessica to the hospital? That he was accepting responsibility for her?

Had he ever stopped feeling responsible for her?

"I thought he was your husband," the police officer said again.

"I am," Kade said, and heard the same firmness in his voice as that day that felt as if it was so long ago when he had said, "I do."

Jessica felt a shiver travel up and down her spine.

Her husband.

She watched Kade standing there, so close she could smell the familiar heady scent of him, his arms folded firmly over the deepness of that chest. He looked grim and formidable when he took that stance.

And even with that intimidating scowl drawing his dark brows down and pulling the edges of his mouth? Kade was the most magnificently made man Jessica had ever encountered. And she was pretty sure the female police officer wasn't immune to that fact, either.

Jessica had never tired of looking at him, not even when their relationship had become so troubled. Sometimes it had made her anger even more complicated that she still liked to look at him when he was so aggravating!

But gazing at him now, she felt resignation. This morning Kade had on a beautifully cut summer suit that she was certain was custom made. With it he had on a plain white shirt, possibly Egyptian cotton, and a subdued, expertly knotted tie, the slight luster of it screaming both silk and expense.

The ensemble made him look every inch the president and CEO of one of Calgary's most successful companies. Despite a rather mundane name, Oilfield Supplies did just that. It supplied the frantic oilfield activity of Alberta and beyond. With Kade's work ethic, ambition and smarts, the company's rise, in the past few years, had been mercurial.

And yet there was nothing soft looking about the man. There was none of the slender build or office pallor of a desk worker about him. He had learned his business from the bottom up, working on rigs to put himself through university. Despite the beautiful clothing, that rugged toughness was still in the air around him. Kade Brennan, with those long legs and those broad shoulders, and that deep chest, radiated pure power.

He had mink-dark hair. It managed, somehow, to look faintly unruly, no matter how short he cut it. And right now, that was very short.

He was clean shaven—Jessica had never known him not to be—and the close shave showed off the masculine perfection of his face: great skin, high cheekbones, straight nose, full lips, faintly jutting chin.

And his damn eyes, sexy and smoldering, were the deep sapphire of the ocean water. It was a color she had seen replicated only once, off the southernmost tip of the Big Island of Hawaii, where they had gone for their honeymoon.

But well before she'd had that reference point, from practically the moment she had met him, Jessica had spent an inordinate amount of time dreaming what their baby would look like. Would it have his eyes or hers, or some incredible combination of both?

The knife edge of that familiar pain was worse than the pain that throbbed along the length of her arm, despite the ice packs splinted in with her limb that were supposed to be giving her relief from pain.

Her husband.

She could feel her heart begin a familiar and hard tattoo at all that had once meant, and at all she knew about this man, the delicious intimacies that only a wife could know.

That he had ticklish toes, and loved the smell of lemons, and that if you kissed that little groove behind his ear, he was putty—

Jessica made herself stop, annoyed that she had gone *there* so swiftly. With everything between them, how was it she could feel this when she saw him? As if she had made the slow, chugging climb up the roller coaster and was now poised at the very summit, waiting to plunge down?

With everything between them, it felt like a betrayal of herself that she could feel such a deep and abiding hunger for the familiar feeling of his arms around her, for the scrape of his cheek across her own, for his breath in her ear, for the gentle savagery of his lips claiming her lips and his body claiming her body.

Her husband.

She felt weak. Where was her newfound sense of herself when she needed it most? Where was her fledgling self-respect? Where was her feeling that her life was working, and that she could have dreams she had set aside when Kade had walked away from her?

Jessica had discovered she could be responsible for her own dreams. It was really much easier without the complications of a man! In fact, she had decided the things she was dreaming would be so much more attainable without a man, especially one like him, who was just a little too sure that he knew the right answers for everybody.

Jessica was certain Kade would not approve of the secret she held inside herself. It was a secret that gave her pure joy, just as once an ultrasound picture tucked in a pocket close to her heart had. She had made a decision to adopt a baby.

It was at the very initial stages, little more than a thought, but she wanted things between her and Kade finalized before she even started the application process. She reminded herself that she needed to be strong for this meeting with Kade, and she despised the unexpected weakness of desire.

She'd rehearsed for a week before she'd called him, striving for just the right all-business tone of voice, planning this morning's meeting so carefully…

Of course, being caught in the middle of a breaking and entering had not been part of her plan! She could not believe, in all the chaos, she had totally forgotten he would be coming.

That was it. That explained the way she was feeling right now. She'd just had quite the shock. The pain in her arm was throbbing mercilessly, and despite denying it to the medic, it was possible she'd hit her head in the scuffle. Maybe, just maybe, a tiny bit of weakness in the department of her husband was acceptable.

Except right now she needed to be strong around him, not weak!

She stole another look at him. There was no missing how ill at ease the store made him. Something in his closed expression even suggested anger. At that realization, that he was angry, something in her hardened. She had known he might react like this when she'd invited him here.

And she had told herself firmly that it was a test she needed to pass. Divorcing Kade, not just on paper, but with her heart, would involve not caring what he liked or didn't like about her choices.

Her lawyer was absolutely right. It was time to tie up some loose ends in her life. And the lawyer was not even aware of *all* the reasons why it had become so important. Her lawyer knew only about her thriving business. Her decision to adopt was a secret, for now.

But it was a secret that required her to acknowledge that Kade Brennan, the husband she had been separated from for more than a year, was one gigantic loose end!

"What happened here?" Kade asked, but typical Kade, he wasn't asking. He was demanding, ready to take charge.

And she was never going to admit what a relief it would be to let him. "Really, Kade, it's none of your business."

The female officer, in particular, looked taken aback at her tone. "I thought he was your husband," she said again, almost plaintively.

"We're nearly divorced," Jessica explained, trying for the cavalier note of a career woman who didn't care, but she had to physically brace herself from flinching from the word.

Divorced.

She'd rehearsed that word, too, trying to take the bitter edge out of it, the sense of loss and finality and failure.

"Oh." If she was not mistaken, Officer—Jessica squinted at her name tag—Kelly took to that information like a starving hound scenting a bone.

"What happened here?" Kade asked again.

Jessica glared at him. To her relief, the medic announced they were ready to go, and she was wheeled out past Kade before having to give in to his demand for answers. Behind her, to her annoyance, she could hear the police officer filling him in on what had happened. She glanced back to see the female officer blinking helpfully at Kade and checking her notes.

"She came in to do paperwork this morning, six o'clock. Someone broke in around seven thirty."

"Don't come to the hospital," Jessica called over her shoulder, feeling a childish desire to get in the last shot. "I don't need you."

She glanced back one more time just as they crossed through her doorway to outside, where throngs of people seemed to be gathered in front of her house. But she didn't really even notice. What she noticed was that her arrow had hit home.

Kade looked momentarily stricken by her words.

That she didn't need him.

And instead of feeling happy that she had drawn blood, she felt sick about it, and some little demon inside her had to try to repair it, and let him know he was needed after all.

"Actually, Kade, can you find a way to secure everything? Please?"

Really, after her remark that she didn't need him, he should tell her to go get stuffed. But he didn't.

"And if you could put up a closed-for-the-day sign over that broken window I'd be most appreciative."

He snorted, but didn't say no.

"I can't just leave things. The door is broken. He could come back. Anybody could come in and just start helping themselves to everything in here."

All her hopes and dreams. It was a strange twist that she was being forced to ask Kade to rescue them.

"Never mind," Jessica said, appalled that she had even asked him. "I'll call someone."

She didn't need him. She didn't! Why was she giving him this mixed message: "I need you. I don't need you." She had the stunning realization she was not as clear of her soon-to-be ex-husband as she thought she was!

"I'll look after it," he said.

She should have protested harder, but there was no denying what a relief it was to have Kade Brennan, her husband for a little while longer, say that he would look after things.

CHAPTER THREE

JESSICA WAS WHEELED out to the ambulance, and Kade prowled through her shop looking for items to repair her door. Finally, in a back drawer in a tiny kitchen area he found a hammer and regarded it thoughtfully.

"This isn't really a hammer," he muttered to himself. "It's more like a toy, a prop for one of her fake nurseries."

In a dank cellar, he found some old boards. Thankfully, they had nails in them that he could pull and reuse. Why did women never have the essentials? Nails, screwdrivers, hammers, duct tape?

He boarded up the broken front door and found a square of thick wood to write a few words on.

He had to nail it up over the broken window because of the lack of duct tape. A determined thief could still get in, but the repair, though not pretty, actually looked quite a bit more secure than her old door with its paned glass.

He surveyed his work briefly, and recognized it as temporary but passable. Then he called his personal assistant, Patty, to tell her he would be very late today, if he made it in at all. "I need you to find me a simple surveillance system. I think there's a kind that alerts to your phone. And then could you find a handyman? I need a door fixed, a window replaced and that surveillance system installed. Have him call me for the details.

"And also if you could have my car dropped at Holy Cross Hospital? Whoever brings it can just give me a call when they get there, I'll meet them for keys." He listened for a moment. "No, everything is fine. No need for concern."

Kade walked out to Memorial Drive and was able to flag a cab to take him to the hospital.

He found Jessica in a wheelchair, in a waiting room in the X-ray department.

"How are you doing?"

It was obvious she was not doing well. Her face was pale, and she looked as if she was going to cry.

He could not handle Jessica crying. There was nothing he hated more than the helplessness that made him feel. To his detriment, he had not reacted well to her tears in the past.

He felt ashamed of the fact that she felt it necessary to suck in a deep, steadying breath before she spoke to him.

"They've done an X-ray. I'm just waiting for the doctor. It is broken. I'm not sure if they can set it, or if it will need surgery." She looked perilously close to tears.

Kade fought an urge to wrap his arms around her and let her cry. But he'd never been good with tears, and it felt way too late now to try to be a sensitive guy. It would require him to be a way better and braver man than he knew how to be.

She knew his weaknesses, because she set her shoulders and tilted her chin. "You didn't have to come."

He shrugged. "Your store is secure," he told her. "I put up a sign."

The struggle—whether to be gracious or belligerent—

was evident in her eyes. Graciousness won, as he had known it would. "Thank you. What did it say?"

"Baby bummer, temporarily closed due to break-in."

A reluctant smile tickled her lips, and then she surrendered and laughed. "That's pretty good. Even though it's a major bummer, not a baby one."

Kade was pretty pleased with himself that he had made her laugh instead of cry.

"It could have been a much more major bummer than it was," he said sternly. "Tell me what happened."

Jessica couldn't help but shiver at the faintly dangerous note in Kade's voice. She could not be intimidated by it!

"Isn't it fairly obvious what happened?" she asked coolly. "I was doing some paperwork, and there was a break-in."

"But he came through the front door."

"So?"

"Is there a back door?" Kade asked. That something dangerous deepened in his tone.

"Well, yes, but we just surprised each other. Thankfully, I called 911 as soon as I heard the glass break."

"Don't you think you could have run out the back door and called 911 from safety?"

Jessica remembered what she didn't like about Kade. Besides everything. She needed a good cry right now and she was sucking it back rather than risk his disapproval. On top of that, he was a big man at work. It made him think he knew the answers to everything.

Which was why she didn't even want him to know about adoption. He was certain to have an opinion about that that she would not be eager to hear.

"Hindsight is always twenty-twenty," she informed him snootily.

"How did you end up hurt?" Kade asked.

Jessica squirmed a bit.

"Um, we scuffled," she admitted. "I fell."

"You scuffled?" Kade asked, incredulous. "You *scuffled* with a burglar? I would have thought it was hard to scuffle while running for the back door."

"I was not going to run away," she said.

"That is nothing to be proud of."

"Yes," she said, "it is. Don't you dare presume to tell me what to be proud of."

From their shared laughter over the bummers of life just moments ago to this. It was just like the final weeks of their marriage: arguments lurked everywhere.

"Why are you proud of it?" he asked, that dangerous something still deepening in his tone, that muscle jerking along the line of his jaw that meant he was *really* annoyed.

"I'm proud I took on that scrawny thief," Jessica said, her voice low, but gaining power. "I lost my mother when I was twelve. I've lost two babies to miscarriage."

And she had lost Kade, not that she was going to mention that. In some ways the loss of him had been the worst of all. The other losses had been irrevocable, but Kade was still there, just not there for her.

"Sorry?" he said, reeling back slightly from her as if she had hit him with something. "What does that have to do with this?"

"I am not losing anything else," she said, and could hear the tautness in her own voice. "Not one more thing."

He stared at her, and she took a deep breath and continued.

"You listen to me, Kade Brennan. I am not surrendering to life anymore. I am not going to be the hapless victim. I am making the rules, and I am making my own life happen."

Kade was shocked into silence, so she went on, her tone low. "So if that means scuffling with someone who was trying to take one more thing from me, then so be it."

"Oh, boy," he said, his voice low and pained. "That's not even sensible."

"I don't care what you think is sensible," she said with stubborn pride.

Though, she did plan to be more sensible soon. Naturally, there would be no more scuffling once she had adopted a baby. She would think things all the way through then. She would be the model of responsible behavior.

She hoped there were no questions about how one would handle a break-in on the adoption application.

"So you weren't running for the back door," he deduced, regaining himself. "Not even close."

"Nope." The new Jessica refused to be intimidated. She met his gaze with determination. She was not going to be cowed by Kade. She was not one of his employees. She was nearly not even his wife. In a little while, they would practically be strangers.

At the thought, a little unexpected grayness swirled inside her—she was willing to bet that was a result of her injury, a bit of shock—but she fought it off bravely.

"I was not letting him get away," Jessica said. "The police were coming."

For a moment he was stunned speechless again. He clenched that muscle in his jaw tighter. She remembered she hated that about him, too: the jaw clenching.

His voice rarely rose in anger, but that muscle, leaping along the hard line of his jaw, was a dead giveaway that he was *really* irritated about something.

"Are you telling me—" Kade's voice was low and dangerous "—that you not only scuffled with the burglar, but you tried to detain him?"

"He was a shrimp," Jessica said defiantly.

"In case you haven't looked in the mirror recently, so are you. And he could have had a knife! Or a gun!" So much for his voice rarely being raised in anger.

"I wasn't going to stand by and let him steal from me!" At the look on Kade's face, she backed down marginally. "Okay, so maybe I didn't think it all the way through." Something that was definitely going to have to change once she embraced motherhood.

"Maybe?"

She was not sure why she felt driven to defend herself, even when she knew Kade was right and she was wrong. Not just defend herself, but goad him a little bit.

"Break-ins started on this block a few nights ago. No one can sleep at night. We all go down there and check our businesses. That business is everything to me now. It's my whole life."

He heard the unspoken, she was sure. That the business had replaced him as her whole life.

The jaw muscle was rippling beneath the line of his skin. She watched it, fascinated despite herself. He was *really* angry.

"You've been going down there in the middle of the night to check your business?"

It didn't seem nearly as clever now with Kade glaring at her.

"Yes, I have," she said, refusing to back down. "And I'll probably do it again tonight, since he got away."

Well, actually, she probably wouldn't, but there was no sense Kade thinking he could order her around, could control her with even a hint of his disapproval. Those days were over.

"You are not going down there tonight," Kade said. "For God's sake, Jessica, haven't you ever heard of security cameras?"

"Of course I've thought of security cameras. And security companies. But the options are many and the selection is huge," she said. "I've been trying to figure out what is best for me and my budget. Not that that is any of your business. And you don't have any say in how I decide to handle it. None whatsoever. You and I only have one thing left to discuss. And that is our divorce."

And unbidden, the thought blasted through her that *that* was a major bummer.

And the doctor, a lovely young woman, chose that moment to come out, X-rays in hand, and say, "Mr. and Mrs. Brennan?"

Mr. and Mrs. Brennan. That should not fill her with longing! That should not make Jessica wonder if there would ever be another Mrs. Brennan taking her place.

It was over. Their brief marriage was over. They were getting divorced. Kade's life was no longer any of her business, just as hers was no longer any of his.

She would probably change her name back to Clark. She could be Ms. Clark instead of Mrs. Brennan. The baby would be a Clark.

She wasn't thinking about a first name. She knew better than that. Or at least she should know better than that. A memory knifed through her: Kade and her poring over the baby-name books. Deciding on Lewis for a boy and Amelia for a girl.

And then the first miscarriage. And somehow, she could see now, in retrospect, what she had not seen then. From the moment Kade had asked her not to name that little lost baby, a crack had appeared between them.

No, she was determined to enjoy the success of her baby nursery design business and her new storefront as a means to an end. She could have it all.

She could fill her life with the thrill of obtaining those adorable outfits no other store would carry, those one-of-a-kind over-the-crib mobiles, those perfect lamb-soft cuddly teddy bears that everyone wanted and no one could find.

And someday, maybe sooner than later, the outfits would be for her own baby. She would design a nursery for her own baby.

"Don't," he'd whispered when she had started painting the walls of their spare room a pale shade of lavender the second time. "Please don't."

But now she didn't need his approval. She could do it all her way. She could finally, finally be happy. All the pieces were in place.

Weren't they? If they were, why did Jessica feel a sudden desire to weep? It was that crack on her head. It was the throbbing in her arm. It was her day gone so terribly wrong, nothing according to her plan.

"Mr. and Mrs. Brennan?" the doctor asked, again, baffled by the lack of response.

"Yes," Kade said.

"No," Jessica said at the very same time.

He looked stubborn, a look Jessica remembered well.

She didn't think she should admit a sudden urge to kill him in front of the doctor, so she shrugged. "We're nearly divorced," she informed the doctor. "He was just leaving."

Kade gave her a look, and then got to his feet and prowled around the small waiting area.

"Well, if you could come with me."

Jessica stood up from the wheelchair to follow the doctor. She wobbled. Kade was instantly at her side.

"Sit down," he snapped.

Really, she should not tolerate that tone of voice from him, that tendency to bossiness. But the sudden wooziness she felt left her with no choice.

Kade pushed her down the hallway with the doctor, and they entered a small examining room. The doctor put the X-rays up on a light board.

"It's not a complicated break," she said, showing them with the tip of her pen. "It's what we call a complete fracture. I'm going to set it and cast it. I think you'll be in the cast for about four weeks and then require some therapy after to get full mobility back."

Four weeks in a cast? But that barely registered. What registered was that this was her arm with the bone, showing white on the X-ray, clearly snapped in two. Her wooziness increased. She had to fight an urge to put her head between her knees.

"Is it going to hurt?" Jessica whispered, still not wanting Kade to see any sign of weakness from her.

"I wish I could tell you no, but even with the powerful painkiller I'm going to give you, yes, it's going to hurt. Do you want your husband to come with you?"

Yes, part of Jessica whimpered. But that was the part she to fight! Aware of Kade's eyes on her, she tilted her chin. "No, I'm fine. Kade, you don't have to wait."

CHAPTER FOUR

YOU DON'T HAVE to wait was not quite as firm as *you can leave now.* Jessica forced herself not to look back at him as the doctor took her to a different room. But she had to admit she felt grateful that he did not appear to be leaving.

A half hour later, her arm in a cast and immobilized in a sling, with some prescription painkillers and some instructions in her other hand, Jessica was pushed by a nurse back to the waiting area. Her feeling of wooziness had increased tenfold.

Because she actually felt happy that Kade was still there. He sprang from a chair as soon as he saw her, and then shoved his hands into his pockets.

"You didn't have to wait," Jessica said in stubborn defiance of the relief.

"I'll make sure you get home safely," he said. "I had someone from the office drop off my car for me while I waited. I'll bring it around to that door over there."

And then, before she could protest on a number of fronts—that she didn't need him to drive her and that she was going back to work, not home—he was gone.

She didn't want to admit how good his take-charge attitude felt sometimes. By the time he'd arrived at the door, she'd realized there was no way she was going to work. She was also reluctant to concede how good it felt when he held open the door of his car for her and she slid from the wheelchair into its familiar luxury. Moments later, with the wheelchair returned, he put the car in gear and threaded through what was left of the morning rush with ease.

Why did she feel glad that he didn't have a different car? She shouldn't care at all. But he'd bought the car after they'd graduated from university, well before he'd been able to afford such a thing.

"But why?" she'd asked him when he had come and shown it to her. The high-priced car had seemed as if it should not be a priority to a recent university graduate.

"Because when I marry you, this is what we're driving away in."

And then he'd shown her the ring he couldn't afford, either. Three months later, with the roof down and her veil blowing out the back, they had driven away to a shower of confetti and their cheering friends.

One of her favorite wedding pictures was of that scene, the car departing, a just-married sign tacked crookedly to the back bumper that trailed tin cans on strings. In that picture Kade had been grinning over his shoulder, a man who had everything. And she had been laughing, holding on to her veil to keep it from blowing off, looking like a woman embracing the wildest ride of her life.

Which marriage had definitely turned out to be, just not in the way she had expected. It had been a rollercoaster ride of reaching dizzying heights and plummeting into deep and shadowy valleys.

Jessica took a deep breath. She tried to clear her head of the memories, but she felt the painkilling drugs were impeding her sense of control. Actually, she did not know which impaired her judgment more: sitting in the car, so close to Kade, or the drugs.

She had always liked the way he drove, and though it felt like a weakness, she just gave herself over to enjoying it. The car, under his expert hand, was a living thing, darting smoothly in and out of traffic.

They pulled up in front of the house they had once shared. It was farther from downtown than her business, but still in a beautiful established southwest neighborhood with rows of single-story bungalows, circa 1950.

Oh, God, if getting in his car had nearly swamped her with memories, what was she going to do if he came into the house they had once shared? There was a reason she had asked him to meet her at her business.

"Kade," she said firmly, wrestling the car door open with her left arm, "we need to get a divorce."

Kade made himself turn and look at her, even though it was unexpectedly painful having her back in the passenger seat of the car.

He forced himself to really look at her. Beneath the pallor and the thinness, he suspected *something*.

"What aren't you telling me?"

She wouldn't look at him. She got the car door open, awkward as it was reaching across herself with her left arm.

"You could have waited for me to do that," he said, annoyed, but she threw him a proud glare, found her feet and stepped out.

But her fighting stance was short-lived. She got a confused look on her face. And then she went very white. And stumbled.

He bolted from the car and caught her just as her legs crumpled underneath her. He scooped her up easily and stared down at her. And there he was, in the predicament he would have least predicated for the day—with Jessica's slight weight in his arms, her body deliciously pliant against his, her eyes wide on his face. She had a scent that was all her own, faintly lemony, like a chiffon pie.

She licked her lips, and his eyes moved to them, and he remembered her taste, and the glory of kissing Jessica.

She seemed to sense the sudden hiss of energy between them and regained herself quickly, inserted her good hand between them and shoved. "Put me down!"

As if he had snatched her up against her will instead of rescuing her from a fall. He ignored her and carried her up the walkway to the house.

Their house.

He was not going to carry her across the threshold. The memory of that moment in their history was just too poignant. He set her down on the front steps and her legs folded. She sat down on the top stair, looking fragile and forlorn.

"I don't feel well and I don't know where my keys are," she said.

He still had one, but he wasn't sure if he should use it. It felt presumptuous. It didn't feel as if he should treat it like his house anymore.

"I must have left my purse at the shop," she said, trying to get up.

"Sit still for a minute," he said.

It wasn't an order, just a suggestion, but she folded her

good arm over the one in the sling. He half expected she might stick her tongue out at him, but she didn't.

"You've lost weight," he said, watching her sit on the stoop.

"A little," she admitted, as if she was giving away a state secret. "You know me. Obsessed about my projects. Right now it's launching Baby Boomer. Sometimes I forget to eat."

He frowned at that. She was always obsessed about something. Once, it had been about him.

"What's your sudden panic to get a divorce?" he asked.

She choked and glared at him. "Over a year is not a sudden panic."

"Have you met someone?" His voice sounded oddly raw in his own ears.

Jessica searched his face but he kept his features cool.

"Not that it is any of your business, but no." She hesitated. "Have you?"

He snorted. "No, I'm cured, thanks."

"I am, too!" She hesitated again, not, he guessed, wanting to appear too interested in his life. "I suppose you're playing the field, then?"

"What? What does that mean, exactly?"

"Seeing lots of women."

He snorted and allowed himself to feel the insult of it. Jessica was painting him as a playboy? "You have to know me better than that."

"You live in that building. It has a reputation."

"The condominium has a reputation?" he asked, astounded. "The building I live in? River's Edge?"

"It does," she said firmly. "Lots of single people live there. Very wealthy single people. It has a pool and that superswanky penthouse party room. The apartments are posh."

"How do you know all that?" he asked.

She turned red. "Don't get the idea I've been sneaking around spying on you."

"That is the furthest from any idea I would ever get about you," he said drily.

"The newspaper did a feature on it."

"I must have missed that."

"It seems like a good place for a single guy to live. One who is, you know, in pursuit of fun and freedom."

That was what Jessica thought he was in pursuit of? Jeez. Well, let her think it. How could it be that she didn't know him at all?

"Rest assured—" he could hear the stiffness in his voice "—I live there because it is a stone's throw from work, which by the way is where I spend the majority of my waking hours." He hesitated, not wanting to appear too interested in her life, either. "So are *you* playing the field?"

"Don't be ridiculous," she said.

"How come it's ridiculous when I ask but not when you ask?" And there it was, the tension between them, always waiting to be fanned to life.

"I already told you I'm obsessed with my business. I don't have time for anything else."

"So you are not in a new relationship, and apparently not looking for one. You want a divorce why?"

She sighed with what he felt was unnecessary drama. "We can't just go on indefinitely like this, Kade."

He wanted to ask why not but he didn't.

"All those hours I spend working are paying off. My business is moving to the next level."

He raised an eyebrow at her.

"I did over a hundred thousand in internet sales last year."

He let out a low appreciative whistle. "That's good."

"I think it could be double that this year with the store-front opening."

So she was moving up as well as on. Well, good for her. No sense admitting, not even to himself, how happy he was that her moving on did not involve a new guy moving in.

"My lawyer has advised me to tie up any loose ends."

He managed, barely, not to wince at being referred to as a loose end. "So your lawyer is afraid of what? That you'll be wildly successful and I, as your legal partner, will come in and demand half your business?"

"I suppose stranger things have happened," she said coolly.

"I think my business is probably worth as much as your business if we were going to start making claims against each other."

"We both know your business is probably worth a hundred times what my little place is worth. It's not about that."

"What's it about, then?" He was watching her narrowly. He knew her so well. And he knew there was something she wasn't telling him.

She sighed heavily. "Kade, we don't even have a separation agreement. We own this house together. And everything in it. You haven't even taken a piece of furniture. We need to figure things out."

He rolled his shoulders and looked at *their* house, the hopeless little fixer-upper that she had fallen in love with from the first moment she had laid her eyes on it.

"It's like the cottage in *Snow White*," she had said dreamily.

It hadn't been anything like the cottage in *Snow White*. Except for the decorative shutters, with hearts cut out of them, the house had been an uninspired square box with ugly stucco. The only thing Snow Whitish about it? It needed seven dwarfs, full-time, to help with its constant need for repair.

She had not done one thing to the exterior since he had left. They hadn't been able to afford too much at the time, so they had rented one of those spray-painter things and redone the stucco white. The black shutters and door had become pale blue.

"Isn't the color a little, er, babyish?" he had asked her of the pale blue.

Her sigh of pure delight, as if the color was inviting a baby into their house, seemed now, in retrospect, as if it might have been a warning.

Their strictly cosmetic changes were already deteriorating.

Was it the same inside as it had been? Suddenly he felt driven to know just how much she had moved on. It felt as if he needed to know.

He looked on his chain and acted surprised. "I have a key."

And a moment later he was helping her into the home they had shared. He had thought she would, if sensible, rip out every reminder of him.

But she was the woman who had scuffled with a burglar, and she had not done the sensible thing.

Their house was relatively unchanged. He thought she might have tried to erase signs of him—and them—but no, there was the couch they had picked out together, and the old scarred wooden bench she had fallen in love with and used as a coffee table. She hadn't even gotten rid of the oversize fake leather burgundy recliner with the handy remote control holder built into it. He had thought it would go. When people had come over she had referred to it, apologetically, as the guy chair, her nose wrinkled up with affectionate resignation. She had even named it Behemoth.

In fact, as far as Kade could see, the only change was that the bench contained only a mason glass jar spilling purple tulips. It was not covered with baby magazines. Oh. And there was one other thing changed. Their wedding pictures, her favorite shots in different-size frames, were not hung over the mantel of the fireplace. The paint had not faded where they had hung, and so there were six empty squares where once their love for each other had been on proud display.

The fireplace didn't actually work. He remembered their excitement the first time they had tried to light it, the year's first snow falling outside. The chimney had belched so much black smoke back into the house they had run outside, choking on soot and laughter. There was still a big black mark on the front of it from that.

He led her through the familiar space of the tiny house to the back, where the kitchen was. One day, they had hoped to knock out a wall and have open concept, but it had not happened. He made her sit at the table, another piece of furniture they had bought together at the second-hand stores they had loved to haunt on Saturday mornings. Without asking her, he fetched her a glass of water, finding the glasses with easy familiarity.

He remembered trying to paint the oak cabinets white in an effort to modernize the look of the kitchen. It had been disastrous. They had fallen asleep tucked against each other, propped against a cupboard, exhausted, covered in more paint than the cabinets. The cabinets looked as awful as they always had, the old stain bleeding through the white. They'd never bothered to try painting them again. The truth was, he liked them like that, with their laughter and ineptitude caught for all time in the hardened paint dribbles. And he thought she probably did, too.

The memories all felt like a knife between his eyes.

CHAPTER FIVE

BUT OF COURSE, Kade knew, those happy memories of renovation disaster had all happened before everything went south. After Jessica had discovered she was pregnant the first time, renovation had slammed to a halt.

Chemicals. Dust. The possibility of stirring up mouse poo.

Jessica took a sip of the water, watching him over the rim. "We need to make a decision about the house."

"You can have it," he said. "I don't want it."

"I don't want you to give me a house, Kade," she said with irritating patience, as if she was explaining the multiplication tables to a third grader. "I actually don't want this house. I'd like to get my half out of it and move on."

She didn't want the house with the fireplace that didn't work and laughter captured in the paint dribbles? She'd always loved this house, despite its many flaws.

There was something more going on that she was not telling him. He always knew. She was terrible at keeping secrets.

"I'll just sign over my half to you," he repeated.

"I don't want you to give it to me." Now she sounded mad. This was what their last weeks and months together had been like. There was always a minefield to be crossed between them. No matter what you said, it was wrong; the seeds were there for a bitter battle.

"That's ridiculous. Who says no to being given a house?"

"Okay, then. I'll give it to you."

"Why are you being so difficult?"

He could not believe the words had come out of his mouth. Their favorite line from *Beauty and the Beast*. In the early days, one of them had always broken the fury of an argument by using it.

For a moment, something suspiciously like tears shone behind her eyes, but then the moment was gone, and her mouth was pressed together in that stubborn "there is no talking to her now" expression.

"Can't we even get divorced normally?" she asked a little wearily, sinking back in her chair and closing her eyes.

"What does that mean?" he asked, but was sorry the minute the words were out of his mouth.

Of course, what it meant was that they hadn't been able to make a baby *normally*.

But thankfully, Jessica did not go there. "Normal— we're supposed to fight over the assets, not be trying to give them to each other."

"Oh, forgive me," he said sarcastically. "I haven't read the rule book on divorce. This is my first one."

Then he realized she was way too pale, and that she wasn't up for this. "You're not feeling very good, are you?"

"No," she admitted.

"We need to talk about this another time."

"Why do you always get to decide what *we* need?"

That stung, but he wasn't going to get drawn into an

argument. "Look, you've had a tough morning, and you are currently under the influence of some pretty potent painkillers."

She sighed.

"You should probably avoid major decisions for forty-eight hours."

"I'm perfectly capable of making some decisions."

"There is ample evidence you aren't thinking right. You've just refused the offer of a house."

"Because I am not going to be your charity case! I have my pride, Kade. We'll sell it. You take half. I take half."

He shrugged, and glanced around. "Have you done any of the repairs that needed doing?"

Her mutinous expression said more than she wanted it to.

"Nothing is fixed," he guessed softly. "You're still jiggling the toilet handle and putting a bucket under the leak in the spare bedroom ceiling. You're still getting slivers in your feet from the floor you refuse to rip out, even though it was going to cost more to refurbish it than it would to put in a new one."

"That's precisely why I need to sell it," she said reasonably. "It's not a suitable house for a woman on her own."

Again, he heard something Jessica was not telling him.

"We'll talk about selling the house," he promised. "We'll probably get more for it if we do some fixes."

He noted his easy use of the word *we*, and backtracked rapidly. "How about if I come back later in the week? I'll have a quick look through the house and make a list of what absolutely has to be done, and then I'll hire a handyman to do it. My assistant is actually tracking one down to fix the door on your shop, so we'll see how he does there."

"I think the real estate agent can do the list of what needs to be done."

She'd already talked to a real estate agent. He shrugged as if he didn't feel smacked up the side of the head by her determination to rid herself of this reminder of all things *them*.

"Your real estate agent wants to make money off you. He is not necessarily a good choice as an adviser."

"And you are?"

He deserved that, he supposed.

"Okay. Do it your way," Jessica said. "I'll pay half for the handyman. Do you think you could come in fairly quickly and make your list? Maybe tomorrow while I'm at work?"

He didn't tell her he doubted she would be going back to work tomorrow. Her face was pale with exhaustion and she was slumped in her chair. No matter what she said, now was not the time for this discussion.

"I'm going to put you to bed," Kade said. "You're obviously done for today. We can talk about the house later." He noticed he carefully avoided the word *divorce*.

"I am exhausted," she admitted. "I do need to go to bed. However, you are not putting me to bed." She folded her one arm up over her sling, but winced at the unexpected hardness of the cast hitting her in the chest.

"I doubt if you can even get your clothes off on your own."

She contemplated that, looked down at her arm in the sling. He knew at that moment, the reality of the next four weeks was sinking in. In her mind, she was trying to think how she was going to accomplish the simple task of getting her clothes off and getting into pajamas.

"I'll go to bed in my clothes," she announced.

"Eventually," he pointed out, "you're going to have to figure out how to get out of them. You're going to be in that cast for how long?"

"A month," she said, horror in her features as her new reality dawned on her.

"I'll just help you this first time."

"You are not helping me get undressed," she said, shocked.

He felt a little shock himself at the picture in his mind of that very shirt sliding off the slenderness of her shoulders. He blinked at the old stirring of pure fire he felt for Jessica. She was disabled, for God's sake.

It took enormous strength to wrestle down the yearning the thought of touching her created in him, to force his voice to be patient and practical.

"Okay," Kade said slowly, "so you don't want me to help you get undressed, even though I've done it dozens of times before. What do you propose?"

Her face turned fiery with her blush. She glared at him, but then stared at her sleeve, bunched up above the cast, and the reality of trying to get the shirt off over the rather major obstacle of her cast-encased arm seemed to settle in.

"Am I going to have to cut it off? But I love this blouse!" She launched to her feet. He was sure it was as much to turn her back to him as anything else. She went to the kitchen drawer where they had always kept the scissors and yanked it open. "Maybe if I cut it along the seam," she muttered.

He watched her juggle the scissors for a minute before taking pity on her. He went and took the scissors away and stepped in front of her. Gently, he took her arm from the sling, and straightened the sleeve of the blouse as much as he could.

There was less resistance than he expected. Carefully, so aware of her nearness and her scent, and the silky feel of her skin beneath his fingertips, he took the sharp point of the scissors and slit the seam of the sleeve.

She stared down at her slit-open sleeve. "Thanks. I'll take it from here."

"Really? How are you going to undo your buttons?"

With a mulish expression on her face, she reached up with her left hand and tried to clumsily shove the button through a very tight buttonhole.

"Here," he said. "I'll help you."

She realized she could not refuse. "Okay," she said with ill grace. "But don't look."

Don't look? Hell's bells, Jessica, we belong to each other. Instead of getting impatient, he teased her. "Okay. Have it your way." He closed his eyes and placed his hand lightly on her open neckline. He loved the feel of her delicate skin beneath his fingertips. Loved it.

"What are you doing?" she squeaked.

"Well, if I can't look, I'll just feel my way to those buttons. I'll braille you. Pretend I'm blind." He slid his hand down. He felt her stop breathing. He waited for her to tell him to stop, but she didn't.

It seemed like a full minute passed before Jessica came to her senses and slapped his hand away.

He opened his eyes, and she was looking at him, her eyes wide and gorgeous. She licked her lips and his gaze went to them. He wanted to crush them under his own.

That old feeling sizzled in the air between them, the way it had been before her quest for a baby had begun.

"Keep your eyes open," she demanded.

"Ah, Jessica," he said, reaching for her buttons, "don't look, but keep my eyes open. Is that even possible?"

"Try your best," she whispered.

"You are a hard woman to please." But, he remembered, his mouth going dry, she had not been a hard woman to please at all. With this memory of how it was to be together, red-hot between them, his fingers on her buttons was a dangerous thing, indeed.

Kade found his fingers on the buttons of her shirt. She stopped breathing. He stopped breathing.

Oh, my God, Jessica, he thought.

He did manage to keep his eyes open and not look. Because he held her gaze the whole time that he undid her buttons for her. His world became as it had once been: her. His whole world was suddenly, beautifully, only about the way the light looked in her hair, and the scent of her, and the amazing mountain-pond green of her eyes.

His hands slowed on her buttons as he deliberately dragged out the moment. And then he flicked open the last button and stepped back from her.

"There," he said. His voice had a raspy edge to it.

She stood, still as a doe frozen in headlights. Her shirt gapped open.

"You want me to help you get it off?"

She unfroze and her eyes skittered away from his and from the intensity that had leaped up so suddenly between them.

"No. No! I can take it from here."

Thank God, he thought. But he could already see the

impracticality of it. "I'm afraid you'll fall over and break your other arm struggling out of those clothes," he told her. "The blouse is just one obstacle. Then there's, um, your tights."

"I can manage, I'm sure." Her tone was strangled. Was she imagining him kneeling in front of her, his hands on the waistband of those tights?

He took a devilish delight in her discomfort even while he had to endure his own.

"And I'm not sure what kind of a magician you would have to be to get your bra off with your left hand," he said.

She looked stricken as she went over the necessary steps in her mind.

"If you let me help you this time…" Kade suggested, but she didn't let him finish.

"No!"

"Okay." He put his hands in the air—cowboy surrender. And suddenly it didn't seem funny anymore to torment her. It just reminded him of all they'd lost. The easy familiarity between them was gone. The beautiful tension. The joy they had taken in discovering each other's bodies and the secrets of pleasing each other. In those first early days, he remembered chasing her around this little house until they were both screaming with laughter.

She blushed, and it seemed to him each of those losses was written in the contrived pride of her posture, too. Jessica headed for the hallway, the bedroom they had shared.

If he followed her there, there was probably no predicting what would happen next. And yet he had to fight down the urge to trail after her.

What was wrong with him? What could happen next? She was on drugs. Her arm was disabled. She was being deliberately dowdy.

The simple truth? None of that mattered, least of all the dowdy part. Around Jessica, had he ever been able to think straight? Ever?

"While you're in there," he called after her, trying to convince her, or maybe himself, that he was just a practical, helpful guy, and not totally besotted with this woman who was not going to be his wife much longer, "you can pick what you're going to wear for the next four weeks very carefully."

"And while you're out there, you can start making a list of the fixes. Then you won't have to come back later."

To help her. He would not have to come back later to help her. He mulled that over. "I'm not sure how you can do this on your own. Think about putting on tights one-handed. It would probably be even more challenging than getting them off."

"I can go bare legged," she called.

"I don't even want to think about how you'll get the bra on," he said gruffly. He couldn't imagine how she was going to struggle into and out of her clothes, but that was not a good thing for him to be imagining anyway.

CHAPTER SIX

JESSICA BOLTED THROUGH her bedroom and into the safety of her bathroom. She did not want Kade thinking about her bra, either!

But the reality of her situation was now hitting home.

Oh, there were practical realities. How was she going to manage all this? Not just dressing, which was going to be an inconvenience and a major challenge, but everything? How was she going to take a shower, and unpack boxes at Baby Boomer? How was she going to butter toast, for heaven's sake?

But all those practical realities were taking a backseat to the reality of how she had felt just now with Kade's hand, his touch warm and strong and beautiful, on her neck, and then on her buttons.

That was just chemistry, she warned herself. They had always had chemistry in abundance. Well, not always. The chemistry had been challenged when they—no, she—had wanted it to respond on cue.

Still, it was easier to feel as if she could control the unexpected reality of Kade being in her home—their home—while she was comfortably locked in her bathroom.

Just to prove her control, she locked the door. But as

she heard the lock click, she was very aware that she could not lock out the danger she felt. It was inside herself. How did you lock that away?

"Focus," Jessica commanded herself. But life seemed suddenly very complicated, and she felt exhausted by the complications. She wanted out of her clothes and into her bed.

She wanted her husband out of her house and she wanted the stirring of something that had slept for so long within her to go back to sleep!

Even if it did make her feel alive in a way she had not felt alive in a long, long time. Not even the excitement and success of her business had made her feel like this, tingling with a primal awareness of what it was to be alive.

Even the most exciting thing in her life—contemplating adopting a baby, and starting a family of her own—had never made her feel like this!

"That's a good thing," she told herself, out loud. "*This* feeling is a drug, a powerful, potent, addicting drug that could wreck everything."

But what a beautiful way to have it wrecked, a horrible uncontrollable little voice deep inside her whined.

"Everything okay in there?"

"Yes, fine, thanks." No, it wasn't fine. *Go away. I can't think clearly with you here.*

"I thought I heard you mumbling. Are you sure you're okay?"

"I'm fine," she called. She could hear a desperate edge in her own voice. Jessica was breathing hard, as if she had run a marathon.

Annoyed with herself, she told herself to just focus on one thing at a time. That one thing right now was removing her blouse. By herself.

Her nightie was hanging on the back of the bathroom door. She should not feel regret that the nightwear was mundane and not the least sexy. She should only be feeling thankful that it was sleeveless.

For a whole year, she had not cared what her sleepwear looked like. As long as it was comfortable she hadn't cared if it was frumpy, if it had all the sex appeal of a twenty-pound potato sack.

For a whole year, she had told herself that not caring what she slept in, that not spending monstrous amounts of money on gorgeous lingerie, was a form of freedom. She had convinced herself it was one of the perks of the single life.

"Focus on getting your blouse off!" she told herself.

"Jessica?"

"I'm okay." She hoped he would not hear the edge in her voice. Of course, he did.

"You don't sound okay. I told you it was going to be more difficult than you thought."

What? Getting dressed? Or getting divorced?

One of the things that was so annoying about Kade? He had an aggravating tendency to be right.

"Focus," Jessica commanded herself. She managed to shrug the blouse off both her shoulders, and peeled the sleeve off her left arm with her teeth. But when she tried to slide the newly slit sleeve over the cast, it bunched up around it, and refused to move.

By now, Jessica was thoroughly sick of both Kade's tendency to be right and the blouse. It wasn't one of her favorites anymore. How was she going to ever wear it again without imagining his hands on the buttons?

She tugged at it. Hard. It made a ripping sound. She liked that sound. She tugged at it harder.

"Argh!" She had managed to hurt her arm.

"Okay in there?"

"Stop asking!"

"Okay. There's no need to get pissy about it!"

She didn't want him telling her what to get pissy about! That was why she needed to divorce him.

She investigated the blouse. It was bunched up on the cast, and she had tugged at it so hard it was stuck there. She was afraid she was going to hurt her arm again trying to force it back off. Gentle prying was ineffectual. It refused to budge. The shoulder was too narrow to come down over the cast, and the fabric had ripped to the seams, but the seams held fast.

"That will teach me to buy such good quality," Jessica muttered, then waited for him to comment. Silence. One-handed, she opened every drawer in the bathroom looking for scissors. Naturally, there were none.

She would just have to forge ahead. So with the blouse hanging off her one arm increasing her handicap substantially, and by twisting herself into pretzel-like configurations, she managed to get the tights off. And then the skirt. She was sweating profusely.

Once the bra was off, she thought, it would be fairly simple to maneuver the nightgown over her head.

She reached behind her with her left hand and the bra gave way with delightful ease. She stepped out of it and let it fall in the heap with her tights and skirt.

The nightgown should be simple. If she left it hanging up as it was on the back of the bathroom door, she could just stick her head up under it, and it would practically put itself on. She grunted with satisfaction as she managed to get inside her nightie, put her left hand through the armhole and release it from its peg.

The nightie settled around her like a burka, her head covered, her face out the neck hole. That was okay. This angle should be good for getting her right arm up through the right armhole.

She tried to get her casted arm up. The nightie shifted up over her head as she found the right armhole and shoved. Of course, the blouse bunched around the cast prevented it from clearing the hole. It snagged on something.

So she was stuck with her arms in the air, and her head inside her nightgown.

She wiggled. Both arms. And her hips. Nothing happened.

With her left hand, she tried to adjust the nightie. She tugged down the neckline. Now half her head was out, one eye free. She turned to the mirror and peered at herself with her one uncovered eye. Her nightgown was hopelessly caught in her blouse, and her arm was stuck over her head.

And it hurt like the blazes.

She plunked herself down on the toilet seat and wriggled this way and that. She was sweating again.

There was a knock at the door.

She went very still.

"I made that list."

"Good," she croaked.

"Nothing on it I didn't expect. What do you think about the floors?"

She could not think about floors right now! She grunted as she tried again to free herself from her nightgown.

"Everything okay in there, Jessica?"

"I told you to stop asking!"

"I heard a thumping noise. You didn't fall, did you?"

"No."

"Are you okay?"

"Um—"

"It's a yes-or-no answer."

"Okay, then," she snapped with ill grace. "No." She unlocked the door.

He opened it. He stood there regarding her for a moment. She regarded him back, with her one eye that was uncovered, trying for dignity, her nightie stuck on her head, and her arm stuck in the air. "Don't you dare laugh," she warned him.

He snickered.

"I'm warning you."

"You are warning me what?" he challenged her.

"Not to laugh. And don't come one step closer."

Naturally, he ignored her on both fronts. Naturally, she was relieved, about him coming over anyway. Her arm was starting to ache unbearably. The smile on his lips she could have lived without.

Because there was really nothing quite as glorious as Kade smiling. He was beautiful at the best of times, but when that smile touched his lips and put the sparkle of sunshine on the sapphire surface of his eyes, he was irresistible.

Except she had to resist!

But then the smile was gone. Kade was towering over her. It occurred to her, from the draft she felt and the sudden scorching heat of his eyes, that the nightie was riding up fairly high on her legs.

Wordlessly, the smile gone, his expression all intense focus, he reached for where the blouse was stuck in the right-hand armhole of her nightgown. He began to un-wind it. It gave easily to the ministrations of his fingers.

She said nothing.

"You see," he said softly, "there's nothing you can threaten me with that will work. Because the worst has already happened to me."

"What's that?" she demanded. How could he say the worst had happened to him when she was the one sitting here, humiliatingly trapped by her own clothing?

"You're divorcing me," he said softly. And then his face hardened and he looked as if he wanted to choke back the words already spoken.

CHAPTER SEVEN

THE NIGHTGOWN BROKE FREE, and her casted arm went through the right hole and the rest of the garment whispered around her. She used her left hand to tug the hem down to a decent level over her legs.

He bent his head and put his teeth on the fabric of her blouse, and the stubborn seam released. With one final, gentle tug that did not hurt Jessica's arm at all, the blouse was free from the cast.

"A good tailor can probably fix that," he said, laying the destroyed blouse in her lap.

"I'm not divorcing you," she said. "We're divorcing each other. Isn't that what you want?"

He found where her sling was discarded on the floor and looped it gently over her head.

"It seems to be what you want all of a sudden," he said. "There's something you aren't telling me, isn't there?"

She felt suddenly weak, as if she could blurt out her deepest secret to him. How would it feel to tell him? *Kade, there is going to be a baby after all.*

No, that was not the type of thing to blurt out. What would be her motivation? Did she think it would change things between them? She didn't want them to change because of a baby. She wanted them to change because he loved her.

What? She didn't want things to change between them at all. She was taking steps to close this door, not reopen it! She was happy.

"Happy, happy, happy," she muttered out loud.

"Huh?"

"Oh. Just thinking out loud."

He looked baffled, as well he should!

"Go to bed," he told her. "We'll talk later. Now is obviously not the time."

He had that right! Where were these horrible, weak thoughts coming from? She needed to get her defenses back up.

With what seemed to be exquisite tenderness, he slipped her cast back inside the sling, adjusted the knot on the back of her neck.

His touch made her feel hungry for him and miss him more than it seemed possible. He put his hand on her left elbow and helped her up, and then across the bathroom and into the bedroom.

He let go of her only long enough to turn back the bedsheets and help her slide into the bed. She suddenly felt so exhausted that even the hunger she felt for her husband's love felt like a distant pang.

He tucked the covers up around her, and stood looking down at her.

"Okay," she said. "I'm fine. You can leave."

He started to go, but then he turned back and stood in the bedroom door, one big shoulder braced against the frame. He looked at her long and hard, until the ache came back so strong she had to clamp her teeth together to keep herself from flicking open the covers, an invitation.

Just like that, the intimacies of this bedroom revisited her. His scent, and the feel of his hands on her heated skin, his lips exploring every inch of her.

"Are you okay?" he asked. "You're beet red."

Flushed with remembered passion, how embarrassing.

She would do well to remember all that passion had not been able to carry them through heartbreak and turbulence.

She had bled all the passion out of this bedroom. She had become, she knew, obsessed with having a baby after the two miscarriages. It had become so horrible. Taking temperatures and keeping charts, and their lovemaking always faintly soured with her desperation.

Seeing him standing in the doorway, she remembered she had stood in that very spot watching him pack his things after their final night together.

"Please don't," she'd whispered.

"I can't stay."

"But why?"

Those cruel words that were forever a part of her now.

"Jessica, you've taken all the fun out of it."

"Out of making love?" she had asked him, stricken.

"Out of everything."

These were the things she needed to remember when a weak part of her yearned, with an almost physical ache, to be loved by him. To be held by him. To taste his lips again, and to taste faint salt on his skin after they'd made love. To feel the glory of his well-defined muscles under her fingertips. To smell him fresh out of the shower, to laugh with him until she could barely breathe for the ecstatic joy of it.

No, she needed to remember the pain, not the glory, the loneliness and the disappointment, and all the hurtful things. She needed to remember when she had needed him—when she had felt so fragile it had seemed as if a feather falling on her could have cracked her wide-open—Kade had been unavailable in every way.

"I'm fine," she said to Kade now. "Please go."

He heard the coolness in her tone and looked offended by it, but she told herself she didn't care. She told herself she felt nothing but relief as she heard him close the door of the house behind him, and then lock the dead bolt with his key.

She told herself she didn't care that he had gone and that she was alone again. For a woman who was happy, happy, happy, she felt an overwhelming need to cry. With her good arm she grabbed her pillow and put it over her face to try to stifle her desire.

Desire. Why had that unfortunate word popped into her head? This further evidence of her weakness made her fight harder not to cry.

It was weak—it was not the woman she wanted to be. Today hardly even rated as a bad day. She'd had two miscarriages. *Those* had been bad days. She'd had the husband she loved madly leave her. *That* had been a bad day.

But despite her every effort to talk herself out of them, the tears came, and they came hard, and they came for every bad day Jessica had ever had.

Kade left the house and stood on the front step for a moment. There was a little peekaboo view of the downtown skyline. It was the only place on the property that had any kind of a view, and he and Jessica used to sit out here with a glass of wine on a summer's night, planning the deck they would build someday to capitalize on their sliver of a view.

But that had been before the pregnancy quest. Then wine, along with renovations, had been off her list.

He didn't want to go there.

He glanced at his watch and was shocked how early it was in the day. It wasn't even noon yet. It felt as if he had put in a full day, and a hard day, too. Still, there was a place he could go when he didn't want to go *there* for that walk down memory lane.

Work.

He called his assistant. The handyman had already been dispensed to Jessica's business. If he went and liked the guy's work, he could surrender the list. It might minimize encounters like the one he had just had.

He decided he liked the handyman, Jake, and he liked his work. Patty had provided him with the surveillance and security system she had found, and it was already installed when Kade arrived.

"It's really cool," Jake said. "It's motion activated, but you can program it to only send an image to your phone if a door or window is touched. Give me your phone number."

Kade had the fleeting thought it should be Jessica's number that he gave him, but on the other hand, how could he trust her not to rush right down here if her phone alerted her to an intruder?

He gave him his number, and they chortled like old friends as they experimented with setting the alarm and then touching the door, watching their images come up on Kade's phone. Along with the alarm system, a new door was nearly installed, and Jake had matched the old one very closely and even gotten one with shatterproof glass. He was reinforcing the frame so that the dead bolt would not break away.

But somehow when Kade left, the list for the fixes at the house he and Jessica shared was still in his pocket. He had not surrendered it to the obviously very capable handyman.

Why? He suspected it was not because he had not got an answer from her about the floors.

He mulled it over as he drove into the office. Somewhere between her house and there, he had decided he was doing the fixes himself.

But why?

He wasn't particularly handy. The state of the kitchen cupboards over there and the fireplace that did not work were ample evidence of that.

Then he knew. It was time to finish it. Not just the house, but all that house represented. It was time to finish his relationship with Jessica. She was absolutely 100 percent right about that.

And as much as he wanted to, he could not hand those finishes off to someone else. It would be cowardly. And he sensed it would leave him with a sense of incompletion that he could never outdistance.

He would go over there, and he would do all the fixes on the list in his pocket, and then they would get a real estate agent in to appraise the place, and then they would put a for-sale sign on it, and it would sell, and that last thing that held them together would be done.

And how should he feel about that?

"Happy, happy, happy," he said.

Though when Jessica had muttered that, obviously under the influence of whatever, she had looked about the furthest thing from happy! And he was aware that happy, happy, happy was about the furthest thing from how he was feeling, too.

But that just showed him how true it was and how urgent. They needed to be done. He called his assistant and did something he had not done for a long, long time.

He asked her to clear his weekend.

It wasn't until he hung up the phone that he was aware that, for someone who wanted to finish things, another motivation lurked just behind his need to fix the house.

Was Jessica going to be okay after being mugged? Not her arm. That would heal. But her. She had always had that artistic temperament, ultrasensitive to the world.

If he knew Jessica—and he did—she was not nearly as brave as she was trying to be.

So, on Saturday morning, feeling a little foolish in his brand-new tool belt, Kade knocked on the door of the house he had shared with Jessica. He was certain she had said she would be at work, but she opened the door.

He could see why she wasn't at work. She would scare people away from her fledgling business in the getup she had on. She was wearing a crazy sleeveless dress that was at least four sizes too large for her.

But, in truth, it was her face that worried him. Just as he suspected, her drawn features hinted she might not be doing well. There was the gaunt look of sleeplessness about her, as well as dark circles under her eyes.

"It's a maternity dress. I have three of them." Her tone was defensive. "They're easy to get on. See the buttons down the front? That is a very hard thing to find in a dress."

"I didn't say anything." Her arm was in the sling. At least she was following doctor's orders.

"But getting dressed was not that easy, even with the buttons. I'm running late."

He noticed her cast had been decorated with all kinds of signatures and drawings.

In college, she had always been surrounded by friends. But then marriage had done something to her. Her world, increasingly, had become about him and their house. When the pregnancy quest had begun, Jessica had quit the job she'd had since earning her arts degree. Admittedly, it had not been the best job. She had barely made minimum wage at that funky, fledgling art gallery in east Calgary.

At first, he'd liked it that Jessica was home, and doted on him. He'd liked it quite a lot, actually. Maybe he'd liked it enough he'd encouraged it. Who didn't want to come home to fresh-baked bread, or roast beef and Yorkshire pudding or three dozen chocolate-chip cookies still warm out of the oven?

Who didn't want to come home to the most beautiful woman in the world waiting for him, with some newly inventive way of showing she loved him? Once it had been rose petals floating in a freshly drawn tub. Another time it had been a candlelit wine tasting in the back garden, a garden that she had single-handedly wrested from a weedy demise.

But slowly, all her devotion had begun to grate on him. He was so aware that Jessica's world was becoming smaller and smaller: paint colors for rooms rather than canvases. She was always trying new recipes. She discovered shopping online and was constantly discovering useless bric-a-brac that he was supposed to share her enthusiasm for.

It had pierced even his colossal self-centeredness that she was becoming a shadow of the vibrant person she had once been. The obsession with the baby had just intensified the sense he didn't know who she was anymore.

She'd started buying things for a baby they didn't have: little shoes just too adorable to pass up, hand-crocheted samplers for the walls of a nursery they didn't have yet. The magazine racks—God forbid a magazine was left conveniently out—were stuffed with parenting magazines.

She was forever showing him articles on the best baby bottles, and strollers, and car seats. She wanted him to go over fabric samples with her because she had found a seamstress to custom make the crib bedding. But it didn't matter which one he picked. The next day she had more for him to look at. She was acquiring a collection of stuffed animals that would soon need a room of their own, not to mention require them to take out a second mortgage to pay for them all.

"Jessica," he remembered shouting at her, "nobody pays three hundred dollars for a teddy bear."

She had looked crushed, and then unrepentant.

The anger, he knew in retrospect, though he had no idea at the time, had nothing to do with the teddy bear. It had to do with the fact he felt responsible for the awful metamorphosis taking place in her. It had to do with the fact that he was aware, in her eyes, he was not enough for her.

She brought him back to the present. "You didn't have to say anything about the dress. I can see in your face how you feel about it."

He was fairly certain it was the memory of the three-hundred-dollar-teddy-bear fight that had been in his face, so he tried to banish those thoughts and stay in the mo-

ment. "I'm not sure why you would wear something so…
er…unflattering."

"Because I don't care what you think, that's why!"

Or, he thought looking at her, she was trying very,
very hard to make it appear that she didn't care what he
thought.

CHAPTER EIGHT

"I LIKE THE CAST, though," Kade told Jessica.

And he did. He liked it that she had a bigger world again. All the scribbling on the cast was evidence of friends and coworkers and a life beyond the house. Okay, it grated a bit that she had managed to make a bigger world without him, and somehow it was still about babies.

"The dress is what I could get on by myself. See? Buttons down the front."

"About the dress," he said, deadpan. "Are they all that color? What would you call that color?"

"Pink?" she suggested.

"Nausea, heartburn, indigestion..." It was the slogan of a famously pink stomach-relief medication.

"The other ones are worse—"

"No, no, they can't be."

"Spiced pumpkin and real-woods camo."

"A camo maternity dress? I guess my next question would be, how are sales?"

"They are very, very popular."

"Tell me it ain't so," he groaned.

"They are part of an extraoversize line."

"Look, you are scaring me with the visual."

"Well, your visual is a little scary, too," she said,

standing back from the door to let him by her. "A tool belt? And what is that you're driving?"

"I borrowed a truck."

"A truck worthy of a camo-wearing pregnant lady, too."

"I needed it for the vibrating floor sander I rented to refinish the floors."

"A floor sander. The scariness increases. You always thought we should just replace the floors," she reminded him.

"You always thought we should refinish them."

"But it doesn't matter now!" she said, but it felt as if it did. It felt as if it was part of all that was unfinished. In the house, and between them. But Kade did not tell her that.

"What do you know about refinishing a floor?" she asked, looking at her watch.

"Oh, ye of little faith," he said. "I went on the internet. It's easier than you think."

Jessica looked insultingly doubtful.

"I think that refinishing will be less time-consuming than ripping out the old floor and putting down a new one," he told her. He didn't add it might be more in keeping with his skill set.

"Why are you tackling it? Why didn't you just hire someone? That guy you hired to install my door was excellent. By the way, I owe you some money for that."

"Yeah, whatever."

She looked as if she was going to argue, but then remembered she already was in the middle of one argument with him and decided to stick to that one. "I mean this is not exactly your line of work, Kade. It's certainly not in keeping with your current lifestyle."

"What lifestyle is that?" he asked her.

"You know."

"I don't."

"CEO—chief everything officer—at a prestigious company, resident of River's Edge."

"I already told you I work all the time."

"That's exactly what I'm trying to say. You work all the time, and not at renovations. You have a very sophisticated lifestyle. You move in very high-powered circles. I don't understand why you want to do this."

"I started it," he said grimly. "And I'm going to finish it."

She looked at him, and he knew she got it. She got it at every level that he had meant it at.

"Well, I'd love to stay and help—"

He could tell she meant it to sound sarcastic, but instead they both heard the wistfulness there, and Jessica blushed.

"—but I have to go to work. It already took me nearly forty-five minutes longer to get ready than I thought it would, and my part-time staffer can only stay until noon today."

"You slept in," he guessed.

Jessica looked as if she was going to protest, but then didn't. She sighed. "I had trouble sleeping."

"I thought you would."

"What? Why?"

"There aren't very many people who could walk away from being assaulted without being affected by it. And you've always been more sensitive than the average person anyway."

She smiled wanly and gave in, just a little bit, to the fact that he was her husband. He *knew* her. "I'm okay till I lie down, then I feel as if I hear glass breaking. I jump at the sound of the furnace turning on, and that tree branch outside the bedroom scraping the window. Then, since I'm awake anyway, I contemplate how to protect my shop, and hate how helpless I feel."

He drew in a deep breath. The warrior in him wanted to devote his life to protecting her.

But she looked as abashed at her confessions as he was at his reaction to them. Jessica glanced again at her watch. "Yikes! Would you look at the time! Sorry, again. I can't help."

"It doesn't matter. There is a lot of legwork before I actually do anything. I have to move furniture before I get started on the floors."

She cast a look at Behemoth. She was obviously thinking moving furniture was a two-person job, but he had also rented a dolly this morning with that recliner specifically in mind.

But Jessica surprised him. The practicalities of moving furniture were not what was on her mind.

"Remember the day we brought that home?" she asked softly.

These were the conversations he didn't want to have. Because the truth was that he remembered everything.

"You protesting the whole way home how ugly it was," Kade reminded her. He thought her exact words had been that it didn't fit with her *vision* for their house. He hadn't become totally jaded with the vision yet. Or maybe he had started to, because he had brought home the chair over her strenuous protests.

"And then we couldn't get it in the door. It weighs about a thousand pounds—"

"Well, maybe fifty," he corrected her wryly.

"And I was trying to hold up one end of it and you were trying to stuff it through the door. I told you it was a sign the house did not want it, and then you shoved extrahard. The frame of the door cracked and Behemoth catapulted into the house and nearly crushed me."

"Except I saved you," he said.

She looked at his face. Her eyes were very wide. She looked as if she was going to step toward him.

Suddenly, he remembered how they had celebrated getting that chair into the house. On the chair. And she had seemed affectionately tolerant of Behemoth after that.

The memory was between them, liquid and white-hot. It didn't mean anything that she still had the chair, did it?

"Go to work," Kade said gruffly, deliberately stepping back from her. "You probably wouldn't be of any help in your delicate state anyway."

Too late, he realized that a delicate state usually referred to pregnancy, and that, of course, was the topic that was a minefield between them.

Thankfully, she seemed a little rattled, as he was himself, by the Behemoth memory. He didn't intend to share the secret of the furniture-moving dolly with her. She would come home, and the floors would be completely done, and the furniture back in place and she would be filled with complete admiration for his adeptness in all things masculine.

And she would be so sorry things had not worked between them.

That thought blasted through his brain from nowhere that he could discern.

"Where should I put the furniture?" he asked hastily.

"Oh. Good question. Try the guest room. I use it as an office. It probably has the most room in it right now."

"Okay."

She cast one last rather insultingly doubtful look around the living room, but then looked at her watch and made a squeaking noise. She disappeared and came back in a few minutes, her look improved ever so slightly by a nice handbag, ultrahigh heels and dark glasses that hid the circles under her eyes.

"All right," she called. "Good luck. See you later."

Then she turned and, with her heels clacking sexy defiance of that horrible dress, went through the kitchen and out the back door. The door seemed to snap shut behind her. Was he mistaken, or had she been eager to get away from him?

Jessica could not wait to get out of that house! Her husband was an attractive man. His executive look—the tailored suits and linen shirts and silk ties, the manicured nails and the beautifully groomed hair—was enough to make any woman give him a second glance.

And yet the man he was this morning felt like *her* Kade. Casual in jeans faded to nearly white, his plaid shirt open at the beautiful column of his throat, his sleeves rolled up over the carved muscle of his forearms, a faint shadow of whiskers on his face. It was who he had been in private—dressed down, relaxed, so, so sexy.

Add to that the tool belt riding low on his hips, his easy confidence about pitting all that masculine strength against Behemoth…

Behemoth. Back in the day. When everything was still *fun*.

Good grief, she had wanted to just throw herself

against him this morning, feel his heart beating beneath her cheek, feel his arms close around her.

The robbery had left her far more rattled than she ever could have believed. Her sleep was troubled. She started at the least sound. Her mind drifted back to that morning if she let down her guard for even a second. And she felt dreadfully alone with the stress of it.

It was making her weak. The fact that he *knew* how she would react made her lonely for him, even though the sane part of her knew wanting to lean on Kade was an insane form of weakness. She had already tried that once, and he wasn't good at comforting her. Probably what had stopped her from throwing herself at him this morning was uncertainty. Would he have gathered her to him, rested his chin on the top of her head, folded his arms around her? Or would he, after an uncomfortable moment of tolerating her embrace, have stepped away?

She did not think it would be a good idea to make herself vulnerable to Kade again.

But even with that resolve strong within her, Jessica arrived at work feeling rattled.

Her stomach was in knots.

"Good grief," said Macy, her part-time staffer, stopping in her tracks. "Where'd you get that dress?"

"You know perfectly well I got it from the rack of Poppy Puppins at the back."

"It looks horrible on you."

Jessica didn't want to look horrible. She hated it that Kade had seen her looking horrible, even though she had deliberately worn the outfit to let him know she did not care one whit what he thought of her.

Sleep deprivation, obviously, was kicking in, plus it was some kind of reaction to being the victim of a crime, just as Kade had said, because Jessica felt as if she was fighting not to burst into tears.

"It has buttons on the front!" Jessica exclaimed for the second time that day. Ignoring the pitying look from Macy, she headed to office and slammed the door behind her.

She could not focus, even before she had *the* thought. *The* thought made her stomach feel as if it had become the lead car on the world's biggest roller coaster. It plunged downward and then did a crazy double loop. She bolted out of her office and into the store.

"Jessica? What's wrong?"

Jessica stared at Macy, not really seeing her. This was the thought that was tormenting her: Had she told Kade to put the furniture in the guest room? But she used that room as an office! And if she was not mistaken, she had the names of adoption agencies and lawyers who specialized in that field strewn all over the desk.

"Are you okay?" Macy asked. She dropped a tiny stuffed football and rushed to Jessica's side. "Are you going to faint?"

Jessica looked down at the bill of lading she still had clutched in her hand. She did feel terribly wobbly. "I think I'm okay," she said doubtfully.

"I was supposed to babysit for my sister at noon, but if you want, I'll see if my mom can do it instead."

Jessica was ashamed that her distress, her weakness, was that obvious to her employee. But her soon-to-be ex-husband had always had a gift for rattling her world, in one way or another.

What did it matter if he knew she was contemplating adoption? But at some deep, deep level, she did not want him to know.

So though usually Jessica would have said a vehement no to an offer like Macy had just made, she didn't. Usually, she would have pulled herself together. She could just phone and tell Kade to put Behemoth in her bedroom instead of the office.

She looked at her watch. He'd been there, in her house, for an hour and a half. It was possible he was already in the office, poring over her personal papers, uncovering her secrets.

"Oh, Macy, could you? I'd be so grateful." She shoved the bill of lading into Macy's hand.

And it wasn't until Jessica was halfway home that she realized she had not even waited for Macy's answer, but had bolted out the door as if her house was on fire.

Which, in less than half an hour, it would be.

CHAPTER NINE

JESSICA PULLED UP to the front of her house. She usually parked in the back, but such was her sense of urgency, she had decided to cut seconds by parking out front instead.

Her sense of her life spiraling out of her control deepened at what awaited her. All the living room furniture was on the front lawn, with the exception of Behemoth, which, as she already knew, could not fit through the front door. At least she hoped the furniture on the front lawn indicated there had been no invasion of her office.

Gathering herself, Jessica went up the steps. The front door to her house was open. She peered in. Her living room was emptied of furniture.

Kade was glaring down at some instructions in his hand. There was a machine there that looked like a huge floor polisher, only it had a bag attached to it, like a lawn mower. Though it felt like further weakness, she stood there for a minute regarding him, loving the look of him.

He looked big and broad and strong. He looked like the kind of man every woman dreamed of leaning on. But that was what Jessica needed to remember.

When she had needed someone to lean on, and when that person should have been her husband? Kade had not been there. At first he had just been emotionally absent, but then he had begun working longer and longer hours, until he was physically absent, too.

By the time Kade had made it official and moved out, her abandonment by her husband had already been complete.

Remembering all that as a defense against how glorious he looked right now, Jessica cleared her throat.

"It's not for sale," he said, without looking up.

"What?"

He did look up then. "What are you doing back?" he asked with a frown.

"What's not for sale?"

"The furniture. People keep stopping and asking if there's a yard sale. The coffee table is generating quite a lot of interest."

"I always told you it was a good piece."

He was silent for a moment. She knew she had left herself wide-open for him to tease her about what a *good piece* meant to him as opposed to what it meant to her. When he didn't follow that thread—once he had found teasing her irresistible—she was not sure how she felt. But it was not relieved.

"If Behemoth was out there," Kade said, "people would be throwing their money at me. I'd be at the center of a bidding war. The newspaper would probably be here by now to find out what all the fuss on Twenty-Ninth Avenue was about."

"Which brings me to my next question," Jessica said. "Why exactly is everything out on the lawn?"

He lifted a shoulder. "Faster to toss it out there than move it all down the hall."

"Toss?" she said.

"I meant gently move."

Despite the fact it meant he had been careless with her possessions, no matter what he said—and what was to stop anyone from taking whatever they wanted?—she felt relief that he had obviously not been anywhere near the spare bedroom that served as her office. She would know by looking at him if he had seen that adoption stuff, but obviously he was preoccupied with the machine in front of him.

It didn't surprise her that he would throw her things out on the lawn if that was faster than maneuvering them down the hallway. He had always had intensity of focus. When he wanted something, he simply removed the obstacles to getting it. It had made him a tremendous success in business.

It was how he had wooed her. She had been bowled over by him. But then that same attitude had become a toxin in their relationship.

A baby wasn't going to happen? Cut your losses and move on.

"How come you're home?" he asked again.

"Things were slow," she, who never told a fib, lied with shocking ease. "I shut it down a bit early. It seemed to me I should be helping out here. After all, I started it, too."

"I don't really see how you can help. You're kind of handicapped at the moment." He regarded her with a furrowed brow. "You still look not quite right. Pale. Fragile."

"I'm fine."

He brightened as he thought of a use for her. "I know what you could do! You could order pizza. Is Stradivarius still around the corner? God, I've missed that pizza. I haven't had it since—"

His voice trailed away. *Since you left me.* Had he missed her? At all? Or had even pizza rated higher than her?

It didn't matter. Their lives were separate now. She was moving on. Which reminded her of why she had rushed home. And it was not to order him a pizza!

She sidled by Kade. She passed close enough to him to breath in the wonderful familiar scent of him, mixed with something unfamiliar. Sawdust from the floor?

It was tempting to lean just a little closer and breathe deeply of the intoxication that was his scent. But she didn't.

"I'll just go, um, freshen up." She didn't mean changing her clothes. Changing clothes had become a rather daunting undertaking with one arm out of commission. What she really meant was she would go to her office and put her life away from his prying eyes just in case he did make it in there.

Behemoth, it turned out, was in the bathroom, not her office. It would be necessary to climb over it if she was really freshening up, which she wasn't. How far did she need to take the ruse? Did she need to climb over that thing and flush the toilet?

It seemed as if it would be endangering her other arm, and unnecessarily, because when she glanced back down the hall, Kade was not paying the least bit of attention to her.

As always.

The thought was edged with so much bitterness she could practically taste it, like chewing on a lemon peel.

Jessica went into her office. The papers were all out, just as she had remembered, but they were undisturbed. She slid them into the top drawer of the desk. She considered locking it, but it fell under the category of him not paying any attention to her. She doubted Kade would find her interesting enough to pry into her closed desk.

"Interesting placement of Behemoth," she said when she came back into the living room.

"I was thinking it might start a trend. Every man would like a recliner in the bathroom. Some kind of recliner-toilet combination is probably a million-dollar idea just waiting to be developed."

"That is gross."

"It isn't. It's combining practicality with extreme luxury. You have to admit there is nothing particularly comfortable or luxurious about a toilet seat."

She remembered this about him with an ache of longing: that easy irreverence that made her want to be stuffy and disapproving, but she always gave in and laughed instead.

She could feel her lips twitching. He saw it, too.

"Think about it," Kade pressed on. "We could offer designer colors. Pickled pumpkin and redneck camo. We could throw in a free matching dress with every purchase."

She tried to be stern. She giggled. He smiled at her giggle. She succeeded in smothering her giggle. He succeeded in smothering his smile.

"I think," she said severely, Mother Superior to misbehaving novice, "we should try to get the floors done before we tackle anything else together."

"Oh, right. Okay. So come and look at this."

She went over to where he was glaring at the floor. "What do you think?"

"About what?"

"That was what I was afraid of," he groaned. "I already sanded this part. Not much is happening. I just went out and got a different grit of sandpaper. I'm going to try it again. Cover your ears."

Obediently, Jessica put her hands over her ears. The machine roared to life. It was like standing next to a jackhammer.

To her relief, Kade stopped it after a few seconds. "Better," he said, "but still…" A light came on in his face. "It's not heavy enough."

"Huh?"

"The sander. It isn't heavy enough to really dig into those floors. Get on."

"What?"

"Come on. Sit on the front of it."

"Have you lost your mind?"

"You wanted to help. You can't do much with your arm like that. Come sit on the sander."

Why hadn't she just gone and ordered a pizza? Against her better judgment, she moved a little closer. "Sit on it?" She tapped it. "Here?"

He nodded eagerly.

Oh, jeez, it had always been hard not to get caught up in his enthusiasm.

She kicked off her shoes, gathered her skirt underneath her and sat down regally on the sander. She planted her feet firmly on a part of it that looked like a front fender. "Do not do anything that will jeopardize my other arm," she warned him.

"Don't worry." Grinning happily, he started the sander. A quiver ran through her. And then a tremble.

"Oh, my God." Her voice came out shaking, as if she was trying to talk from under water. In the midst of an earthquake. With her good hand, she clutched wildly at the side of the sander. She braced her front feet.

"Ready?"

Ready? *Sheesh, Jessica, run for your life!* Instead, she clung like a bronc rider waiting for the gate to open. She nodded her head.

The machine lurched across the floor.

"That's better," Kade called. "It's working!" He swung the huge machine slowly back and forth over the floor.

"I feel like I'm on one of those machines from a seventies gym," she yelled. Her voice sounded as if she was a cartoon character. Her whole body was vibrating crazily. She could see the flesh on her arms and legs jiggling rapidly.

She started to laugh. Even her laughter was shaking. Kade also gave a shout of pure glee.

He abandoned the slow sweeping motions in the corner and swiveled the machine outward. He raced across the living room, pushing the machine in front of him. Jessica glanced over her shoulder. A wide swath of sanded wood showed behind them, like the wake behind a boat.

They rocketed toward the front door.

An older woman put her head in. Her glasses slipped down her face and her mouth fell open. She was followed by her husband. His mouth fell open, and he grabbed her arm and tried to push her back out the door, as if protecting her from a sight unsuitable for a lady.

She was having none of it, though. She stood her ground, taking in the sight, wide-eyed.

Kade jerked the machine to a halt so quickly Jessica was nearly launched. He turned off the machine. Jessica pulled her skirt down—the vibrating had made it ride dangerously up her thigh—and tried to quit laughing.

An undignified snort, caused by the suppressed laughter, came out of her mouth.

"Yes?" Kade asked their visitors, his voice dignified, as if not a thing was amiss.

"Uh, we were wondering if there's a yard sale," the man said when it was evident his wife was still shocked speechless. "We wondered about the bench."

"Not for sale," Kade said, and then Jessica heard a familiar wickedness enter his tone. "However, I'll give you a good deal on the world's best vibrator."

The woman staggered backward out the door. The man's mouth fell open so hard, his chin hit his chest.

"Sorry to disturb you," he cried as he backed out the door after his wife.

Jessica waited until they were gone. She glared up at the man who was her husband, but she could not stir any genuine annoyance with him. Instead, she remembered how funny and spontaneous he was, she remembered that irreverent edge to his humor.

A smile was tickling his lips. And then she remembered that oh-so-familiar grin. And realized she had never really forgotten that.

Kade gave a shout of pure delight and devilment. And then the laughter spilled out of Jessica, too, and they were both laughing. Hard. Until they were doubled over with it, until the walls of their little house rang with it.

Until the laughter flowed between them like a river that connected them to everything they had once been.

CHAPTER TEN

KADE LOOKED AT Jessica and realized how much he loved to make her laugh. He always had. That was what he had missed most when their relationship had begun to go sideways. Her laughter.

"Goodness," Jessica said a little breathlessly. "I have not laughed like that in a very long time."

"Me, either," he admitted.

"It reminds me of when we were younger," she said.

"Me, too."

"Before…" Her voice faded away. But he knew what she meant. Before the loss of the first baby. And then the second one. Her laughter had leached out of her like bloodred wine leaking from a wineskin with a small puncture in it.

And when she had stopped laughing, and when he had realized how powerless he was to fix that, nothing had seemed worth laughing about to him anymore, either.

Now he watched as she scrambled off the sander, brushing at that ugly skirt with her good arm. The laughter had lightened the strained look around her eyes and mouth.

But when she faced him, a different kind of strain was

there. And it wasn't, for once, the strain of remembering everything that had transpired between them.

This had been lost, too, this deep and delicious sense of awareness of each other. Or maybe not lost. Maybe it had gone underground, like a creek that ran below the surface. It didn't matter that right now, Jessica's surface was encased in that thoroughly revolting dress. Kade could see, with utter ease, to what was underneath. And not her underwear. Her spirit. He could sense that beautiful, sensual awareness of each other, a longing to touch and explore.

In their marriage, it felt as if that had gone, too. It had gone the same place the laughter had gone—into that lonely abyss. It was as if the raft of life that they had shared had snapped in two, and they had stood by helplessly, with no paddles, drifting farther and farther away, not able to stop it.

"Why babies?" he asked softly.

"What?"

She actually looked frightened by the question.

"Why Baby Boomer? Why is your business about all things baby when that caused us so much heartache?"

"Oh." She relaxed visibly. "I'm not sure it was even intentional. You know some of my friends had seen the nursery you and I—" Her voice drifted away and she squinted, as if looking at something in the distance. Then she cleared her throat. "Nicole Reynolds asked me if I could do something for her. A mural on the wall of her nursery. It was a forest scene, with rabbits and birds and a deer. It was an immersion and it kind of snatched me back from the brink. Gave me purpose and a reason to get up in the morning. I liked being part of what was hap-

pening in their family, that circle of joy and expectation.
It just kind of snowballed."

He was so aware he had caused her that pain. Well,
not all of it. The miscarriages had put her in a space he
couldn't reach. And then she'd wanted to try again. To
plunge herself into that pool of misery he could not rescue her from again. He'd thought it was his job to make
her happy. To make her world perfect. At some point, to
his grave detriment, he had given up trying.

"I'm sorry, Jessie. I'm sorry it wasn't me who snatched
you back from the brink."

Her eyes skittered to him and then away. For a moment
it looked as if she would cross that abyss between them,
throw herself into his embrace, come home.

But that moment passed even before he recognized
completely what was blooming inside him.

Hope.

Shouldn't he know by now that that was the worst trap
of all? To hope?

She seemed to recognize it, because smiling way too
brightly, she said, "How about if I go order that pizza
now?"

"Oh, yeah, sure."

She retreated to the kitchen; he looked at the floors.
With the extra weight on the sander, wood had disappeared quickly. The wood was bare, but wavy. If he put
a level on it, it would probably rock like the little horse
in one of her nursery displays. He was fairly certain that
the damage caused by her wild ride on the sander was
something wood filler could not fix.

But he was aware of *liking* this kind of problem over
the other kind. The baffling problems of the heart.

"What kind of pizza?" she called.

"The usual," he said, before he remembered they really didn't have a usual anymore, not since their lives had become unusual.

But she didn't miss a beat, and he heard her talking into the phone, ordering a half pepperoni and mushroom and a half anchovies and pineapple and ham.

He went into the kitchen and watched her. The afternoon sunshine was painting her in gold. Even in that horrible dress, she looked beautiful. He remembered what it was to share a life with her and felt the pang of intense loss.

And suspected she was feeling it, too. Jessica had hung up the phone, but she had all the old take-out menus out of the kitchen drawer—she'd actually allowed them to have a junk drawer—and was studying them hard.

"You're too heavy," he said when she glanced up at him.

"Excuse me? Then maybe pizza isn't the right choice!"

"Oh, for heaven's sake. Not like that."

"Not like what?"

"You," he said, and could hear the gruff sincerity in his voice, "are perfect. You are too heavy for the sander! We dug some pretty good ruts in the floor."

"Oh." She blushed and looked back at the menus. She was pleased that he thought she was perfect. And he was pleased that he had pleased her, even though the road they were on seemed fraught with danger. "You should have hired it out."

"Very unmanly," he said.

"You," she said, and he could hear the sincerity in her voice, "couldn't be unmanly if you were wearing this dress."

He was pleased that she thought he was manly,

though the sense of danger was hissing in the air between them now.

She was right, and not just about the manly part. He should have hired the floor job out. The truth, he wouldn't have missed those moments of her laughter for the world. Even if the floor was completely wrecked, which seemed like a distinct possibility at the moment, that seemed a small price to pay.

"I just need something lighter than you to put on the sander." He deliberately walked away from the building tension between them and went out the back door to their toolshed. He found an old cinder block. He didn't miss the look on her face when he came back in hefting it, as her eyes found the bulge of his biceps and lingered there for a heated moment.

He slowed marginally, liking her admiration of his manliness more than he had a right to. Then he went into the living room and found and pitted himself against a nice comforting problem, one that he could solve. How did you get a cinder block to sit on a sander?

Kade finally had it attached, and restarted the machine. It wasn't nearly as much fun as waltzing around the room with Jessica. And it wasn't nearly as dangerous, either.

Or that was what he thought until the precise moment he smelled smoke. Frowning, he looked toward the kitchen. They were having pizza. What was she burning?

He shut off the sander, and went into the kitchen doorway, expecting crazily to find her pulling burned cookies from the oven. She had gone through a cookie phase when she had made her world all about him. Who had known there were so many kinds of cookies?

Once or twice, he had tried to distract her from her

full-scaled descent into domestic divahood. He had crossed the kitchen, breathed on her neck, nibbled her ear...

He remembered them laughing when he'd lured her away and they'd come back to cookies burned black. She had taken them out of the oven and thrown the whole sheet out into the yard...

But now there were no cookies. In fact, Jessica was standing right where he had left her, still studying all the take-out menus as if each one represented something very special. Which it did, not that he wanted to go there now. Kade did not want to remember Chinese food on the front steps during a thunderstorm, or a memorable evening of naked pad thai, a real dish that they had eaten, well, in the spirit of the name.

"Don't distract me," he snapped at her, and that earned him a wide-eyed look of surprise.

"What are you burning?"

"I'm not burning anything."

He turned away from her, sniffing the air. It wasn't coming from in here, the kitchen. In fact, it seemed to be coming from the living room. He turned back in and the sanding machine caught his attention. A wisp of something curled out of the bag that caught the sawdust coming off the floor.

And in the split second that he was watching it, that wisp of phantom gray turned into a belch of pure black smoke.

"The house is on fire!" he cried.

"That's not funny," she said.

He pushed by her and opened the cupboard by the stove—thank God she had not moved things around—and picked up the huge canner stored there. He dashed to the sink, then remembered the canner didn't fit well under the faucet. He tilted it precariously and turned on the water. It seemed it was filling in slow motion.

She sniffed the air. "What the—"

He glanced back at the door between the kitchen and the living room. A cloud of black smoke billowed in, up close to the top of the door frame.

"Get out of the house," he yelled at her. He picked up the pot and raced out to the living room. The first flame was just shooting out of the sawdust bag on the sander. He threw the pot of water on it. The fire crackled, and then disappeared into a cloud of thick black smoke that was so acrid smelling he choked on it.

He threw the pot on the floor, and went to Jessica, who, surprise, surprise, had not followed his instructions and had not bolted for the door and the safety of the backyard. She was still standing by the menus with her mouth open.

He scooped her up. He was not sure how he managed to think of her arm under these circumstances, but he did and he was extracareful not to put any pressure on her injured limb. He tucked her close to his chest—and felt a sense, despite the awful urgency of this situation, of being exactly where he belonged.

Protecting Jessica, looking after her, using his superior strength to keep her safe. She was stunned into silence, her green eyes wide and startled on his face.

And then he felt something sigh within her and knew she felt it, too. That somehow she belonged here, in his arms.

He juggled her to get the back door open, then hurtled down the back steps and into the yard. With reluctance, he let her slide from his arms and find her own feet.

"Is the house on fire?" she asked. "Should I call 911?"

"I want you to make note of the technique. First, you get to a safe place, then you call 911."

"But the phone's in there."

"I have one," he tapped his pocket. "But don't worry. The fire's out. I just didn't want you breathing that black guck into your lungs."

"My hero," she said drily. "Rescuing me from the fire you started."

"It wasn't exactly a fire," he said.

She lifted an eyebrow at him.

"A smolder. Prefire at best."

"Ah."

"The sander must be flawed. Sheesh. We could sue them. I'm going to call them right now and let them know the danger they have put us in." He called the rental company. He started to blast them, but then stopped and listened.

He hung up the phone and hung his head.

"What?"

Kade did not want to admit this, but he choked it out. "My fault. You need to check the finish that was on the floor before you start sanding. Some of the finishes become highly flammable if you add friction."

She was smiling at him as if it didn't matter one bit. "You've always been like that," she said. "Just charge ahead, to hell with the instructions."

"And I'm often left cleaning up messes of my own making," he said. "I'm going to go back into the house. You stay out here. Toxins."

"It's not as if I'm pregnant," she said, and he heard the faint bitterness and the utter defeat in those words.

And there it was, the ultrasensitive topic between

them. There was nothing to say. He had already said everything he knew how to say. If it was meant to be, it would be. Maybe if they relaxed. It didn't change how he felt about her. He didn't care about a baby. He cared about her.

So he had said everything he could say on that topic, most if it wrong.

And so now he said nothing at all. He just laid his hand on her cheek, and held it there for a moment, hoping she could *feel* what he had never been able to say.

CHAPTER ELEVEN

JESSICA DID SEEM to be able to feel all those things he had never been able to say, because instead of slapping his hand away, she leaned into it, and then covered it with her own, and closed her eyes. She sighed, and then opened her eyes, and it seemed to him it was with reluctance she put his hand away from her.

And so they went into the house together and paused in the doorway.

"Wow, does that stink," Jessica said. She went and grabbed a couple of dish towels off the oven handle. "We need these over our faces, not that I can tie them."

Kade took the towels from her and tied one over the bottom half of her face and one over his.

"Is mine manly?" he asked. "Or did I get the one with the flowers on it?"

He saw her eyes smile from under her mask. Now Jessica was in an ugly dress *and* had her face covered up. But the laughter still twinkled around the edges of her eyes, and it made her so beautiful it threatened to take his breath away far more than the toxic cloud of odor in the room.

Firmly, Kade made himself turn from her, and aware he looked ridiculous, like an old-time bandito, surveyed the damage to the living room.

All that was left of the sander bag was ribbons of charred fabric. They were still smoking, so he went over and picked up the sander and threw it out the front door, possibly with a little more force than was necessary. It hit the concrete walkway and pieces shot off it and scattered.

"That gave me a manly sense of satisfaction," Kade said, his voice muffled from under the dish towel. He turned back into the room.

The smile deepened around her eyes. How was this that they had narrowly averted disaster, and yet it felt good to be with her? It was as if a wall that had been erected between them was showing signs of stress, a brick or two falling out of it.

There was a large scorch mark on the floor where the sander had been, and a black ugly film shining with some oily substance coated the floor where he had thrown the water. The smoke had belched up and stained the ceiling.

"I think the worst damage is the smell," Kade said. "It's awful, like a potent chemical soup. I don't think you're going to be able to stay here until it airs out a bit."

"It's okay. I'll get a hotel."

"You're probably going to have to call your insurance company. The smell is probably through the whole house. Your clothes have probably absorbed it."

"Oh, boy," she said, "two claims in one week. What do you suppose that will do to my premiums?" And then she giggled. "It's a good thing the furniture is on the lawn. It won't have this smell in it. Do you think I'm going to have to repaint?"

"You don't have to go to a hotel," he said. "I've got lots of room."

Son, I say, son, what are you doing?

She hesitated. There was a knock at the door.

"Pizza," they said together.

Jessica contemplated what she was feeling as Kade looked after the pizza delivery. He cocked his head slightly at her, a signal to look at the delivery boy, who was oblivious, earbuds in, head bobbing. He didn't seem to even notice that he was stepping over a smoldering piece of machinery on the front walkway to get to the door. If he noticed the smell rolling out of the house, it did not affect his rhythm in any way.

As they watched the pizza boy depart, she felt like laughing again. That was impossible! She'd had two disasters in one week. She should be crying, not feeling as if an effervescent bubble of joy was rising in her.

Shock, she told herself. She was reacting to the pure shock of life delivering the unexpected. Wasn't there something just a little bit delightful about being surprised?

"Of course I can't stay with you, Kade," she said, coming to her senses, despite the shock of being surprised. "I'll get a hotel room. Or I can stay with friends."

"Why don't we go to my place and eat the pizza? You don't make your best decisions on an empty stomach. We'll figure it out from there."

Other than the fact it, once again, felt good to be *known*, that sounded so reasonable. She was hungry, and it would be better to look for a place to live for the next few days on a full tummy. What would it hurt to go to his place to have the pizza? She had to admit that she was curious about where Kade lived.

And so she found herself heading for the borrowed truck, laughing at the irony of him carefully locking the door when all her furniture was still on the lawn. Except for her precious bench, which at the last moment, she made him load into the box of the truck, they just left everything there.

She suspected leaving her furniture on the lawn was not nearly as dangerous as getting into that truck with him and heading toward a peek at his life.

His condo building sat in the middle of a parklike setting in a curve in the Bow River. Everything about the building, including its prime nearly downtown location, whispered class, wealth and arrival. There was a waterfall feature in the center of the circular flagstone driveway. The building was faced in black granite and black tinted glass, and yet was saved from the coldness of pure modern design by the seamless blending of more rustic elements such as stone and wood in the very impressive facade.

A uniformed doorman came out when Kade pulled up in front of the posh entryway to the building.

"Hey, Samuel, can you park this in the secured visitor area for me?"

Kade came and helped her out of the truck, and she was aware of the gurgle of the waterfall sliding over rocks. Something in the plantings around it smelled wonderful. Honeysuckle?

If the doorman was surprised to have a pickup truck to park among the expensive sports cars and luxury vehicles, it certainly didn't show in his smooth features.

"It's underground," Kade said to Jessica, when the truck had pulled away. "You don't have to worry about your bench."

The truth was she was so bowled over by her surroundings, the bench had slipped her mind.

Though the incredible landscape outside should have prepared her for the lobby, she felt unprepared. The entryway to the building was gorgeous, with soaring ceilings, a huge chandelier and deep distressed-leather sofas grouped around a fireplace.

No wonder he had never come home.

"Wow," Jessica said, gulping. "Our little place must seem pretty humble after this. I can see why you were just going to give it to me."

Kade looked around, as if he was puzzled. "I actually didn't pick the place," he said. "The company owns several units in here that we use for visiting executives. One was available. I needed a place to go and we had one vacant. I rent it from the company."

She cast him a glance as they took a quiet elevator up to the top floor. He really did seem oblivious to the sumptuous surroundings he found himself in. Once off the elevator, Kade put a code into the keyless entry.

"It's 1121," he said, "in case you ever need it."

She ducked her head at the trust he had in her—gosh, what if she barged in when he was entertaining a girlfriend?—and because it felt sad that she knew she would never need it. Well, unless she did stay for a couple of days until the disaster at her place was sorted.

Already, she realized with wry self-knowledge, her vehement no to his invitation was wavering.

Maybe that wasn't so surprising. Kade was charming, and he could be lethally so. She needed to remember charm was not something you could take to the bank in a relationship.

He opened the door and stood back.

"Oh, my gosh," Jessica said, stepping by him. The sense of being seduced, somehow, increased. She found herself standing in a wide entryway, floored in huge marble tiles. That area flowed seamlessly into the open-space living area, where floor-to-ceiling windows looked out over the park and pathways that surrounded the Bow River.

The views were breathtaking and exquisite, and she had a sense of being intensely curious and not knowing where to look first, because the interior of the apartment was also breathtaking. The furnishings and finishes were ultramodern and high-end. The kitchen, on the back wall of the huge open space, was a masterpiece of granite and stainless steel. A huge island had the cooktop in it, and a space-age stainless-steel fan over that.

"Let's eat," Kade said. He'd obviously gotten used to all this luxury. The fabulous interior of his apartment didn't create even a ripple in him. "Maybe on the deck? It's a nice night. I'll just get some plates."

Jessica, as if in a dream, moved out fold-back glass doors onto the covered terrace. It was so big it easily contained a sitting area with six deeply cushioned dark rattan chairs grouped together. On the other side of it sat a huge rustic plank table with dining chairs around it. It looked as if it could sit eight people with ease.

Huge planters contained everything from full-size trees to bashful groups of purple pansies. She took a seat at the table and wondered about all the parties that had been hosted here that she had not been invited to. She looked out over the river.

She felt as if she was going to cry. The apartment screamed to her that he had moved on. That he had a life she knew nothing about. After all their closeness this afternoon, she suddenly felt unbearably lonely.

Kade came out, juggling dishes and the pizza.

"What?" he said, sliding her a look as he put everything down.

"Your apartment is beautiful," she said, and could hear the stiffness in her own voice.

"Yeah, it's okay," he said. She cast him a look. Was he deliberately understating it?

"The kitchen is like something out of a magazine layout."

He shrugged, took a slice of pizza out of the box and laid it on her plate, from the pepperoni half, just as if they had ordered pizza together yesterday instead of a long, long time ago.

"I think I'll look for open concept in my next place," she said. She bit into the pizza and tried not to swoon. Not just because the pizza was so good, but because of the memories that swarmed in with the flavor.

"Don't," he said.

Swoon over pizza?

"It's not all it's cracked up to be, open concept."

"Oh," she said, relieved. "You don't like it?"

"You can't be messy. Everything's out in the open all the time. Where do you hide from your dirty dishes?"

"That would be hard on you," Jessica said. She remembered painful words between them over things that now seemed so ridiculous: toothpaste smears on the sink, the toilet paper roll put on the "wrong" way. "But I didn't see any dirty dishes."

"Oh, the condo offers a service. They send someone in to clean and make the beds and stuff. You don't think I'm keeping all those plants alive, do you?"

"Very swanky," she said. "Kind of like living at a hotel."

"Exactly. That is probably why this place," Kade said, "has never felt like home."

Jessica felt the shock of that ripple through her. This beautiful, perfect space did not feel like home to him?

"I've missed this pizza," he said.

"Me, too," she said. But she knew neither of them was talking about pizza. They sat out on his deck and watched the light change on the river as the sun went down behind them. The silence was comfortable between them.

"I should go," she finally said. "I have to make some phone calls. It's probably getting late to call a friend for tonight. I'll go to a hotel and arrange something for the rest of the week."

"You shouldn't bother. It sounds as if it's going to be a lot of hassle. There is lots of room here. There's a guest room."

Logically, Jessica knew she could not stay. But it felt so good to be here. It felt oddly like home to her, even if it didn't to Kade. Maybe it was because she was aware that, for the very first time since she had been attacked in her business, she felt safe.

And so tired. And relaxed.

Maybe for her, home was where Kade was, which was all the more reason to go, really.

"Okay," she heard herself saying, without nearly enough fight. "Maybe just for one night."

The logical part of her tried to kick in. "I should have packed a bag. I don't know why I didn't think of it."

"I told you," Kade said with an indulgent smile, "you don't think well when you're hungry. I thought of it, but then I wondered if your stuff was going to smell like that burning sander. Don't worry. Like I said, the place is set up for visiting execs. The bathrooms are all stocked up with toothbrushes and toothpaste and shampoo and stuff. And you don't need pajamas."

She could feel her eyebrows shoot up into her hairline.

He laughed. "The guest bedroom has its own en suite, not that I was suggesting you sleep naked. You can borrow one of my shirts."

Good grief, he was her husband. Why would she blush like a schoolgirl when the word *naked* fell, with such aggravating ease, from his gorgeous lips?

CHAPTER TWELVE

"AND WHAT SHOULD I do for clothes tomorrow?" Jessica asked. Her voice felt stiff with tension.

But Kade did not seem tense at all. He just shrugged, and then said, his tone teasing, "We will figure something out. It's not as though we could do worse than what you have on."

We.

She ordered herself not to give in to this. It was a weakness to let him look after her. It was an illusion to feel safe with him.

But she did. And she was suddenly aware she had not really slept or even eaten properly since the break-in. Exhaustion settled over her.

"One night," she decided. "My place will probably be aired out by tomorrow."

"Probably," he said insincerely.

"I think I have to go to bed now."

"All right. I'll show you the way, and find you a shirt to wear for pajamas."

"I'll put away the dishes."

"No, I'll do it. I've gotten better at picking up behind myself."

Was that true, or would the maid come and pick up

after them tomorrow? She found she just didn't care. She was giving herself over to the luxurious feeling of being looked after. Just for one night, though!

And then she found herself led down a wide hallway and tucked inside a bedroom that was an opulent symphony of grays. She went into the attached bathroom. Her mouth fell open. There was a beautiful bathtub shaped like an egg in here. And double sinks and granite, and a walk-in shower. And this was the guest room.

Why did she feel such comfort that he didn't feel as at home here as he had in the humble little wreck of a house they had shared?

Just tired, she told herself. As promised, there was everything she needed there, from toothbrushes to fresh towels.

When she went out of the bathroom, she saw he had left a shirt on the bed for her. Unable to stop herself, she buried her face in it, and inhaled the deep and wonderful scent of her husband. She managed to get the oversize buttons undone on the dress and get it off.

She pulled his shirt on. His buttons weren't quite so easy to do up, but she managed. When she noticed they were done up crooked, she didn't have the energy to change them. She tumbled into the deep luxury of that bed, looked out the window at the lights of the city reflecting in the dark waters of the river and felt her eyes grow heavy.

She realized, for the first time since her shop had been broken into and she had been injured in her ill-advised scuffle with the perpetrator, she was going to get to sleep easily. She suspected she would sleep deeply.

Only it wasn't really the first time in a week.

It was the first time in a year.

* * *

Kade was so aware that Jessica was right down the hallway from him. He wished he would not have made that crack about her sleeping naked.

Because a man did not want to be having naked thoughts about the wife he still missed and mourned.

But he had developed ways of getting by all these painful feelings. He looked at his watch. Despite the fact Jessica was in bed—she had always handled stress poorly, and he suspected she was exhausted—it was still early.

And he had his balm.

He had work. Plus, he had nearly wrecked her house today. He needed to look after that. He liked the sense of having a mission. This time, though, he decided to call the guy who had fixed her shop door, at least for the floors.

Jake, like all good carpenters and handymen in the supercharged economy of Calgary, was busy.

But willing to put a different project on hold when he heard Jessica's situation, and that Jessica's furniture was currently residing on the lawn.

His attitude inspired confidence, and Kade found himself sharing the whole repair list with him. Jake promised to look at it first thing in the morning, even though it was Sunday, and get back to him with a cost estimate and a time frame.

"Can she stay out of the house for a couple of days? The floor sanding and refinishing causes a real mess. It's actually kind of a hazardous environment. Even the best floor sander can't contain all the dust, and it's full of chemicals. Plus it'll be easier for me to work if she's not there."

"Oh, sure," Kade said, thinking of Jessica staying here

a few days. She probably wouldn't. She would probably insist on getting a hotel.

But for a little while longer, anyway, he was still her husband. And he liked having her here, under his roof. He liked how protective he felt of her, and how he felt as if he could fix her world.

So he gave Jake the go-ahead.

As he disconnected his phone, Kade realized he needed to remember, when it came to larger issues, there was a lot he could not fix. This sense of having her under his protection was largely an illusion. They had tried it over the fire of real life, and they had been scorched.

Tomorrow, he would get up superearly and be gone before she even opened her eyes. He would solve all the helpless ambivalence she made him feel in the way he always had.

He would go to work.

He would, a little voice inside him said, abandon his wife. The same as always.

But it didn't quite work out that way. Because in the night, he was awakened to the sound of screaming.

Kade bolted from his bed and down the hall to her door. He paused outside it for a minute, aware, suddenly, he was in his underwear.

He heard a strangled sob, and the hesitation was over. He opened her door, and raced to her side. The bedside lamp was a touch lamp, and he brushed it with his hand.

Jessica was illuminated in the soft light. She was thrashing around, her hair a sweaty tangle, her eyes clenched tightly shut. When the light came on, she sat up abruptly, and the jolt to her arm woke her up.

She looked up at him, terrified, and then the terror melted into a look he could have lived for.

Had lived for, once upon a time, when he still believed in once upon a time.

"Are you okay?" he asked softly.

"Just a dream," she said, her voice hoarse.

He went into the adjoining bathroom and found a glass wrapped in plastic that crinkled when he stripped it off. Again, he was reminded this place was more like a hotel and not a home. He filled the glass and brought it to her.

She was sitting up now, with her back against the headboard, her eyes shut. "Sorry," she said.

"No, no, it's okay." He handed her the water. "How long have you been having the nightmares?"

"Since the break-in." She took a long drink of water. "I dream that someone is breaking into my house. My bedroom. That I wake up and—" She shuddered.

Kade felt a helpless anger at the burglar who had caused all this.

"Are you in your underwear?" she whispered.

"Yeah." He wanted to say it was nothing she had never seen before, but she looked suddenly shy, and it was adorable.

"You know I don't own a pair of pajamas," he reminded her.

He sat down on the bed beside her. Everything about her was adorable. She looked cute and very vulnerable in his too-large shirt with the buttons done up crooked. Her hair was sticking up on one side, and he had to resist the temptation to smooth it down with his hand. He noticed her eyes skittered everywhere but to his bare legs.

Sheesh. How long had they been married?

She seemed as if she might protest him getting in the bed, but instead, after a moment's thought, she scooted over, and he slid his legs up on the mattress beside her.

He felt the soft familiar curve of her shoulder touching his, let the scent of her fill up his nose.

"I'm sorry about the nightmares," he said.

"It's silly," she said. "I think I'm getting post-traumatic stress disorder. It's shameful to get it for a very minor event."

"Hey, stop that. You were the victim here. The person who should be ashamed is whoever did this. Jessica, do these people not have any kind of conscience? Decency? Can they not know how these stupid things they do for piddling sums of money reverberate outward in a circle of pain and distress for their victims?"

He felt her relax, snuggle against him. "I feel sorry for him."

He snorted. "You would."

"I don't think you or I have ever known that kind of desperation, Kade."

Except that was not true. When she had wanted to have that baby, he had been desperate to make her happy. Desperate. And her own desperation had filled him with the most horrifying sense of helplessness.

He reached over and snapped off the light. His hand found her head, and he pulled it onto his shoulder, and stroked her hair.

"Go to sleep," he said softly. "I'll just stay with you until you do. You're safe. I'll take care of you. Why don't you lie back down."

"In a minute," she said huskily. "You know what this reminds me of, Kade?"

"Hmm?"

"Remember when we first met, how I was terrified of thunderstorms?"

"Yeah," he said gruffly, "I remember."

"And then that one night, a huge electrical storm was moving over the city, and you came and got me out of the bathroom where I was hiding."

"Under the sink," he recalled.

"And you led me outside, and you had the whole front step set up. You had a blanket out there, and a bottle of wine, and two glasses, and we sat on the step.

"At first I was terrified. I was quivering, I was so scared. I wanted to bolt. The clouds were so black. And the lightning was ripping open the heavens. I felt like Dorothy in the *Wizard of Oz*, as if I could be swept away.

"And then you put your hand on my shoulder, as if to hold me to the earth. You told me to count the seconds between the lightning bolt and the thunder hitting and I would know how far away the lightning strike was."

He remembered it all, especially her body trembling against his as the storm had intensified all around them.

"It kept getting closer and closer. Finally, there was no pause between the lightning strike and the thunder, there was not even time to count to one. The whole house shook. I could feel the rumble of the thunder ripple through you and through me and through the stairs and through the whole world. The tree in the front yard shook."

"Yeah, I remember."

"The whole night lit up in a flash, and I looked at you, and your face was illuminated by the lightning. You weren't even a little bit afraid. I could tell you loved it. You loved the fury and intensity of the storm. And suddenly, just like that, I wasn't afraid anymore. I loved it, too. Sitting out on the front steps with you, we sipped that wine, and cuddled under that blanket, and got soaked when the rain came."

She was silent for a long time.

"And after that," he said gently, "every time there was a storm, you were the first one out on that step."

"It's funny, isn't it? It cost nothing to go sit on those steps and storm watch. They came from nowhere. We couldn't plan it or expect it. And yet those moments?"

"I know, Jessica," he said softly. "The best. Those moments were the best."

"And today," she said, her voice slightly slurred with sleep, "today was a good day, like that."

"I nearly burned your house down."

"Our house," she corrected him. "You made me laugh. That made it worth it."

It made him realize how much pain was between them, and how much of it he had caused. He had a sense of wanting, somehow, to make it right between them. It bothered him, her casual admittance that she did not laugh much anymore. It bothered him, and he accepted responsibility for it.

So it could be a clean goodbye between him and Jessica. They could get a divorce without acrimony and without regret. So they could remember times like that, sitting in the thunderstorm, and know they had been made better for them. Not temporarily. But permanently.

He was a better man because of her.

CHAPTER THIRTEEN

PERHAPS, KADE THOUGHT, he was not the man he had wished to be or hoped to be, but still, he was better than he had been. Because of her, and because of the love they had shared.

Was there a way to honor that before they said good-bye? What if tomorrow, Sunday, he wasn't going to go to work after all?

Kade could tell something had shifted. Her head fell against his chest heavily, and he heard her breathing change.

And he knew he should get up and move, but there was something about this moment, this unexpected gift of his wife trusting him and being with him, that felt like one of those best moments ever, a moment just like sitting on the front step with her watching thunderstorms.

And so he accepted that he was reluctant to leave it. And eventually he fell asleep, sitting up, with Jessica's sweet weight nestled into him and the feel of the silk of her hair beneath his fingers.

Jessica woke to the most luxurious feeling of having slept well. The sun was spilling in her bedroom window. When she sat up and stretched, she saw that through the enor-

CARA COLTER   115

mous windows of the bedroom, she had a view of the
river and people jogging down the paths beside it.

Had she dreamed Kade had come into her room and
they had talked about thunderstorms? It seemed as if she
must have, because things had not been that easy between
them for a long, long time.

And yet, when she looked, she was pretty sure the
bedding beside her had been crushed from the weight
of another person.

Far off in that big apartment, she heard a familiar
sound.

Kade was whistling.

She realized she was surprised he was still here in the
apartment. She glanced at the bedside clock. It was after
nine. Sunday was just another workday for Kade. Usually he was in the office by seven. But not only was he
here, he sounded happy.

Like the Kade of old.

There was a light tap on the door, and it swung open.
Jessica pulled the covers up around her chin as if she
was shy of him.

"I brought you a coffee."

She *was* shy of him. She realized she had not dreamed
last night, because she had a sudden and rather mouthwatering picture of him in his underwear. Thankfully, he
was fully dressed now, though he was still off the sexi-
ness scale this morning.

It was obvious that Kade was fresh out of the shower,
his dark hair towel roughened, a single beautiful bead of
water sliding down his cheek to his jaw. Dressed in jeans,
he had a thick white towel looped around his neck, and
his chest and feet were deliciously bare.

She could look at that particular sight all day: the

deepness of his chest, the chiseled perfection of his muscles, the ridged abs narrowing and disappearing into the waistband of jeans that hung low on slender hips. Her mouth actually went dry looking at him standing there.

He came in and handed her the coffee. It smelled wonderful—though not as wonderful as his fresh-from-the-shower scent—and she reached out for it. Their fingers touched, and the intensity sizzled in the air between them.

She knew that no part of last night had been a dream. He had slipped onto the bed beside her, and they had talked of thunderstorms, and she had fallen asleep with his big shoulder under her head.

She took a steadying sip of the coffee. It was one of those unexpectedly perfect moments. Kade had always made the best coffee. He delighted in good coffee and was always experimenting with different beans, which he ground himself. It had just the right amount of cream and no sugar.

He remembered. Silly to feel so wonderful that he remembered how she liked her coffee. The luxury of the bed, the sun spilling in the window, the coffee, him delivering it bare chested—yes, an unexpectedly perfect moment.

"I just talked to Jake," he said, taking a sip of his own coffee, and eyeing her over the rim of it.

"Who?"

"Jake. The contractor who fixed the door at your shop. He's over at your house."

"He's at my house at, what is it, seven o'clock on Sunday morning? How do you get a contractor, especially a good one, to do that?"

"I used my substantial charm."

"And your substantial checkbook?" she asked sweetly.

He pretended to be offended. "He's going to do the list of all the things that need fixing—the leak in the roof and the toilet handle and the floors, which really need refinishing now. And he'll fix the new smoke damage on the ceiling, too. That's the good news."

"Uh-oh, there's bad news."

"Yeah. There always is, isn't there? It's going to take him the better part of a week to get everything done. And he says it will go a lot smoother if you aren't there."

She concentrated hard on her coffee. "Oh," she finally squeaked out. A week of this? Coffee delivered by a gorgeous man whom she happened to know intimately? Who had joined her last night in bed in his underwear? She'd be a basket case. "Look, obviously I can't stay here. I'll call a friend. Or get a hotel."

"Why is it obvious you can't stay here?" he asked.

"Kade, we're getting a divorce. We're supposed to be fighting, not setting up as roommates." Certainly she should not be feeling this way about the near nudity of a man she was about to divorce!

"'From where the sun now stands, I will fight no more forever,'" he said softly.

"I hate it when you quote Chief Joseph." No, she didn't. She loved it. She loved it as much as she loved that he had made her coffee exactly as she liked it, without even having to ask.

She loved that he remembered she had once bought a piece of art—that they couldn't afford—with a part of that quote as its name. She remembered that he hadn't been mad. He'd turned the piece over in his hands—a shard of gourd, burned with an Appaloosa galloping across it toward the sun—and he'd smiled and said, "Worth starving for a few weeks."

And, of course, they hadn't starved.

But of course, that had been at the beginning, when her staying home and having a house of her own and a husband to look after had been so novel. Later, it seemed as if Kade was nothing but annoyed when she bought things for the house. She thought of reminding him of that.

But it seemed too petty. She slid him a look now. Was he quoting that because they were turning over a new leaf? Because they were not going to squabble anymore?

Everybody squabbled when they got divorced.

"You want to do something fun today?" he asked. "Since fixing the house has been removed from our list?"

No, she did not want to do something fun! She wanted to get a divorce. She wanted to sell the house they had shared. She wanted to cut ties with him. She wanted to adopt a baby and get on with her life, without him. Fun? Who had fun in the middle of a divorce?

"I thought I took the fun out of everything," she said. She put the coffee down and folded her arms over the largeness of his shirt, which she suddenly wished was at least a little sexy. She recognized the treachery of her thoughts.

He looked bewildered. "You took the fun out of everything?"

"That's what you said. The day you left."

Kade looked genuinely shocked. "I didn't say that."

"Yes, you did." The words, in fact, felt burned into her, as if they had become part of who she was.

"Are you sure?"

"Oh, yeah."

He looked genuinely distressed, but she found she couldn't let it go.

"So," she said, trying for a bright, light note, "what do you do for fun? You're probably an expert at it, now that the dead weight isn't around your neck anymore."

"Jessica, I don't remember saying that. It must have been one of those mean, in-the-heat-of-the-moment things. I'm sorry."

She shrugged, as if it didn't matter one little bit, as if she had not mulled over those words every single day for a year.

"So if we *were* going to do something fun today— and I'm not saying that we are—what would you suggest?" Did it sound as if she was forgiving him? *Was* she forgiving him? "Remember, I have one arm out of commission. Skydiving is out. Ditto for rock climbing. And bull riding."

"I said that? That you took the fun out of everything?"

"Yes! And then you packed your bag, and you left, and you never looked back."

"I thought you'd call, Jessica."

"Why would I call? You were the one who left." She hesitated. She tried to strip any hurt from her voice. "I thought you'd call."

"I didn't know what to say."

"Neither did I. I wasn't going to beg you to come back."

"Why would you beg me to come back?" he asked wearily. "And I guess that's why I didn't call, either. We had reached a complete impasse. We were utterly and exhaustingly miserable. We just seemed to go in endless circles. You wanted a baby. I'd had enough."

She could see the very real pain in his face. For the first time? Had she really been so wrapped up in herself and what she wanted that she could not see what it was doing to him? She'd accused him of being insensitive to her, but she saw now it had been a two-way street. She felt an odd little shiver of awareness go up her spine.

"So," Jessica said carefully, trying to navigate the minefield between them without getting blown up, "answer the question. What do you do with a one-armed woman for fun?"

His eyes fastened on her lips.

"Stop it," she said.

"Stop what?" he asked innocently.

"Looking at me like that. I think *that* would be quite a challenge one armed."

"What?" he asked innocently.

"You know."

He smiled wickedly. "I think *that* could be quite a lot of fun.

"I think it would be darn near impossible."

"I don't. I like a challenge. I like figuring things out."

Good grief, she could not stay here for days with this kind of delicious sensual tension in the air between them.

"I could start by offering to help you shower," he said, his voice a low growl.

She threw the pillow at him. It was a clean miss, but he dodged anyway, managing to save his coffee. He laughed and made a face at her. "So are we agreed? We'll do something fun today?"

"I suppose, if you promise to be good," she said warningly, reaching for the other pillow.

"Do I have to? Okay, okay." And then he backed away from her, closed the door and was gone.

She freshened up in the bathroom and put on the maternity dress. When she saw her reflection in the full-length mirror of his opulent guest bathroom, she felt she had succeeded just a little too well in her goals.

She had wanted to look as if she didn't care! She was not sure she had wanted to look quite this bad! She looked like a waif abandoned outside an orphanage. Still, defiantly, refusing to give in to the temptation to win his approval in any way, least of all by trying to make herself attractive to him, she stepped out of the bathroom.

The truth was she hadn't brought anything else anyway. She had thought her stay here was going to be brief. Given the shakiness of her resolve, looking pathetic seemed as if it could only be a good thing.

He was behind the kitchen counter putting croissants—obviously freshly delivered—on a plate.

"Wow. Excuse me while I pluck out my eyes. I'd forgotten the full ugliness of that dress. Or maybe I blocked it. Trauma."

"It is not that bad." He still had not put on a shirt. In the "life was unfair" department, this seemed to rate quite high: that he wanted to pluck out his eyes and she wanted to gaze at him endlessly.

"It is. That bad. Believe me. At least its awfulness helps me figure out the agenda for the day. We need to go shopping first."

"I am not going shopping. I love this dress." She didn't actually. She thought it was quite hideous. "I'm sorry you'll be embarrassed by me, but that's the way it is."

"I'm not embarrassed by you. But in the 'find something to be grateful for' department—"

She squinted at him suspiciously. He was not a "find something to be grateful for" kind of guy.

"I'm just glad you didn't bring the camo one. If we end up in the woods today, I don't want to misplace you."

"What are the chances we'll end up in the woods?"

"Anything can happen when you just let the day unfold."

She should not feel nearly as thrilled by that as she did! But spontaneity had not been part of her world for a long time, and Jessica suddenly felt eager for it.

CHAPTER FOURTEEN

ONE THING THAT Jessica remembered about Kade with complete fondness was that he always seemed open to what the world could bring him.

They had a simple breakfast at his apartment. He had had the still-steaming croissants and preserves delivered, and they sat out on the terrace and ate in the new warmth of the spring light. What was it about spring that brought hope to even the most wounded heart?

He seemed to forget she looked ugly. She seemed to forget he looked gorgeous. The old comfort rose up between them.

They talked as if nothing had ever gone wrong between them. It was like the old days, when spending time with him felt as if she was spending time with her best friend. The conversation flowed easily and naturally, words spilling out of them, as if they were anxious to catch up. They talked about mutual friends, his aunt Helen and her cousin Dave. They talked a bit about their businesses.

And then they left his place and walked downtown. Jessica became self-consciously aware of the ugliness of her dress again as she walked beside him. Kade was dressed casually in a sports shirt and summer khaki pants, and yet she could not help but notice how he got *that* look from women. Interested. Admiring. Hungry for a taste of that particular delight. They would glance at her, too, and then dismiss her.

When he came around to her good arm and his hand found hers, her own sense of hunger deepened. She was so aware of how much she had missed this, the small intimacies that made a relationship, the feel of his hand, strong, closing possessively around her own, sending that message to all who passed: *taken*.

She was determined to make a go of it on her own, but that simple thing, him taking her hand, filled her with a longing that felt physical in its intensity, like a shiver going up and down her spine that would not go away.

If she was smart, she would drop his hand and turn and run.

But smart seemed to have abandoned her. She wanted these moments. It felt as if she was stealing them to store away, as a part of her, for when she did not have him anymore. She actually felt thankful that *these* memories might overlay the old ones. Their history, leading up to the separation, was so filled with bitterness and anger and frustration that it had become as if the dark colors of a new painting had completely obliterated the light of the old painting that existed right underneath it.

They entered the downtown. It was a beautiful day so they avoided the Plus 15 Skywalk and instead strolled the pedestrian mall on Stephen Avenue. Downtown did not have its weekday bustle, the throngs of men and women in business attire, but there was still a colorful conglomeration of shoppers and activities on the streets.

A cowboy-hatted busker had set up close to Stephen Avenue Walk and was singing lustily. They stopped and watched for a few minutes. Kade dropped a five into his guitar case and they moved on.

They enjoyed the historic sandstone buildings of one of Canada's few designated National Historic Sites. Calgarians had been conducting their commerce here on Eighth Avenue for over a hundred years. They passed the building where Kade worked, in the heart of Calgary's financial district, and then walked along the column-fronted arcade of the very impressive Hudson's Bay Company building. The building had always anchored Calgary's downtown core.

"How about there?"

She looked at the store Kade had paused to point out. It was a tiny but very upscale boutique called Chrysalis, which Jessica knew of but had never set foot in. "I can't go in there."

"Why?"

Mostly because of how she was dressed right now! "I can't afford anything in there."

"I can."

"No."

"Come on. It will be fun. Remember that scene we liked in that movie?"

"Pretty Woman?" she guessed.

He nodded happily. "Let's reenact that."

"I'm no Julia Roberts," she said, but she could feel herself being drawn into his playfulness. Where had all the playfulness gone between them?

"You are way better than her," he said, and he looked at her with such genuine male appreciation that she nearly melted.

They went into the shop. It was understated and tasteful. But the salesclerk was a very chic young woman with an outrageous purple streak in her blond hair. She rushed at them, probably, Jessica thought, to get rid of her, the same as in the movie.

"My first customers of the day," she said gleefully. Then she eyed Jessica with the look of a seasoned fashion aficionado. Rather than judgment or snobbery, Jessica sensed friendliness and very genuine concern. "What is that you are wearing?"

In a tone that should be reserved for "I'm so sorry to hear about the death in your family."

"I'm having a little trouble with my arm," Jessica said defensively.

"Even so, you're lovely! And just a little bit of a thing. You have to show off your assets!" She cast Kade a look that clearly said, "Especially if you are with a guy who looks like that," and that she clearly considered him an asset worth keeping.

"Thank you. We'll just have a quick look around," Jessica said.

"No, no, *no*. I am going to guide you through your Chrysalis experience."

"Oh, dear," Jessica mumbled, and sent Kade a pleading look. *Get me out of here.* But Kade folded his arms over his chest and shrugged slightly. *Let's just go with it.*

"I will have you fixed up in no time. In fact, I will love working with you. Caterpillar to butterfly, as our name suggests. I'm Holly, by the way."

The girl's enthusiasm was so genuine that Jessica could not even stir herself to annoyance at being called, basically, an insect pupa.

"Usually, I would ask about your lifestyle, but today I think you're looking for some things that are easier to get in and out of, aren't you?"

Kade frowned at Holly. "We were hoping for some-one more like the salesclerk in *Pretty Woman*. You know? If you could just be snotty, and then I flash my gold card at you and you fall all over yourself trying to help us out."

Holly laughed. "Well, I like the gold card part. And I always fall all over myself trying to help people out." She looked at Jessica. "How would you feel if I just put you in a change room and found some things that I think would work for you?"

Jessica should be insulted. She was obviously being told she could not be trusted to pick out her own things, but given the dress she had on, could she blame the girl?

"I like to encourage everyone to let me pick some things for them," Holly said. "You know, people get in shopping ruts."

Out of the corner of her vision, Jessica saw Kade roll his eyes at the near religious fervor Holly apparently had for the shopping experience.

Undaunted, Holly went on. "They pick variations of the same thing for themselves over and over. Sometimes a fresh eye can be amazing. And then, you can model what I pick out for you for your extremely handsome boyfriend."

"Husband," Kade said. "Though I like the handsome part."

"Oh, sorry. No rings," Holly said. She squinted at him. "Though you look as though you've had one on recently."

Jessica's gaze flew to Kade's ring finger. Sure enough, a white band of skin marked where his wedding ring had been. The band had been there recently, obviously, since such marks faded rather quickly. What did it mean that he had worn his ring so recently?

Stay in the moment, she ordered herself sternly. She had one mission today. To have fun. To let go. To be free. And if she ended up, with Holly's help, looking a little bit better than she looked right now, she'd go with that, too.

For once, Jessica felt no desire at all to hide behind their upcoming divorce.

She followed Holly obediently to the back of the store. There was a classy sitting area there for Kade, complete with a comfy deep upholstered chair and a huge flat-screen TV. Holly handed him the remote, and then shooed Jessica into an opulent change room.

Minutes later, she was back. "I don't mean to be presumptuous, but I brought you this." She held up a bra. "Front closing."

And sexy as all get out. Jessica took the bra with her good hand and suddenly ached to put it on. To give herself permission to be feminine and beautiful.

She had not felt like a beautiful woman since her husband had left her. Despite career success, somehow she carried loneliness and defeat within her.

A thought, unwelcome, came out of nowhere.

Had she been planning on using a child to combat her pervasive feeling of inadequacy? She shook off the shadow that passed over her. Today was just about fun. She had given herself over to introspection quite enough in the past year.

"You are a lifesaver," Jessica told Holly, and then surrendered to the process. She allowed herself to be spoiled completely. Holly did have an exceptional eye for fashion, and along with the bra, she had soon provided Jessica with a stack of clothing topped by a filmy jade silk top.

None of it was anything Jessica would have chosen

for herself. She had become the master of understated. Almost all her clothes were in neutrals, grays and taupes, as if, she realized with a start, she was trying to make herself invisible.

Jessica fingered the silk and felt a pure and simple longing. To be pretty.

It occurred to her she had not cared about being pretty since long before Kade had left her. Since she had lost the second baby.

"This will be amazing with your eyes. And look— Velcro fasteners!"

"You found a top with a Velcro closure? Is this really silk? Where's the price tag?"

"Your Prince Charming out there told me to take the price tags off."

"Humph," she said, but she didn't feel nearly as annoyed as she should have. She didn't have to buy it, she reminded herself. She just had to have fun with it.

Soon, the ensemble was completed with an easy-to-pull-on skirt with a flirty hemline and a delicate pair of sandals that Jessica could just slip her feet into.

"You look awesome," Holly said. "Go show him."

Jessica stared at herself in the mirror. "Um, I think I look a bit too young." Plus, the blouse was extremely sheer, which explained Holly bringing a sexy bra with it.

"Nonsense."

"This looks like something a teenager would wear. Don't you think the skirt is a little, um, short? Not to mention the blouse is a little, er, see-through."

"When you have legs like that? Show them off, girlfriend. Same with your other assets. Now go show him! He'll let you know how right that look is for you."

Feeling strangely shy about sharing this oddly intimate moment with Kade, the same as she had felt this morning sharing space with him, Jessica exited the change room. Kade had found a football game on TV and didn't even look impatient. He looked content.

And then he noticed her. He flipped off the sound. His eyes darkened. She suddenly didn't care how short the skirt was or if the blouse was see-through. She did a saucy little spin.

"Wow," he said, his voice hoarse. "You look incredible. Two thumbs-up to that one."

Jessica didn't just feel beautiful for the first time in a long time. She felt sexy. It felt unbelievably good to feel sexy with no agenda, no calendar lurking in the back of her mind, no temperature to take. It felt, well, fun. And after that, she just gave herself over to the experience completely.

It was fun, having Holly help her in and out of outfits, and then modeling them for Kade, who was a great audience. He raised his eyebrows, and did low wolf whistles and louder ones. He made her feel as if she was not only sexy and beautiful, but as if she was the only woman in the world he felt that way about.

But even so, Jessica had to draw the line somewhere, and she drew it at an evening dress Holly hauled in.

"I have absolutely nowhere to wear such a thing," she said. Still, she touched it wistfully. Like everything in Chrysalis, the cut and the fabric were mouthwatering. "I won't be able to get it on over my arm."

"Sure you will," Holly said. "It's back fastening, so I'll just drop it over your head, like this, and poof. Ooh, butterfly."

It took a bit more work for them to get her arm out

the sleeve, but then she was standing there looking at herself, stunned.

Her hair was flyaway from all the in-and-out of trying on clothes, but somehow that added to the sense of electricity in the air. The dress, the color of licking flame, fit her like a glove, then flared out at the bottom in a mermaid hemline.

"Here." Holly crouched at her feet. "Let me slip these on you."

As if in a dream, Jessica lifted one foot and then the other. She stared at herself in the mirror. The heels had added three inches to her height. The cast and sling on her arm might as well have disappeared, the outfit was so attention grabbing, especially with a very deep, plunging neckline.

Holly stood back and looked at her with satisfaction. "*This* is exactly what I envisioned from the moment you walked through the door. Go show him."

Should she? What was the point? It didn't feel fun anymore. It felt strangely intense, almost like the moment she had walked toward him down that long aisle in her wedding dress.

She was going to protest, but when Holly held open the door for her, Jessica sucked in her breath and walked out. Holly slid away.

Kade didn't look right away. "Don't drop it!" he yelled at the TV. And then he turned and saw her. Without taking his eyes off her, he turned off the remote. The television screen went blank. He stood up. His mouth fell open and then he shut it, and rocked back on his heels, looking at her with eyes narrowed with passion.

This was what she had missed when that moment she had glided down the aisle toward him had been replaced by the pressures of everyday living, by disappointments, by hurts, by misunderstandings.

"Jessie," he whispered.

This was what she had missed. She leaned toward him.

CHAPTER FIFTEEN

JESSIE LEANED TOWARD HIM, looking at him with heavy-lidded eyes.

*Pretty woman...walking down the street...*The music seemed to explode into the small dressing room and waiting area. Jessica gasped and put her hand to her throat, wobbled on the high heels.

Kade was in front of her instantly, looking down at her with concern.

"Sorry," she said. "I keep startling from loud noises."

He cocked his head at her. The room flooded with Roy Orbison's distinctive vocals. Kade took one step closer to her. He held out his hand, and she didn't hesitate, not for one second. She took his hand. Kade drew her to him and rocked her against him.

And then, as if they had planned it, as if they had never stopped dancing with each other, they were moving together. Even though the tempo of the song was fast, they did not dance that way.

They slow danced around the waiting area, their bodies clinging to each other, their gazes locked. The music faded, but they didn't let go, but stood very still, drinking each other in, as if they could make up for a whole year lost.

Holly burst in. "How cool was that, that I found—" She stopped. "Whoa. You two are *hot*."

Kade's arms slid away from Jessica. He stepped back. He swept a hand through his hair. "We'll take it," he said.

"That dress?" Holly said.

"No. Everything. Every single thing she tried on."

Jessica's mouth opened, but the protest was stuck somewhere in her throat, and not a single sound came out. She turned and went back into the change cubicle.

"Wear this one," Holly suggested, following her in. She dug through the pile of clothing to the very first outfit Jessica had tired on, the jade top and skirt.

But she didn't want to wear that one. Her world felt totally rattled by what had just happened, by how spontaneously she and Kade had gone into each other's arms. She wanted to feel safe again.

"Where's the dress I came in here with?"

Holly giggled. "He told me to throw it away."

"What?"

"Yeah, he said to grab it at my first opportunity and dispose of it."

"And you just listened to him? That's outrageous."

"He's very masterful," Holly said with an unapologetic sigh. "Besides—" she winked "—he's the one with the credit card."

Jessica thought of the frank male appreciation in his eyes as she had modeled her new outfits, and she contemplated how she was feeling right now.

Alive. One hundred percent in the land of the living, the life force tingling along the surface of her skin. Did she really want to go back to safety? To reclaim that familiar wooden feeling she had lived with for so long?

Why not, just for today, embrace this? That she was

alive? And that her life was alight with the unexpected element of fun? And with the unexpected sizzle of attraction between her and the man she had married.

They left the store with Kade's arms loaded with parcels, and with her feeling fresh and flirty and like a breath of spring in the first outfit she had tried on. He had paid for everything.

"I'll pay you back," she said. He had insisted on buying every single thing she had donned, even the evening gown.

Since the theme of the day was fun, she'd given in. But buying the gown? That was just silly. She had nowhere to wear an evening gown. Her future plans did not involve anything that would require formal wear. In fact, she needed to be stocking up on comfy pants and sweatshirts that could hold up to baby puke and other fluids associated with the delights of motherhood.

But she had been so caught up in the moment, and the dress had made her feel so uncharacteristically glamorous—sexy, even—that she had actually wanted to be silly. She had wanted to purchase that piece of silk and gossamer that had made her feel better than a movie star.

She should have protested more—she knew that when the bill was totaled—but the look in his eyes when he had seen her had sold every single outfit to her. She'd had a ridiculous sense of *needing* those clothes, though in her heart, she knew what she wanted was the look in his eyes. "Once we sell the house, I'll pay you back," she said firmly.

"Whatever. Hey, this stuff is already heavy. Look. There's one of those rickshaw things being pulled by a bike. Have you ever been in one of those?"

"No."

He juggled the packages to his left arm, put his two fingers to his lips and let out a piercing whistle. The driver, a fit-looking twentysomething guy, pulled over.

"Where to?"

"Ah, we aren't sure yet. I think we need you for the day. Have you got a day rate?"

"I do now!"

Jessica knew she should have protested when the driver named his rate, but somehow she just couldn't. She and Kade piled into the narrow seat of the rickshaw, squished together, all their packages bunched in with them.

"Where to?"

"We need a picnic lunch," Kade decided. "And a bottle of wine. And a forest. Maybe Yan's for the lunch. Do you feel like Szechuan?"

She thought of all those menus she had sorted through yesterday, each one representing a memory. She loved Szechuan-style Chinese food. "Two orders of ginger beef," she reminded him.

Their driver took off across the downtown, darting in and out of traffic, getting them honked at, shaking his fist and yelling obscenities at drivers of vehicles.

It was hysterically funny, and she could not stop laughing. That wondrous feeling of being alive continued to tingle along the surface of her skin.

"You're going to get us killed," she said with a laugh as a cab they had cut off laid on the horn. She clung to Kade's arm as the rickshaw swayed violently, and then their driver bumped up on a curb. "Or get my other arm broken."

He twirled an imaginary moustache. "Ah, getting

you right where I want you. Helpless. And then I can ply my lethal charms against you."

Kade flopped down on the blanket that he had purchased. The driver had found them a quiet spot on Prince's Island, and had managed to make himself scarce while Kade and Jessica enjoyed their picnic under a leafy tree, with the sound of the river in the background. Now, after too much food, and most of a bottle of wine, Kade felt sleepy and relaxed.

"Two orders of ginger beef," he moaned. "It's masochistic."

"Nobody was forcing you to eat it."

"You know why we always have to buy two, though." *Always*, as if there was not a yearlong blank spot in their relationship, as if they could just pick up where they had left off. He considered where they had left off, and thought, despite his current level of comfort with Jessica, why would they want to?

"Yes, we always have to buy two because you eat the first one by yourself, and most of the second one."

"Guilty," he moaned. "My tummy hurts, Jessie."

"And three spring rolls," she reminded him. "And most of the sizzling rice." Despite the sternness in her tone, when he opened one eye, she was smiling. She looked as utterly content as he could remember her looking in a long, long time.

He lifted up his shirt and showed her his tummy. She sighed, and scooted over beside him, that teeny-tiny skirt hitching way up her legs, and rubbed his stomach with gentle hands.

"Ah," he said, and closed his eyes. Maybe it was because he had not slept well last night, or maybe it was because he had eaten too much, or maybe it was because his world felt right for the first time in over a year, but with a sigh of contentment, he went to sleep.

When he woke up, she was sleeping curled up beside him. He slid his arm around her shoulders and pulled her into his side, being careful of her arm.

"Did we fall asleep?" she asked.

"Yeah."

"Is our driver still here? Or did he take off with all my new stuff?"

Kade got up on one elbow. He could see the rickshaw over by the riverbank. When he craned his head, he could see the driver tapping earnestly at his phone with his thumbs.

"I haven't paid him yet. He's not going anywhere." He slid his own phone out of his pocket and checked the time. "Holy, it's four o'clock already."

"It's been a perfect day," she said.

"Agreed. What was the best part for you? The shopping? I love the long dress."

"I don't have a single place to wear a dress like that," she said. "I shouldn't have bought it."

"Yes, you should have. I want you to accept it as a gift from me. You can pay me back for the rest of that stuff if you insist—"

"Which I do!"

"But I want to buy that dress."

"Why do you want to buy me a dress that I probably will never wear?"

"Wear it around the house. Put a movie on, and wear it to watch it. Eat popcorn in it."

She laughed. "That seems eccentric and foolhardy. What if I got butter on it?"

"That's what I liked about it. You know what it reminded me of, Jess?"

"No. What?" She held her breath.

"It reminded me of those paintings you used to do, the ones that were all swirling colors and amazing motion."

"I haven't thought about those for years," she said.

"Save the dress and wear it to the unveiling of your first art show."

She laughed a little nervously. "I'm not having a first art show."

"But that's what I've always wondered. Where did that part of you go?"

"I paint murals," she said. "That's my creative outlet."

"I don't think bunnies on walls do justice to your gifts," he said.

"I don't care what you think!" she snapped. "Sorry. Let's not ruin the moment with you telling me how to live my life."

She was right. This was not any of his business, not anymore. Maybe it never had been.

"Is there any ginger beef left?" he asked wistfully.

"No."

"How about sizzling rice?"

And then the moment of tension was gone, and she laughed and passed him the container. It seemed like the most natural thing in the world to go home to his place together. And then to say good-night with unnatural formality and to go to their separate bedrooms.

The next morning, they both got up. He ordered croissants again. She came out to eat one in the too-large shirt.

"I guess I should have been shopping for pajamas instead of evening dresses," she said.

What kind of kettle of worms would it open up, he

wondered, if he said he liked what she had on—his shirt—way better than pajamas?

"Are you coming back here after you've finished work?" he asked her. He was holding his breath waiting for her reply.

"I guess," she said, and he heard in her voice the very same things he was feeling. What were they reopening, exactly, by living under the same roof? What were they moving toward? Were they putting a framework in place for their future relationship? Was it possible they could be one of those rare amicably divorced couples who were friends?

He hoped things would become clear in the next few days, because he did not like uncertainty. And at the moment, his future seemed murky, like looking into a most uncooperative crystal ball.

CHAPTER SIXTEEN

MONDAY, AFTER WORK, Jessica returned to Kade's apartment. She was somewhat ashamed that she had not done a single thing to make new living arrangements for herself. And now here she was, aware she was waiting for the door of the apartment to open.

Why? Kade never came home at regular hours. What was she waiting for? Hadn't this been part of their whole problem? That she waited, as if her whole life depended on him, and he had a whole life that had nothing to do with her?

Surely she'd come further than this, still waiting for him to come home! It was pathetic, and she was not being pathetic anymore. And so, instead of sitting in the apartment, she went and explored his building.

There was a good-size pool that they were conducting a kayaking class in, and beside that was a climbing wall. She went and sat on a bench and watched people climb the wall.

A good-looking man came over and introduced himself as Dave and asked her if she was going to try it.

She held up her arm. "Already did," she said, deadpan. He laughed and flirted with her a bit, and she realized whatever had happened when she had put on all those clothes had been good. She was wearing one of her new outfits, and it seemed to fill her with confidence she hadn't had for some time. Dave went up the wall, obviously showing off, and she was content to let him.

She watched for a while, and decided as soon as her arm got better, she would try climbing. The wall looked really fun.

After doing a thorough tour of the building and the gorgeous gardens outside, which included that impressive waterfall at the front, she wandered back to the apartments.

Kade was there. Did he look pleased when she let herself in using the code he had given her?

"Hey," he said. "How was your day?"

"Oh, I struggled through."

"Work late?"

"Oh, no, I've been back for a while. I thought I'd check out your building. It's great. I love the climbing wall."

"Really? I've never been on it. Is that one of the outfits we bought yesterday?"

"Yeah, I've had lots of comments on it. A guy named Dave, down at the climbing wall, stopped to talk to me. I don't think he normally would have mistaken me for his type."

She felt just the littlest thrill of pleasure that Kade could not hide his annoyance at Dave's attention.

"Want to order something for dinner? I don't have much here to cook." He snapped his fingers. "Unless you want an omelet."

He'd always made the best omelets.

"Perfect," she said.

And it was perfect. After dinner they watched the

news together, and it felt so utterly easy, as if they were an old married couple.

Which they were, sort of.

Of course, when they'd been a newly married couple, they hadn't sat around watching television. They couldn't keep their hands off each other. Later, when that stage had passed—or when she'd killed it, by bringing out the dreaded chart—they had played cards sometimes in the evening.

She suddenly longed for that.

"You have a deck of cards, Kade?"

"Why? You want to play strip poker?" he asked with such earnest hopefulness she burst out laughing.

"No!"

"How about a strip Scrabble game, then?"

"How about just an ordinary Scrabble game?" she said, trying not to encourage him by laughing.

"Can we use bad words?"

"I suppose that would be okay. Just this once."

"How about if we use only bad words?"

She gave him a slug on his arm. "That falls into the 'give him an inch and he'll take a mile' category."

Suddenly, she wanted to play a bad-words Scrabble game with him. She wanted to not be the uptight one, the stick-in-the-mud. "A bad-words Scrabble game it is," she said.

"I don't actually have a Scrabble board."

"That figures."

"But I bet we can find it on the computer."

And so that was what they did, sat side by side on his sofa, playing a bad-words Scrabble game on the computer until she was laughing so hard it felt as if she could die from it.

"So," he said casually, after he had just played *phaut*, "tell me why you want a divorce all of a sudden."

"I told you, it's not all of a sudden."

"But there's something going on."

And, maybe he'd done this on purpose, reminded her of what it was like to have a best friend, because she wanted to tell him. Crazily, she wanted to know what he thought.

"I'm thinking of adopting a baby," she said quietly.

He was staring at her. "Aw, Jess," he said, not as if he was happy for her, but as if he pitied her.

"What does that mean?" she asked.

"It's the Old English spelling of *fart*," he said. "*P-h-a-u-t*. You can challenge it if you want. But you miss a turn if you're wrong."

She had just told him something very important! How could he act as if the stupid word he'd made up was more engrossing?

"Not *that*. What does 'aw, Jess' mean?"

"Never mind. I'm sorry I said it."

She saw, suddenly, that he was using his stupid made-up word as a way not to get into it with her. "No, I want you to tell me."

"But then when I do, you'll be mad," he said, confirming his avoidance strategy.

"Will I?" When had she become that person? The one who invited opinions, but then was angry if they were not what she wanted to hear? She wanted it not to be a truth about her, but in her gut, she knew it was.

"You don't want to hear what I have to say, but maybe I'm going to say it anyway, for the sake of the baby."

She felt as if she was bracing herself.

"A baby isn't supposed to fill a need in you, Jessica," he said quietly. "You're supposed to fulfill its needs."

Jessica felt the shock of it. She felt as if she should be very, very angry with him. But she was not. Instead, she remembered the revelation she'd had in the change room of Chrysalis, the one she had tried to shake off.

That she was using a child to try to fight off her own pervasive feeling of inadequacy. Instead of being angry with Kade, Jessica was, instead, sharply aware she had carried a certain neediness in her since the death of her mother. The miscarriages had made it worse.

So Kade had called a spade a spade. She saw, from the look on his face, it was not a put-down at all. She had a deep sense of his courage, that he had handed her a simple truth, knowing it might make her angry, but also believing she needed to hear it. And maybe also believing she would know what to do with it.

Jessica remembered how before she had hated everything about Kade, she had loved everything about him. And this was one of the things she had loved, that he had a way of seeing right to the heart of things. He would have shrugged it off, uncomfortable, if she called it intuition, but that was exactly what it was.

It was part of what made him so good at business. He was brilliantly insightful. Before things had gone sideways between them, Jessica had loved his input, so different from her own.

"I've been too blunt," he said. "I'm sorry."

"No, Kade," she said, "it's what I needed to hear, even if it's not what I wanted to hear."

She suspected this was why she had not wanted to tell him about the adoption, because he could shed a light on her plans that could change everything.

"You and I," she said, "we've always been so different. It's as if we each have the pieces of half of a puzzle.

It's when we're together that we can piece together the whole thing."

She thought of those adoption papers at home, and it occurred to her this was what he had shown her: she was still wanting a baby to fill gaps in her life.

She had probably never been less ready for a baby than she was right now.

"I'm very tired now," she whispered, feeling as if she was holding the remnants of another shattered dream within herself. "I'm going to bed."

"Jess, I'm sorry. I didn't want to hurt you."

She smiled wanly. "Oh, Kade, I don't think we ever wanted to hurt each other. And yet, somehow we always do."

And yet, over the next few days it was as if something had broken free between them; a wall of ice had crumbled, and what was held behind it flowed out. As they shared his beautiful space, there were moments of spontaneous laughter. And quiet companionship. As they shared meals and memories and old connections, they rediscovered their comfort with one another. And caught glimpses of the joy they had once shared. And relaxed into that rare sensation of having found someone in the world with whom it was possible to be genuine.

And so when Jake called Kade on Thursday afternoon and told him that the house was done, Kade felt not happy that the work had been finished so quickly, but a sense of loss. He wanted to give Jake a list of ten more things to do. No, a hundred. No, a thousand.

He brought her the news after work. Jessica had arrived at the apartment before him. She was wearing one of the outfits they had bought together—a lively floral-print dress with a belt and a wide skirt that reminded him of something someone might wear to dance the jive.

She had her arm out of the sling and was wiping down his counters. Once it had bugged him so much that she felt driven to wipe up every crumb.

But now, watching her, he could see it gave her a kind of contentment to be bringing order to her space, and he found he liked watching her.

She looked up and saw him standing there, and she smiled a greeting.

"Hey! You are not supposed to be out of that sling yet."

"You know me."

It was the most casual of statements, but it filled him with some sense of satisfaction that, yes, he did know her.

"I could not handle the mess on the counter. I needed both hands free to wring out the dishcloth."

"You've always been such a stickler for tidy."

"I know. You used to protest daily, *too many rules.*"

"Did I? I don't remember that."

Jessica cast Kade a look. Could he really not remember the mean things he had said to her?

"You called me the sock Nazi," she remembered ruefully. Was she hoping he would apologize? He didn't. He cocked his head at her, and looked at her in that way that made her stomach do the roller-coaster thing.

"I couldn't understand the changes in you," he said. "We said 'I do' and overnight you went from being this kind of Bohemian free-spirited artist to Martha Stewart's understudy."

"And you," she reminded him, "resisted me at every turn. It drove me crazy. If I put out a laundry hamper, you would throw your dirty clothes on the floor beside it."

It had driven her crazy that she had been creating this perfect little nest for them—a perfect world, really—and he'd resisted her at every turn. He'd left his socks in the living room. He'd hung his towels crooked in the bathroom. He'd left dishes in the sink, and if he'd been working outside and forgot something in the house, he'd just traipsed in, leaving a pathway of leaves and grass and mud in his wake.

"I know I could be inconsiderate," he said, but he didn't sound very remorseful. "I felt as if you were trying to control me all the time, I felt as if you thought the way you wanted to live was the only correct way, and what I wanted, to be a little relaxed in my own space, didn't count at all."

Jessica felt shocked by that. It was certainly true. She had always wanted things her way.

"And then I'd come home from working all day, and you'd have some elaborate meal all prepared and candles on the table and the best dishes out. I would have been just as happy with a hamburger and my feet up on the coffee table in front of the TV. Not that I was allowed to put my feet up on the coffee table, even though it was really a bench that was sturdy enough to have survived one war, a fire and two floods."

She was aghast at the picture he was painting. He looked as if he was going to stop, but now that the floodgates were open, he was completely unable to.

"I wanted to talk to you the way we had always talked—about ideas and dreams and your art. I wanted to laugh with you and be lighthearted.

"But suddenly all you wanted to talk about was paint

colors for the nursery and could we please get a new sofa, and did I think there was too much tarragon in the recipe. *Tarragon*, Jess."

And so this was how their relationship had started to show cracks, she thought. She had known it was all going dreadfully wrong.

"I wanted to shake you, and say, 'Who are you and what the hell have you done with Jessica?'"

It wasn't until after he'd gone from her life that she realized how stupid it had been to make an issue out of the very things she then had missed.

"But you—" Jessica's defensive response died on her lips. She considered the possibility he was right. Instead of feeling defensive, she let what he had just said sink in. Suddenly, for the first time, it occurred to her maybe she should be the one who was sorry. If she was going to move on, if she was going to be a good parent—no, a great parent—to a child someday, she had to start working on herself now. And part of that meant facing her role in the relationship going wrong.

Up until this point, had she really told herself she had no part in it? That it was all his fault?

"What happened to you?" he asked. "And worse, what did I have to do with it?"

"Nothing," she said softly, and with dawning realization. "You had nothing to do with it. I think, Kade, ever since my mom died, I longed to have *that* world again.

"I was only twelve when she was diagnosed with a rare form of cancer. She went from diagnosis to dead in three weeks."

"I know that," he said, reminding her he knew so much about her.

"But what you didn't know—maybe what I didn't

even know until this minute—was that I wanted my world back. After she died, it was just my dad and my brother and me. Everything went south. The house was a catastrophe. We ate takeout and macaroni and cheese. I couldn't even invite a friend over, our house was such a disaster. I wanted my lovely, stable family back."

"Oh, Jessie," he said. "I probably should have figured that out."

"And then we got married," she said slowly, "and I already had this idea in my head what a perfect life looked like, and I set out to make our life together look like that. And when I could sense you were dissatisfied, I thought it was because we needed to take the next step—to solidify ourselves as a family."

"You decided you wanted to have a baby."

"Didn't you want to have a baby?" she asked.

"Of course I did," he reassured her. "But maybe not for me. I wanted you to be happy. It didn't seem as though paint chips and the creative use of tarragon were making you happy. It certainly didn't seem as though I was making you happy."

CHAPTER SEVENTEEN

So HERE WAS a painful truth looking Jessica in the face. She'd had a wonderful husband who loved her, and somehow she had managed to manufacture misery.

Not that their challenges had not been real, but why hadn't she been able to focus on everything that was right and good, instead of working away at the tiny cracks until they had become fractures between Kade and her?

As painful as this conversation was, Jessica was relieved by it. This was the conversation they had needed to have a year ago, when everything had fallen apart so completely between them. Maybe if they had had it even before that, they could have stopped things from progressing to a complete fallout.

"When the first miscarriage happened," Jessica admitted softly, "I think it was a cruel reminder of what I'd already learned from my mother's illness—I was not in control of anything. And yet instead of surrendering to that, I fought it hard. The more out of control I felt, the more I started trying to control everything. Maybe especially you."

"Jessica," Kade said, and his voice was choked, "I always saw the failure as mine, not yours."

Her eyes filled with tears. It was not what she needed to hear, not right now, just as she was acknowledging her part in their marriage catastrophe.

"When I married you," Kade said, his voice low and pain-filled, "it felt as if that was a sacred vow and that I had found my lifelong duty. It was to protect you. To keep you safe. To stop bad things from happening. I felt as if my love should be enough to protect us—and you—from every storm.

"When it wasn't? When the growing chasm between us was made impassable by the two miscarriages, I could not enter your world anymore. I felt as if I was losing my mind. Those miscarriages, those lost babies, made me admit to myself how powerless I was. I couldn't do the most important thing I'd ever wanted to do. I could not save my own babies.

"And that compounded the fact I was already dealing with a terrible sense of failure at lesser levels."

"What levels?" she asked.

"I had failed to even make you happy. I wanted you to stop trying to get pregnant. But you wouldn't. It made me feel as if I was not enough to meet your needs. It felt as if the bottom fell out of our whole world. When you wanted to keep trying—keep subjecting yourself and us to that roller-coaster ride of hope and joy and grief and despair—I just couldn't do it. And so I retreated to a world where I could be in control."

"And abandoned me," she whispered.

"Yes," he said quietly. "Yes. Yes, I did abandon you. But I think not nearly so thoroughly as you abandoned yourself. It was as if a baby was going to become your whole reason and your whole life."

She realized that she had not been ready then, and she

was not really ready now, either. She began to cry. She had vowed no more losses, and now she faced the biggest one of all. Somehow in marriage, she had lost herself. She had become the role she played instead of the person she was.

Kade had always hated tears.

Always. If they argued and she started crying, he left.

Except when they had lost the first baby. They had crawled into bed together and clung to each other and wept until there were no tears left.

But after that, it was as if he steeled himself against that kind of pain, against feeling so intensely ever again. Even after the devastation of the loss of the second baby, he had been capable of only a few clumsy claps on the shoulder, a few of the kinds of platitudes she had come to hate the most.

It had seemed as if her grief had alienated him even more, had driven him away even more completely.

The tears trickled down her cheeks. She could not stop them now that they had been let loose.

She expected him to do what he had always done: escape at the first sign of a loss of control on her part. But he didn't.

"Jessie," Kade said softly. "In retrospect, we weren't ready for those babies. Neither of us was. We thought our relationship was on firm ground, but at the first stress, it fractured, so it wasn't. Babies need to come into a stronger place than that."

He came and he put his arms around her. He drew her deep against him, doing what she had needed so desperately from him all along. He let her tears soak into his shirt.

"I'm okay now," she finally sighed against him. "Thank you."

"For what?" he growled.

"For holding me. It's all I ever needed. Not for you to fix things, but for you to be there, as solid as a rock, when things went sideways."

He looked at her. He nodded. She could see the regret in his face. She could see that he got it. Completely.

And then something changed in his eyes, and he reached down and lifted a tear off her cheek with his finger, and scraped his thumb across her lip.

Jessica could feel the move into the danger zone. And she should have stepped back from it. But she could not.

A part of her that would not be controlled missed him—and missed this part of their life together—with a desperation that made her think she knew how heroin addicts felt. The *need* overshadowed everything. It overpowered common sense and reason. It certainly overpowered the need to be in control and the need to be right.

They were all gone—common sense and reason, control and the need to be right. They were gone, and in their place his thumb scraping across her lip became her whole world. Her lips parted, and she drew his thumb into her mouth. His skin tasted of heaven.

He went very still. She gazed up at him. And then she stood on her tiptoes, and she pulled his head down to her. She kissed that beautiful, familiar little groove behind his ear. He groaned his surrender and placed his hands on each side of her face and looked down at her, and then lowered his mouth to hers.

Welcome.

Welcome home.

His hunger was as apparent as hers. He crushed her lips under his own. His tongue found the hollow of her mouth, and she melted against him as he devoured her. His lips moved away from hers and he anointed the hollow of her throat and the tip of her nose and her eyelids.

"Jessica," he said hoarsely. "Oh, Jessica."

He scooped her up in his arms and went to the hallway to his bedroom. He tapped open the partially closed door with his foot, strode across the room and laid her on his king-size bed. It gave luxuriously under her weight. She stared up at him.

And wanted her husband, Kade, as she had never wanted anything else in her entire life. The wanting sizzled in her belly, and curled around her heart, and came out her lips as a moan of desire and invitation. She held out her good arm to him.

And he came willingly down to her, laying his body over hers, careful to hold his weight off her broken wing. He found the lobe of her ear and nipped it with delicate precision. He rained tiny kisses down on her brow and her nose and her cheeks and her chin.

Finally, when she was gasping with wanting and longing, he captured her lips and nuzzled teasingly. And then he took her lips more deeply, laying his claim, stoking the fire that was already there to white-hot.

"I am going to melt," she said hoarsely.

"Melt, then," he whispered. "Melt, and I will come with you."

His mouth on hers became a fury of possession and hunger. His tongue plunged the cool cavern of her mouth, exploring, darting, resting, tasting. He left her mouth and trailed kisses down the open collar of her shirt. He laid his trail of fire down her neck and onto her breastbone. His fingers found the buttons of her blouse and released them one by one. His lips found the nakedness of her flesh where it mounded above her bra, then blazed down the rise of her ribs to the fall of her belly. His lips went to all the places on her that only his lips had ever been before.

She did not melt. Rather, the heat built to a near explosion. The first of July, Canada Day, was weeks away, but the fireworks had begun already. They started, always, with the smaller ones, delightful little displays of color and noise, smoke and beauty. But they built and built and built to a fiery crescendo that lit the entire sky and shook the entire world.

It was obvious from the need that ached within her, from the way her body arched against him in welcome and anticipation, that this particular set of fireworks was heading toward only one possible climax.

"My arm— I don't know…" she whispered. It was her only uneasiness. She felt no guilt and no regret. He was her husband, and they belonged to each other in this way. They always had.

Kade took his weight off her and drank her in deeply.

"Do you want to do this?" he asked, and his voice was a rasp of raw need.

She knew her answer, her certainty, was in her face, and vibrating along the whole length of her body.

"I do. It's just with my arm like this, I don't know how we're going to manage," she said.

"I do," Kade whispered, his voice a growl of pure and sensual need. He had, intentionally or not, echoed their vows. *I do.* "Do you trust me, Jessie?"

"Yes."

"I know exactly how we are going to do this," he told her.

And he did. And so did she.

When they were done, in the sacred stillness that followed, the truth hit her and hit her hard.

It was not that she loved her husband again. It was that she had never stopped. Cradling the warmth of that truth to her, in the arms of her beloved, *home* for the first time in more than a year, Jessica slept.

Kade woke deep in the night. Jessica was asleep beside him, curled tightly against him, like a puppy seeking warmth. He felt tenderness toward her unfurl in him with such strength it felt as if his throat was closing. He'd known, in some deep place inside himself, ever since he'd seen the police cars in front of her store that morning, that he still loved her.

That he could not imagine a world without her. Not just *a* world. *His world.*

Something buzzed by his ear, and Kade realized it was that sound that had woken him up, and he was momentarily confused. His phone was automatically set to Do Not Disturb during the evening hours. He picked it up off the nightstand and squinted at it. It was four-thirty in the morning.

The phone buzzed again, vibrating in his hand. It was not his normal ring. Suddenly it occurred to him they had programmed the alarm at Baby Boomer to this phone to override his do-not-disturb settings. He unlocked the screen. Sure enough, there was a live-feed image of someone at the door of Baby Boomer.

Glancing at Jessica and seeing how peaceful she looked, Kade slipped from the bed, grabbed his clothes off the floor and went out into the hall. He called 911, with his phone tucked in against his ear, pulling on his pants at the same time. He explained what was happening, but the operator sounded particularly bored with his news of an alarm going off and a possible break-in in progress.

He thought of Jessica with her arm immobilized and he thought of her ongoing sleep disturbances and about the way she startled every time there was a loud sound. Even in the cubicle of the dress shop, when the music had started unexpectedly, she had nearly jumped out of her skin. Thinking of that, Kade felt really, really angry. Dangerously angry.

Jessica needed to know that he would look after her. That he would protect her. If her world was threatened, he would be there. He would put his body between her and a bullet if he had to.

And so, like a soldier getting ready to do battle for all he believed in, Kade went out the apartment door, got in his car and headed at full speed to her store.

At first it appeared no one was there. But then he noticed the newly repaired door hanging open and a sliver of light moving inside the store.

Without a single thought, he leaped from the car and took the stairs two at a time. He burst in the door and raced across the room and tackled the shadowy figure by the cash register.

Jessica was right. The thief was scrawny! Holding him in place was ridiculously easy. The anger at all the grief this guy had caused Jessica seemed to seep out of him. The thief was screaming, "Please don't hurt me."

He seemed skinny and pathetic, and just as Jessica had guessed, desperate with a kind of desperation Kade did not know.

Kade heard sirens and saw flashing lights, and moments later the police were in the doorway, telling *him* to put his hands in the air. It seemed to take forever to sort it all out, but finally, he finished filling out reports and doing interviews.

It was now nearly seven. Jessica was probably awake and probably wondering where he was.

He called her, and could hear the anxiety in her voice as soon as she answered the phone.

"Where are you?"

"The alarm at your business alerted to my phone a couple of hours ago. I headed over here."

"*You* answered the alarm?"

"Well, I called the police, but I just wanted to make sure they caught him." He laughed, adrenaline still coursing through his veins. "You were right, Jessie. He was scrawny."

She cut him off, her voice shrill. "You caught the thief?"

"Yeah," he said proudly.

"But you are the one who lectured me about being foolhardy!"

He frowned. He wanted to be her hero. He wanted her to know her world was safe with him. Why didn't she sound pleased? Why wasn't she getting the message?

"You could have been killed," she said. "He could have had a gun or a knife. You're the one who pointed that out to me."

"Jessica, it all worked out, didn't it?"

"Did it?" she said, and he did not like what he heard in her voice. "Did it, Kade?"

"Yes!"

"Kade, being in a relationship means thinking about the other person."

"I *was* thinking about you."

"No, you weren't."

"How about if you don't tell me what I was thinking about? We had a great night last night. It doesn't mean you own me. It doesn't mean you get to control me. You know what this conversation feels like? *Here we go again*."

"Does it?" she said, and her voice was very shrill. "Well, try this out—here we *don't* go again!"

And she slammed down the phone. He stared at his phone for a long time, and finally put it back in his pocket. He already knew, when he got back to his apartment, she would be gone.

CHAPTER EIGHTEEN

JESSICA HUNG UP the phone. She was shaking violently. She hugged herself against the feeling of being cold.

And she faced an awful truth about herself. Her courage was all used up. She did not have one drop left. This love made her feel so vulnerable, and she did not want to feel that way anymore.

She thought of how it had been last night, of Kade's heated lips anointing every inch of her fevered flesh.

In the cold light of dawn, her heart swelled with loving him.

But it didn't feel good at all. It felt as if that love could not make her whole and could even destroy what was left of her.

It was her curse: her mother, whom she had loved so deeply, taken from her. And then each of those babies, whom she had loved madly and beyond reason, without even having met them, gone from this earth.

Loving Kade felt as if it was leaving herself open to one more loss. And he could be reckless. Impulsive. Look what he had just done! That could have been a far different phone call. It could have been the police calling to tell her Kade was dead.

Was he right? Was she trying to control him? Whatever—she had a deep sense that she could not sustain one more loss.

Quietly, Jessica walked through his beautiful apartment. With each step a memory: pizza and warm croissants and sitting on the sofa and playing a Scrabble game. She went back to the guest room, put on the nearest thing she could find, but left all the rest of the clothing they had bought together, because it, too, held too many memories.

Of dancing with him in Chrysalis. She should have recognized the danger right that second, before rickshaw rides, and Chinese food in the park, and falling asleep on a blanket with the trees whispering their names. Before it had all built to that moment last night of unbridled passion, of *hoping* for the most uncertain thing of all.

The future.

Feeling like a thief who had stolen the most precious thing of all, a moment of the pure pleasure of love, Jessica slipped out the door of Kade's empty apartment and locked it behind her. She went down to the lobby and had the concierge call her a cab.

In minutes, she was being whisked through the dawn-drenched city. As soon as they pulled up in front of her house, she wished that she had thought to go to a hotel.

Because this was more of them, of her and of Kade. It was the house they had chosen together and lived in together and loved in together.

And fought in together, she reminded herself, and watched love make that torturous metamorphosis to hate.

She could not survive that again. She could not survive losing him again.

When she let herself in the house, she felt relief. It wasn't really *their* house anymore. Though all her familiar furniture was back, except her bench, which was still in the back of a truck somewhere, everything else felt new.

Except Behemoth, which seemed to be squatting on the new floor glaring accusingly at her.

It even smelled new, of floor varnish and paint. The floors glowed with soft beauty; the walls had been painted a dove gray. The soot was gone from where they had tried to use the fireplace that one time, and it was gone off the ceiling.

Jessica went through to the kitchen, and it was as she had dreaded. She reached up and touched the cabinets. The oak stain was no longer bleeding through the white, and that, more than anything else, made her feel like crying.

She kicked off her shoes and passed her bedroom. There would be no going back to bed. She was sure of that. She went to her office and slid open the desk drawer.

Jessica took out all the documents she needed to start filling out to begin the adoption procedure, to get on with her dreams of a life in a way that did not involve him.

But as she stared at the papers, she realized she was terrified of everything that love meant, and especially of the built-in potential for loss and heartbreak.

She was not whole. She had never been whole. She had brought a neediness to her and Kade's relationship that had sucked the life out of it. And if she did not get herself sorted out, she would do the same to a child.

She thought of putting the documents back in the desk drawer, but it seemed to her they would be just one more thing to move, to sort through when the time came to leave here. It seemed to her she was not at all sure what she wanted anymore.

She dumped the papers in the garbage, and then she went and sat on the couch and hugged her knees to herself, and cried for who she was not, and what she was never going to have.

Finally, done with crying, done with Kade, done with dreams, she called the real estate office. An agent was there promptly, and Jessica calmly walked through the house with him as he did his appraisal. She felt numb and disconnected, as if the agent was on one side of a thick glass wall, and she was on the other. She didn't really care what price he put on the house. In fact, she barely registered the number he had given her. She gave him the listing, signed the papers, and he pounded the for-sale sign into her lawn.

She kept hoping her phone would ring, but it didn't. She and Kade had arrived at the same place, all over, an impasse that neither of them would be willing to cross. If it was a good thing, why did she feel so bereft?

After she had watched the agent pound the sign in in front of her house, she went outside and invited him to come by Baby Boomer and do the very same thing.

In the brutal light of this heartbreak, Jessica could see herself all too clearly. The business had risen from her neediness, from her need for something outside herself to fill her. It had been part of that whole obsession that she had not been able to let go of, not even after it had cost her her marriage to the man she loved.

Jessica expected to feel sad when the for-sale sign went up in front of Baby Boomer.

Instead, she felt relief. She felt oddly free.

It was going to be different now. She thought about what she really wanted, and she remembered when she had first met Kade, before she had lost herself, who she had been. An artist, not drawing pictures of bunnies on nursery walls, but drawing from a place deep within her.

That night, after she had closed the shop for the day, she went into the art-supply store next door. As soon as she walked in the door, the smells welcomed her—the smell of canvases and paints and brushes.

It smelled of home, she told herself firmly, her true home, the self she had walked away from again and again and again.

But home conjured other images: Kade laughing, and Kade with his feet up on the coffee table, and Kade's socks on the floor, and Kade opening a box of pizza, and her sitting on a sander laughing so hard she cried. She shook that off impatiently.

She had made her vow, her new vow. And it was not to have and to hold. The vow she intended to obey was that she would not lose anything else. Not one more thing. And that meant not doing anything that would open her to loss.

Possibly more than any other single thing, loving Kade fell into that category.

Over the next weeks Jessica had to relearn a terribly hard lesson: you didn't just stop loving someone because you wanted to, because it had the potential to hurt you.

Love was always there in the background, beckoning, saying you can have a larger life if you risk this. But she thought maybe it was from living in the house they had shared together that she could not shake her sense of grief and torment.

Not even painting could fill her.

So she did other things she had always wanted to do and held back from. She signed up for a rock-climbing course, and a kayaking program, and a gourmet-cooking class. She had a sense of needing to fill every second so that she would not have time to think, to be drawn into the endless pool of grief that was waiting to drown her. Jessica was aware she was searching frantically to find things she could be passionate about that did not involve that sneaky, capricious, uncontrollable force called love.

But the more she tried to do, the more exhausted she became. If these efforts to fill her life were right, wouldn't she feel energized by them, instead of completely drained? At rock climbing, her limbs were so weak she could not hold herself on the wall. At kayaking—which was only in a local swimming pool for now—she fell out of the kayak and had a panic attack. At cooking class, she took one taste of her hollandaise sauce and had to run to the bathroom and be sick.

The feeling of weakness progressed. Jessica felt tired all the time. She had fallen asleep at work. She cried at the drop of a hat. Her stomach constantly felt as if it was knotted with anxiety.

Obviously, she had been absolutely correct when she had told him, "Here we *don't* go again." She took this as evidence that she was doing the right thing. If she was having this kind of reaction to a weeklong reunion with her husband, what would happen to her if they tried it for another year? Or two? And *then* it didn't work? Obviously, she could not survive.

"You need to go see a doctor," Macy said to her after finding her fast asleep, her head on her arms on her desk. "Something is wrong with you."

And so she went to see the doctor. She knew nothing was wrong with her. Love was not an ailment a doctor could cure. You could not take a pill to mend a broken heart. The doctor ordered a raft of tests, and Jessica had them all done, knowing nothing would come of it.

But then the doctor's office phoned and asked her to come back in. There were test results they needed to discuss with her in person.

And that was when she knew the truth. Jessica knew that, like her mother, she was sick and dying. Thank God she had not proceeded with her adoption idea. Thank God she had not proceeded with loving Kade.

It was just another confirmation that she could not allow herself to love. People could leave her, but she could leave people, too. It was all just too risky.

The doctor swung into the room, all good cheer. Jessica guessed he'd had a fantastic golf game that completely overrode the news he was about to give her.

She waited for him to remember the gravity of breaking it to someone that they were dying.

But that foolish grin never left his face!

"I have wonderful news for you," he said. "You're pregnant."

She stared at him. Life was too cruel. All those years of charts and temperatures and schedules, and now she was pregnant. Plus, she knew a terrible truth. Being pregnant did not necessarily mean walking away with a baby at the end.

Hadn't she decided she was unsuited for motherhood? She called Macy and told her she wouldn't be in for the rest of the day. She went home.

Her real estate agent was on the steps. "I've been trying to call you all morning. We have an offer on your house! A great offer."

Numbly she signed the paper he shoved at her. She went into the house and closed the door. Despite all her efforts to control everything, to keep change at bay, everything was changing anyway.

What was she going to tell Kade?

Nothing. He would feel trapped. He would feel as if he had to do the honorable thing, be sentenced to a life of bickering with her.

No. There had been no pretense in their last night together. He did love her. She knew that.

And now they were in the same place all over again. Where that love would be tested by life. What would make it different this time? If they lost another baby, how would it be any better this time?

"It won't," Jessica told herself. "It won't be better. It will be worse."

She lay down on the couch and cried and cried and cried. She hoped she had cried until there were no tears left, but from experience, she knew. There were always tears left. There was always an event waiting to blindside you, waiting to make you find that place where you had hidden a few extra tears.

CHAPTER NINETEEN

KADE DISCONNECTED FROM the phone call. He was part owner in his and Jessica's house, so he had been notified. It had just sold. Jessica, apparently, could not even tell him that herself. That had been a secretary at the real estate company asking him to come in and sign some documents.

He had not seen or heard from Jessica since that night when they had made love, and then he had made the fateful decision to go and tackle the breaking and entering at her business himself.

For a guy who thought he had the emotional range of a rock, he was stunned by how he felt.

Angry. And then sad. Frustrated. Powerless. And then sad some more.

He loved his wife. He loved her beyond reason. They were two intelligent people. Why could they not build a bridge across this chasm that divided them?

He mulled over the news about the house. What was he going to do now? Should he be the one to try to cross the minefield between them? A man had to have his pride.

But it seemed to Kade pride might have had quite a bit to do with why they could not work things out in the first place.

Maybe a man didn't have to have his pride.

Maybe a man having his pride really had nothing to do with being strong, with doing what needed to be done, with doing the right thing. Maybe a man had to swallow his pride.

Jessica, Kade knew, would never take the first step toward reconciliation, and for a second he felt angry again.

But then he relived her voice on the phone that morning of the break-in. It occurred to him that Jessica had not been trying to control him. She had been genuinely terrified.

Suddenly, he felt ashamed of himself. Wasn't this part of what was destroying them? Pride? Okay, it was a guy thing. It was always all about him. Even when he told himself it was about her. For example, he would go and save her store. But it had really been about him. He'd wanted to be the hero. He'd wanted to see her eyes glowing with admiration for him.

Maybe it was time for him to grow up.

To see things through her eyes, instead of through the warp of his own colossal self-centeredness.

She had been terrified.

And right from the beginning, from the day he had first seen her again, after she had tried to take out the thief herself at her store, she had given him clues where all that terror came from.

I lost my mother when I was twelve. I've lost two babies to miscarriage. I am not losing anything else. Not one more thing.

Kade had seen what losing those babies had done to her. He had seen the intensity of her own love tear her apart.

He had seen photos of her when she was a girl. In her

fifth-grade class photo, she had been grinning merrily at the camera, all leprechaun charm and joyous mischief. But by the following year, when her mother had died, she had looked solemn and sad, the weight of the whole world on her shoulders.

He tried to imagine her at twelve, her sense of loss, her sense of the world being a safe place being gone.

The loss of each of those babies would have triggered that old torment, that sense of the world not being safe.

As would the man she loved putting himself at risk.

And suddenly, he despised himself. So what if she tried to control him?

"Kade," he said and swore to himself. "Don't you get it? It's not all about you."

He loved her. He loved Jessica Clark Brennan, his wife, beyond reason. He had cut her loose to navigate her heartbreaks on her own. When she had disappeared into that dark world of her own heartache, instead of having the courage to go in with her, to help her find her way back out, he had abandoned her.

That was not love.

But how was he going to make her see that he understood that now? He suspected she had spent the past weeks building up her defenses against him—against love. How was he going to knock them back down?

They had just sold a house together. The most natural thing in the world would be to bring a bottle of champagne over there and celebrate with her.

And it was time for honesty. Not pride. Pride didn't want her to know how he felt, pride did not want to be vulnerable to her.

But love did. Love wanted her to know how he felt and love wanted to be vulnerable to her.

Pride had won throughout their separation.

Now it was time to give love, their love, a chance. A second chance.

With his mind made up, a half hour later, Kade knocked on the door of the house they had shared. He saw Jessica come to the window, and then there was silence. For a moment, he thought she was not going to open the door.

But then she did.

What he saw made him feel shattered. She was in one of those horrible dresses again. He thought she had been kidding about one being available in camo, but no, she hadn't been. Aside from the horror of the dress, Jessica looked awful—tired and pale and thin.

"Hello, Jessica," he said quietly. His voice sounded unnatural to him.

"Did you come to get your check?"

"My check?" he asked, genuinely confused. Obviously there would be no money yet from a house that had barely sold.

"I told you I'd pay you for those clothes from Chrysalis once the house sold."

"You didn't even take the clothes with you."

"What? Are you wearing them?"

"Are you crazy?"

"Because if you're not, I'm paying for them."

"Okay," he said. "I am, then. Wearing them."

Just a glimmer of a smile, before she doused it like a spark of a fire in a tinder-dry forest. Still, despite her look of studied grimness, was there a shadow of something in her eyes? Something that she did not want him to see? Despite all her losses, and despite the fact she wanted not to, he could tell she *hoped*.

And her hope, to him, was the bravest thing of all.

"Well, then, did you bring back my bench?"

"No."

"What are you doing here, then?"

"Isn't it obvious? I brought a bottle of champagne. I thought we should celebrate the sale of our house."

"Oh."

"This is the part where you invite me in," he told her gently.

"What if I don't want you to come in?" she said.

But he could still see that faint spark of hope in her eyes.

"We still have some business to complete, Jessie." Ah, she'd never been able to resist him when he called her Jessie.

She stood back from the door, her chin tilted up in defiance of the hope he had seen in her eyes. He went in.

He tried to hide his shock at what he found inside the house. The house was not a reflection of Jessica. And it wasn't just that the floors had been refinished, either. There were things out of place. There was a comforter and a pillow on the sofa. Empty glasses littered the coffee table. There were socks on the floor.

Really? It was all very frightening. "Are you okay?" he asked her.

She went and sat down on the sofa, crossed her arms over her chest in defense. Against him. "I'm fine. What do you want to discuss?"

"Ah." He went through to the kitchen with his bottle of wine. "How's your arm?" he called. Maybe that was the explanation for the mess. She was not completely able-bodied.

"It's okay. The cast has been off for a bit. I have some exercises I do to strengthen my muscles."

The corkscrew was in a familiar place. How was it this kitchen felt so much more like home than his own masterpiece of granite and stainless steel? He opened the bottle, got glasses down and poured. He hated it that the cabinets had been fixed.

He went back and handed her a wineglass, and sat down beside her. He noticed the black soot stain up the front of the fireplace had been fixed, too.

It was as if their memories were being erased, one by one. "Here's to the sale of the house," he said.

"To moving on," she agreed hollowly. But she set her glass down without taking a sip.

He took a sip of his own wine, watching her carefully over the rim of his glass. A bead of perspiration broke out over her lip, and her face turned a ghastly shade of white.

He set his glass down and reached for her, afraid she was going to tumble off the sofa. "Jessica?"

She slid away from his touch and found her feet. She bolted for the bathroom, and didn't even have time to shut the door. The sound of her getting violently sick filled the whole house.

No wonder the place was a wreck. She wasn't feeling well.

She came back into the room, looking weak and wasted. She sat on the couch, tilted her head against the back and closed her eyes.

"Why did you say you were fine? Why didn't you just tell me you had the flu?"

"Sorry," she mumbled. "I should have told you. I don't want you to catch anything."

Her eyes were skittering all over the place. She was

a terrible liar. She had the same look on her face right now that she'd had the year she'd denied buying him the golf clubs he'd wanted for a long time, when she really had.

But why would she lie about having the flu? Or maybe the lie would be that she didn't want him to catch anything.

He looked at her hard. After a long time, she looked back at him, proud and…right beneath that, what? *Scared?* Of what? Him?

Kade felt a strange stillness descend on him, the kind of stillness you might feel in a church with sun pouring through a stained glass window.

He *knew.* He knew right to the bottom of his soul. Jessica was pregnant. He was being given a second chance.

She looked away. "Yeah," she finally said, the word obviously an effort from the lie inherent to it. "The flu."

"Uh-huh."

Her eyes flew to his face, then moved away again.

"You're pregnant, aren't you, Jessica?"

She was silent for a bit and then she sighed with a kind of relief. "Imagine that," she said quietly. "All those charts and temperatures and schedules, all that taking all the fun out of it, and then one night. One single night…"

"Are you happy at all?" he asked her quietly.

"It's pretty hard to be happy when you're terrified," she said. "You know what the cruelest irony is, Kade? I'd just realized, with your help, that I am not ready for a baby!"

It came out very close to a wail of pure panic.

"Aw, Jess," he said quietly, "maybe that *is* when you are ready. When you can see your own imperfections and embrace them. Maybe it's when you can see it's an imperfect world, and instead of trying to impose perfection on it, you just embrace that, too. Maybe that's the only real lesson we can give a baby. It's the one I learned from the failure of us. The world is not going to be perfect. Life is not going to be easy. I can't control everything. But together, with love for each other, we can handle whatever it throws at us."

"We?" she whispered.

"Jessie, I am not leaving you alone with this. And maybe that's what I really wanted to say that night when you told me you were planning to adopt a baby. Not that you weren't ready, or that you had issues to work on, because who could ever be ready for a baby? And who does not have issues to work on? I guess what I was trying to say that night was that it's a lot to take on alone. I didn't want to think about you taking it on without me. It's going to take two people, stumbling through, to bring this baby into the world.

"I'm going to be there for you this time."

Her eyes went to his face, and this time they stayed there, wide and hopeful. She wanted to believe—the capacity for hope was there—but she was frightened, too. And who could blame her?

"I know my track record stinks," he said.

She didn't disagree with that.

"And I know I can't protect you from life. Or from loss. I know we're months away from holding a baby in our arms, and I know you're scared this is going to end like all the other times. All I can really protect you from is walking through difficult times alone."

She was crying now.

"Jessica, I've been given a second chance to be a better man. And I'm taking it. I'm proving to you—and to myself—that I can live up to those vows we took. I remember those vows. I remember each word of them. So listen to me. Because I'm doing this again. And I'm doing it right this time."

His voice was hoarse with emotion, almost a whisper at first, and then with it growing stronger and stronger, he spoke.

"I, Kade Brennan, take you, Jessica, to be my wife, my heart and my soul, my companion through life and my one and only love. I will cherish you and I will nurture a friendship based in trust and honor. I will laugh with you and, especially, I will cry with you. I will love you faithfully, today, tomorrow and forever. Through the best and the worst, through the difficult and the easy, whatever may come, I will always be there for you. I have given you my hand." Kade held out his hand to her, cleared his throat and said, "I have given you my hand to hold, and so I give also my life into your keeping."

To him, it seemed like forever that she looked at him, her eyes sparkling with unshed tears. And then her hand slipped into his, as if it had never left it, as if this was where her hand was meant to be.

Jessica spoke. Her voice was husky and tears were set free and flowed down her face, just as they had that day all those years ago, when he had cherished her tears instead of seeing them as a sign of his own powerlessness.

She said, "I, Jessica Clark-Brennan, take you, Kade, to be my husband, my heart and my soul, my companion in life and my one and only true love. I will cherish you and I will nurture our friendship, based in trust and honor. I will laugh with you, and, yes, I will cry with you. I will love you faithfully, today, tomorrow and forever.

Through the best and the worst, through the difficult and the easy, whatever may come, I will always be there. I have given you my hand to hold, and so I give also my life into your keeping."

She had her knuckles in her eyes, scrubbing like a child who just wanted the tears to go away.

But that was their past. Her tears had upset him and made him feel helpless and hopeless, and so he had turned away. And so she had begun to try to hide how she felt from him, the very one she should have been able to lean on, the one she should have been able to be completely transparent and completely herself with.

Not this time. This time he was walking right into the fire. He slid over on the sofa and crossed the small space that remained between them. Gently, he scooped her up and put her on his lap. She did not resist. She sighed against him as if she had waited her whole life for this moment.

To feel safe, to feel looked after, to feel as if there was a slight possibility everything would be okay. He tucked her head into his shoulder, and felt her tears soak through his shirt.

It wasn't until a long time later that he realized that it was not only her tears soaking his shirt. His own, locked inside him for way too long, had joined hers.

He could not know how this pregnancy would end. But he did know, however it concluded, they were in this together this time. For all time.

"I love you," he said. "Jessie, I love you."

And then he held his breath.

Until he heard the words he needed to hear.

"Kade, I love you."

At that precise moment, the sound of her voice and

her words washed over him, and he felt like a desert that had not seen rain for the longest time. He felt as if the moisture had come, fallen on the parched place that was his soul. He could feel the color and the life seeping back into his world.

CHAPTER TWENTY

"HEY, I LIKE IT."

"The dress?" Jessica said, turning to Kade. She was teasing. She knew he hated this dress, and every dress from her Poppy Puppins collection. But it did great as a paint smock, and it covered her growing girth beautifully. Jessica watched him shrug out of his jacket at the door.

"Of course not that dress." He wrinkled his nose. "I have to find your secret cache of those dresses. Every time I throw one out, three more appear."

She laughed. It was the small things that she had come to love the most: him coming through the door at night, playing a Scrabble game together, watching TV and eating popcorn together, him licking her fingers, slick with butter.

Sometimes she wondered, if they had never had a bad spell, if she had never known what it was like to live without him as part of her daily life, would she love these little things as much as she did? Would she have known to appreciate them?

She had moved into his place at River's Edge after her house had been turned over to the new owners. Eventually, after the baby was born, they would buy a house for the three of them.

But at the moment, they were both cautious about making decisions based on a baby. This caution remained, even though her due date was looming large. They didn't even have a nursery, and the guest room was untouched. No lavender paint or murals this time. No crib, no mobiles, no teddy bears.

They had a beautiful handmade crate they could line with blankets and put beside their bed. When the time came. She loved the idea of the baby sleeping next to them, so close they could breathe in each other's breath, exchange air, become even more a part of one another.

Kade came over and put his hand on the gentle swell of her belly under the paint smock.

He put his head down and spoke directly to her stomach. "Hello, baby. Do you hear me in there? Moving," he said with satisfaction. "A football player."

"Or a ballerina."

"Nah, it's a boy."

It was only in the past few weeks that they had dared to play this game, so afraid were they of jinxing this incredibly magical and miraculous experience. But this time, the fear was different. They would lie awake with it, deep into the night, holding hands, leaning on each other.

They had chosen not to know the sex of their child. This baby was a miracle, boy or girl. Besides, it was endlessly fun debating it, even as they carefully avoided the baby sections of the stores. It was like a superstition, but she did not care. She was not buying one thing for that baby until she had held it in her arms.

She had barely set foot in Baby Boomer since selling it to Macy. But she knew Macy had her covered. She knew there was a shelf there filled with things Macy was quietly selecting for her: bottles and blankets and tiny disposable diapers and little outfits. *If* the time came this time—that hope fluttered in Jessica's chest, they were so close now, and the doctor smiled and shook his head at Jessica's fears—they had a whole nursery that could be put in a box and delivered to them.

There was an unexpected new dimension to Jessica's relationship with Macy and with her old place of business.

Macy was selling paintings almost as fast as Jessica could produce them. Jessica was working largely in abstract, the colors and motion flowing out of her like rivers of light. It was as if this part of her, dammed up for too long, was bursting forth now that it had been set free.

And for some reason, that kind of art appealed to people shopping for baby stuff, not for nurseries, necessarily, though there was a whole move away from the cute traditional look of babies' rooms.

No, people having babies these days, and especially the ones who shopped at an upscale store like Baby Boomer, were largely established professional couples. They had whole gorgeous big houses to decorate, not just nurseries.

And the name Jessica Brennan was causing a surprising stir in the Calgary art scene.

"I like it," Kade said. Having greeted the baby, he turned his attention to the canvas. "What's it called?"

She didn't have a studio. The light pouring through the windows of his apartment had proved perfect. When it was too strong, she closed the curtains and had lights set up to point to the canvas. Between the canvases, paints, lights and paint tarps on the floor, the place looked very messy. Add to that a sock of Kade's, menus out on the counter and magazines on the coffee table, and the effect was one of moderate disarray. And she loved it.

Kade had, with gentle strength, helped her probe the origins of that terrible need to feel in control.

Perhaps, she thought, eyeing their space, she had gone a little too far the other way.

She lifted her shoulder. *Oh, well.*

She turned her attention to the canvas. She was not sure where this came from, this endless current of inspiration, but she was pretty sure it came from love.

"Today it's called *Joy Rising.*" She shrugged. "Who knows if it will still be called that tomorrow."

"Joy Rising," Kade said, and stood back from it.

The backdrop of the canvas was a light gray neutral. The rest of it was filled with hundreds of bubbles—like soap bubbles—rising, starting small at the bottom left of the canvas, growing larger at they reached the right-hand corner.

"It's good," he said. "Now, what's for dinner?"

It was a standing joke between them, a light tease about what she liked to call her Martha Stewart phase. "The pizza menu is on the counter."

He laughed.

And his laughter shivered along her spine. They had almost lost this. They had almost walked away from it. And that was what made it even more precious today.

And maybe that was what all loss did, if you were brave, if you were open to its lessons. Maybe all loss sharpened your sense of the now, of the gifts of this very moment.

He had moved over and was studying the menu.

"Kade?"

"Huh?"

Jessica put her hand to her swollen belly. "Ah."

He was at her side in an instant, scanning her face.

"It's time," she said. "Oh, my God, it's time."

And even this moment, with intense ripples of pain possessing her body, was awash with light, with joy rising. Jessica looked into the face of the man who was her husband, and she read the strength there and knew, together, whatever happened next, it would be just fine.

Kade woke up. His neck was sore. He had fallen asleep in the chair. For a moment, he was disoriented, but then he heard a little sound, like a kitten mewing, and it all came back to him.

His eyes adjusted to the dark, and there they were. His wife and his daughter, the baby on Jessica's chest.

He had thought over the past few months with Jessica as they came together as a couple again, as they celebrated their second chance, that he had come to know the depth and breadth of love completely.

Now, looking at his child, he knew he had only kidded himself. He had only scratched the surface of what love could be.

The baby made that mewing sound again.

Jessica stirred but did not wake.

Jessica. How could someone that tiny, someone who appeared that fragile, be so damned brave? Men thought they were courageous, but that was only until they'd seen a baby born. And then they had to admit how puny their strength was, how laughable this thing they had passed off as courage was.

Courage certainly was not tackling a thief!

Kade got up from his chair. Jessica needed to rest. She

had done her bit. Thirteen hours of the most unbelievable pain Kade could imagine.

How he had wanted to take that pain from her, to take her place.

But that was one of the lessons of this remarkable second chance. He could not take her pain away. He could not fix everything, or really, even most things.

He had to be there. He had to stand there in his own helplessness, and not run from it. He had to walk with her through her pain, not try to take it away from her. Admitting his own powerlessness sometimes took more courage than anything he had ever done before.

The baby mewed again, and stirred again.

He touched the tiny back of his baby girl. It was warm beneath his fingers. He could feel the amazing miracle of the life force in that tiny little bundle.

He had been the first to hold her, the nurse showing him how. He had looked into that tiny wrinkled face, the nose crunched and the eyes screwed tightly shut in outrage, and he had recognized her.

Love.

Love manifest.

And so, summoning his courage, he lifted the baby off the gentle rise and fall of his wife's sleeping chest.

He could hold her in the palm of one hand, his other hand supporting her neck, as the nurse had shown him.

Destiny.

They had decided to call her Destiny.

Her eyes popped open, a slate gray that the nurse had told him would change. They didn't know yet if she would have green eyes like Jessica's or blue like his, or some amazing combination of both.

The nurse had said, too, that this little baby probably could not see much.

And yet, as Kade held her, her eyes seemed to widen with delighted recognition.

"That's right, sweetie, it's me. Daddy."

Daddy. The word felt incredibly sweet on his tongue, and the baby squirmed in his hand. He drew her close to his chest and went and sat back down on the chair, awkwardly stroking her back.

He was so aware of how tiny she was, and helpless. How she was relying on him.

He felt a moment's fear. The world always seemed to be in such a fragile state. The weather changed and wars broke out, and floods came and fires.

People could be fragile, too, held in the trance of long-ago hurts, hiding the broken places within them.

There was so much that he was powerless over, and yet this little girl would see him as all-powerful. Her daddy.

This was what he needed to teach her: that yes, the world could be fragile and easily broken. And people could be fragile and easily broken, too.

But there was one thing that was not fragile, and that was not easily broken.

And that thing was love.

It was the thread that ran, strong, through all the rest. It was what gave strength when strength failed, what gave hope when it was hopeless, what gave faith when there was plenty of evidence that it made no sense at all to have faith. It was what healed the breaks, and made people come out of the trance and embrace all that it was to be alive.

"Welcome to this crazy, unpredictable, beautiful, amazing life," Kade whispered to his little girl. "Welcome."

He closed his eyes, and when he opened them, Jessica's hand was on his shoulder, and she was awake, looking at them both.

"I need to confess something to you," Kade growled.

"What?"

"I've broken one of my vows to you."

"Impossible," she whispered.

"No. You are not my one and only true love anymore. I have two of you now."

And the smile on Jessica's face—radiant, a smile that shamed the very sun—said it was worth it. Every piece of pain they had navigated was worth it.

Because it had brought them here.

To this place. To this moment.

Where they knew that all else might pass away, but that love prevailed.

* * * * *

HER PREGNANCY SURPRISE

SUSAN MEIER

I'd like to thank my editors, Katinka Proudfoot
and Suzy Harding, and also
Senior Editor Kim Young, for helping me
turn Grace and Danny's story into a real keeper.

CHAPTER ONE

"YOU AREN'T planning on driving back to Pittsburgh tonight, are you?"

Danny Carson walked into the third floor office of his Virginia Beach beach house talking to Grace McCartney, his newest employee, who stood behind his desk, hunched over her laptop. A tall brunette with bright violet eyes and a smile that lit the room, Grace was smart, but more than that she was likable and she genuinely liked people. Both of those qualities had helped enormously with the work they'd had to do that weekend.

Grace looked up. "Would you like me to stay?"

"Call it a debriefing."

She tilted her head to one side, considering the suggestion, then smiled. "Okay."

This was her real charm. She'd been working every waking minute for three days, forced to spend her entire weekend assisting Danny as he persuaded Orlando Riggs—a poor kid who parlayed a basketball scholarship into a thirty-million-dollar NBA deal—to use Carson Services as his financial management firm. Not only was she away from her home in Pittsburgh and her friends, but she hadn't gotten to relax on her days off. She could be annoyed that he'd asked her to stay another night. Instead she smiled. Nothing ruffled her feathers.

"Why don't you go to your room to freshen up? I'll tell Mrs. Higgins we'll have dinner in about an hour."

"Sounds great."

After Grace left the office, Danny called his housekeeper on the intercom. He checked his e-mail, checked on dinner, walked on the beach and ended up on the deck with a glass of Scotch. Grace took so long that by the time Danny heard the sound of the sliding glass door opening behind him, Mrs. Higgins had already left their salads on the umbrella table and their entrées on the serving cart, and gone for the day. Exhausted from the long weekend of work, and belatedly realizing Grace probably was, too, Danny nearly suggested they forget about dinner and talk in the morning, until he turned and saw Grace.

Wearing a pretty pink sundress that showed off the tan she'd acquired walking on the beach with Orlando, she looked young, fresh-faced and wholesome. He'd already noticed she was pretty, of course. A man would have to be blind not to notice how attractive she was. But this evening, with the rays of the setting sun glistening on her shoulder-length sable-colored hair and the breeze off the ocean lightly ruffling her full skirt, she looked amazing.

Unable to stop himself he said, "Wow."

She smiled sheepishly. "Thanks. I felt a little like celebrating Orlando signing with Carson Services, and though this isn't exactly Prada, it's the best of what I brought."

Danny walked to her place at the table and pulled out her chair. "It's perfect." He thought about his khaki trousers, simple short-sleeved shirt and windblown black hair as he seated her, then wondered why he had. This wasn't a date. She was an employee. He'd asked her to stay so he could give her a bonus for the good job she'd done that week, and to talk to her long enough to ascertain the position into which he should promote her—also to thank her for doing a good job. What he wore should be of no consequence. The fact that it even entered his head nearly made him laugh.

He seated himself. "Mrs. Higgins has already served dinner."

"I see." She frowned, looking at the silver covers on the plates on the serving cart beside the table, then the salads that sat in front of them. "I'm sorry. I didn't realize I had stayed in the tub so long." She smiled sheepishly again. "I was a little more tired than I thought."

"Then I'm glad you took the extra time." Even as the words tumbled out of his mouth, Danny couldn't believe he was saying them. Yes, he was grateful to her for being so generous and kind with Orlando, making the athlete feel comfortable, but the way Danny had excused her lateness sounded personal, when he hardly knew this woman.

She laughed lightly. "I really liked Orlando. I think

he's a wonderful person. But we were still here to do a job. Both of us had to be on our toes 24/7."

When she smiled and Danny's nerve endings crackled to life, he realized he was behaving out of character for a boss because he was attracted to her. He almost shook his head. He was so slow on the uptake that he'd needed an entire weekend to recognize that.

But he didn't shake his head. He didn't react at all. He was her boss and he'd already slipped twice. His "wow" when he'd seen her in the dress was inappropriate. His comment about the extra time that she'd taken had been too personal. He excused himself for those because he was tired. But now that he saw what was happening, he could stop it. He didn't date employees, but also this particular employee had proven herself too valuable to risk losing.

Grace picked up her salad fork. "I'm starved and this looks great."

"Mrs. Higgins is a gem. I'm lucky to have her."

"She told me that she enjoys working for you because you're not here every day. She likes working part-time, even if it is usually weekends."

"That's my good fortune," Danny agreed, then the conversation died as they ate their salads. Oddly something inside of Danny missed the more personal chitchat. It was unusual for him to want to get friendly with an employee, but more than that, this dinner had to stay professional because he had things to discuss with her. Yet he couldn't stop the surge of disappointment, as if he were missing an unexpected opportunity.

When they finished their salads, he rose to serve the main course. "I hope you like fettuccini alfredo."

"I love it."

"Great." He removed the silver covers. Pushing past the exhaustion that had caused him to wish he could give in and speak openly with her, he served their dinners and immediately got down to business. "Grace, you did an exceptional job this weekend."

"Thanks. I appreciate the compliment."

"I intend to do more than compliment you. Your work secured an enormous account for Carson Services. Not only are you getting a bonus, but I would like to promote you."

She gaped at him. "Are you kidding?"

Pleased with her happy surprise, Danny laughed. "No. Right now you and I need to talk a bit about what you can do and where in the organization you would like to serve. Once we're clear, I'll write up the necessary paperwork."

She continued to stare at him slightly openmouthed, then she said, "You're going to promote me anywhere I want to go?"

"There is a condition. If a situation like Orlando's ever comes up again, where we have to do more than our general push to get a client to sign, I want you in on the persuading."

She frowned. "I'm happy to spend time helping a reluctant investor see the benefits of using your firm, but you don't need to promote me for that."

"The promotion is part of my thank-you for your assistance with Orlando."

She shook her head. "I don't want it."

Positive he'd heard wrong, Danny chuckled. "What?"

"I've been with your company two weeks. Yet I was the one chosen for a weekend at your beach house with Orlando Riggs—a superstar client most of the men and half of the women on staff were dying to meet. You've already given me a perk beyond what employees who have been with you for years have gotten. If there's an empty position somewhere in the firm, promote Bobby Zapf. He has a wife and three kids and they're saving for a house. He could use the money, and the boost in confidence from you."

Danny studied her for a second, then he laughed. "I get it. You're joking."

"I'm serious." She took a deep breath. "Look, everybody understood that you chose me to come with you this weekend because I'm new. I hadn't worked with you long enough to adopt your opinions, so Orlando knew that when I agreed with just about everything you said I wasn't spouting the company party line. I hadn't yet heard the party line. So I was a good choice for this. But I don't want to be promoted over everybody's head."

"You're worried about jealousy?"

She shook her head. "No! I don't want to take a job that should go to someone else. Someone who's worked for you for years."

"Like Bobby Zapf."

"In the two weeks I spent at the office, I watched

Bobby work harder than anybody else you employ. If you want to promote somebody he's the one."

Danny leaned back in his chair. "Okay. Bobby it is." He paused, toyed with his silverware, then glanced up at her, holding back a smile. He'd never had an employee turn down a promotion—especially not to make sure another person got it. Grace was certainly unique.

"Can I at least give you a bonus?"

She laughed. "Yes! I worked hard for an entire weekend. A bonus is absolutely in order."

Continuing to hold back a chuckle, Danny cleared his throat. "Okay. Bonus, but no promotion."

"You could promise to watch my performance over the next year and then promote me because I'd had enough time to prove myself."

"I could." He took a bite of his dinner, more pleased with her than anybody he'd ever met. She was right. In his gratitude for a weekend's work, he had jumped the gun on the promotion. She reeled him in and reminded him of the person who really deserved it. If he hadn't already been convinced she was a special person, her actions just now would have shown him.

Grace smiled. "Okay. It's settled. I get a bonus and you'll watch how well I work." Then as quickly as she'd recapped their agreement, she changed the subject. "It's beautiful here."

Danny glanced around. Darkness had descended. A million stars twinkled overhead. The moon shone like a silver dollar. Water hit the shore in white-foamed waves.

"I like it. I get a lot of work done here because it's so quiet. But at the end of the day I can also relax."

"You don't relax much, do you?"

Lulled by the sounds of the waves and her calming personality, Danny said, "No. I have the fate of a company that's been around for decades on my shoulders. If I fail the company fails and the legacy my great-grandfather sweated to create crumbles into nothing. So I'm focused on work. Unless relaxation happens naturally, it doesn't happen."

"I don't relax much, either." She picked up her fork again. "You already heard me tell Orlando I grew up the same way he did. Dirt poor. And in the same away he used his talent to make a place for himself, I intend to make a place for myself, too."

"Here's a tip. Maybe you shouldn't talk your bosses out of promotions?"

"I can't take what I don't deserve." She wiggled her eyebrows comically. "I'll just have to make my millions the old-fashioned way. I'll have to earn them."

Danny laughed and said, "I hate to tell you this, but people who work for someone else rarely get rich. So if you want to make millions, what are you doing working for me?"

"Learning about investing. When I was young I heard the theory that your money should work as hard for you as you work for it. Growing up, I didn't get any experience seeing how to make money work, so I figured the best place to get the scoop on investing was at an investment firm." She smiled, then asked, "What about you?"

"What about me?"

She shrugged. "I don't know. Anything. Did you want your family's business? Were you a happy child? Are you happy now?" She shrugged again. "Anything."

She asked the questions then took a bite of her dinner, making her inquiry into his life seem casual, offhand. But she'd nonetheless taken the conversation away from herself and to him. Still, she didn't seem as if she were prying. She seemed genuinely curious, but not like a bloodhound, like someone trying to become a friend.

He licked his suddenly dry lips and his heart rate accelerated as he actually considered answering her. A part of him really wanted to talk. A part of him *needed* to talk. Two years had passed. So much had happened.

He took a breath, amazed that he contemplated confiding in her, yet knowing he wouldn't. Though he couldn't ignore her, he wouldn't confide. He'd never confide. Not to her. Not to anyone.

He had to take the conversation back where it belonged. To business.

"What you see is who I am. Chairman of the Board and CEO of Carson Services. There isn't anything to talk about."

She blinked. "Really?"

"From the time I was six or eight I knew I would take over the company my great-grandfather started. I didn't have to travel or experiment to figure out what I wanted. My life was pretty much mapped out for me and I simply followed the steps. That's why there's not a lot to talk about."

"You started training as a kid?"

"Not really training, more or less being included in on conversations my dad and grandfather thought were relevant."

"What if you didn't like investing?"

"But I did."

"It just sounds weird." She flushed. "Sorry. Really. It's none of my business."

"Don't be sorry." Her honesty made him laugh. More comfortable than he could remember being in years, he picked up his fork and said, "I see what you're saying. I was lucky that I loved investing. I walked into the job as if it were made for me, but when my son—"

He stopped. His chest tightened. His heart rate kicked into overdrive. He couldn't believe that had slipped out.

"But your son what?"

"But when my son began to show artistic talent," he said, thinking quickly because once again the conversation had inadvertently turned too personal. And this time it was *his* fault. "I suddenly saw that another person might not want to be CEO of our company, might not have the ability to handle the responsibility, or might have gifts and talents that steer him or her in a different direction. Then the company would have to hire someone, and hiring someone of the caliber we would require would involve paying out a huge salary and profit sharing. The family fortune would ultimately deplete."

She studied him for a second, her gaze so intense Danny knew the mention of his son had her curious. But he wouldn't say any more about Cory. That part of his life was so far off-limits that he didn't even let himself think about it. It would be such a cold, frosty day in hell that he'd discuss Cory with another person that he knew that day would never come.

Finally Grace sighed. "I guess you were lucky then—" she turned her attention back to her food "—that you wanted the job."

Danny relaxed. Once again she'd read him perfectly. She'd seen that though he'd mentioned his son, he hadn't gone into detail about Cory, and instead had brought the discussion back to Carson Services, so she knew to let the topic go.

They finished their dinner in companionable conversation because Grace began talking about remodeling the small house she'd bought when she got her first job two years before. As they spoke about choosing hardwood and deciding on countertops, Danny acknowledged to himself that she was probably the most sensitive person he'd met. She could read a mood or a situation so well that he didn't have to worry about what he said in front of her. A person who so easily knew not to pry would never break a confidence.

For that reason alone an intense urge to confide in her bubbled up in him, shocking him. Why the hell would he want to talk about the past? And why would he think that any woman would want to hear her boss's marital horror stories? No woman would. No *person* would. Except maybe a gossip. And Grace wasn't a gossip.

After dinner, they went inside for a drink, but Danny paused beside the stairway that led to his third-floor office suite.

"Bonuses don't pass through our normal accounting. I write those checks myself. It's a way to keep them completely between me and the employees who get them. The checkbook's upstairs. Why don't we just go up now and give you your bonus?"

Grace grinned. "Sounds good to me."

Danny motioned for Grace to precede him up the steps. Too late, he realized that was a mistake. Her perfect bottom was directly in his line of vision. He paused, letting her get a few steps ahead of him, only to discover that from this angle he had a view of her shapely calves.

He finished the walk up the stairs with his head down, gaze firmly fixed on the Oriental carpet runner on the steps. When he reached the third floor, she was waiting for him. Moonlight came in through the three tall windows in the back wall of the semidark loft that led to his office, surrounding her with pale light, causing her to look like an angel.

Mesmerized, Danny stared at her. He knew she was a nice person. A *good* person. He also knew that was why he had the quick mental picture of her as an angel and such a strong sense of companionship for her. But she was an employee. He was her boss. He needed to keep his distance.

He motioned toward his office suite and again she preceded him. Inside, he sat behind the desk and she gingerly sat on the chair in front of it.

"I think Orlando Riggs is the salt of the earth," Danny said as he pulled out the checkbook he held for the business. "You made him feel very comfortable."

"I felt very comfortable with him." She grimaced. "A lot of guys who had just signed a thirty-million-dollar deal with an NBA team would be a little cocky."

"A little cocky?" Danny said with a laugh. "I've met people with a lot less talent than Orlando has and a lot less cash who were total jerks."

"Orlando seems unaffected."

"Except that he wants to make sure his family has everything they need." Danny began writing out the check. "I didn't even realize he was married."

"And has two kids."

Kids.

Danny blinked at the unexpected avalanche of memory just the word kids brought. He remembered how eager he'd been to marry Lydia and have a family. He remembered his naive idea of marital bliss, and his chest swelled from the horrible empty feeling he got every time he realized how close he'd been to fulfilling that dream and how easily it had all been snatched away.

But tonight, with beautiful, sweet-tempered, sincere Grace sitting across the desk, Danny had a surprising moment of clarity. He'd always blamed himself for the breakdown of his marriage, but what if it had been Lydia's fault? He'd wanted to go to counseling. Lydia had simply wanted to go. Away from him. If he looked at the breakdown of his marriage from that very thin perspective, then the divorce wasn't his fault.

That almost made him laugh. If he genuinely believed the divorce wasn't his fault then—

Then he'd wasted years?

No. He'd wasted his life. He didn't merely feel empty the way he'd been told most people felt when they lost a mate; he felt wholly empty. Almost nonexistent. As if he didn't have a life. As if every day since his marriage had imploded two years ago, he hadn't really lived. He hadn't even really existed. He'd simply expended time.

Finished writing the check, Danny rose from his seat. It seemed odd to think about feeling empty when across the desk, eager, happy Grace radiated life and energy.

"Thank you for your help this weekend."

As he walked toward her, Grace also rose. He handed her the check. She glanced down at the amount he'd written, then looked up at him. Her beautiful violet eyes filled with shock. Her tongue came out to moisten her lips before she said, "This is too much."

Caught in the gaze of her hypnotic eyes, seeing the genuine appreciation, Danny could have sworn he felt some of her energy arch to him. If nothing else, he experienced a strong sense of connection. A rightness. Or maybe a purpose. As if there was a reason she was here.

The feeling of connection and intimacy could be nothing more than the result of spending every waking minute from Friday afternoon to Sunday night together, but that didn't lessen its intensity. It was so strong that his voice softened when he said, "No. It isn't too much. You deserve it."

She took a breath that caused her chest to rise and fall, calling his attention to the cleavage peeking out of the pink lace of her dress. She looked soft and feminine, yet she was also smart and sensitive. Which was why she attracted him, tempted him, when in the past two years no other woman had penetrated the pain that had held him hostage. Grace treated him like a person. Not like her rich boss. Not like a good catch. Not even like a guy so far out of her social standing that she should be nervous to spend so much one-on-one time. But just like a man.

"Thanks." She raised her gaze to his again. This time when Danny experienced the sense of intimacy, he almost couldn't argue himself out of it because he finally understood it. *She* felt it, too. He could see it in her eyes. And he didn't want to walk away from it. He *needed* her.

But then he saw the check in her hands and he remembered she was an employee. An affair between them had consequences. Especially when it ended. Office gossip would make him look foolish, but it could ruin her. Undoubtedly it would cost her her job. He might be willing to take a risk because his future wasn't at stake, but he couldn't make the decision for her.

CHAPTER TWO

DANNY cleared his throat. "You're welcome. I very much appreciated your help this weekend." He stepped away and walked toward the office door. "I'm going downstairs to have a drink before I turn in. I'll see you in the morning."

Grace watched Danny go, completely confused by what was happening between them. For a few seconds, she could have sworn he was going to kiss her and the whole heck of it was she would have let him.

Let him? She was so attracted to him she darned near kissed him first, and that puzzled her. She should have reminded herself that he was her boss and so wealthy they were barely on the same planet. Forget about being in the same social circle. But thoughts of their different worlds hadn't even entered her head, and, thinking about them now, Grace couldn't muster a reason they mattered.

Laughing softly, she combed her fingers through her hair. Whatever the reason, she couldn't deny the spark between her and Danny. When Orlando left that afternoon, Grace had been disappointed that their weekend together had come to an end. But Danny had asked her to stay one more night, and she couldn't resist the urge to dress up and hope that he would notice her the way she'd been noticing him. He'd nearly ruined everything by offering her a promotion she didn't deserve, but he showed her that he trusted her opinion by taking her advice about Bobby Zapf.

The real turning point came when he mentioned his son. He hadn't wanted to talk about him, but once Danny slipped him into the conversation he hadn't pretended he hadn't. She had seen the sadness in his eyes and knew there was a story there. But she also recognized that this wasn't the time to ask questions. She'd heard the rumor that Danny had gone through an ugly divorce but no report had mentioned a child from his failed marriage. Nasty divorces frequently resulted in child custody battles and his ex-wife could very well make him fight to see his son, which was undoubtedly why he didn't want to talk about him.

But tonight wasn't the night for probing into a past that probably only reminded him of unhappy times. Tonight, she had to figure out if he felt for her what she was beginning to feel for him. The last thing she wanted was to be one of those employees who got a crush on her boss and then pined for him for the rest of her career.

And she wouldn't get any answers standing in his third floor office when he was downstairs!

She ran down the steps and found him in the great room, behind the bar, pouring Scotch into a glass.

He glanced up when she walked over. Though he seemed surprised she hadn't gone to her room as he'd more or less ordered her to, he said, "Drink?"

Wanting to be sharp and alert so she didn't misinterpret anything he said or did, Grace smiled and said, "No. Thanks."

She slid onto one of the three red leather bar stools that matched the red leather sofas that sat parallel to each other in front of the wall of windows that provided a magnificent view of the Atlantic Ocean. A black, red and tan Oriental rug between the sofas protected the sand-colored hardwood floors. White-bowled lights connected to thin chrome poles suspended from the vaulted ceiling, illuminating the huge room.

Danny took a swallow of his Scotch, then set the glass on the bar. "Can't sleep?"

She shrugged. "Still too keyed up from the weekend I guess."

"What would you normally do on a Sunday night?"

She thought for a second, then laughed. "Probably play rummy with my mother. She's a cardaholic. Loves any game. But she's especially wicked with rummy."

"Can't beat her?"

"Every once in a while I get lucky. But when it comes to pure skill the woman is evilly blessed."

Danny laughed. "My mother likes cards, too."

Grace's eyes lit. "Really? How good is she?"

"Exceptional."

"We should get them together."

Danny took a long breath, then said, "We should."

And Grace suddenly saw it. The thing that had tickled her brain all weekend but had never really surfaced. In spite of her impoverished roots and his obviously privileged upbringing, she and Danny had a lot in common. Not childhood memories, but adult things like goals and commitments. He ran his family's business. She was determined to help her parents out of poverty because she loved them. Even the way they viewed Orlando proved they had approximately the same beliefs about life and people.

If Danny hadn't asked for her help this weekend, eventually they would have been alone together long enough to see that they clicked. They matched. She knew he realized it, too, if only because he'd nearly slipped into personal conversation with her four times at dinner, but he had stopped himself. Probably because she was an employee.

It was both of their loss if they weren't mature enough to handle an office relationship. But she thought they were. Her difficult childhood and his difficult divorce had strengthened each of them. They weren't flip. They were cautious. Smart. If any two people could have an office relationship without it affecting their work, she and Danny were the two. And she wasn't going to miss out on something good because, as her boss, Danny wouldn't be the first to make a move.

She raised her eyes until she caught his gaze. "You know what? Though you're trying to fight it, I think you like me. Would it help if I told you I really like you, too?"

* * *

For several seconds, Danny didn't answer. He couldn't. He'd never met a woman so honest, so he wasn't surprised that she spoke her mind. Even better, she hadn't played coy and tried to pretend she didn't see what was going on. She saw it, and she wanted to like him as much as he wanted to like her.

And that was the key. The final answer. She wanted to like him as much as he wanted to like her and he suddenly couldn't understand why he was fighting it.

"It helps enormously." He bent across the bar and kissed her, partly to make sure they were on the same page with their intentions, and partly to see if their chemistry was as strong as the emotions that seemed to ricochet between them.

It was. Just the slight brush of their lips knocked him for a loop. He felt the explosion the whole way to his toes.

She didn't protest the kiss, so he took the few steps that brought him from behind the bar and in front of the stool on which she sat. He put his hands on her shoulders and kissed her deeply this time, his mouth opening over hers.

White-hot desire slammed through him and his control began slipping. He wanted to touch her, to taste her, to feel all the things he'd denied himself for the past two years.

But it was one thing to kiss her. It was quite another to make love. But when he shifted away, Grace slid her hand around his neck and brought his lips back to hers.

Relief swamped him. He'd never had this kind of an all-consuming desire to make love. Yet, the yearning he felt wasn't for sexual gratification. It was to be with Grace herself. She was sweet and fun and wonderful...and beautiful. Having her slide her arms around him and return his kisses with a passion equal to his own filled him with an emotion so strong and complete he dared not even try to name it.

Instead he broke the kiss, lifted her into his arms and took her to his bed.

The next morning when Grace awoke, she inhaled a long breath as she stretched. When her hand connected with warm, naked skin, her eyes popped open and she remembered she'd spent the night making love with her boss.

Reliving every detail, she blinked twice, waiting for a sense of embarrassment or maybe guilt. When none came she smiled. She couldn't believe it, but it was true. She'd fallen in love with Danny Carson in about forty-eight hours.

She should feel foolish for tumbling in over her head so fast. She could even worry that he'd seen her feelings for him and taken advantage of her purely for sexual gratification. But she wasn't anything but happy. Nobody had ever made love to her the way he had. And she was sure their feelings were equal.

She yawned and stretched, then went downstairs to the room she'd used on Friday and Saturday nights. After brushing her teeth and combing her hair, she ran back to Danny's room and found he was still sleeping, so she slid into bed again.

Her movements caused Danny to stir. As Grace

thanked her lucky stars that she had a chance to fix up a bit before he awoke, he turned on his pillow. Ready, she smiled and caught his gaze but the eyes that met hers were not the warm brown eyes of the man who had made love to her the night before. They were the dark, almost black eyes of her boss.

She remembered again the way he'd made love to her and told herself to stop being a worrying loser. Yes, the guy who ran Carson Services could sometimes be a real grouch, but the guy who lived in this beach house was much nicer. And she was absolutely positive that was the real Danny.

Holding his gaze, she whispered, "Good morning."

He stared at her. After a few seconds, he closed his eyes. "Tell me we didn't make a mistake."

"We did not make a mistake."

He opened his eyes. "Always an optimist."

She scooted closer so she could rest her head on his outstretched arm. "We like each other. A lot. Something pretty special happened between us."

He was silent for a few seconds then he said, "Okay."

She twisted so she could look at him. "Okay? I thought we were fantastic!"

His face transformed. The caution slipped from his dark eyes and was replaced by amusement. "You make me laugh."

"It's a dirty job but somebody's got to do it."

Chuckling, he caught her around the waist and reversed their positions. But gazing into her eyes, he softened his expression again and said, "Thanks," before he lowered his head and kissed her.

They made love and then Danny rolled out of bed, suggesting they take a shower. Gloriously naked, he walked to the adjoining bathroom and began to run the water. Not quite as comfortable as he, Grace needed a minute to skew her courage to join him, and in the end wrapped a bedsheet around herself to walk to the bathroom.

But though she faltered before dropping the sheet, when she stepped into the shower, she suddenly felt bold. Knowing his trust was shaky because of his awful divorce, she stretched to her tiptoes and kissed him. He let her take the lead and she began a slow exploration of his body until he seemed unable to handle her simple ministrations anymore and he turned the tables.

They made love quickly, covered with soap and sometimes even pausing to laugh, and Grace knew from that moment on, she was his. She would never feel about any man the way she felt about Danny.

CHAPTER THREE

WHEN Grace and Danny stood in the circular driveway of his beach house, both about to get into their cars to drive back to Pittsburgh, she could read the displeasure in his face as he told her about the "client hopping" he had scheduled for the next week. He wanted to be with her but these meetings had been on the books for months and he couldn't get out of them. So she kissed him and told him she would be waiting when he returned.

They got into their vehicles and headed home. He was a faster driver, so she lost him on I-64, but she didn't care. Her heart was light and she had the kind of butterflies in her tummy that made a woman want to sing for joy. Though time would tell, she genuinely believed she'd found Mr. Right. She'd only known Danny for two weeks, and hadn't actually spent a lot of that time with him since he was so far above her on the company organizational chart. But the weekend had told her everything she needed to know about the real Danny Carson.

To the world, he was an ambitious, demanding, highly successful man. In private, he was a loving, caring, normal man, who liked her. A lot.

Yes, they would probably experience some problems because he owned the company she worked for. He'd hesitated at the bar before kissing her. He'd asked her that morning if they'd made a mistake. But she forced herself not to worry about it. She had no doubt that once they spent enough time together, and he saw the way she lived her beliefs, his worries about dating an employee would vanish.

What they had was worth a few months of getting to know each other. Or maybe the answer would be to quit her job?

The first two days of his trip sped by. He called Wednesday morning, and the mere sound of his voice made her breathless. Though he talked about clients, meetings, business dinners and never-ending handshaking, his deep voice reminded her of his whispered endearments during their night together and that conjured the memory of how he tasted, the firmness of his skin, the pleasure of being held in his arms. Before he disconnected the call, he whispered that he missed her and couldn't wait to see her and she'd all but fainted with happiness.

The next day he didn't call, but Grace knew he was busy. He also didn't call on Friday or Saturday.

Flying back to Pittsburgh Sunday, Danny nervously paced his Gulfstream, fighting a case of doubt and second thoughts about what had happened between him and Grace. In the week that had passed, he hadn't had a spare minute to think about her, and hadn't spoken with her except for one quick phone call a few days into the trip. The call had ended too soon and left him longing to see her, but after three days of having no contact, the negatives of the situation came crowding in on him, and there were plenty of them.

First, he didn't really know her. Second, even if she were the perfect woman, they'd gone too far too fast. Third, they worked together. If they dated it would be all over the office. When they broke up, he would be the object of the same gossip that had nearly ruined his reputation when his marriage ended.

He took a breath and blew it out on a puff. He couldn't tell if distance was giving him perspective or calling up all his demons. But he did know that he should have thought this through before making love to her.

Worse, he couldn't properly analyze their situation because he couldn't recall specifics. All he remembered from their Sunday night and Monday morning together were emotions so intense that he'd found the courage to simply be himself. But with the emotions gone, he couldn't summon a solid memory of the substance of what had happened between them. He couldn't remember anything specific she'd said to make him like her— like? Did he say like? He didn't just like Grace. That Sunday night his feelings had run more along the lines of a breathless longing, uncontrollable desire, and total bewitching. A man in that condition could easily be

seduced into seeing traits in a woman that weren't there
and that meant he had made a horrible mistake.

He told himself not to think that way. But the logical
side of his brain called him a sap. He'd met Grace two
weeks before when she'd come to work for his company,
but he didn't really know her because he didn't work
with new employees. He worked with their bosses. He
said hello to new employees in the hall. But otherwise,
he ignored them. So he hadn't "known" her for two
weeks. He'd glimpsed her.

Plus, she'd been on her best behavior for Orlando.
She had been at the beach house to demonstrate to
Orlando that Carson Services employed people in the
know. Yes, she'd gone above and beyond the call of duty
in her time with Orlando, making him feel comfortable,
sharing personal insights—but, really, wasn't that her
job?

Danny took a long breath. Had he fallen in love with
a well polished persona she'd pulled out to impress
Orlando and simply never disengaged when the basketball star left?

Oh Lord!

He sat, rubbed his hands down his face and held
back a groan. Bits and pieces of their Sunday night
dinner conversation flitted through his brain. She'd
grown up poor. Could only afford a house that needed
remodeling. She wanted to be rich. She'd gone into investing to understand money.

He *had* money.

Technically he was a shortcut to all her goals.

He swallowed hard. It wasn't fair to judge her when she wasn't there to defend herself.

He had to see her. Then he would know. After five minutes of conversation she would either relieve all his fears or prove that he'd gone too fast, told her too much and set himself up for a huge disappointment.

The second his plane taxied to a stop, he pulled out his cell phone and called her, but she didn't answer. He left a message but she didn't return his call and Danny's apprehensions hitched a notch. Not that he thought she should be home, waiting for him, but she knew when he got in. He'd told her he would call. He'd said it at the end of a very emotional phone conversation in which he'd told her that crazy as it sounded, he missed her. She'd breathlessly told him she missed him, too.

Now she wasn't home?

If he hadn't given her the time he would be landing, if he hadn't told her he would be calling, if he hadn't been so sappy about saying how much he missed her, it wouldn't seem so strange that she wasn't home. But, having told her all those things, he had the uncontrollable suspicion that something was wrong.

Unless she'd come to the same conclusions he had. Starting a relationship had been a mistake.

That had to be it.

Relief swamped him. He didn't want another relationship. Ever. And Grace was too nice a girl to have the kind of fling that ended when their sexual feelings for each other fizzled and they both eagerly walked away.

It was better for it to end now.

Content that not only had Grace nicely disengaged
their relationship, but also that he probably wouldn't run
into her in the halls because their positions in the
company and the building were so far apart, he went to
work happy. But his secretary buzzed him around ten-
thirty, telling him Grace was in the outer office, asking
if he had time for her.

Sure. Why not? Now that he'd settled everything in
his head, he could handle a debriefing. They'd probably
both laugh about the mistake.

He tossed his pencil to the stack of papers in front
of him. "Send her in."

He steeled himself, knowing that even though his
brain had easily resolved their situation, his body might
not so easily agree. Seeing her would undoubtedly
evoke lots of physical response, if only because she
was beautiful. He remembered that part very, very well.

His office door opened and she stepped inside.
Danny almost groaned at his loss. She was every bit as
stunning as he remembered. Her dark hair framed her
face and complemented her skin tone. Her little pink
suit showed off her great legs. But he wasn't meant for
relationships and she wasn't meant for affairs. Getting
out now while they could get out without too much dif-
ficulty was the right thing to do.

"Good morning, Grace."

She smiled. "Good morning."

He pointed at the chair in front of his desk, indicating she should sit. "Look, I know what you're going
to say. Being away for a week gave me some perspec-

tive, too, and I agree we made a mistake the night we slept together."

"What?"

Confused, he cocked his head. "I thought you were here to tell me we'd made a mistake."

Holding the arms of the captain's chair in front of his desk, she finally sat. "I came in to invite you to dinner."

He sat back on his chair, knowing this could potentially be one of the worst conversations of his life. "I'm sorry. When you weren't home last night when I called, I just assumed you'd changed your mind."

"I was at my mother's."

"I called your cell phone."

She took a breath. "And by the time I realized I'd hadn't turned it on after I took it off the charger, it was too late for me to call you back." She took another breath and smiled hopefully. "That's why I came to your office."

He picked up his pencil again. Nervously tapped it on the desk. "I'm sorry. Really. But—" This time he took the breath, giving himself a chance to organize his thoughts. "I genuinely believe we shouldn't have slept together, and I really don't want to see you anymore. I don't have relationships with employees."

He caught her gaze. "I'm sorry."

That seemed to catch her off guard. She blinked several times, but her face didn't crumble as he expected it would if she were about to cry. To his great relief, her chin lifted. "That's fine."

Pleased that she seemed to be taking this well—

probably because his point was a valid one—bosses and employees shouldn't date—he rose. "Do you want the day off or something?"

She swallowed and wouldn't meet his gaze. She said, "I'm fine," then turned and walked out of his office.

Danny fell to his seat, feeling like a class-A heel. He had hurt her and she was going to cry.

Grace managed to get through the day with only one crying spurt in the bathroom right after coming out of Danny's office. She didn't see him the next day or the next or at all for the next two weeks. Just when she had accepted that her world hadn't been destroyed because he didn't want her or because she'd slept with him, she realized something awful. Her female cycle was as regular as clockwork, so when things didn't happen on the day they were supposed to happen, she knew something was wrong.

Though she and Danny had used condoms, they weren't perfect. She bought an early pregnancy test and discovered her intuition had been correct. She had gotten pregnant.

She sat on the bed in the master suite of her little house. The room was awash with warm colors: cognac, paprika, butter-yellow in satin pillows, lush drapes and a smooth silk bedspread. But she didn't feel any warmth as she stared at the results of the EPT. She had just gotten pregnant by a man who had told her he wanted nothing to do with her.

She swallowed hard and began to pace the honey-yellow hardwood floors of the bedroom she'd scrimped, saved and labored to refinish. Technically she had a great job and a good enough income that she could raise a child alone. Money wasn't her problem. And neither was becoming a mother. She was twenty-four, ready to be a mom. Excited actually.

Except Danny didn't want her. She might survive telling him, but she still worked for him. Soon everybody at his company would know she was pregnant. Anybody with a memory could do the math and realize when she'd gotten pregnant and speculate the baby might be Danny's since they'd spent a weekend together.

He couldn't run away from this and neither could she.

She took a deep breath, then another, and another, to calm herself.

Everything would be fine if she didn't panic and handled this properly. She didn't have to tell Danny right away that she was pregnant. She could wait until enough time had passed that he would see she wasn't trying to force anything from him. Plus, until her pregnancy was showing, she didn't have to tell anybody but Danny. In six or seven months the people she worked with wouldn't necessarily connect her pregnancy with the weekend she and Danny together. They could get out of this with a minimum of fuss.

That made so much sense that Grace easily fell asleep that night, but the next morning she woke up dizzy, still exhausted and with an unholy urge to vomit. On Saturday morning, she did vomit. Sunday morning, she couldn't get out of bed. Tired, nauseated and dizzy beyond belief, she couldn't hide her symptoms from anybody. Which meant that by Monday afternoon, everybody would guess something was up, and she had no choice but to tell Danny first thing in the morning that she was pregnant. If she didn't, he would find out by way of a rumor, and she couldn't let that happen.

Grace arrived at work an hour early on Monday. Danny was already in his office but his secretary had not yet arrived. As soon as he was settled, she knocked on the frame of his open door.

He looked up. "Grace?"

"Do you have a minute?"

"Not really, I have a meeting—"

"This won't take long." She drank a huge gulp of air and pushed forward because there was no point in dilly-dallying. "I'm pregnant."

For thirty seconds, Danny sat motionless. Grace felt every breath she drew as the tension in the room increased with each second that passed.

Finally he very quietly said, "Get out."

"We need to talk about this."

"Talk about this? Oh, no! I won't give credence to your scheme by even gracing you with ten minutes to try to convince me you're pregnant!"

"Scheme?"

"Don't play innocent with me. Telling the man who

broke up with you that you're pregnant is the oldest trick in the book. If you think I'm falling for it, you're insane."

Grace hadn't expected this would be an easy conversation, but for some reason or another she had expected it to be fair. The Danny she remembered from the beach house might have been shocked, but he would have at least given her a chance to talk.

"I'm not insane. I am pregnant."

"I told you to get out."

"This isn't going to go away because you don't believe me."

"Grace, I said leave."

His voice was hard and cold and his office fell deadly silent. Knowing there was no talking to him in that state and hoping that after she gave him a few hours for her announcement to sink in he might be more amenable to discussing it, Grace did as he asked. She left his office with her head high, controlling the tears that welled behind her eyelids.

The insult of his reaction tightened her chest and she marched straight to her desk. She yanked open the side drawer, withdrew her purse and walked out of the building as if it were the most natural thing in the world for her to do. When she got into her car, she dropped her head to her steering wheel and let the tears fall.

Eventually it would be obvious she hadn't lied. But having Danny call her a schemer was the absolute worst experience she'd ever had.

Partially because he believed it. He believed she would trick him.

Grace's cheeks heated from a sudden rush of indignation.

It was as if he didn't know her at all—or she didn't know him at all.

Or maybe they didn't know each other.

She started her car and headed home. She needed the day to recover from that scene, but also as sick as she was she couldn't go back to work until she and Danny had talked this out. Pretty soon everybody would guess what had happened. If nothing else, they had to do damage control. There were lots of decisions that had to be made. So when she got home she would call her supervisor, explain she'd gotten sick and that she might be out a few days. Then she and Danny would resolve this *away* from the office.

Because she had written down his home number and cell number when he left the message on her answering machine the Sunday night he'd returned from his business trip, Grace called both his house and his cell that night.

He didn't answer.

She gave him forty-eight hours and called Thursday morning before he would leave for work. Again, no answer.

A little more nervous now, she gave him another forty-eight hours and called Saturday morning. No answer.

She called Monday night. No answer.

And she got the message. He wasn't going to pick up her calls.

But by that time she had something a little more serious to handle. She couldn't get well. Amazed that she'd even been able to go to work the Monday of her encounter with Danny, she spent her days in bed, until, desperate for help and advice, she told her mother that she was pregnant and sicker than she believed was normal. They made a quick gynecologist appointment and her doctor told her that she was simply enduring extreme morning sickness.

Too worried about her baby to risk the stress of dealing with Danny, Grace put off calling him. Her life settled into a simple routine of forcing herself out of bed, at least to the couch in her living room, but that was as far as she got, and watching TV all day, as her mother fussed over her.

Knowing the bonus she'd received for her weekend with Orlando would support her through her pregnancy if she were frugal, she quit her job. Swearing her immediate supervisor to secrecy in their final phone conversation, she confided that she was pregnant and having troubles, though she didn't name the baby's father. And she slid out of Carson Services as if she'd never been there.

She nearly called Danny in March, right before the baby was born, but, again, didn't have the strength to handle the complexities of their situation. Even though he would be forced to believe she hadn't lied, he might still see her as a cheat. Someone who had tricked him. She didn't know how to explain that she hadn't, and after nine months of "morning sickness" she didn't give a damn. A man who behaved the way he had wasn't her perfect partner. His money didn't make him the special prize he seemed to believe he was. It was smarter to focus on the joy of becoming a mother, the joy of having a child, than to think about a guy so hurt by his divorce that he couldn't believe anything anyone told him.

When Sarah was born everything suddenly changed. No longer sick and now responsible for a child, Grace focused on finding a job. Happily she found one that paid nearly double what she'd been making at Carson Services. Because her parents had moved into her house to help while she was pregnant, she surprised them by buying the little bungalow down the street. Her mother wanted to baby-sit while Grace worked. Her dad could keep up both lawns. And the mortgage on the new house for her parents was small.

Busy and happy, Grace didn't really think about Danny and before she knew it, it was September and Sarah was six months old. Everything from baby-sitting to pediatrician appointments was taken care of. Everyone in her little family was very happy.

And Grace wondered why she would want to tell Danny at all.

But holding Sarah that night she realized that this situation wasn't about her and Danny anymore. It was about Sarah. Every little girl had a right to know her daddy.

The following Saturday evening, Grace found herself craning her neck, straining to read the small sophisti-

cated street signs in the development that contained
Danny's house. It hadn't been hard to find his address.
Convincing herself to get in the car and drive over had
been harder. Ultimately she'd come to terms with it not
for Danny's sake, but for Sarah's. If Grace didn't at least
give Danny the chance to be a dad, then she was no
better than he was.

She located his street, turned onto it and immediately
saw his house. Simple stone, accented by huge multi-
paned windows, his house boasted a three-car garage
and space. Not only was the structure itself huge, but
beyond the fence that Grace assumed protected a
swimming pool, beautiful green grass seemed to stretch
forever before it met a wall of trees. Compared to her
tiny bungalow, his home was a palace.

She parked her little red car in his driveway, got out
and reached into the back seat to unbuckle Sarah.
Opting not to put her in a baby carrier, Grace pulled her
from the car and settled her on her arm.

Holding her squirming baby and bulky diaper bag,
she strode up the stone front walk to Danny's door,
once again noting the differences in their lifestyles per-
sonified by decorative black lantern light fixtures and
perfect landscaping.

Grace shook her head, trying to stop the obvious
conclusion from forming, but she couldn't. She and
Danny were different. Too difference to be together.
Why hadn't she recognized that? He probably had.
That's why he'd told her he didn't want to see her. They
weren't made for each other. Not even close. And he'd

now had fifteen months to forget her. She could have to explain the entire situation again, and then face another horrible scene.

Still, as much as she dreaded this meeting, and as much as she would prefer to raise Sarah on her own, she knew it wasn't fair for Sarah to never know her father. She also knew Danny should have the option to be part of his daughter's life. If he again chose not to believe Grace when she told him Sarah was his child, then so be it. She wouldn't beg him to be a father to their baby. She wouldn't demand DNA testing to force him in. If he wanted a DNA test, she would comply, but as far as she was concerned, she was the one doing him the favor. If he didn't wish to acknowledge his child or be a part of Sarah's life that was his decision. She wasn't going to get upset or let him hurt her again. If he said he wanted no part of her or her baby, this time Grace and Sarah would leave him alone for good.

Again without giving herself a chance to think, she rang the doorbell. Waiting for someone to answer, she glanced around at his massive home, then wished she hadn't. How could she have ever thought she belonged with someone who lived in this part of the city?

The door opened and suddenly she was face-to-face with the father of her child. Though it was Saturday he wore dress slacks and a white shirt, but his collar was unbuttoned and his tie loosened. He looked relaxed and comfortable and was even smiling.

Then his eyes darkened, his smile disappeared and

his gaze dropped to Sarah, and Grace realized he remembered who she was.

She took a breath. "Can we come in?"

The expression in his eyes changed, darkening even more, reminding Grace of a building storm cloud. For the twenty seconds that he remained stonily silent, she was positive he would turn her away. For those same twenty seconds, with his dark eyes condemning her, she fervently wished he would.

But without saying a word, he pulled open his door and stepped aside so she could enter.

"Thank you." She walked into the echoing foyer of his big house, fully expecting this to be the worst evening of her life.

CHAPTER FOUR

As Grace brushed by Danny, a band of pain tightened his chest. At first he thought the contraction was a result of his anger with Grace, fury that she'd continued with her pregnancy scheme. He wondered how she intended to get around DNA since he would most certainly require the test, then he actually looked at the baby in her arms, a little girl if the pink one-piece pajamas were any indication. She appeared to be about six months old—the age their baby would be if he had gotten Grace pregnant that Sunday night at his beach house. More than that, though, the baby looked exactly as Cory had when he was six months old.

Danny stood frozen, unable to do anything but stare at the chubby child in Grace's arms. Suddenly the baby smiled at him. Her plump lips lifted. Her round blue eyes filled with laughter. She made a happy gurgling sound that caused playful spit bubbles to gather at the corners of her mouth. She looked so much like Cory it was as if Danny had been unceremoniously flung back in time.

Feeling faint, he pointed down the corridor. "There's a den at the end of the hall. Would you please wait for me there?"

Grace caught his gaze with her pretty violet eyes and everything inside of Danny stilled. In a hodgepodge of pictures and words, he remembered bits and pieces of both the weekend they'd spent together with Orlando and the morning he'd kicked her out of his office—wrongly if his assumptions about the baby were correct. In his mind's eye, he saw Grace laughing with Orlando, working with him, making him comfortable. He remembered her soft and giving in his arms. He remembered her trembling when she told him she was pregnant, and then he remembered nothing but anger. He hadn't given her a chance to explain or even a sliver of benefit of the doubt. He'd instantly assumed her "pregnancy" was a ruse and wouldn't hear another word.

"I don't think we want to be interrupted," he said, grasping for any excuse that would give him two minutes to come to terms with some of this before he had to talk to her. "So I need to instruct my housekeeper that we're to be left alone."

She pressed her lips together, nodded and headed down the hall. Once Danny saw her turn into the den, he collapsed on the bottom step of the spiral staircase in his foyer and dropped his head to his hands.

They were shaking. His knees felt like rubber. Pain ricocheted through him and he squeezed his eyes shut. In vivid detail, he saw Cory's birth, his first birthday party, and every Christmas they'd had together. He remembered his giggle. He remembered his endless questions as he grew from a toddler into a little boy. He remembered how he loved garbage trucks and mailmen.

Pain overwhelmed him as he relived every second of the best and worst six years of his life and then realized he could very well go through it all again. The first birthday. Laughing, happy Christmases. Questions and curiosities. And pain. One day he was a doting dad and the next he was living alone, without even the possibility of seeing his son again.

He fought the anger that automatically surged up in him when the thought about his marriage, about Lydia. In the past year, his sense of fair play had compelled him to examine his marriage honestly and he had to admit that Lydia hadn't been a horrible shrew. *He* hadn't been a terrible husband. Their marriage hadn't ended because he and his ex-wife were bad people, but because they'd hit a crossroad that neither had anticipated. A crossroad where there had been no choice but to separate. They had once been the love of each other's life, yet when their marriage had begun to crumble, they'd both forgotten the eight good years, only remembered their horrible final year, and fought bitterly. They'd hurt each other. Used Cory as a weapon. And both of them had walked away damaged.

Remembering that only made his upcoming showdown with Grace more formidable. He and Grace didn't have two years of courtship and six years of marriage to look back on to potentially keep them from hurting each other. So how did he expect their confrontation to turn out any better than his fight with Lydia had?

He didn't.

He wouldn't shirk his responsibility to Grace's baby. But he had learned enough from the past that the key to survival was not being so in love with his daughter that she could turn into Grace's secret weapon.

Finally feeling that he knew what he had to do, Danny rose from the step, went to the kitchen and told his housekeeper he and Grace weren't to be disturbed, then he walked to the den.

Unfortunately he couldn't keep the displeasure out of his voice when he said, "Let me see her."

Grace faced him. "Save your anger, Danny. I was the one left to have this baby alone. I was so sick I had to quit my job and depend on my parents to basically nurse me for nine months. The bonus you gave me went to support me until I had Sarah and could go back to work. I was sick, exhausted and worried that if anything went wrong when she was born I wouldn't be able to pay for proper care. You could have helped me through all of that, but you never even followed up on me. So the way I see this, you don't have anything to complain about."

She was right, of course. It didn't matter that he was still hurting from the end of his marriage when she told him she was pregnant. He hadn't for two seconds considered Grace or her feelings. Still, he had no proof that she was the innocent victim she wanted him to believe she was. The weekend they'd spent together, he'd made himself an easy mark for a woman he really didn't know. He'd never wanted another relationship, let alone a child. And now he had one with a stranger. A woman he genuinely believed had tricked him.

"What made it all worse was wondering about your reaction when I did bring Sarah to you." She sat on the leather sofa in the conversation area, laid the gurgling baby on the cushion and pulled the bonnet ribbon beneath the little girl's chin, untying the bow.

Danny's breathing stuttered as he stared at the baby. *His daughter.* A perfect little pink bundle of joy. She punched and pedaled her legs as Grace removed her bonnet.

Grace's voice softly intruded into his thoughts. "I understood when you told me you didn't want to see me anymore. I had every intention of respecting that, if only because of pride. But this baby was both of our doing."

Sarah spit out her pacifier and began to cry.

Grace lifted the little girl from the sofa cushion and smoothed her lips across her forehead. "I know. I know," she singsonged. "You're hungry."

She rose and handed the baby to Danny. "Can you take her while I get her bottle?"

Panic skittered through him and he backed away. He hadn't held a baby since Cory.

To his surprise Grace laughed. "Come on. She won't bite. She doesn't have teeth yet."

"I've…I'm…I just—"

Realizing he was behaving like an idiot, Danny stopped stuttering. He wasn't an idiot. And he would always think of Cory every time he looked at Sarah, but there was no way he'd admit that to Grace. She already knew enough about him and he didn't know half as much about her. Seeing Cory every time he looked at Sarah would be his cross to bear in private.

He reached out to take the baby, but this time Grace pulled her back.

"Sit," she said as if she'd thought his hesitancy was uncertainty about how to hold the baby. "I'll hand her to you."

Deciding not to argue her assumption, Danny lowered himself to the sofa and Grace placed the baby in his arms. "Just set her bottom on your lap, and support her back with your left hand."

He did that and the baby blinked up at him, her crying becoming sniffles as she lost herself to confusion about the stranger holding her.

Staring at her mutely, Danny identified. The first time he'd seen Cory was immediately after he'd slid into the doctor's hands. He'd been purple and wrinkled and when the doctor slapped his tiny behind he'd shrieked like a banshee. The little girl on Danny's lap was clean and now quiet. The total opposite of her half brother.

Grace pulled a bottle from her diaper bag. Dripping formula onto her wrist, she checked the bottle's temperature and said, "Can I take this to your kitchen and warm it?"

"Go back to the foyer, then turn right. The door at the end of the hall leads to the kitchen. My housekeeper is there. She'll help you."

Grace nodded and left.

Danny glanced down at the blue-eyed, rather bald baby. He took a breath. She blinked at him again, as if still confused.

"I'm your father."

She cocked her head to the right. The same way Cory used to. Especially when Danny would tell him anything about Carson Services, about responsibility, about carrying on the family name, as if the idea of doing anything other than paint was absurd.

Remembering Cory's reaction tightened Danny's chest again, but this time it wasn't from the memory of how, even as a small child, Cory had seemed to reject the idea of taking over the family business. Danny suddenly realized this little girl was now the one in line to run Carson Services. Grace might not know it, but Danny did.

Grace ran to the kitchen and didn't find a housekeeper, but she did locate a microwave into which she quickly shoved the bottle. She'd never seen a person more uncomfortable with a baby than Danny appeared to be, which was surprising considering he had a son, but she wasn't so insensitive that she didn't realize that meeting Sarah hadn't been easy for him.

She'd been preoccupied with Sarah's needs and hadn't factored Danny's shock into the equation. But having watched his facial expression shift and change, she realized that though he might not have believed Grace when she told him she was pregnant he seemed to be accepting that Sarah was his.

When the timer bell rang, she grabbed the bottle and

headed back to his den. Walking down the hall she heard Danny's soft voice.

"And that's why mutual funds are better for some people."

Grace stopped just outside the door.

"Of course, there are times when it's more logical to put the money of a conservative investor in bonds. Especially a nervous investor. Somebody who can't afford to take much risk. So you always have to question your investor enough that you can determine the level of risk his portfolio and personality can handle."

Standing by the wall beside the door, Grace twisted so she could remain hidden as she peered inside. Sarah gripped Danny's finger and stared up at him. Her blue eyes sharp and alert. Danny appeared comfortable, too, holding the baby loosely on his lap, and Grace realized that talking about something familiar was how Danny had overcome his apprehensions. Still, stocks? Poor Sarah!

"It's all about the individual. Some people are afraid of the stock market. Which is another reason mutual funds are so great. They spread the risk over a bunch of stocks. If one fails, another stock in the fund could sky-rocket and balance everything out."

If it had been under any other circumstances, Grace would have burst out laughing. Danny looked up and saw her standing there. He grimaced. "Sorry. I didn't know what else to talk about."

She shrugged. "I guess it doesn't really matter. All a baby really cares about is hearing your voice." She walked into the room and lifted Sarah from Danny's lap.

Nestling the baby into the crook of her arm, she added, "When in doubt, make up something. Maybe a story about a bunny or a bear. Just a short little anything."

Danny didn't reply, but rose and walked to the window. "You should be the one to sit."

Not about to remind him that there was plenty of space for both of them on the leather sofa, Grace took the place he had vacated. With two silent parents, the sound of Sarah greedily sucking filled the room.

"I almost wish you hadn't brought her to me."

Grace hadn't forgotten that he'd broken up with her before she told him she was pregnant. Still, that was his tough luck. He'd created a child and she wasn't letting him pretend he hadn't.

"She's your child."

"Yes. And I know you think there are all kinds of reasons that's great, but you're not going to like the way this has to play out."

"The way this has to play out?"

"I have to raise my daughter."

Not expecting that, Grace stared at his stiff back. But rather than be offended by his defiant stance, she remembered the feeling of his corded muscles beneath her fingertips. The firmness of his skin. Her own shivers of delight from having his hands on her.

Reaction flared inside her but she quickly shook it off. She wouldn't let herself fall victim to his charm again. Too much was at stake. She didn't know the official definition of "raise his daughter," but it sounded as if he intended to get more than a Saturday afternoon with Sarah every other weekend. There was no way Grace would let him take Sarah and ignore her. He hadn't ever wanted her. If he took her now, it would probably be out of a sense of duty to his family.

Still, if Grace argued, if she didn't handle this situation with kid gloves, her reply could sound like an accusation and accusations only caused arguments. She did not want to argue. She wanted all this settled as quickly and amicably as possible.

"It's good that you want to be involved—"

Danny suddenly turned from the window and caught her gaze, but Grace couldn't read the expression in his eyes and fell silent. She didn't know what he was thinking because she didn't know him. Not at all. She hadn't worked with him long enough to even know him as a boss. With Orlando he had been fun and funny. But when she'd told him about being pregnant he'd been hard, cold, unyielding. As far as she knew he had two personalities. A good guy and a bad guy and she had a sneaking suspicion few people saw the good guy.

"I want my daughter to live with me."

"Live with you?" *Grace* would be the one getting a visit every other Saturday afternoon? He had to be joking. Or insane.

"I've got money enough and clout enough that if I take you to court I'll end up with custody."

Grace gaped at him. It had been difficult to bring her child to meet him. As far as she was concerned, he could have stayed out of their lives forever. She was only here for Sarah's sake. Trying to grasp that he wanted to take Sarah away from her was staggering. Could his money really put Grace in a position where she'd be forced to hand over her innocent, defenseless baby daughter to a complete stranger? A man who didn't even want her?

She pulled in a breath and said, "That's ridiculous."

"Not really. When I retire, the option to take over Carson Services will be Sarah's. She'll need to be prepared. Only I can prepare her."

"But your son—"

"Never wanted the job. It falls to Sarah."

Overwhelmed, Grace shook her head. "This is too much in one day. I never even considered the possibility that you wanted to know I'd had a baby. Yet the day you find out, you're suddenly demanding custody."

"I don't have any other choice."

Grace sat in stunned silence. The whole hell of it was he didn't want Sarah. He wasn't asking for any reason except to fulfill a duty. Which was just wonderful. Grace would lose the baby she adored to a man who didn't want her, a man who intended to *train* her for a job. Not to love and nurture her, but to assure there was someone to take over the family business.

The injustice of it suffocated Grace at the same time that she understood it. Danny might not want Sarah, but he had a responsibility to her and to his family.

She wondered if he really needed to live with Sarah to teach her, then unexpectedly understood his side again. Preparing to take over a family fortune required more than a formal education. It required knowledge of family history and traditions. It required social graces. It required building social relationships.

All of which Grace didn't have. Sarah had to live with him at least part of the time.

Part of the time.

Suddenly inspired, Grace said, "You know what? I think I have a compromise."

"I don't compromise."

No kidding.

"Okay, then maybe what I have is a deal to propose."

His eyes narrowed ominously. "I don't need a deal, either."

"Well, listen anyway. The problem I see is that you don't know Sarah—"

"Living together will take care of that."

"Just listen. You don't know Sarah. I don't think you really want her. You're asking for custody out of a sense of duty and responsibility not to her but to your family, and, as bad as it is for my cause, I understand it. But as Sarah's mother I can't let you take my baby when you don't want her. So what I'm going to propose is that you come to live with Sarah and me for the next two weeks."

His face scrunched in confusion. "How exactly would that help?"

"If nothing else, in two weeks, I'll get to know you and you'll get to know her. Especially since I don't have a housekeeper or nanny. You and I will be the ones to care for her."

His shrewd brown eyes studied her, as if he were

trying to think of the catch. Since there was no catch, Grace continued.

"The deal is if you can spend two weeks with us, learning to care for her, and if at the end of that two weeks I feel comfortable with you having her, I won't contest *shared* custody. Week about. I get her one week. You have her the next. That way, as she gets older, you can schedule the functions you think she needs to be involved in, and I won't have to give her over to you permanently."

Danny shook his head. "Grace—"

"I won't give her over to you permanently. Not for any reason. Not any way. The best you'll get from me is week about and only if I believe you can handle her."

"You're not in a position to name terms," Danny said, shaking his head. "I can beat you in court."

"And then what?" Grace asked barely holding onto her temper. This time yesterday he didn't know he had a daughter. This time last year he didn't want to even hear Grace was pregnant. He couldn't expect her to hand over their child. She'd spend every cent of money she had before she'd recklessly hand over her baby to a man who didn't want Sarah, a man who probably would keep his distance and never love her.

"Say you do beat me in court. What are you going to do? Pass off your daughter's care to nannies, and let her be raised by a stranger when she could be spending that time with her mother? Is that your idea of grooming her? Showing her how to walk all over people?"

He ran his hand along the back of his neck.

She had him. They might not have spent much time

together, but she'd noticed that when he rubbed the back of his neck, he was thinking.

"It sure as hell isn't my idea of how to teach her," Grace said quietly, calming down so he would, too. "If nothing else, admit you need some time to adjust to being her dad."

He sighed. "You want *two* weeks?"

"If you can't handle her for two weeks, how do you expect to have her permanently?"

Danny said nothing and Grace retraced her argument, trying to figure out why two weeks made him hesitate. A person who wanted full custody couldn't object to a mere two-week stay with the same baby he was trying to get custody of —

Unless he wasn't worried about two weeks with Sarah as much as he was worried about two weeks with Grace. The last time they'd spent three *days* together they'd ended up in bed.

The air suddenly filled with electricity, so much that Grace could almost see the crackles and sparks. Memories—not of his accusations when she told him she was pregnant, but his soft caresses that Sunday night and Monday morning—flooded her mind and the attraction she'd felt the weekend they'd spent together returned full force.

But she didn't want it. She did not want to be attracted to this man. He'd come right out and said he didn't want a relationship with her. Plus, he had clout that she didn't have. Grace needed all her facilities to fight for Sarah's interests. She couldn't risk that he'd push her around in court the way he'd steamrolled her when she told him she was pregnant.

The reminder of how he'd kicked her out of his office without hearing her out was all she needed. Her chin came up. Her spine stiffened. She would never, ever trust him again. She would never give in to the attraction again.

"You're perfectly safe with me. Our time together was a mistake. I wouldn't even speak to you were it not for Sarah."

He remained silent so long that Grace sighed with disgust. He hadn't had a clue how painful his words had been to her. He hadn't cared that she could have misinterpreted everything he'd said and drawn the conclusion that he'd had his fun with her but she wasn't good enough to really love. He'd been so wrapped up in his own wants and needs that he never considered hers.

Or anyone's as far as Grace knew.

Another reason to stay the hell away from him.

"I mean it, Danny. I want nothing to do with you and will fight tooth and nail before I let you take Sarah even for weekends if only because you're a virtual stranger."

Obviously controlling his anger, he looked at the ceiling then back at her. "If I spend two weeks with you and the baby you won't contest shared custody," he said, repeating what he believed to be their arrangement.

"*If* by the end of those two weeks I believe you'll be good to Sarah."

Sarah had stopped sucking. Grace glanced down to see the baby had fallen asleep in her arms. "If you wish, we can have our lawyers draw up papers."

"Oh, I *will* have my lawyer write an agreement."

"Great. Once we get it signed we can start."

"You'll have it tonight. Do you have an e-mail address?"

"Yes."

"Watch your computer. You'll have the agreement before you go to bed. You can e-mail me directions to your house and I'll be there tomorrow."

CHAPTER FIVE

WHEN GRACE received Danny's e-mail with their agreement as an attachment, she realized that no matter how simple and straightforward, she couldn't sign any legal document without the advice of counsel. She replied saying she wanted her own lawyer to review the agreement before she signed it, expecting him to be angry at the delay. Instead he was surprisingly accommodating of her request.

She spoke with a lawyer Monday morning, who gave her the go-ahead to sign, and e-mailed Danny that she had executed the agreement and he could sign it that evening when he arrived at her house.

Busy at work, she didn't give Danny or the agreement another thought until she walked into the foyer of her little bungalow and saw something she hadn't considered.

The downstairs of her house had an open floor plan. Pale orange ceramic tile ran from the foyer to the back door. An oatmeal-colored Berber area rug sat beneath the burnt-orange tweed sofa and the matching love seat, delineating that space. Similarly the tan, brown and black print rug beneath the oak table and chairs marked off the dining area. A black-and-tan granite-topped breakfast bar separated the living room from the kitchen, but because there were no cabinets above it, people in the kitchen were clearly visible from any point downstairs.

Grace wasn't afraid that Danny wouldn't like her home. She didn't give a damn if he liked it or not. What troubled her was that with the exception of the two bedrooms, both upstairs, there was nowhere to hide. Anytime they were downstairs they would technically be together.

"Well, Sarah," she said, sliding the baby out of her carrier seat and giving her a quick kiss on the cheek. In her yellow one-piece outfit, Sarah looked like a ray of sunshine. "I guess it's too late to worry about that now."

As the words came out of her mouth, the doorbell rang, and Grace winced. If that was Danny, it really was too late to worry about the close quarters of her house now.

Angling the baby on her hip, Grace walked to the door and opened it. Danny stood on her small porch, holding a garment bag, with a duffel bag sitting beside his feet. Dressed in jeans and a loose-fitting sport shirt, he looked comfortable and relaxed, reminding her of their time together at his beach house.

A sudden avalanche of emotion overtook her. She had really fallen hard for him that weekend. Not just because he was sexy, though he was. He had an air of power and strength that—combined with his shiny black hair, piercing black eyes and fabulous body—

made him one of the sexiest men Grace had ever met. Staring into his eyes, she remembered the way he made love to her. She remembered their pillow talk and their one phone conversation. He had definitely felt something for her that weekend, too, but in the one short week he was out of town he'd lost it. He hadn't believed her when she told him she was pregnant. He'd kicked her out of his office. And now they were here. Fighting over custody of a baby he hadn't wanted.

"This house doesn't look big enough for two people, let alone three."

"It's got more space than you think," Grace said, opening the door a little wider so he could enter, as she reminded herself she had to do this because she couldn't beat him in court. "It looks like a ranch, but it isn't. There are two bedrooms upstairs."

"Yeah, they're probably no bigger than closets."

Grace told herself she could do this. She'd dealt with grouchy Danny every time she'd spoken to him—except for that one weekend. The person she'd met that weekend was more likely the exception and grouchy Danny was the rule. She wasn't about to let their two weeks begin with her apologizing.

Ignoring his closet comment, she said, "Let's take your bags upstairs and get them out of the way."

Grace turned and began walking up the steps, and, following after her, Danny got a flashback of following her up the steps of his beach house. It intensified when he glanced down at the steps to avoid looking at her shapely legs. The memory was so clear it made him dizzy, as if he were stepping back in time.

But he wasn't. They were here and now, fifteen months later. She'd had his child. She might have done it without him, but ultimately she'd brought the baby to him. And why not? As far as Grace knew little Sarah could inherit a fortune—even before Danny was dead if she became the CEO of Carson Services when Danny retired.

He didn't want even a portion of the family fortune to go to an opportunist, but his threat of taking Grace to court to get full custody had been empty. An attempt to pressure her into giving him their daughter. Then Grace had come up with a compromise and to Danny's surprise it really did suit him. He could train Sarah without paying off her mother.

Plus, he no longer had the worry that a custody battle gave her reason to dig into his past.

All he had to do was spend two weeks with Grace, a woman who he believed tricked him.

At the top of the steps, Grace turned to the right, opened a door, and stepped back so he could enter the room. To his surprise, Grace was correct, the bedroom was more spacious than he'd thought from the outward appearance of the house. Even with a double bed in the center of the room, a knotty pine armoire and dresser, and a small desk in the corner, there was plenty of space to walk.

He hesitantly said, "This is nice."

"We have to share the bathroom."

He faced her. She'd taken a few steps into the room, as if wanting to be available to answer questions, but not exactly thrilled to be in the same room with him. Especially not a bedroom.

Her soft voice triggered another batch of beach house memories. Grace telling him to promote someone else. Grace looking like an angel in front of the upstairs widows. Grace ready to accept his kiss…

He shoved the memories out of his brain, reminding himself that woman probably didn't exist. "I'll keep my things in a shaving kit. I won't take up any room."

She turned away from him with a shrug. Walking to the door, she said, "It doesn't matter one way or the other to me."

He couldn't tell if she intended to insult him or prove to him that his being there had no meaning to her beyond their reaching an accord about custody, but the indifference he heard in her voice was just fine with him. He didn't want to be involved with her any more than she wanted to be involved with him.

Which should make for a fabulous two weeks.

He tossed his duffel bag on the bed and walked the garment bag to the closet before going downstairs. At the bottom of the steps, he realized that the entire first floor of the house was open. He could see Grace puttering in the compact kitchen and Sarah swinging contentedly in the baby swing sitting in the space between the dining area and living room.

Walking to the kitchen, he said, "Anything I can help you with?"

"You're here for Sarah. So why don't you amuse her, while I make dinner?"

"Okay." Her cool tone of voice didn't affect him because she was correct. He was here for Sarah. Not for Grace. Not to make small talk or plans or, God forbid, even to become friendly.

He glanced at the cooing baby. A trip to the department store that morning to arrange for baby furniture to be delivered to his house had shown him just how behind the times he had become in the nine years that had passed since Cory was a baby. Playpens were now play yards. Car seats had become downright challenging. He didn't have to be a genius to know that if the equipment had changed, so had the rules. He wouldn't do anything with Sarah without asking.

"Should I take her out of the seat?"

Pulling a salad bowl from a cabinet, Grace said, "Not when she's happy. Just sit on the floor in front of her and chat."

Chat. With a baby. He'd tried that the day Grace brought Sarah to his house and hadn't known what to say. Obviously he had to think of something to talk about other than investing. But he wasn't sitting on the floor. After a quick look around, he grabbed one of the oak ladder-back chairs from the table in the dining room section and set it in front of the swing.

"Hey, Sarah."

She pulled the blue plastic teething ring from her mouth and cooed at him. He smiled and settled more comfortably on the chair as he studied her, trying to think of something to say. Nothing came. She gurgled contently as she waved her arms, sending the scent of baby powder through the air to his nose. That brought a burst of memories of Cory.

He'd been so proud of that kid. So smitten. So enamored with the fun of having a baby that he'd thought his life was perfect. Then Cory had shown artistic ability and Lydia wanted to send him to special school. Danny had thought she was jumping the gun, making a decision that didn't need to be made until Cory was older.

Taking a breath, Danny forced himself back to the present. He had to stop thinking of Cory. He had to focus on Sarah. He had to create an amicable relationship so their time together would be happy and not a horrible strain.

Then he noticed that the one-piece yellow thing she wore made her hair appear reddish brown. "I think somebody's going to be a redhead."

The baby gooed. Danny smiled. Curious, he turned toward the kitchen. "My parents are French and English. So I don't think the red hair comes from my side of the family. How about yours?"

Grace grudgingly said, "Both of my parents are Scottish."

"Well, that explains it."

Danny's comment fell on total silence. Though he was here for Sarah, he and Grace had two long weeks to spend together. He might not want to be her friend, but he didn't want to be miserable, either. Studying Grace as she ripped lettuce and tossed it into a bowl, he swore he could see waves of anger emanate from her.

It might have been her idea to share custody, but she clearly didn't want to spend two weeks with him any more than he wanted to spend two weeks with her. He'd forced her hand with the threat of taking her baby away.

Taking her baby away.

He hadn't really looked at what he was doing from her perspective and suddenly realized how selfish he must seem to her.

"Had I gone for full custody, I wouldn't have shut you out of her life completely."

"No, but you would have demanded that she live with you and I'd be the one with visitation."

She walked over to him and displayed a plate with two steaks. "I'm going to the back deck to the grill." She waited a heartbeat, then said, "You're not afraid to be alone with her, are you?"

As if any man would ever admit to being afraid of anything. "No. But I'm guessing you're a better choice to stay inside with her, which means I should grill the steaks."

"Great." She handed him the plate. "I'll finish the salad."

She pivoted and returned to the kitchen without waiting for his reply. Danny rose from his seat and walked out to the deck. He agreed with her nonconversation policy. There was no point in talking. She didn't like him. And, well, frankly, he didn't like her.

He dropped the plate of steaks on a small table and set the temperature on the grill. Still, whether he agreed with her or not, not talking guaranteed that the next two weeks would be two of the longest of his life. Torture really. Maybe payback for his not believing her? He slapped the steaks on the grill rack.

That was probably it. Payback. But what Grace didn't realize was that the way she treated him was also proof that she wasn't the sweet innocent she'd pretended to be.

He almost laughed. What a mess. All because he couldn't keep his hands off a woman. He'd never make *that* mistake again.

He closed the lid and looked out over the expanse of backyard. Grace didn't have a huge space but what she had was well tended. Her bungalow was neat and clean, newly remodeled. Her yard was well kept. He hoped that was an indicator that Grace would take good care of Sarah during the weeks she had her.

He heard a giggle from inside the house. Turning, he saw he hadn't shut the French doors. He ambled over and was just about to push them closed when he heard Grace talking. "So, somebody needs to go upstairs and get a fresh diaper."

She lifted the baby from the swing and rubbed noses with her. "I swear, Sarah, there's got to be a better system."

The baby laughed. Danny sort of chuckled himself. A person would think that after all the generations of babies, somebody, somewhere would have thought of a better system than diapers.

"Let's take care of that. Then we'll feed you something yummy for dinner."

The baby giggled and cooed and Danny felt a quick

sting of conscience for worrying about Sarah when she was in Grace's care. Grace obviously loved the baby.

He took a quick breath. She might love the baby but there was a lot more to consider in child rearing than just love. Grace was on trial these next two weeks every bit as much as he was. He wouldn't be convinced she was a good mom, just because she was sweet. She wasn't sweet. As far as he knew she was a conniver. She could have seen the French doors were open and put on a show with the baby for him to see.

He closed the doors and checked the steaks. They were progressing nicely. He sat on one of the deck chairs. The thick red, yellow and tan striped padding felt good to his tired back and he let his eyelids droop. He didn't raise them again until he heard the French doors open.

"How's it going?" Grace asked quietly. Sarah sat on her forearm, once again chewing the blue teething ring.

Danny sat up. "Fine. I was just about to peek at the steaks." He poked and prodded the steaks, closed the lid and chucked Sarah under the chin. "You're just about the cutest kid in the world, aren't you?"

Sarah giggled and cooed and Grace regretted her decision to bring the baby with her when she checked on him. When she least expected it, he would say or do something that would remind her that she'd genuinely believed he was a nice, normal guy the weekend they'd spent at the beach house. Volunteering to help her in the kitchen when he first came downstairs hadn't been expected. His wanting to know Sarah's heritage had struck her as adorable. And now he looked perfectly natural, perfectly comfortable on her back deck.

But he was also here to convince Grace that he would be able to care for Sarah. Technically he was on good behavior. She refused to get sucked in again as she had at the beach house.

She turned to go back into the house, but he said, "Grace?" And every nerve ending she had went on red alert. He had a sexy quality to his voice that was magnified when he spoke softly. Of course, that took her back to their pillow talk the night they had slept together and that made her all quivery inside.

Scowling because she didn't want to like him and did want to let him know that if he thought he could charm her he was wrong, she faced him. "Yes?"

"You never told me how you wanted your steak."

Feeling embarrassment heat her cheeks, she quickly turned to the door again. "Medium is fine."

With that she walked into the house. She put Sarah in her high chair and rummaged through the cupboards for a jar of baby food, which she heated. By the time she was done feeding Sarah, had her face cleaned and the rubber teething ring back in her chubby hands, Danny brought in the steaks.

"Salad is on the counter," she said, as she laid plates and silverware on the table. "Could you bring that in, too?" Her new strategy was to put him to work before he could volunteer. This way, he wouldn't seem nice, he would only be following orders.

He did as she asked and they sat down at the table,

across from each other, just as they had been sitting that Sunday night at his beach house. She'd dressed up, hoping he would notice her. But tonight, on the trip upstairs to change Sarah's diaper, she'd put on her worst jeans, her ugliest T-shirt. What a difference fifteen months made.

"Your house is nice."

"Thank you."

Silence reigned for another minute, before Danny said, "So, did you buy it remodeled like this?"

She bit back a sigh, loath to tell him anything about herself. More than that, though, they'd discussed this that night at the beach house. He'd forgotten. So much for thinking she'd made any kind of impression on him

"It was a wreck when I bought it."

"Oh, so you did the remodeling—I mean with a contractor, right?"

"No. My cousin and I remodeled it." And she'd told him that, too.

He smiled. "Really?"

Grace rose from her seat. "You know what? I'm really not all that hungry and it's time for me to get Sarah bathed and ready for bed." She smiled stiffly. "If you'll excuse me."

Alone at the table Danny quietly finished his steak. If Grace was going to continually take Sarah and leave the room, maybe he shouldn't cancel tomorrow's dinner engagement? He drew in a breath, then expelled it quickly. He couldn't dodge or fudge this commitment. He wanted at least shared custody of his daughter, and Grace had handed him the way to get it without a custody battle that would result in her investigating his past and probably result in him losing all but scant visitation rights. So he couldn't leave. He had to be here every minute he could for the next two weeks.

The problem was he and Grace also had to be together. He'd thought they could be at least cordial, but this was what he got for his positive attitude. The silent treatment. Well, she could save herself the trouble if she intended to insult him. His ex-wife had been the ultimate professional when it came to the silent treatment. Grace would have to go a long way to match that.

But when he'd not only finished eating his dinner and stacking the dishes in the dishwasher and Grace still hadn't come downstairs, he wondered if maybe she couldn't give Lydia a tip or two in the silent treatment department. Angry, because the whole point of his being here was to spend time with his daughter, Danny stormed up the steps. He stopped outside Grace's bedroom door because it was ajar and what he saw compelled him to rethink everything.

Though Grace's bedroom was pretty, decorated in warm colors like reds, yellows and taupe, a big white crib, white changing table and two white dressers took up most of the space. Still, there was enough adult furniture pushed into the room's corners that Danny could almost envision how she probably had her room before the baby was born. When she met him, she had had a pretty house, a sanctuary bedroom and a budding career. When she got pregnant, she'd lost her job. When she actually had Sarah, most of her pretty house had become a nursery.

"Oh, now, you can't be sleepy yet."

Grace's soft voice drifted out into the hallway.

"You still need to spend some time with your daddy."

Danny swallowed when he heard himself referred to again as a daddy. He was only getting used to that.

"I know you're tired, but just stay awake long enough to say good-night."

She lifted Sarah from the changing table and brushed her cheek across the baby's little cheek. Mesmerized, Danny watched. He'd forgotten how stirring it was to watch a mother with her baby.

"Come on," Grace said, turning to the door. Danny jumped back, out of her line of vision.

Thinking fast, he leaped into his room and quickly closed the door. He counted to fifty, hoping that gave her enough time to get downstairs, then opened the door a crack and peered out into the hall. When he found it empty, he walked downstairs, too. Grace sat on the sofa, Sarah on her lap.

"Can I hold her before she goes to bed?"

"Sure."

She made a move to rise, but Danny stopped her. "I'll take her from your lap."

Grace nodded and Danny reached down to get Sarah. Lifting her, he let his eyes wander over to Grace and their gazes caught. Except now he knew why he was no longer dealing with the sweet, innocent woman he'd slept with at the beach house. Her life had changed so much that even if she hadn't tricked him, she couldn't be the same woman. She'd gotten pregnant to a stranger. He'd rejected her. She'd lost her job and was too sick to get another. She'd had her baby alone. Any of those would have toughened her. Made her cynical. Maybe even made her angry.

No. She was no longer the woman he knew from the beach house.

CHAPTER SIX

DANNY awakened to the sounds of the shower. Grace was up before him and already started on her day. He waited until the shower stopped, then listened for the sounds of the bathroom door opening before he got out of bed, slipped on a robe and grabbed his shaving kit.

In the hall he heard the melodious sounds of Grace's voice as she spoke to Sarah and laughed with her. He stopped. Her soft laughter took him back to their weekend at the beach house. He shook his head and walked into the bathroom. He had to stop remembering. As he'd realized last night, that Grace no longer existed. Plus, they had a child. Sarah's future was in their hands. He didn't take that responsibility lightly anymore.

After a quick shower, Danny dressed in a navy suit, ready for a long day of business meetings. He jogged down the stairs and was immediately enfolded in the scent of breakfast.

Walking to the small dining area, he said, "Good morning."

Grace breezed away from the table and strode into the kitchen. "Good morning."

Sarah grinned up at him toothlessly. He smiled down at her. "And how are you today?"

Sarah giggled. Danny took a seat at the table. Grace set a dish containing an omelet, two slices of toast and some applesauce in front of him. Suddenly her coolness made sense. He'd forced her to have their baby alone, yet she'd nonetheless suggested shared custody, allowing him into her home to give him the opportunity to prove himself. Even if the Grace who'd seduced him that night no longer existed, the woman who'd taken her place had her sense of generosity. Even to her detriment. She wouldn't cheat him out of time with her daughter. Or use Sarah as a weapon. She was fair and it cost her.

Grace set her dish at the place opposite Danny and sat down. She immediately grabbed her napkin, opened it on her lap and picked up her fork.

Sarah shrieked.

Grace shook her head. "You already ate."

Sarah pounded her teething ring on the high chair tray.

"A tantrum will do you no good," Grace said to Sarah, but Danny was painfully aware that she didn't speak to him. She didn't even look at him.

His chest tightened. She'd been such a fun, bubbly, lively person. Now she was cautious and withdrawn. And he had done this to her.

Grace all but gobbled her breakfast. She noticed that Danny had become quiet as she drank a cup of coffee, but she didn't have time to care. She wasn't entirely sure she would care even if she had time. He'd basically accused her of lying. He clearly believed she'd tricked him. And if both of those weren't enough, he intended to take her child every other week. She didn't want to be his friend. He was only in her house because she couldn't risk that he'd get full custody, and she also wouldn't risk her child's happiness with a grouch. So he was here to prove himself. She didn't have to entertain him.

He was lucky she'd made him breakfast. That was why she was late, and rushing, so if he expected a little morning chitchat, that was his problem.

Having eaten enough food to sustain herself until lunch, Grace rose from her seat and took her dish to the kitchen. To her surprise Danny was right behind her when she turned from the dishwasher. Her heart thudded in her chest, half from surprise, half from being so close to him. He radiated warmth or energy, or something, that made being near him intoxicating. And trouble. His being irresistible was what had caused her to let her guard down in the first place.

He handed her his plate, though most of his food hadn't been eaten.

She took a quick gulp of air to try to rid herself of the breathless feeling and looked up at him. His eyes mirrored an emotion she couldn't quite read, except that he was unsure of what he was supposed to be doing.

"I'm rushing because I'm late. You can stay and finish. Just rinse your plate when you're through and put it in the dishwasher."

"I've had enough," Danny said and as Grace turned away from the dishwasher she saw him glance around her small kitchen. "Since I'm the boss I don't have to worry about being late, so if you'd like I could clean up in here."

In his neat navy blue suit, white shirt and blue print tie, he might look like the guy who ran Carson Services, but he behaved like the Danny Grace had met at the beach house, and that wasn't right. Being attracted to him wasn't right. Even being friendly wasn't right, if only because they were on opposite ends of a custody battle.

"No, thank you," she coolly replied. "It will take me only a minute or two to wipe the skillet and stove. You go on ahead. I'm fine."

"Grace," he said with a chuckle. "It's not a big deal."

"Really?" Try as she might, she couldn't keep the sarcasm out of her voice. "I'm surprised a rich guy like you even knows how to clean a skillet."

He laughed. The sound danced along her nerve endings, reminding her again of how he'd been the night they'd made love. She fought the happy memories by recalling the scene in his office. The one where he'd called her pregnancy a scheme.

"I couldn't exactly take a maid to university. My parents might have gotten me an apartment, but unless I wanted to live in squalor I had to do at least a little straightening up."

Grace felt herself softening to him and squeezed her eyes shut. It was much easier dealing with mean Danny. No expectations were better than unmet expectations.

Opening her eyes, she faced him. "Look, I don't want you to be nice to me. I don't need you to be nice."

"Helping clean up isn't nice. It's common courtesy."

"Well, save it. You're here to prove yourself with Sarah. And you did fine this morning just by saying good morning. You noticed her. You didn't ignore her. You're on the right track."

"I'm not going to let you wait on me while I'm here."

Grace removed her apron and set it on the counter. She didn't have time or the inclination to argue. She also couldn't give a damn what he did. That only tripped memories of a man she was absolutely positive didn't exist. She couldn't get into arguments that tempted her to believe otherwise.

"Fine. Dishcloths are in the bottom drawer."

She walked out of the kitchen and over to the high chair, where she lifted Sarah into her arms before she headed for the stairway.

But from the corner of her eye she could see Danny standing in the kitchen, plate in hand, watching her. He looked totally out of place and equally confused and Grace again fought against emotions she couldn't afford to have.

How could he make her feel like the one in the wrong when he had done such terrible things to her?

After a horrifically long day, Danny finally had ten minutes alone in his office. Though he tried to make a few phone calls before leaving he couldn't. Being with Grace at her house and yet not really being with Grace was driving him crazy. He could not live with someone for two whole weeks who barely spoke to him. Not that he wanted lively conversation, but he couldn't handle being ignored, either. Plus, if they didn't at least discuss Sarah and her care, especially her likes and dislikes, how were these two weeks supposed to prove to Grace that she could relax when Sarah was with him?

Knowing it wouldn't help matters if he were late for dinner that night, Danny stuffed a few files into a briefcase and left early. At her front door, he hesitated. He felt so ill at ease just walking inside that he should ring the bell. But he was living here. The next two weeks this was his home. And maybe walking in would jar Grace into realizing she had to deal with him.

He opened the door and saw Grace on the floor with Sarah, playing peekaboo.

"Hey."

Sarah squealed her delight at seeing him. Grace glanced over. "Hey."

He didn't smell anything cooking and finally, finally saw a golden opportunity. "I was thinking this afternoon that things might go easier if we just went out to dinner." He paused, but she didn't say anything. "On me, of course."

She sighed, lifted Sarah into her arms and rose from the floor. "It's not practical to go out to a restaurant with a baby every night." She walked into the kitchen, Sarah on her hip.

With Grace's reply ringing in his head, Danny looked around again. Two bears sat on the sofa. A baby swing was angled in such a way that the baby inside could be seen from the kitchen, dining room or living room. A high chair sat by the dining table. Blocks were stacked on the buffet. The room smelled of baby powder.

He remembered this now. For the first few years of a baby's life everything revolved around the baby. That had been a difficult enough adjustment for a married couple. But it had to be all-consuming for a single mom. Not just because she didn't have assistance with Sarah, but because it affected everything.

He walked into the kitchen. "Can I help with dinner?"

She pulled a package of hamburger from the refrigerator. "Do you want to grill the hamburgers?"

Eager to do his share, Danny said, "Sure."

He reached for the hamburger, but Grace pointed at his jacket and tie. "You can't cook in that."

He grimaced. "Right."

After changing into jeans and a T-shirt, he took the hamburger from the refrigerator and headed for the back deck and the grill. Grace was nowhere around, but he assumed she and the baby were in her room. Maybe because the baby needed a diaper change.

Gazing out over the short backyard Danny studied the houses near Grace's. Realizing none was as well kept as hers, he remembered her telling him about remodeling her home the night they spent at his beach house. That was why her comments about wanting to be rich hadn't struck him oddly that night. He knew she was a hard worker. But three weeks later when she told him she was pregnant, he'd forgotten how eager she was to earn her way in life. He only remembered that she'd wanted to be rich and he'd assumed the worst.

He'd seduced her, left her for a week, said he didn't want to see her again when he returned, refused to believe her when she told him she was pregnant and then threatened to file for full custody of their baby. While he'd acted on inaccurate "interpretations" of things she'd done, he'd given her five very real reasons to hate him.

It was no wonder she was cool to him. He'd not only misjudged her. He'd behaved like a horrible person.

The sound of a car pulling into her driveway brought him out of his thoughts. He strode to the far end of the deck and glanced around the side of the house just in time to see Grace pulling Sarah from the car seat. With a grocery bag hooked over her arm and Sarah perched on the other, she walked, head down, into the house.

Danny's heart squeezed in his chest. Would he ever stop hurting people?

Grace stepped into her house at the same time that Danny walked in from the deck. "Where did you go?"

"I needed milk and hamburger buns." Carrying Sarah, she went to the kitchen to deposit her purchases.

Danny grabbed the gallon jug that dangled from her hand and put it in the refrigerator. "I could have gone to the store."

"Well, I did."

He sighed. "Grace, I want to help but I can't do things that I don't know need done."

"I didn't ask you to do anything."

But even as the words were coming out of her mouth, Grace regretted them. She slid Sarah into the high chair and turned to face Danny. He might be a difficult person, but she wasn't. And she refused to let him turn her into one.

"Here's the deal. I'm accustomed to being on my own. There's no point in breaking that habit because you'll only be here for another twelve days. So don't worry about it. Okay?"

He nodded, but he kept looking at her oddly as if she'd just discovered the secret to life. He continued to steal peeks at her all through dinner, making her nervous enough that she chattered to Sarah as they ate their hamburgers and salads, if only to bring some sound into the room.

When she could legitimately slip away to feed Sarah a bottle and put her to bed, she felt as if she were escaping a prison. She extended her alone time with a long, soothing shower, but rather than slip into her usual nightgown and robe she put on sweatpants and a T-shirt and shuffled downstairs to watch a little TV to unwind before trying to sleep.

She had just turned off all the lights and settled on the sofa with a cup of cocoa, when Danny came down the steps.

Seeing her curled up on the couch, he paused. "Sorry."

He pivoted to go back upstairs and Grace said, "Wait." She didn't want to be his friend. She didn't want to like him. She most certainly didn't want to get romantically involved with him. But she couldn't take the silence anymore and she suspected he couldn't, either.

"You don't have to leave. For the next two weeks this is your home. We might as well get accustomed to each other."

At first he hesitated, but then he slowly made his way down the steps and into the sitting area.

"Would you like some cocoa?"

As he lowered himself to the love seat, he chuckled softly. "I haven't had cocoa in—"

He stopped. Grace suspected that the last time he'd had cocoa it had been with his son, but she was also tired of tiptoeing around his life. He'd told her very little about himself the night they had dinner at the beach house and she'd not pushed him. But if she had to accept him into her house and Sarah's life, then he had to accept her into his. They couldn't pretend his other life didn't exist.

"In?" Grace prompted, forcing him to talk about his son.

"In years." He took a breath and caught her gaze. "Since I had cocoa with my son."

The words hung in the room. Danny kept his gaze locked with Grace's, as if daring her to go further. But she had no intention of delving into every corner of his world. She only wanted them to begin having normal conversations, so the tension between them would ease.

"See. We can talk about both of your children." She rose from the sofa. "Let me make you a cup of cocoa."

Without waiting for his reply, she walked into the kitchen, pulled a small pot from the cupboard by the stove and set it on a burner. Danny lowered himself to one of the stools by the counter, reminding Grace of how she had sat at the beach house bar while he poured himself a glass of Scotch.

Danny suddenly bounced from the seat, as if he'd had the memory, too, and didn't want it. He strode into the kitchen and reached for the refrigerator door handle. "I'll help you."

Removing the cocoa from a cupboard, Grace turned so quickly that she and Danny nearly ran into each other in the compact kitchen.

He caught her elbows to steady her, and tingles of awareness skipped along her skin. This close she could feel the heat of his body. Memories of making love, of how different he had been that night and how happy she had been, flipped through her brain. The sizzle between them was so intense she suddenly wondered what might have happened if they hadn't made love that night. Would the nice guy she'd met at the beach house have pursued her? Would he have remained nice? Would they have discovered differences and gone their separate ways or lived happily ever after?

Pulling her arms away, she turned toward the stove. What might have been wasn't an issue. If she thought about what might have been for too long she might get starry-eyed again and that would be insane. The guy had hurt her and now he wanted her child. She wouldn't be reckless with him again.

"Hand me the milk."

He did.

"Thanks." Exaggerating the task of pouring it into the pan so she didn't have to look at him, she said, "How are things at Carson Services?"

He walked back to the counter, but didn't sit. Instead he leaned against it. "Fine."

"How's Orlando?"

Danny laughed. "Great. He's a dream client. Because he does his homework, we're always on the same page when I suggest he move his money."

"That's so good to hear. I liked him."

"He's asked about you."

Dumping three scoops of cocoa on top of the milk, she grimaced. "What did you tell him?"

Danny shifted uncomfortably. "That you'd moved on."

She heard the stirring of guilt in his voice. Though part of her found it fitting, she couldn't pretend she was innocent. She'd recognized from the beginning that losing her job was one of the potential consequences of a failed relationship between them. So she wouldn't pretend. She would discuss this like an adult.

She faced him. "So you told him the truth."

"Excuse me?"

"What you told him was the truth. I *had* moved on."

He barked a laugh. "Yeah."

Grace walked over to him and stood in front of him, holding his gaze. "We won't survive twelve more days of living together if we don't admit here and now that we both made mistakes that weekend. We don't need to dissect our sleeping together and place blame. But we do need to admit that we *both* made mistakes."

"Okay."

"It is okay because we both moved on."

"Bet you wish you had stayed moved on."

She might be willing to agree to be polite and even friendly, but she didn't intend to discuss nebulous things like regrets. So she fell back on humor to get her out of the conversation. Batting her hand in dismissal, she said, "Nah. What fun is having a nice, quiet life with no one pestering you for custody of your child?"

He laughed again. She turned to leave, but he caught her fingers and stopped her. Her gaze swung back to his.

"You're one of only a few people who make me laugh."

Memory thrummed through her. Her being able to make him laugh had been their first connection. But the touch of his fingers reminded her that they'd taken that connection so much further that night. She remembered the way his hands had skimmed her body, remembered how he'd held her, remembered the intensity of the fire of passion between them.

But in the end, passion had failed them. The only thing they had between them now was Sarah. And everything they did had to be for Sarah.

Grace cleared her throat and stepped back. "We'll work on getting you to laugh more often for Sarah." She pulled her hand away from his, walked to the stove and poured Danny's cocoa into a mug. "So what do you like to watch?"

"Watch?"

"On TV."

He took the mug she handed to him. "Actually I don't watch TV."

"Then you're in for a treat because you get to watch everything I like."

That made him laugh again, and Grace's heart lightened before she could stop it, just as it had their weekend together. But she reminded herself that things at the beach house had not turned out well. And she didn't intend to make the same mistake twice. He needed to be comfortable and relaxed for Sarah. She and Danny also needed to be reasonably decent to each other to share custody. But that was all the further she could let things between them go.

They spent two hours watching crime dramas on television. Danny was oddly amused by them. The conversation remained neutral, quiet, until at the end of the second show the eleven o'clock news was announced and Grace said she was going to bed.

"Ripped from the headline is right," he said, when Grace hit the off button on the remote and rose from the sofa. "That program couldn't have been more specific unless they'd named names."

"That's the show's gimmick. The writers take actual situations and fictionalize them. It's a way to give curious, gossip-hungry viewers a chance to see what might have happened, and how it would play out in court."

Danny said, "Right," then followed her up the stairs. In the little hallway between their closed bedroom doors, Danny put his hand on his doorknob, but he couldn't quite open the door. It didn't seem right to leave her just yet. And that spurred another beach house memory. He hadn't wanted to leave her after he'd given her her bonus. He'd tried to ignore the feeling, but Grace had followed him down to the bar in his great room.

That made him smile. The hall in which they stood was far from great. It was a little square. Only a bit wider than the bar that had separated them at the beach house. He'd closed that gap by leaning forward and kissing her, and he'd experienced one of the most wonderful nights of his life.

And he'd ruined even the pleasant memories he could hold onto and enjoy by not believing her. Not appreciating her.

"Thanks for the cocoa."

She faced him with a smile. "You're welcome."

He took a step away from his door and toward hers. He might not have appreciated her the weekend at the beach house, but tonight he was beginning to understand that she probably had been the woman he'd believed her to be when he seduced her. Everything that had happened between them was his fault. Especially their misunderstandings.

He caught her gaze. "I'm glad you moved on."

He took another step toward her, catching her hand and lifting it, studying the smooth skin, her delicate fingers. He recalled her fingers skimming his back, tunneling through his hair, driving him crazy with desire, and felt it all again, as if it were yesterday.

"I'm a lot stronger than I look."

Her words came out as a breathy whisper. The same force of attraction that swam through his veins seemed to be affecting her. In the quiet house, the only sound Danny heard was the pounding of his heart. The only thought in his mind was that he should kiss her.

Slowly, holding her gaze, watching for reaction, he lowered his head. Closing his eyes, he touched his lips to hers. They were smooth and sweet, just as he remembered. Warmth and familiarity collided with sexual hunger that would have happily overruled common sense. Their chemistry caused him to forget everything except how much he wanted her. How happy she made him. How natural it was to hold her.

But just when he would have deepened the kiss, she stepped away.

"This is what got us into trouble the last time." She caught his gaze. "Good night, Danny."

And before he could form the words to stop her, she was behind her closed bedroom door.

CHAPTER SEVEN

DANNY awoke feeling oddly refreshed. He opened his eyes, saw the sunny yellow bedroom around him and was disoriented until he remembered he was living with Grace.

Grace.

He'd kissed her, but she'd reminded him that was what had gotten them into trouble the last time. And he didn't think she was talking about creating Sarah. Sarah wasn't trouble. Sarah was a joy. Their "trouble" was that they had slept together when they didn't know each other, which was why he hadn't trusted her enough to continue the relationship, and why he hadn't believed Grace when she told him she was pregnant. He'd thought she was lying to him. Tricking him. Because he didn't know her well enough to realize Grace would never do something like that.

He now knew his accusations were the product of an overly suspicious mind, but he also had to admit to himself that he hadn't changed much from the man who had dismissed her as a liar. Yes, he'd gotten past the tragedies of his life and to the outside world he appeared normal. And he really could be normal at work, normal with friends, normal with a woman only looking for an evening of entertainment. But his divorce had soured him on commitment. He wasn't marriage material. He wasn't even a good date for anyone who wanted anything other than a fun night out or no-strings-attached sex. Forget about being the right guy for someone as wonderful as Grace. She deserved better. Even he knew it.

She needed a husband. A mate. Someone to share her life. He was not that guy.

He rolled out of bed and tugged on his robe. But once the slash belt was secured, he stopped again. He'd nearly forgotten he was sharing a bathroom.

Sharing a bathroom.

Watching TV.

And happy.

How long had it been since he could say he was happy? Years. He'd accustomed himself to settling for surface emotions, convinced that if he loved anything, life would yank it away. But though he might not believe he could make a commitment to a woman, living with Grace made him consider that he could love Sarah and he could be a real dad. Especially since Grace was kind enough, honest enough, fair enough that she was willing to share custody. Not as adversaries, but as two friends. Both having the best interests of their little girl at heart. And without a hearing that would air his less-than-perfect past.

He grabbed his shaving kit, opened his bedroom door and glanced down the short hall. The bathroom door was open and Grace wasn't anywhere to be seen. Good. He didn't want to bump into Grace dressed only in a robe. As she'd reminded him last night, kissing— or more appropriately runaway emotions and hormones—had gotten them into trouble the last time. He wasn't going to make the same mistake twice. Getting romantically involved had cost them. He'd lost a good employee and someone who probably would have turned into a friend.

And he'd hurt her.

He wouldn't let himself forget that. He also wouldn't let himself hurt her again. He could say that with absolute certainty because he wouldn't get involved with her again. That was a promise he was making to himself.

He showered and shaved and was back in his bedroom before he heard the sound of Grace's alarm. Removing a suit from the garment bag he'd hung in the closet, he heard Sarah's wailing and Grace's words of comfort. He put the suit back in the closet, and yanked on jeans and a T-shirt, listening to Grace soothing Sarah as she carried her downstairs. He heard Grace quietly return upstairs and knew that the lack of crying meant Sarah was sucking her bottle.

He listened for the sound of Grace's door closing and then sneaked downstairs. It had been years since he'd made his "world famous" blueberry pancakes, but if anybody ever deserved a little treat, it was Grace.

After taking a last peek to be sure her black skirt and print blouse were in the proper position, Grace shifted away from her full-length mirror to lift already-dressed Sarah from her crib. But as she turned, the scent of something sweet stopped her.

Whatever it was it smelled like pure heaven.

Her mouth watered.

She grabbed Sarah and rushed down the steps. In the kitchen, dressed in jeans and a T-shirt and wearing a bib apron, stood Danny.

"What is that smell?"

He turned with a smile. "Pancakes. My one and only specialty."

"If they taste as good as they smell, they are absolutely your specialty."

"Oh, they do."

The ringing endorsement—combined with the growling of Grace's tummy—had her scampering into the dining area. She slid Sarah into her high chair and went to the kitchen to retrieve plates from the cupboard. "More stuff you learned while at school?"

He winced. "Not really. These are the only thing I can cook. Unless you count canned soup and fried eggs."

Avoiding her eyes, he set two fluffy blueberry pancakes on each of the two plates she held. Grace took them to the table. She set her dish at the seat beside the high chair and the second across the table from her.

The night before he'd kissed her and just the memory of that brought a warm fuzzy somersault feeling to her empty tummy. She hadn't let the kiss go too far. But there was something between them.

Something special. Something sharp and sexual. It wasn't something that would go away with the press of a button, or just because it complicated things. And today he'd made her breakfast. Though she appreciated it, she also knew she had to tread lightly. She didn't want to get involved with him again and he was tempting her.

Danny brought the syrup to the table and sat across from her. "I think there are some things you and I need to discuss."

Her stomach flip-flopped again. The last thing she wanted was to talk about their one-night stand. Or whatever it was that had happened between them. But disliking him hadn't worked to keep them apart. So maybe it was best to talk?

"Okay."

He took a breath. "All right. Here's the deal. That kiss last night was wrong and I don't want you to have to worry about it happening again."

She looked across the table at him, her heart in her throat, and praying her eyes weren't revealing the pain that brought. She also didn't think getting involved was a good idea, but he hadn't needed to say the words.

"The truth is I know you deserve better than me."

Grace blinked. That wasn't at all what she was expecting and she had absolutely no idea how to reply.

"The night we slept together, I was going through a bad time," he said, glancing down at his pancake before catching her gaze again. "Not that that makes what happened right, but I think it might help you to understand that now that I'm past those personal problems, I can see I misjudged you and I'm sorrier than I can ever say."

Grace took a breath. Once again he was talking about himself, but not really about anything. Still his apology was a big step for them. "Okay."

"Okay you understand or okay you accept my apology?"

She took another breath. Her gut reaction was to accept his apology, but she simply didn't trust him. He had a powerful personality. He might say that she needn't worry about him kissing her again, but she didn't believe either of them could say that with absolute certainty. There was something between them. Chemistry, probably. Hormones that didn't listen to reason. She was afraid that if she accepted his apology and told him she understood it would open the door to things she couldn't control. Things neither one of them could control.

Before she could answer, Danny said, "I hate excuses for bad behavior, but sometimes there are valid reasons people do all the wrong things." He took a breath. "Because that weekend was the two-year anniversary of my son's death, I wasn't myself."

Grace blinked. "What?"

"Cory had died two years before. Six months after his accident my wife and I divorced. I spent the next year and a half just going through the motions of living."

Shocked into silence, Grace only stared at him.

"That weekend you reminded me of happiness." He combed his fingers through his hair. "I don't know.

Watching you with Orlando and hearing the two of you make jokes and have a good time, I remembered how it felt to be happy and I began to feel as if I were coming around." He caught her gaze. "You know…as if I were ready to live again."

Stuck in the dark place of trying to imagine the crushing blow of the death of a child and feeling overwhelmed at even the thought, Grace only nodded.

"But I'd always believed you and I had gone too far too fast by making love the very first weekend we really even spoke, and when I went away for that week of client hopping my doubts haunted me. I started imagining all kinds of reasons you'd sleep with me without really knowing me, and some of them weren't very flattering." He took a breath. "When you told me you were pregnant it just seemed as if every bad thing I had conjured had come true." He held her gaze steadily. "I was wrong and I am sorry."

Grace swallowed hard. She'd left the beach house happy, thinking she'd found Mr. Right and believing all things good would happen for them. But Danny had left the beach house worried about the potential bad. It was no wonder neither of them had seen the other's perspective. They were at two ends of a very broad spectrum.

"I'm sorry, too. I was so happy I didn't think things through. Had I known—"

Sarah pounded on her tray with a squeal. Grace grimaced. "I forgot to feed her."

Danny calmly rose. "I can get that."

Grace's first instinct was to tell him to sit back down.

Their discussion wasn't really over. But wasn't it? What else was there to say? He was sorry. She was sorry. But they couldn't change the past. She didn't want a relationship. He'd hurt her and she rightfully didn't trust him. And he didn't want a relationship. Otherwise he wouldn't have promised not to kiss her again. There was nothing more to say. The discussion really was over.

"Do you remember how to make cereal?" Grace asked.

"The stuff in the box with a little milk, right?"

She nodded.

"I can handle it."

He strode into the kitchen and Grace took several long, steadying breaths.

His child had died.

She had always believed that nothing he could say would excuse the way he treated her when she told him she was pregnant.

But this did.

It didn't mean she would trust her heart to him, but it did mean she could forgive him.

That night Grace had dinner nearly prepared when Danny arrived. She directed him upstairs to change while she fed Sarah some baby food and by the time Sarah had eaten, Danny returned wearing jeans and a T-shirt. He looked as relaxed as he had their night at the beach house. Confession, apparently, had done him a world of good.

Incredibly nervous, Grace fussed over the salads.

Now that she knew about Danny's son everything was different. She almost didn't know how to treat him. His admissions had opened the door to their being friends, and being friendly would work the best for Sarah's sake. But could two people with their chemistry really be friends?

While Grace brought their salads to the table, Danny took his seat.

"You know, we never have gotten around to discussing a lot of things about Sarah."

Glad for the neutral topic, Grace said, "Like what?"

"For one, child support."

"Since we'll each have Sarah two weeks a month, I don't think either one of us should be entitled to child support. So don't even think of filing for any."

He laughed. "Very funny."

A tingle of accomplishment raced through her at his laughter, but she didn't show any outward sign of her pleasure. Instead she shrugged casually. "Hey, I make a decent salary. How do I know it wasn't your intention to file?"

"You never did tell me where you got a job."

"I work for a small accounting firm. Johnson and O'Hara."

"So you do okay financially?"

"Yeah." Grace smiled. "Actually they pay me double what your firm did."

He chuckled. "You got lucky."

"Yes, I did."

He glanced into the kitchen, then behind himself at

the living room. "And you seem to know how to use your money wisely."

"I bought this house the day I got my first job."

"The night I was grilling, I remembered you told me about remodeling your house while we ate that Sunday night at the beach house." He smiled across the table at her, and Grace's stomach flip-flopped. Lord, he was handsome. And nice. And considerate. And smart. And now she knew he wasn't mean-spirited or selfish, but wounded. Life had hurt him and he needed somebody like her to make him laugh.

Oh God, she was in trouble!

"You did a good job on the remodel."

"My cousin did most of it." Shifting lettuce on her dish, Grace avoided looking at him. "I was the grunt. He would put something in place, tack it with a nail or two then give me the nail gun to finish."

"It looks great." He took another bite of salad.

But Grace was too nervous to eat. She couldn't hate him anymore. But she couldn't really like him, either.

Or could she?

By telling her about his son, he'd both explained his behavior and proved he trusted her.

But he'd also said she didn't need to worry about him kissing her anymore.

Of course, he might have said that because she'd pushed him away the night before, reminding him that kissing only got them in trouble.

They finished their salads and Grace brought the roast beef, mashed potatoes and peas to the table. Unhappy with being ignored, Sarah pounded her teething ring on her high chair tray and screeched noisily.

"What's the matter, Sarah Bear," Grace crooned, as she poured gravy onto her mashed potatoes. Sarah screeched again and Grace laughed. "Oh, you want to sit on somebody's lap? Well, you can't."

She glanced at Danny. "Unless your daddy wants to hold you?"

Danny said, "Sure, I'll—"

But Grace stopped him. "No. You can't hold a baby in front of a plate with gravy on it. You would be wearing the gravy in about twenty seconds."

"If you want to eat your dinner in peace, I could take her into the living room, then eat when you're done."

He was so darned eager to please that Grace stared at him, drawing conclusions that made her heart tremble with hope. There was only one reason a man wanted to please a woman. He liked her. Which meant maybe Danny had only promised not to kiss her again because she'd stopped him, not because he didn't want to kiss her anymore.

Or she could be drawing conclusions that had absolutely no basis in fact.

"I'm fine. I like having Sarah at the table. When I said you might want to hold her I was just teasing her."

"Oh, okay."

Determined to keep her perspective and keep things light and friendly, Grace turned to the high chair. "So, Miss Sarah, you stay where you are."

"What's that thing your mother's got you wearing?"

Danny asked, pointing at the fuzzy swatch of material in the shape of a stuffed bear that had been sewn onto Sarah's shirt.

"It's a bear shirt."

Danny's fork stopped halfway to his mouth and he gave Grace a confused look. "What?"

"A bear shirt." Grace laughed. "From the day she was born, my dad called her Sarah Boo Beara…then Sarah Bear. Because the name sort of took, my parents buy her all kinds of bear things." She angled her fork at the bear on Sarah's shirt. "Push it."

"Push it?"

"The bear. Push it and see what happens."

Danny reached over and pushed the bear on Sarah's shirt. It squeaked. Sarah grinned toothlessly.

Danny jumped as if somebody had bitten him. "Very funny."

"It makes Sarah laugh and some days that's not merely a good thing. It's a necessity."

"I remember."

Of course, he remembered. He'd had a son. Undoubtedly lots of things he did for Sarah or things Sarah did would bring back memories for him. If he needed anything from Grace it might not be a relationship as much as a friend to listen to him. Just listen.

"Would you like to talk about it?"

Danny shook his head. "Not really."

Okay. She'd read that wrong. She took a quiet breath, realizing she'd been off base about him a lot, and maybe the smart thing here would be to stop trying to guess what he thought and only believe what he said. Including that he wouldn't be kissing her anymore. So she should stop romanticizing.

"If you ever do want to talk, I'm here."

"I know." He toyed with his fork then he glanced over at her with a wistful smile. "I sort of wonder what might have happened between us if I'd told you everything the morning after we'd slept together, as I had intended to."

Her heart thudded to a stop. "You were going to tell me?"

He nodded. "Instead the only thing I managed to get out was that I had to go away for a week." He paused, glancing down at the half-eaten food on his plate. "I really shouldn't have slept with you that night. I was still raw, but fighting it, telling myself it was time to move on. And I made a mistake."

"You don't get sole blame for that. I was the one who went down to the bar."

"Yeah, but I was the one who knew I wasn't entirely healed from my son's death and my divorce. The whole disaster was my fault."

"It takes two—"

"Grace, stop. Please."

His tone brooked no argument—as if she'd been pushing him to talk, when she hadn't—and Grace bristled. Though he'd said he didn't want to talk about this, he'd been the one to dip their toes into the conversation. Still, because it was his trouble, his life, they were discussing, he also had to be the one with the right to end it. "Okay."

He blew his breath out on a long sigh. "I'm not trying to hide things or run from things, but I just plain don't want to remember anymore. I'm tired of the past and don't like to remember it, let alone talk about it. I like living in the present."

"I can understand that."

"Good." He set his fork on his dish. "So do you want help with the dishes?"

She almost automatically said no, but stopped herself. Giving him something to do made life easier for both of them. "Sure."

He rose, gathering the plates. She lifted the meat platter and walked it to the refrigerator. The oppressive tension of the silence between them pressed on her chest. If the quiet was difficult for her, she couldn't even imagine how hard it was on Danny. Knowing he didn't want to think, to remember, she plunged them into the solace of chitchat.

"So what did you do at work today?"

Danny turned on the faucet to rinse their dishes. "The same old stuff. What did you do?"

"I'm in the process of reviewing the books for a company that wants to incorporate."

That caught his interest. "Oh, an IPO."

Grace winced at the excitement in his voice. "No, a small family business. The corporation will be privately held. The principals are basically doling out shares of stock to the family members who made the company successful, as a way to ensure ownership as well as appropriate distribution of profits."

"Ah."

"Not nearly as exciting as investing the fortunes of famous athletes, but it's good work. Interesting."

"Have you begun to do any investing for yourself?"

His question triggered an unexpected memory of telling him she'd gone to work for his investment firm because she wanted to learn about investing to be rich. The heat of embarrassment began to crawl up her neck. She'd meant what she said, but given everything that had happened between them, her enthusiastic pronouncement had probably fed the fire of his suspicions about her.

They'd really made a mess of things that night.

She walked back to the dining room table and retrieved the mashed potato bowl. "I'm working on getting the house paid off. So I haven't had a lot of spare cash."

"Since we'll be splitting expenses for Sarah, you should have some extra money then, right?"

She shrugged. "Maybe."

"Grace, I want to pay my fair share. And I can be pretty stubborn. So no maybes or probablys or whatevers. Let's really be honest about the money."

"Okay."

He stacked the dishes in the dishwasher. "Okay. So once we get everything straightened out I would like to open an account for you at Carson Services."

Grace laughed. "Right. Danny, even if I have spare cash from our sharing expenses for Sarah, I'm not sure I'll have more than a hundred dollars a month or so."

"A hundred dollars a month is good."

"Oh, really? You're going to open an investment account with a hundred dollars?"

He winced. "I thought I'd open it with a few thousand dollars of my own money. You know, to make up for what you've spent to date and you could add to it."

Grace sighed. "You told me to stop talking about the past and I did. So now I'm going to tell you to stop fretting about the money."

"But I—"

"Just stop. I don't want your money. I never did. When I said I wanted to be rich that night at the beach house, I was actually saying that I wanted my parents and me to be comfortable." She motioned around her downstairs. "Like this. This is enough. I am happy. I do not want your money. Can you accept that?"

He held her gaze for several seconds. Grace didn't even flinch, so that he would see from her expression that this was as important to her as no longer discussing the past was for him.

"Yes, I accept that."

"Okay."

Sliding under the covers that night, Grace was still annoyed by their money discussion. Not because he wanted to pay his fair share, and not even because she had brought his suspicions about her on herself, but because that one memory opened the door to a hundred more.

She remembered what it felt like to be with him. He'd made her feel so special. Wonderful. Perfect.

Warmth immediately filled her. So did the sense that she'd had during their weekend together. That they fit. That they were right for each other. She had been so happy that weekend, but she also remembered that *he'd* been happy too.

Was she so wrong to think *she* brought out the nice guy in him? And was it so wrong to believe that there was a chance that the nice guy could come out and stay out forever? And was it so wrong to think that maybe— just maybe—if the nice guy stayed out forever they could fall in love for real? Not fall into bed because they were sexually attracted. But fall in love. For real. To genuinely care about each other.

She didn't know, and she couldn't even clearly analyze the situation because they'd slept together and that one wonderful memory clouded her judgment.

Plus she'd already decided she wouldn't be second-guessing him anymore. He'd said she didn't have to worry about him kissing her again.

He didn't want her. She had to remember that.

CHAPTER EIGHT

GRACE awakened to the scent of pancakes and the sound of Sarah slapping her chubby hands against the bars of her crib.

"I'm coming."

She groggily pulled herself out of bed and lifted Sarah into her arms. Rain softly pitter-pattered on the roof. The scent of blueberry pancakes wafted through the air. It would have been a perfect morning except Grace had tossed and turned so much the night before that she'd slept in.

Though she had said she didn't want to get accustomed to having Danny around, after dressing Sarah for the day, she padded downstairs and into the kitchen area.

"Hey."

Danny looked up from the newspaper he was reading at the kitchen counter. "Good morning."

"I'm sorry, but I slept in. Could you take her?"

"And feed her?"

Grace nodded.

"Sure. Come on, Sarah Bear."

Sarah easily went to Danny and Grace turned and walked back though the living room, but at the stairs she paused, watching Danny as he held Sarah with one arm and prepared her cereal with the other. Rain continued to tap against the roof, making the house cozy and warm. Breakfast was made. She would have privacy to dress. It all seemed so perfect that Grace had a moment of pure, unadulterated sadness, realizing that *this* was what sleeping together too soon had cost them.

She drew in a breath and ran upstairs. There was no point crying over spilled milk. No point wishing for what might have been. And no way she could jeopardize the comfort level they had by yearning for a romance. Particularly with a man who so desperately needed to do things at his own pace, in his own way.

She showered, dressed and returned downstairs. Sarah sat in her high chair and cooed when Grace approached. Danny rose from the dining room table and walked into the kitchen.

"I'll microwave your pancakes. Just to warm them up."

"Thanks."

"Want some coffee?"

"Yes, but I'll get it." She laughed. "I told you, I don't want to get too accustomed to having help."

He leaned against the counter and crossed his arms on his chest. "We could share the nanny I hire."

She held up her hands to stop him. "Don't tempt me."

"Why not? What else is she going to do during the weeks you have Sarah?"

"Take yoga."

He burst out laughing. "Come on, Grace, at least think about it."

She poured herself a cup of coffee, then grabbed the cream from the refrigerator. "The part of me that wants help is being overruled by the part of me that loves the one-on-one time with Sarah."

He nodded. "Okay. Makes sense."

She turned and smiled at him. "Thanks."

He returned her smile. "You're welcome."

For a few seconds, they stood smiling at each other, then Grace's smile faded and she quickly turned away. She really liked him, and that triggered more phero-mones than a thousand bulging biceps. They were better off when she had disliked him, before his explanation and apology. Now instead of disagreeing and keeping their distance they were becoming friends, getting close, and she was wishing for things she couldn't have.

"By the way, my lawyer called this morning."

Brought back to the present by a very timely re-minder, Grace faced him. "Oh, yeah?"

Danny winced. "Yeah. The guy's a nut. He called me while he was shaving. He actually woke me." The mi-crowave buzzer rang. Unfolding his arms, Danny pushed away from the counter. "He asked about the progress on our agreement. I told him that you had told me you contacted a lawyer, and that lawyer had told you it was okay to sign, so you signed it, right?"

The casual, cozy atmosphere of Grace's little house shifted. Tension seeped into the space between them with words left unsaid. He hadn't signed their agreement. She had. But he hadn't. And it worried his lawyer. Or maybe it worried *him* and he used the call from his lawyer as a cover?

She swallowed, calling herself crazy for being suspicious. Shared custody was *her* idea. "I signed it."

"Great. Give it to me and I'll sign it, then we'll be set. According to my lawyer, once we have that in place we won't even need a hearing." Plate of warm pancakes in his hand, he faced her. "We simply begin sharing custody."

His pancakes suddenly looked like a bribe, and Grace froze, unable to take them from his hand. Until she reminded herself that Danny had nothing to gain by being nice to her. If anything *she* benefited from any agreement that kept them out of court.

She forced a smile and took the plate from his hands. "Sounds good. It's upstairs. I'll get it."

He glanced at his watch, then grimaced. "I have an early meeting today so unless you want your pancakes to get cold again, how about if you get it for me tonight. Tomorrow's Saturday, but I can take it to work on Monday and sign it in front of my secretary who can witness it. Then we'll make copies."

Calling herself every sort of fool for being suspicious, Grace walked to the table. "That sounds good." Eager to make up for her few seconds of doubt, she added, "But it's on top of my dresser. You could get it."

He waved a hand in dismissal. "We'll handle it tomorrow."

Grace drove to work, feeling like an idiot for mistrusting him. But walking from the parking garage, she reminded herself that it wasn't out of line for her to be suspicious of him. She might be prone to a little too much second-guessing about him, but he hadn't really told her a lot about his life. And he stopped the discussion any time they began to edge beyond surface facts.

Plus, *they* had a past. An unusual, unhappy past. He mistrusted her. When she told him she was pregnant, he kicked her out of his office. After that, she never tried to contact him again because she hadn't trusted him. She only took the baby to him for Sarah's sake. She hadn't expected him to want visitation, let alone have a hand in raising their daughter. But he did. He wanted full custody and had agreed to shared custody. To get Grace to give him that, he had to prove himself. Everything they'd done had been a negotiation of a sort.

She shouldn't magically feel that things between them had been patched up.

Except that he'd trusted her enough to tell him about his son.

Didn't that count as at least a step toward mended fences?

Yes, it did. Yet even knowing that he had good reason to be off his game something bothered her. Something in her gut said that Danny was too eager about their agreement and accepting shared custody, and she had no idea why.

Grace couldn't come up with a solid answer, even though the question popped into her head a million times that day. She returned home that evening edgy and annoyed, tired of running this scenario through her brain. Shared custody and the agreement had been *her* idea. She'd already signed the agreement. Week about with Sarah was the fair thing to do in their circumstance. The man had offered her the use of his nanny. He'd told her about his son. Yet something still nagged at her.

It didn't help that Sarah was grouchy. After a quiet and somewhat strained dinner, Danny excused himself to go to his room to work on a project that needed to be completed on Monday morning. Grace tried to stack the dishes in the dishwasher with Sarah crying in her high chair, but her patience quickly ran out. She lifted the baby and carried her up to Danny's room.

"Can you watch her while I finish clearing the kitchen?"

Looking too big for the little corner desk Grace had in her spare room more for decorative purposes than actual use, Danny faced her. "Grace, I—"

"Please." Grace marched into the room. "I know you have to get this project done for Monday morning, but I had a miserable day and I just need a few minutes to clean up." She dropped Sarah onto his lap. "When the dishes are done, I'll take her again."

With that she walked out, closing Danny's bedroom door behind her, leaving nothing but silence in her wake.

Danny glanced down at the little girl on his lap. "One of us made her angry and since I've been up here and you were the one with her in the kitchen, I'm blaming you."

Sarah screeched at him.

"Right. You can argue all you want but the fact remains that I was up here and you were down there with her."

He rose from the little desk chair and walked to the door, intending to take the baby to the living room where he and Sarah could watch TV or maybe play on the floor. But even before his hand closed around the knob, he had second thoughts. Grace said she wanted to clean the kitchen, but maybe what she needed was some peace and quiet. He glanced around, unsure of what to do. The room wasn't tiny, but it wasn't a center of entertainment, either.

"Any suggestions for how we can amuse ourselves for the next hour or so?" he asked Sarah as he shifted her into his arms so that he could look down at her. She smiled up at him and his heart did a crazy flip-flop. From this angle he didn't see as much of Cory in her features as he saw Grace. Were he to guess, he would say Sarah's eyes would some day be the same shade of violet that Grace's were.

She rubbed her little fist across her nose, then her right eye, the sign babies used when they were sleepy. Danny instinctively kissed the top of her head.

She peeked up and grinned at him and this time Danny's heart expanded with love. Not only had Sarah grown accustomed to him, but also he was falling in love with her. He was falling in love with the baby, happy living in Grace's home and having feelings for Grace he didn't dare identify. He knew she deserved a better man than he was. He'd made a promise to himself not to hurt her and he intended to keep it.

He looked down at Sarah, who yawned. "On, no, Sarah! You can't fall asleep this early. You'll wake up before dawn, probably ready to play and tomorrow's Saturday, the only day your mom gets to sleep in—"

He stopped talking because inspiration struck him. The thing to do would be to get Sarah ready for bed. That way she wouldn't fall asleep for at least another half hour and who knew? Maybe a bath would revive her? Plus he might make a few brownie points with Grace by keeping them so busy she could relax.

Pleased with that idea, he held Sarah against his shoulder, quietly opened his bedroom door and looked down the hall. Grace was nowhere in sight, and he could still hear the sounds of pots and pans in her kitchen.

He sneaked across the little hall and into her room. Inside he was immediately enfolded in a warm, sheltered feeling, the sense a man got when he felt at home. He squeezed his eyes shut, telling himself not to get so attached to Grace and her things that he again did something they'd both regret. He took a breath, then another and then another, reminding himself of all the reasons being too cozy with her was wrong.

Sarah wiped her nose in his shirt and snuggled into his shoulder, bringing him back to reality.

"No. No," he said, manipulating her into a different position before she could get too comfortable. "You'll be able to go to sleep soon enough if you let your daddy get you ready for bed."

He searched around the room for her baby tub, but

realized it was probably in the bathroom. Remembering that preparation was a parent's best trick when caring for a baby, he decided to get everything ready before he brought his sopping wet baby from the bathroom. He laid a clean blanket on the changing table, then pulled open the top draw of a white chest of drawers that had bears painted on the knobs. Inside were undershirts and socks so tiny they looked about thumb-size. Knowing those were too small, he closed the drawer, and opened the next one, seeking pajamas. He found them, then located the stash of disposable diapers, and arranged them on the changing table.

With everything ready he took Sarah to the bathroom. Holding her with one arm, he filled the baby tub he'd placed inside the regular bathtub, found her soap and shampoo and the baby towel that hung on the rack.

That was when he realized she was fully dressed and he was still wearing his suit trousers. In an executive decision, he pronounced it too late to do anything about his trousers and laid her on the fluffy carpet in front of the tub to remove her clothes.

She giggled and cooed and he shook his head. "Let's just hope you're this happy after I put you in the water."

She grinned at him.

Returning her smile, he lifted her to eye level. "Ready?"

She laughed and patted his cheeks.

"Okay, then." He dipped her into the tub and when she didn't howl or stiffen up, he figured she was one of the babies who loved to sit in water. Grateful, he kept one hand at her back as he wet a washcloth and squeezed a few drops of liquid soap on it, amazed by how quickly baby care was coming back to him.

"So you like the water?" Danny said, entertaining Sarah with chitchat as he washed her, just in case any part of bathtime had the potential to freak her out. She merely gooed and cooed at him, even when he washed her hair. Pleased by his success, he rinsed off all the soapsuds, rolled her in the soft terry-cloth baby towel and carried her back to Grace's room.

Not in the slightest uncomfortable, Sarah chewed a blue rubber teething ring while Danny put on her diaper and slid her into pajamas.

When she was completely dressed, he took her out into the hallway. He heard the sounds of the television—indicating Grace was done filling the dishwasher and probably waiting for the cycle to be complete so she could put everything away—and turned to the stairs, but his conscience tweaked. He'd been here five days and he hadn't done anything more than make pancakes, help with dishes and grill a few things. This was the first time he'd really helped with the baby. It seemed totally wrong to take Sarah downstairs and disturb the only private moments he'd allowed Grace.

He turned and walked back into Grace's bedroom. "So what do we do?"

Sarah rubbed her eyes again.

Danny frowned. He didn't have a bottle for her, but she didn't seem hungry. Or fussy. All she appeared to be was sleepy. Now that they'd wasted almost an hour getting her ready for bed, it didn't seem too early to let her fall asleep. The only question was, could she fall asleep without a bottle?

He remembered a comment Grace had made about making up stories for Sarah, and walked to the bed. If he laid Sarah in her crib, he ran the risk that she'd cry and Grace's private time would be disturbed. It seemed smarter to sit on the bed and tell Sarah a story and see if she'd fall asleep naturally.

He sat. Sarah snuggled against his chest. But sitting on the edge of Grace's bed was incredibly uncomfortable, so he scooted back until he was leaning against the headboard.

"This is better."

Sarah blinked up at him sleepily.

"Okay. Let's see. You clearly like bears since your grandfather blended a bear into your name, so let's make up a story about a bear."

She blinked again. Heavier this time. He scooted down a little further, then decided he might as well lie down, too.

Two hours later, Grace awoke on the sofa. She'd fallen asleep! Danny was going to kill her.

She ran up the steps and to Danny's room, but it was empty. Panicked, she raced across the hall and without turning on the light saw his shadowy form on her bed. She tiptoed into the room and peered down to discover he was not only sleeping on her bed with Sarah, he'd also put the baby in her pajamas for the night.

Both the baby and her daddy slept deeply, comfortably. Little Sarah lay in the space between his chest and his arm, snuggled against him in a pose of trust. Danny looked naturally capable. Grace wished she had a camera.

Careful not to disturb Danny, she reached down and lifted Sarah from his arms. The baby sniffled and stretched, but Grace "Shhed," her back to sleep and laid her in her crib.

Then she turned to her bed, her heart in her throat. Danny looked so comfortable and so relaxed that she didn't want to disturb him. The peaceful repose of his face reminded her of the morning she'd awakened in his bed in the beach house, and she involuntarily sat down beside him.

Unable to help herself, she lovingly brushed a lock of hair from his forehead. She wasn't going to fall into her black pit of recriminations again about sleeping together. She already knew that had been a mistake. No need to continue berating herself. Life had handled their punishment for prematurely sleeping together by using it to keep them apart. What she wanted right now was just a couple of seconds, maybe a minute, to look at him, to be happy he was here, to enjoy the fact that he loved their daughter so she wouldn't have to worry when Sarah was in his care.

She scooted a little closer on the bed, remembered waking up that morning at the beach house, laughed softly at how glad she had been that she'd had the chance to sneak away and brush her teeth before he woke up, and then sighed as she recalled making love in the shower.

She remembered thinking that she'd never love

another man the way she loved Danny and realized it was still true. He had her heart and she wasn't even sure how he'd done it. Except that he was cute, and sweet, and nice, and she desperately wanted to fill the aching need that she could now see he had.

But he wouldn't let her.

And that was what was bothering her. That was why she grabbed onto her suspicions like a lifeline. As long as she mistrusted him, she could hold herself back. But now that he'd told her about his son, explaining his irrational behavior, she had forgiven him. And once she'd forgive him, she'd begun falling in love again.

But he didn't love her. He didn't want to love her. If she didn't stop her runaway feelings, she was going to get hurt again.

After another breath, she lightly shook his shoulder and whispered, "Danny?"

He grumbled something unintelligible and she smiled. Damn he was cute. It really didn't seem fair that she had to resist him.

"Danny, if you don't want to get up, I can sleep in your room, but you'll have to wake up with Sarah when she cries for her two o'clock feeding."

The threat of being responsible for Sarah must have penetrated, because he took a long breath, then groggily sat up.

"Want help getting across the hall?"

He stared at her, as if needing to focus, and reached for her hand, which was still on his shoulder. His fingers were warm and his touch gentle, sending reaction from

Grace's fingertips to her toes. She remembered how sweet his kisses had been. She remembered how giving, yet bold he was as a lover. She remembered how safe she'd felt with him, how loved.

In the silence of the dark night, their gazes stayed locked for what felt like forever, then he put his hands on her shoulders and ran them down her back, along the curve of her waist and up again.

Grace swallowed and closed her eyes, savoring the feeling that she remembered from that summer night. Not sexual attraction, but emotional connection, expressed through physical attraction. Whatever was between them was powerful, but it was also sweet. By caring for Sarah tonight he'd shown her what she'd instinctively understood about him. That deep down he was a good guy. He'd kept Sarah beyond the time he'd needed to for Grace to get her work done, dressed her in pajamas and fallen asleep with the baby in his arms.

He might dismiss it or downplay it, but he couldn't deny it and that meant they were at a crossroad. He liked her enough to do something kind for her. It might be too soon for him to fall in love again. Or he might not want to fall in love again. But he was falling. And she didn't have to tell him she was falling, too. He could surely see it in her eyes.

Gazing into his dark eyes, Grace held her breath, hoping, almost praying he was thinking the same thing she was and that he had the courage to act on it.

CHAPTER NINE

IN THE dark, quiet bedroom that radiated warmth and the comfort of home, Danny stared at Grace. All he wanted to do was crawl under the covers of her bed with her. Not to make love but to sleep. He was tired, but also he simply needed the succor of this night. The peaceful feeling a man got when his baby was tucked away in her crib, sleeping like an angel, and the mother of his baby was tucked under his arm. The desire was instinctive, nearly primal, and so natural he hadn't thought it. It had overtaken him. Almost as if it wasn't something he could stop or change.

But every time he'd given in to his instincts, he'd failed somebody. He'd failed Lydia, he'd failed Cory, and he'd even failed Grace by not believing her when she told him she was pregnant. Did he really want to fail her again?

No.

He backed away from the temptation of Grace, his hands sliding off her in a slow, sad way, savoring every second of her softness for as long as he could before it was gone.

He hadn't said anything foolish like how beautiful she was or how much he had missed her or how the instant closeness they had shared was coming back to him. He hadn't done anything he couldn't take back like kiss her. He could get out of this simply by saying good-night and leaving the room.

"Good night."

She swallowed. "Good night."

And Danny walked out of the room.

Grace sat on the bed. It was still warm from where he lay. She could smell the subtle hint of his aftershave.

She dropped her head to her hands. If she'd needed any more reason to stay away from Danny, he'd given it to her tonight. She'd watched the play of emotions on his face display the battle going on in his brain as he'd stared at her, wanting her, yet denying himself. She could have been insulted or hurt; instead she saw just how strong he was. How determined he could be to deny himself what he wanted, even when it was probably clear to him that she wanted it, too.

And it was her loss. She knew it the whole way to her soul.

For the second time since he'd moved in with Grace, Danny awakened happy. The night before he'd spent time with Sarah and had very successfully cared for her, proving to himself that he didn't need to be afraid about the weeks he would spend with his daughter. He'd also successfully stepped away from temptation with Grace.

He wanted her, but he didn't want to hurt her. Some day she would thank him.

As he dressed, he heard the sounds of Sarah awakening and Grace walking down the stairs to get her a bottle. When he was sure she had returned to her room to dress and get the baby ready for the day, he rushed downstairs, strode into the kitchen and retrieved the ingredients for pancakes.

Twenty minutes later she came down the stairs and he turned from the stove. "Good morning."

Wearing jeans and a pale blue top that made her eyes seem iridescent, Grace carried the baby to her high chair.

"Good morning."

She was beautiful in an unassuming, yet naturally feminine way that always caused everything male in Danny to sit up and take notice. But he didn't mind that. In fact, now that he knew he could control the emotional side of their relationship, he actually liked noticing Grace. What man didn't want to appreciate a beautiful woman?

As she puttered, getting the baby settled in the high chair with a teething ring, Danny looked his fill at the way her T-shirt hugged her full breasts and her blue jeans caressed her bottom. But what really drew him was her face. Her violet eyes sparkled with laughter and her full lips lifted in a smile. If his walking away the night before had affected her, she didn't show it. She was one of the most accepting, accommodating people he'd ever met.

He took a stack of pancakes to the table and she sniffed the air. "Blueberry again."

He winced. "They're my only specialty."

She surprised him by laughing. "You say that as if you'd like to learn to cook."

His reaction to that was so unexpected that he stopped halfway to the kitchen and he faced her again. "I think I do."

She took her seat at the table. "I don't know why that seems so novel to you. Lots of men cook."

But Danny didn't want to cook. He wanted to please Grace. Not in a ridiculous, out-of-control way, but in a way that fulfilled his part of the responsibility. Still, with only a week left in their deal to live together it was too late now to find a class.

Grace plopped a pancake on her plate as Sarah pounded her high chair tray. "You could get a cookbook."

Now that idea had merit.

"Or I could teach you."

And that idea had even more merit. He would get the knowledge he needed to do his part, and he'd have a perfect opportunity to spend time with Grace. Normal time. Not fighting a middle-of-the-night attraction. Not wishing for things he couldn't have. But time to get even more adjusted to having her in his world without giving in to every whim, sexual craving or desire for her softness.

"I'd like that."

She smiled at him. "Great. This morning we'll go shopping for groceries."

Reaching into the cupboard for syrup, he said, "Shopping?"

"Shopping is the first step in cooking. You can't

make what you don't have. If you'd tried to prepare these pancakes tomorrow," she said, pointing at her dish, "you would have been sadly disappointed because the blueberries would have been gone. That's why we're going shopping today."

He didn't really want to go to a store, but she had a point. Unfortunately her suggestion also had a fatal flaw. "How am I going to know what to buy if I don't yet know how to cook anything?"

"I'm going to help you."

"Right."

Sarah screeched her displeasure at being left out of the conversation. Danny took his seat at the table and before Grace could turn to settle the baby, he broke off a small bite of pancake and set it in her open mouth.

She grinned at him.

And Danny felt his world slide into place. What he felt was beyond happiness. It was something more like purpose or place. That was it. He had a place. He had a child, and a friend in his child's mother. In a sense, Grace getting pregnant had given him back his life. As long as he didn't try to make this relationship any more than it was, he had a family of sorts.

In the grocery store, Grace had serious second thoughts about her idea of teaching Danny to cook. He wanted to learn to steam shrimp and prepare crème brûlée. Her expertise ran more along the lines of pizza rolls and brownies. And the brownies weren't even scratch brownies. They were from a boxed mix.

"How about prime rib?"

"I'm not exactly sure how that's made, either."

"We need a cookbook."

"Or we could start with less complex things like grilled steak and baked potatoes."

Standing by the spice counter, he slowly turned to face her, a smile spreading across his mouth. "You don't know how to cook, either."

"That's a matter of opinion. I know the main staples. I can bake a roast that melts in your mouth, fix just about any kind of potato you want and steam vegetables. My lasagna wins raves at reunions—"

"Reunions?"

"You know. Family reunions. Picnics. Where all the aunts and uncles and cousins get together and everybody brings his or her specialty dish, plays volleyball or softball, coos over each other's kids and the next morning wakes up with sore muscles because most of us only play sports that one day every year."

He laughed.

"You've never been to a family reunion?"

"I don't have much of a family. My dad was an only child, and though my mother had two siblings, her brother became a priest and her sister chose not to have kids."

She gaped at him. "You're kidding."

"Why are you so surprised. *Your* parents had only one child."

"My parents had one child because my dad was disabled in an automobile accident. He appears fine and he can do most things, but he never could go back to work. It's why my parents have so little money. We had to live on what my mother could make."

"Oh."

Seeing that he was processing that, Grace stepped over to the spices and pulled out a container of basil. She had to wonder if the reason Danny couldn't seem to love wasn't just the mistake of his marriage, but a result of his entire past. Could a person who'd only seen one marriage, then failed at his own, really believe in love?

"I can also make soup."

"What kind?"

"Vegetable and chicken and dumpling."

"Ah. A gourmet."

"Now, don't get snooty. I think you're really going to like the chicken and dumpling. I have to use a spaetzle maker."

"What the hell is a spaetzle maker?"

His confusion about a cooking utensil only served to confirm Grace's theory that Danny couldn't love because he knew so little about the simple, ordinary things other people took for granted. "It's a fancy word for a kitchen gadget that makes very small dumplings."

"Why don't you just call it that?"

"Because I'm not the one who decided what it's called. It's German or something. Besides, spaetzle maker sounds more official."

"Right."

Grace laughed. She was having fun. Lots of fun. The kind of fun they probably would have had if she and Danny had let their relationship develop slowly. They were so different that they'd desperately needed time to get to know each other, to become familiar with each other's worlds, and to integrate what worked and get rid of what didn't. From Danny's eagerness to learn and his curiosity, it was clear something was missing in his world. And from the way he reacted to the simplicity of her life it was obvious she wouldn't have been able to stay the same if they'd actually had a relationship. That was also why Sarah needed both of them. Neither one of them was *wrong* in the way they lived. It was all a matter of choices.

They spent over double what Grace normally allotted for food, but Danny paid the bill. When she tried to give him her share, he refused it, reminding her that she'd paid for the first week's groceries. Another proof that Danny was innately fair. A good man. Not the horrible man who tossed her out of his office when she told him she was pregnant. But a man trying to get his bearings after the loss of a child.

At two o'clock that afternoon, with Sarah napping and Danny standing about three inches behind her, Grace got out her soup pot.

"Could you watch from a few feet back?"

"I'm curious."

"Well, be curious over by the counter." He stepped away from her and to keep the conversation flowing so he didn't pout, Grace said, "Soup is good on a chilly fall day like this."

Danny leaned against the counter and crossed his arms on his chest. "I think you're showing off."

"Showing off?"

"I doubted your abilities, so you're about to dazzle me with your spaetzle maker."

She laughed. "The spaetzle maker doesn't come into play for a while yet. Plus, there's very little expertise to soup," she said, dropping the big pot on the burner. "First you get a pot."

He rolled his eyes.

"Then you fill it halfway with water." She filled a large bowl with water and dumped the water into the big pot on the stove. "You add an onion, one potato, a stalk of celery and a chicken."

He gaped at her. "You're putting that entire chicken into the pot?"

"Yes."

Now he looked horrified.

She laughed. "Come on. This is how my grandmother did it." While he stood gaping at her, looking afraid to comment, she reached for the chicken bouillion cubes.

His eyes widened. "You're cheating!"

"Not really. The only thing bouillion cubes accomplishes is to cut down on cooking time."

"It's still cheating."

"I'm starting to notice a trend here. You're against anything that saves time."

"I want to learn to cook correctly."

She shrugged. "I need to be able to save time." With everything in the pot, she washed her hands then dried them with a paper towel.

"Now what?"

"Now, I'm going to take advantage of the fact that Sarah's still napping and read."

"Really?"

"Even with the bouillion cubes, the soup needs to cook at least an hour. It's best if we give it two hours." She glanced at the clock on the stove. "So until Sarah wakes I'm going to read."

"What should I do?"

"Weren't you working on something last night?"

He pouted. "Yeah, but I can't go any further because I left an important file at my office."

She sighed. "So I have to entertain you?"

He actually thought about that. For a few seconds Grace was sure the strong man in him would say no. Instead he laughed and said, "Yes. Somebody's got to entertain me."

Grace only stared at him. The night before she would have sworn he was firmly against getting involved with her, but today he was happy to be in her company. It didn't make sense—

Actually it did. The night before they were both considering sleeping together. Today they were making soup. Laughing. Happy. Not facing a life choice. Just having fun in each other's company. No stress. No worries. And wasn't that her real goal? To make him comfortable enough that Sarah's stays with him would be pleasant?

That was exactly her goal. So she couldn't waste such a wonderful opportunity.

"Do you know anything about gardening?"

"No."

"Ever played UNO?"

He gave her a puzzled look. "What's an Uno?"

"Wow, either you've led dull life or I've been overly entertained." Deciding she'd been overly entertained by a dad who couldn't do much in the way of physical things, Grace had a sudden inspiration. "If your mother's an expert at rummy, I know you've played that."

He glanced down at his fingernails as if studying them. "A bit."

"Oh, you think you're pretty good, don't you?"

"I'm a slouch."

"Don't sucker me!"

"Would I sucker you?"

"To get me to let my guard down so you could beat me, yes." She paused, then headed to the dining room buffet and the cards. "If you think you have to sucker me, you must not be very good."

"I'm exceptional."

She grinned. "I knew it."

Just then, a whimper floated from the baby monitor on the counter.

Grace set the cards back in the drawer. "So much for rummy. I'll try to get her back to sleep but I'm betting she wants to come downstairs."

"Why did she wake up so soon?"

"She probably heard us talking. That's why she didn't roll over and go back to sleep. She wants to be in on the action."

"Great. We'll play rummy with her in the high chair."

She paused on her way to the steps. "We could, but wouldn't it be more fun to spend a few minutes with Sarah first?"

He nodded. "Yeah. You're right."

As Grace went up the steps Danny took a long breath. He, Grace and the baby had had a good time shopping. He and Grace had had fun putting away the groceries and getting the soup into the pot. Now they would spend even more time together, and no doubt it would be fun.

He rubbed his hand across the back of his neck. The whole morning had been so easy—so right—that he knew he was correct in thinking that a friendship between him and Grace gave him the family, the connection, he so desperately wanted. But he also knew he was getting too close to a line he shouldn't cross—unless he wanted to fall in love with her and make their family a real family. He didn't want to hurt her, but right now, in his gut, he had an optimistic sense that he wouldn't. And the night before he'd seen in her eyes that she wanted what he wanted. For them to fall in love. She didn't have to say the words for Danny to know that she trusted him. She believed in him. He'd hurt her once, yet she trusted that he wouldn't hurt her again.

She believed in him and maybe the trick to their situation wouldn't be to take this one step at a time, but to trust what Grace saw in him, rather than what he knew about himself.

He walked into the kitchen and lifted the lid from the

pot. He sniffed the steam that floated out and his mouth watered. Even if soup was simple fare and even though he absolutely believed Grace had cheated with the bouillion cube, it smelled heavenly. He'd trusted her about spending two weeks here with her and Sarah, and had acclimated to being in a family again, albeit a nontraditional one. He'd trusted Grace about the soup, and it appeared he would be getting a tasty dinner. He'd trusted her about relaxing with Sarah and he now had a relationship with his daughter.

Could he trust her instinct that he wouldn't hurt her? Or let her down the way he'd let Lydia down?

Grace came down the steps carrying smiling Sarah.

When the baby immediately zeroed in on him, he said, "Hey, kid."

She yelped and clapped her hands.

"She does a lot of screeching and yelping. We've got to teach her a few words."

"Eventually. Right now, I think playing with the blocks or maybe the cone and rings are a better use of our time."

Danny was about to ask what the cone and rings were, but he suddenly had a very vivid memory of them. He saw Cory on the floor, brightly colored rings in a semicircle in front of him. He remembered teaching Cory to pick up the rings in order of size and slide them onto the cone.

And the memory didn't hurt. In fact, it made him smile. Cory had always had an eye for color. Maybe Sarah did, too? Or maybe Danny didn't care how smart

Sarah was or where her gifts were? Maybe his being so concerned about Cory's gifts was part of what had pushed Lydia away from him?

Forcing himself into the present, Danny glanced around. "Where's the toy box?"

"I don't have one. Sarah's toys are in the bottom drawer of the buffet in the dining area."

He walked over to it. "Curse of a small house?"

"Yes. This is the other reason I hesitated to talk with you about opening an investment account for me. I definitely need something with more space and I'm considering buying another house, and if I have extra money that's probably where it will go."

He opened the bottom drawer, found the colorful cone and rings and pulled it out. Returning to the area that served as a living room, he handed Grace the cone and sat on the sofa.

As Grace dumped the multicolored rings on the floor in front of Sarah, Danny cautiously said, "You know, we've never made a firm decision about child support."

She glanced up at him with a smile. "Yes, we did. I told you I wouldn't pay you any."

Her comment made him laugh and suddenly Danny felt too far away. He slid off the sofa and positioned himself on the floor across from Grace with Sarah between them, using the baby as a buffer between him and the woman who—whether she knew it or not—was tempting him to try something he swore he'd never try again. Even the idea of *trying* was new. He was shaky at best about trusting himself, and Sarah's happiness also tied into their situation. He couldn't act hastily, or let his hormones have control.

"Actually I think if we went to court a judge would order me to pay you something. So, come on. Let's really talk about this."

Grace busied herself making sure all the rings were within Sarah's reach. "Okay, if you want to pay something every month, why don't you put a couple hundred dollars a month into a college fund for Sarah?"

"Because she doesn't need a college fund. I can afford to pay for schooling." He took a breath, remembering that the last time they'd broached this subject she'd made him stop—the same way he made her stop when they got too far into his past. But resolving child support for their daughter was different than rehashing a past he desperately needed to forget. They had to come to an agreement on support.

"Look, I know you don't want to talk about this. But we have to. I don't feel right not contributing to her day-to-day expenses."

"I already told you that we're going to be sharing custody," Grace said as she gently guided Sarah's hand to take the ring she was shoving into her mouth and loop it onto the cone. "I will have her one week, but you will have her the next. Technically that's the way we'll share her expenses."

"I'd still like to—"

"Danny, I have a job. My house is nearly paid off. When I sell it, the money I get will be my down payment for the new one. I have a plan. It works. We're fine."

"I know. I just—"

Though Danny had thought she was getting angry, she playfully slapped his knee. "Just for one afternoon will you please relax?"

He peered at her hand, then caught her gaze. "You slapped me."

She grinned. "A friendly tap to wake you up, so you'll finally catch on that I'm right."

This was what he liked about her. She didn't have to win every argument. She also knew when to pull back. *Before* either one of them said something they'd regret, rather than after. It was a skill or sixth sense he and Lydia had never acquired. Plus, she had wonderfully creative ways of stepping away and getting him to step away. Rather than slammed doors and cold shoulders, she teased him. And she let him tease her.

"Oh, yeah? So what you're saying is that friendly tapping between us is allowed?"

"Sure. Sometimes something physical is the only way to get someone's attention."

"You mean like this?" He leaped behind Sarah, caught Grace around the shoulders, and nudged her to the floor in one fluid movement, so he could tickle her.

"Hey!" she yelped, trying to get away from him when he tickled her ribs. "You *had* my attention."

"I had your attention, but you weren't getting my point, so I'm making sure you see how serious I am when I say you should take my money."

She wiggled away from him. "I don't need your money."

"I can see that," he said, catching her waist and dragging her back. "But I want to give it."

He tickled her again and she cried, "Uncle! I give up! Give me a thousand dollars and we'll call it even."

"I gave you more than that for helping with Orlando," he said, catching her gaze. When their eyes met, his breathing stopped. Reminded of the bonus and Orlando, vivid images of their weekend came to Danny. He stopped tickling. She stopped laughing. His throat worked.

In the year that had passed he'd all but forgotten she existed, convinced that she had lied about her pregnancy and left his employ because she was embarrassed that her scheme had been exposed. Now he knew she'd been sick, dependent upon the bonus that he'd given her for expenses and dependent upon her parents for emotional support that *he* should have given her.

"I'm so sorry about everything."

She whispered, "I know."

"I would give anything to make it up for the hurt I caused you."

"There's no need."

He remembered again how she had been that weekend. Happy, but also gracious. She wouldn't take a promotion she hadn't deserved. She wouldn't pry, was kind to Orlando, never overstepped her boundaries. And he'd hurt her. Chances were, he'd hurt her again.

Still, he wanted so much to kiss her that his chest ached and he couldn't seem to overrule the instinct that was as much emotional as it was physical. He liked her.

He just plain liked her. He liked being with her, being part of her life, having her in his life.

He lowered his head and touched his lips to hers, telling himself that if he slid them into a simple, uncomplicated romance with no expectation of grandeur, she wouldn't be hurt. He wouldn't be hurt. Both would get what they wanted.

His mouth slid across hers slowly at first, savoring every second of the physical connection that was a manifestation of the depth of his feelings for her. She answered, equally slowly, as if as hesitant as he was, but also as unable to resist the temptation. When the slight meeting of mouths wasn't enough her lips blossomed to life under his, meeting him, matching him, then oh so slowly opening.

It was all the invitation Danny needed. He deepened the kiss, awash with the pleasure of being close to someone as wonderful as Grace. Happiness virtually sang through his veins. Need thrummed through him. For the first time since she'd brought Sarah to him, his thoughts didn't automatically tumble back to their beach house weekend. They stayed in the present, on the moment, on the woman in his arms and the desire to make love. To touch her, to taste her, to cherish every wonderful second. To build a future.

But the second the future came into play, Danny knew he was only deluding himself. He'd tried this once and failed. He'd lost a child, broken his wife. Spent a year mourning his loss alone in the big house so hollow and empty it echoed around him. He knew the reality of loss. How it destroyed a person. Emptied a life. He couldn't go through it again, but more than that, he wouldn't force Grace to.

CHAPTER TEN

DANNY broke the kiss, quickly rose from the floor and extended his hand to Grace. When she was on her feet, he spun away and Grace's stomach knotted.

"Danny?"

He rubbed both hands down his face. "Grace, this is wrong."

"No, it isn't." Glad for the opportunity to finally discuss their feelings instead of guessing, she walked over and grabbed him by the upper arm, turning him to face her. "This is us. We like each other. Naturally. We're like toast and butter or salt and pepper. We fit."

He laughed harshly. "Fit? Are you sure you want to say you fit with me?"

She didn't hesitate. "Yes."

He shook his head. "Grace, please. Please, don't. Don't fit with me. Don't even *want* to fit with me. If you were smart you wouldn't even want to be my friend."

At that her chin came up. If he was going to turn her away again, to deny her his love, or even the chance to be part of his life, this time she would make him explain. "Why?"

"Because I'm not good for you. I'm not good for anybody."

"Why?"

He raked his fingers through his short black hair. "Stop!"

"No. You say you're not good for me. I say you are. And I will not stop pursuing you."

"Then I'll leave."

"Great. Run. If that's your answer to everything, then you run."

He groaned and walked away as if annoyed that she wouldn't let him alone. "I'm not running. I'm saving you."

"I don't think you are. I also don't think you're a coward who runs. So just tell me what's wrong!"

He pivoted to face her so quickly that Grace flinched. "Tell you? Tell you what? That I failed at my marriage and hurt the woman I adored? Tell you that I don't want to do it again?"

His obsidian eyes were bright with pain. His voice seemed to echo from a dark, sacred place. A place of scars and black memories and wounds. A place he rarely visited and never took another person. Still, broken marriages were common. And though she understood his had hurt him, she also suspected even *he* knew it was time to get beyond his.

Her heart breaking for him, Grace whispered, "How do you know that you'll fail?"

Stiff with resistance, he angrily countered, "How do you know that I won't?"

"Because you're good. You may not know it but I see it every day in how you treat me and how you treat Sarah."

"Grace, you are wrong. I use people. Just ask my ex-wife. She'll tell you I'm a workaholic. If you called her right now, she'd probably even accurately guess that I'm only here because I need to raise my daughter because I need an heir. Carson Services needs an heir."

"Well, she'd be wrong. If you only wanted to raise Sarah because Carson Services needs an heir you could take me to court."

"Unless I didn't want you digging into my past."

That stopped her.

"What if this is all about me not wanting you to take me to court?" he asked, stepping close. "What if there is something so bad in my past that I know even you couldn't forgive it?"

She swallowed. Possibilities overwhelmed her. Not only did having a hidden sin in his past explain why he agreed to live with her and their daughter when letting his lawyers handle their situation would have been much easier, but it also explained why he always stepped back, always denied himself and her.

Still, she couldn't imagine what he could have done. He wasn't gentle and retiring by any means. But he also wasn't cruel or vindictive. He wasn't the kind to take risks or live on the edge. She might have told herself to stop guessing, to quit ascribing characteristics to him he didn't deserve, but she'd also lived with him for a week. Almost fifteen hours a day. She'd seen him *choose* to make breakfast, *choose* to bathe Sarah, *choose* to give Grace breaks. She didn't believe he could be cruel or do something so horrible it couldn't be forgiven.

She took a breath, then another. "I don't think there is something in your past that can't be forgiven."

"What if I told you that I killed my son?"

Her heart in her throat, more aware of the pain that would cause him than any sort of ramification it would have on their relationship, she said, "You couldn't have killed your son."

"It was an accident, but the accident was my fault."

Grace squeezed her eyes shut. An accident that was his fault. Of course. That accounted for so many things in his life and how he had treated her that before this hadn't added up.

But accidents were circumstances that somehow got out of someone's control. He hadn't deliberately killed his child. He couldn't deliberately kill his child. That was why he was so tortured now.

"Danny, it wasn't your fault."

His eyes blazed. "Don't you forgive me! And don't brush it off as if my son's life was of no consequence. I was in charge of him that morning. *I* knew he was in the mood to push me. He wanted to remove the training wheels from his bike and I refused, but he kept arguing, begging, pleading. When my cell phone rang, I should have ignored it. But my natural reaction kicked in, I grabbed it, answered it and gave him the chance to prove to me how good he was on his bike by darting out into the street right into the path of an SUV."

He paused, raked his fingers through his hair again and his voice dropped to a feather-light whisper. "A neighbor hit him. She doesn't come out of her house now. I ruined a lot of lives that morning."

The tick of the clock was the only sound in the room. Grace stood frozen, steeped in his pain, hurting for him.

"Not quite as sure of me now, are you?"

She swallowed. "It wasn't your fault."

He ran his hands down his face. "It was my fault. And I live with it every day. And I miss my son and I remember the look on my wife's face." Seeming to be getting his bearings, he blew his breath out on a long gust and faced her. "And I won't do that to you."

He headed for the stairway. Panicked, knowing they were only at the tip of this discussion, Grace said, "What if I—"

He stopped at the bottom of the steps. His face bore the hard, cold expression she remembered from the day she told him she was pregnant.

"You don't get a choice. You don't get a say. This pain is mine."

He ran up the steps and Grace collapsed on her sofa. Bending forward, she lifted Sarah from the floor and squeezed her to her chest, suddenly understanding why he didn't want her digging into his past. It could give her plenty of grounds to keep him from getting custody—even shared. But it also gave her a foot in the door to keep the baby away from him completely.

And she hated to admit she was considering it. Not because of what had happened with his son, but because he couldn't seem to get beyond it. What did it mean for Sarah that her father wouldn't let himself love again?

She took a breath, knowing her fears were premature because they had another week to live together, another week for him to recognize that though he didn't want to forget his son, he also had a daughter who needed him. She shouldn't jump to conclusions.

But twenty minutes later he came downstairs, suitcases in hand.

"We have another week to live together."

"Grace, I'm done." He shrugged into his jacket. "Besides, I never signed the agreement. This was a mistake anyway."

With that he opened the door, and stepped out, but he turned one final time and looked at Sarah, then his gaze slowly rose to catch Grace's. She saw the regret, the pain, the need. Then she watched him quickly erase it as determination filled his dark eyes. He stepped out into the September afternoon, closing the door behind him with a soft click.

Danny walked into the empty foyer of his huge house and listened to the echo his suitcase made as he set it on the floor, knowing this was the rest of his life, and for the first time totally, honestly, unemotionally committed to accepting it. He wouldn't risk hurting Grace. Telling his story that afternoon, he remembered in vivid detail how unworthy he was to drag another person into his life. Now that Grace knew his mistake, he didn't expect to even get visitation with Sarah. He expected to live his life alone, the perfect candidate to serve Carson Services and pass on the family legacy.

To Sarah. A little girl who wouldn't know him, probably wouldn't know about Carson Services, but who shared his bloodline. When she came of age, Danny would offer her the chance to train to take over the family business, but would Grace let her? No mother would sentence her daughter to even a few hours a week with a cold, distant father.

Walking up the ornate curved stairway of the huge home that went to the next Carson, Danny had to wonder if that wasn't a good thing.

CHAPTER ELEVEN

A MONTH later, seated at the slim wooden table in the hearing room in the courthouse, Danny wasn't entirely sure why he had come to this proceeding. Grace's reasons for being here were a no-brainer. She'd had her lawyer set the hearing to make her case for Danny not getting custody. She could probably get enough reasons on the record to preclude him from even *seeing* their baby again.

But he knew she wouldn't do that. After his confession to her, and a week of wallowing in misery in his lonely house, he'd pulled himself up by his bootstraps and gone back to work like the sharp CEO he was, and his life had fallen into a strong, comfortable routine. Once he'd gotten his bearings and stopped feeling sorry for himself, he'd recognized that *all* was not lost. Grace wouldn't keep Sarah from him. She would be kind enough—or maybe fair enough to Sarah—to let him have visitation, even though she probably hated him.

Some days he hated himself. Blamed himself for the pain he'd caused both him and Grace by letting her believe in him—even if it was for one short week. Had he told Grace right from the beginning that his son was not only dead, but Danny himself was responsible for Cory's accident, Grace would have happily kept her distance. She wouldn't have mourned the loss of his love, as he'd pictured her doing. He wouldn't have again felt the sting of living alone in his big, hollow house, torturously reminded of how it felt to be whole, to be wanted, to have people in his life and a purpose beyond perpetuating the family business.

But if nothing else had come from the week he'd spent with Grace and Sarah, Danny knew Grace would be fair. He thoroughly loved his daughter. He wanted to be part of her life, not just to assure she'd be ready to make a choice about Carson Services, but because he loved having her around. He loved being with her. And she was Danny's last chance at a family. He might never have the good fortune to share his life with Sarah's mother, but he could at least have a daughter.

So he supposed he'd come to this hearing as a show of good faith, proof that if Grace intended to let him have visitation, he wanted it. He suspected that any visitation she granted him would be supervised. He'd been the one in charge when Cory was killed. Grace's lawyer would undoubtedly drop that fact into the proceeding as a way to demonstrate that Danny wasn't a good dad. But he'd take even supervised visitation. At this point, he'd take anything he could get.

Grace entered the hearing room. Wearing an electric-blue suit, with her dark shoulder-length hair swaying around her and her sexy violet eyes shining, she was pretty enough to stop his heart. Yet in spite of how gorgeous she was, Danny's real reaction to her was emotional rather than physical. He'd missed her. They'd spent a total of nine days together. Three at his beach house and six at her house and he missed her. Ached for her. Longed for everything he knew darned well they could have had together, if he hadn't looked away for one split second and changed his destiny.

Grace approached the table with her lawyer, young, handsome, Robby Malloy. The guy Danny's lawyer called pretty boy Malloy. Danny could see why. He had the face of a movie star and carried himself like a billionaire. Danny experienced a surge of jealousy so intense he had to fight to keep himself from jumping from behind the table and yanking Grace away from the sleazy ambulance chaser.

But he didn't jump and he didn't yank. Because as a father his first concern had to be assuring that he was part of his daughter's life. He'd never had the right to care about Grace, about who she dated, or even if she dated.

So why was his blood pressure rising and his chest tightening from just looking at her with another man? Her lawyer no less? A man who may not even be romantically interested, only earning his hourly fee for representing her?

The judge entered the room, his dark robe billowing around him with his every step. Danny followed the lead of his attorney, Art Brown, and rose.

Having not yet taken his seat, Malloy extended his hand to the judge. "Judge Antanazzo."

"Good morning, Mr. Malloy," Charlie Antanazzo boomed. "How's my favorite attorney today?"

Malloy laughed. "Well, I doubt that I'm your favorite attorney," he said, obviously charming the judge. "But I'm great, your honor. This is my client, Grace McCartney."

As Grace shook Judge Antanazzo's hand, he smiled. "It's a pleasure to meet you."

Danny would just bet it was. Not only did the judge smile like any man happy to meet a pretty girl, but also Danny hadn't missed the way the judge took a quick inventory that started with Grace's shiny sable hair and managed to skim her perfect figure and nice legs in under a second.

This time it was a bit harder to refrain from leaping over the desk and yanking her to him.

But that ship had sailed and Danny had to grow accustomed to watching men fawn over Grace. He'd had his chance and he'd blown it. Or maybe it wasn't so much that Danny had had his chance, as much as it was that Danny had destroyed his own life long before he met Grace.

Danny's lawyer finally spoke. "Good morning, your honor," Art said, then shook the judge's hand. "This is my client, Danny Carson."

The judge quickly shook the hand Danny extended and frowned as he looked down at the brown case file he'd brought into the hearing room with him.

"Yes, I know. Danny Carson. CEO of Carson

Services. Let's see," he said, skimming the words in front of him. "Ms. McCartney was in your employ at one time." He continued reading. "She told you she was pregnant. You didn't believe her. Circumstances, including her being sick during the pregnancy, kept her from pursuing the matter. Then she took the baby to you." He read some more. "There's no record of child support." He looked at Danny. "Do you pay child support?"

Danny's lawyer said, "No, your honor, but—"

The judge ignored him. "All right then. This case boils down to a few concise facts. Ms. McCartney told you she was pregnant, brought the child to you and you don't pay child support." He glanced from Danny to Grace and held Grace's gaze. "Am I up to speed?

"There's a little more, your honor," Grace's lawyer said. "Once the court reporter is ready, I'd like to go on the record."

Danny's heart sank. Great. Just great. From the scant information the judge had read, it was pretty clear whose side he was on. Once Danny's past came out, the judge might not even let him have supervised visitation. The urge to defend himself rose up in Danny and this time rather than fight it, he let it take root. All the facts that the judge had read had made him look bad. But he wasn't. Everything he'd done wrong wasn't really a deliberate misdeed. Every one of his "bad" things were explainable—defendable.

He'd *misinterpreted* Grace's not answering the phone the night he'd flown home after his week of client hopping. As a result of that he broke off with her. So, when she came in to tell him she was pregnant, he'd thought it was a ruse to get him back, and he hadn't believed her. And when she left his employ, Danny had thought it was because her scheme had been exposed. He wasn't bad. He wasn't a schmuck. He had made some mistakes. Very defendable mistakes. Technically he could even defend himself about Cory's death.

He took a breath. That wasn't at issue right now. Sarah's custody was.

The lawyers and judge made preliminary statements for the record. Danny studiously avoided looking at Grace by tapping the eraser of his pencil on the desk. Eventually the judge said, "Mr. Malloy, ball's in your court."

"Thank you, your honor. My client would like to testify first."

Danny's lawyer had warned him that preliminary hearings could sometimes seem unofficial, but Danny shouldn't take it lightly because a court reporter would be recording the proceedings. He sat up a little straighter.

Though Grace stayed in her seat at the table, she was sworn in.

Her lawyer said, "Okay, Ms. McCartney, there is no argument between you and Mr. Carson about paternity?"

"No. And if there were we'd get a DNA test. We've agreed to that."

"But there's no need because you know Mr. Carson is the father?"

"Yes. I didn't—hadn't—" She paused, stumbling

over her explanation and Danny frowned, not sure what she was getting at.

"You hadn't had relations," Robbie prompted and Grace nodded.

"—I hadn't had relations with anybody for several months before Danny—Mr. Carson—and I spent a weekend at his beach house."

Danny damned near groaned. Not because it sounded as if he'd taken her to his private hideaway to seduce her, but because for the first time since that weekend he realized how important sleeping with him must have been in her life. She didn't sleep around. Hell, she apparently barely slept with anybody. But she'd been with him that night. She'd smiled at him, made him laugh, made him feel really alive—

Robbie Malloy said, "So why are you here today, Ms. McCartney?" bringing Danny back to the present.

"I'm here today because Mr. Carson and I had a shared custody agreement."

"Briefly, what does the agreement say?"

"That if he could stay at my house for two weeks, basically to learn how to care for Sarah, I would agree to shared custody."

"Did Mr. Carson want shared custody?"

"No. At first he wanted full custody. The agreement we made about shared custody was drafted to prevent us from fighting over Sarah. Shared custody seemed like the fair way to handle things."

"But—"

Grace took a breath. Danny raised his gaze to hers

and she looked directly at him. Which was exactly what he'd intended to make her do. If she wanted to testify against him, then let her do it looking into his eyes.

"But he didn't stay the two weeks."

Danny's eyes hardened.

"Ms. McCartney, is it also correct that he didn't sign the agreement?"

"No, he did not."

"And is that why we're here?"

"Well, I can't speak for Mr. Carson, but the reason I am here is to get it on the record that even though he didn't sign the agreement, or stay the two weeks, I believe Mr. Carson fulfilled its spirit and intent and I feel we should honor it."

"Which means you believe you and Mr. Carson should have shared custody?"

She held Danny's gaze. "Yes."

"You want me to have Sarah every other week?" Danny said, forgetting they were on the record.

"Yes. Danny, you proved yourself."

"I left."

"I know." She smiled slightly. "It doesn't matter. You showed me you can care for Sarah."

Robbie said, "Your honor, that's what we wanted to get on the record. No further questions."

The judge turned to Art. "Do you want to question Ms. McCartney?"

Art raised his hands. "Actually I think we'll let Ms. McCartney's testimony stand as is."

"Does Mr. Carson want to testify?"

Without consulting Danny, Art said, "No."

The judge quickly glanced down at his notes. "Technically you have a custody agreement in place. It's simply not executed. But Ms. McCartney still wants to honor it." He looked at Danny. "Mr. Carson? Do you want to honor the agreement?"

Danny nodded as Art said, "Yes."

The judge made a sound of strained patience, then said, "You're a very lucky man, Mr. Carson. Very lucky indeed."

Staring at Grace, who had begun casually gathering her purse as if what she had just said hadn't been of monumental significance, Danny didn't know what to say. Art spoke for him. "Your honor, when parents share custody it's frequently considered that each is taking his or her share of the financial burden when the child is with him—or her."

The judge closed the file. "Right. As if these two people have equal financial means." He faced Danny. "Don't screw this up." He left the room in a flurry or robes and promises about writing up an order.

Art began gathering his files. "Well, that went much better than expected," he said with a laugh, but overwhelmed with too many emotions to name, Danny watched Grace and her lawyer heading for the door.

Just as Grace would have stepped over the threshold, emotion overruled common sense and he called, "Wait!"

Grace turned and smiled at him.

Danny's throat worked. She was incredibly beautiful and incredibly generous. And he was numb with gratitude. "Why didn't you—"

She tilted her head in question. "Why didn't I what?"

Go for the jugular? Fight? Tell the court about Cory?

"Why are you letting me have Sarah?"

"You're her dad."

"I —" He took a breath. "What if I can't handle her?"

To his amazement, Grace laughed. "You can handle her. I've seen you handle her. You'll be fine."

"I'll be fine," he repeated, annoyed with Grace for being so flip, when the safety of their daughter was at stake. "What kind of answer is that!"

"It's an honest one."

"How can you trust her with me!"

"Are you telling me you're going to put her in danger?"

He glared at her. "You know I won't."

"Then there's no reason you shouldn't have your daughter."

"You trust me?"

She smiled. "I trust you. But if you're nervous, hire a nanny. You've told me at least twice that you were going to do that. So hire somebody."

Danny's heart swelled with joy. He was getting a second chance. He would have something of a family. He swallowed hard. "Okay."

She took two steps closer to him and placed her hand on his forearm. "Or, if you don't want to hire a nanny, you could come home."

Home. Her house *was* home. Warm. Welcoming. He could remember nearly every detail of their six short days. Especially how tempted he was to take what they both wanted. Just as he was tempted now to take what she was offering. A complete second chance. Not just an opportunity to be Sarah's daddy, but a second chance at life. A real life.

But he also knew he was damaged. So damaged it wasn't fair to use Grace as a step up out of his particular hell. He smiled regretfully. "You know you deserve better."

"So you say, but I don't think so. I see the part of you that you're trying to hide, or forget, or punish. I don't see the past."

"You're lucky."

"No, Danny, I'm not lucky. It's time. Time for you to move on." She held out her hand. "Come home with me. Start again."

He stared at the hand she offered. Delicate fingers. Pretty pink fingernails. Feminine things. Soft things. Things that had been missing from his life for so long. A million possibilities entered his head. A million things he would do, *could* do, if he took that hand, took the steps that would put him in Grace's world again. He could teach Sarah to walk. Hear her first word. Hear the first time she called him daddy. Sleep with Grace. Use the spaezle maker. Steal kisses. Share dreams. Spend Christmas as part of a family.

None of which he deserved.

"I can't."

CHAPTER TWELVE

DANNY turned away and though Grace's gut reaction was to demand that he talk to her, she didn't. Tears filled her eyes. Tears for him as much as for the wonderful future he was denying both of them, and she turned around and walked out of the hearing room.

Robbie was waiting. "You okay?"

She managed a smile. "Yeah. I'm fine."

"You're awfully generous with him."

"That's because he's so hard on himself."

"Be careful, Grace," Robbie said, directing her to the stairway that led to the courthouse lobby. "Men like Danny Carson who have a reputation for taking what they want don't like to lose. You may think that by "granting" him shared custody you were doing him and your daughter a kindness, but you had him over a barrel and he knew it. He may have just played you like a Stradivarius. Made you feel sorry for him so that you'd give him what he wanted, since he knew he probably couldn't beat you in court."

"I don't think so. I know Danny better than you do. He wouldn't do something like that."

"You think you know Danny?"

"I *know* Danny."

"Well, you better hope so because what we got on the record today—you saying you believed he was capable of caring for Sarah—negated any possibility we had of using his son's death in future hearings."

Grace gasped. "I would never use his son's death!"

Robbie held up his hand in defense. "Hey, I'm okay with that. Actually I agree that it would be cruel to use his son's death against him. I'm just saying be careful. This whole thing could backfire and you could end up fighting for your own daughter."

"I won't."

Robbie shook his head. "God save me from clients in love."

"It's that obvious?"

"Yes." Holding open one of the two huge double doors of the courthouse entrance, Robbie added, "And if Danny's as smart as everyone claims he is, he'll use it. Better put my number on speed dial."

Reading to Sarah in the rocking chair that night, Grace thought about the look on Danny's face when she stated for the record that she wanted their shared custody agreement upheld.

She shouldn't have been surprised that he expected her to testify against him. He was angry with himself and nothing she said or did could change that. No matter how sad he appeared or how much she'd simply wanted to hug him, she couldn't. A man who couldn't forgive himself, especially for something so traumatic, wasn't ready for a relationship and he might never be. It had broken her heart when he refused her offer to return home. As much for him as for herself.

But at least she had her answer now.

With Sarah asleep in her arms, Grace set the story-book on a shelf of the changing table and rose from the rocker. She laid Sarah in her crib, covered her, kissed her forehead and walked down the steps.

It wasn't going to be easy sharing custody with a man she loved but who could never love her. But she intended to do it. Actually she intended to do the one thing she'd promised herself she wouldn't do the night she rushed down to his beach house bar to see if he felt about her the way she felt about him. She was going to pine for him. She intended to love him forever, quietly, without expectation of anything in return because the real bottom line to Danny's trouble was that nobody had ever really loved him. At least not without expectation of anything in return. His parents expected him to take over the family business. His ex-wife held him responsible for their child's death. The people who worked for him wanted a job. His investors, even investors he considered friends, like Orlando, needed his expertise. Nobody loved him without expectation of anything in return.

So she would be that person. She might never be his wife, but she would be there for him in all the right ways, so that he could see that he was okay and that life didn't always have to be about what he could give somebody.

Two Mondays later when Robbie called and told her that the judge's order had come down, Grace sat quietly and listened as her lawyer explained how she was to have Sarah ready at six o'clock that Friday night. With every word he said, her chest tightened. Her eyes filled with tears. It was easy to say she intended to love Danny without expectation of anything in return when the situation was abstract. But now that shared custody was a reality she suddenly realized loving Danny meant denying herself. At the very least, she would spend every other week without her daughter.

She hung up the phone, glad for four days to prepare herself to see him, and managed to greet him with a smile Friday evening. With Sarah's diaper bag packed and sitting by the door, she put Sarah into his arms.

"Hey, Sarah Bear," he said softly and the baby hit him on the cheek with her rattle. He laughed nervously. "I guess she's forgotten who I am."

"Maybe," Grace said, trying to sound strong and confident, but with Danny standing at her door, refusing to go beyond the foyer, wearing a topcoat and scarf because western Pennsylvania had had its first snowfall of the season, it seemed as if the Danny she loved no longer existed. The guy in jeans and a T-shirt who made pancakes seemed to have been replaced by the man who ran Carson Services.

"We won't need that," Danny said, nodding at the diaper bag, as he struggled to contain Sarah who had begun to wail in earnest and stretched away from Danny, reaching for Grace. "I have a nursery full of things." For the first time since he'd arrived, he met her gaze. "I also hired a nanny."

"Good." Tears clogged Grace's throat when Sarah squealed and reached for her. "Stay with Daddy, Sarah," she whispered, pushing the baby back in Danny's arms, then fussing with Sarah's jacket as she slowly pulled her hands way.

But with her mom this close, Sarah all but crawled out of Danny's arms again, with a squeal that renewed her crying.

Pain ricocheted through Grace. "Maybe we should have broken this up? Had her do an overnight visit or two before we forced her to spend an entire week."

"It's going to be hard no matter how we do it. Let's just get this over with."

He opened the door, not even sparing Grace a glance, taking her daughter.

"If she gives you any trouble, just call," Grace said, trying to keep her voice light and bright as he walked away, but it wobbled.

Already on the sidewalk, striding to his car, Danny said, "We're fine."

And he left.

Watching his car lights as they disappeared into the night, Grace stood on her stoop, with her lawyer's words ringing in her ears, suddenly wondering if Danny really hadn't tricked her.

Could he have put on jeans a few times, made a couple of pancakes and cruelly lured her into loving him, all to take her child?

* * *

Danny entered his home, sobbing Sarah on his arm. "Elise!" he called, summoning his nanny.

She strode into the foyer. Tall and sturdily build, Elise wore a brightly colored knit cardigan over a white blouse and gray skirt. She looked like she could have stepped out of a storybook, as the quintessential nanny.

"Oh, my. This little one's got a pair of lungs!" Elise said with a laugh, and reached out to take Sarah from his arms. But as Danny handed the baby to her nanny, he felt odd about giving over Sarah's care so easily. He remembered that Grace had told him that she didn't want to share his nanny because caring for Sarah was part of her quality time.

After shrugging out of his topcoat, he reached for Sarah again. "Tonight, I'll take care of her."

"But—"

"At least until she adjusts to being here."

Elise took a breath, gave him a confused smile and said, "As you wish."

Danny didn't care what she thought. All he cared about was Sarah. He'd thought hiring a nanny would be the perfect way to help ease Sarah into her new life, but seeing Elise with Sarah felt wrong. Sarah was his responsibility. His little girl. His daughter.

Carrying Sarah into the nursery, Danny thought of Grace. How tears had filled her eyes when Sarah had begun to cry. He'd left quickly, not to cause her pain, but to get all three of them accustomed to this every other Friday night ritual. But he'd hurt her.

Again.

It seemed he was always hurting Grace.

Still, with crying Sarah on his arm, it wasn't the time to think about that. He wrestled her out of her jacket, little black shoes, tiny jeans and T-shirt, then rolled her into a pair of pajamas.

She never stopped crying.

He put her on his shoulder and patted her back, as he walked downstairs and to the refrigerator where he extracted one of the bottles Elise had prepared. Sitting on the rocker in the nursery, he fed her the bottle and though she drank greedily, sniffled remnants of her crying jag accompanied her sucking. The second the bottle came out of her mouth, she began to cry again.

"I'm sorry. I know this is hard. I know you miss your mom, but this is the right thing. Trust me."

He paced the floor with her, trying to comfort her, but as he pivoted to make his third swipe across the room, he saw the books beside the rocker. The designer he'd hired to create the yellow and pink, bear-theme room had strategically stationed books on a low table within reach of the rocker. After sitting again, he took one of the books, opened it and began to read.

"Once upon a time, in a kingdom far away, there lived a princess. Her name was—" He paused, then smiled. "Sarah. Sarah bear."

Sarah's crying slowed.

"She was a beautiful child with blond—reddish-brown curls," he amended, matching the description of the little girl in the book to the little girl in his arms. "And blue eyes."

Her crying reduced to sniffles and she blinked, her confused expression taking him back to the first night he'd cared for her alone—the night Grace had been edgy. The memory caused him to smile. He hadn't wanted to be alone with Sarah. Wasn't sure he could handle her. He'd only kept the baby to please Grace.

He took a breath. This time he was caring for Sarah to *protect* Grace. From him. Adding a failed marriage to ignoring her pregnancy and taking her child wouldn't help anything. He had to remember that.

"The princess lived alone with her father, the king. Her mother had died when the princess was a baby and a governess had been hired. Mrs. Pickleberry had a face puckered in a perpetual frown and Sarah would pretend to be ill, rather than spend time with her when the king was out of the palace performing his royal duties. Each time, when Mrs. Pickleberry would leave her room, sufficiently convinced that Sarah should stay in bed for the day, Sarah would crawl into her window seat, her legs tucked beneath her, her thumb in her mouth, watching, alone, for her father to return."

Danny stopped reading. The king didn't have a choice about leaving his daughter in the care of her governess, but Danny had choices. Lots of them. In the argument they'd had the day Grace brought Sarah to him, Grace had asked if it was better for Sarah to be raised by strangers rather than her mother. Still, that

wasn't what was happening here. Yes, Sarah would be
stuck with a governess—uh, nanny—while Danny was
at work, but he wasn't taking Sarah away from her
mother. Not really. Just every other week.

He glanced down. Sarah was asleep.

Thank God. He didn't think he could take any more
of the story's inadvertent accusations. He laid the baby
in her crib and stood for several minutes, just watching Sarah, basking in the joy of being a dad, considering all the things he could do for Sarah, and
convincing himself that while he had Sarah, Grace
could also do so many things, things she otherwise
didn't have time to do.

But the soft smile that had lit his face suddenly died.
Grace might have time to do tons of different things, but
she wouldn't. She would spend every hour he had
custody worrying about Sarah. Not because Danny
wasn't trustworthy, but because she would miss her.
And only because she would miss her. In fact, right now,
Grace was probably crying, or lonely. And he absolutely couldn't stand the thought of it.

He wasn't the kind of man to hurt people. But his reasoning this time went beyond his own image of himself.
He couldn't stand the thought of Grace missing Sarah
because he loved her. The last thing any man wanted to
do was hurt the woman he loved most in this world. And
yet that was what he always did with Grace. He hurt her.
When he'd met her, he was a broken, empty man. She'd
reminded him of life. That Sunday night at the beach
house, she'd given him a glimpse of what they'd have

together if he could open up. When he couldn't, she'd gracefully accepted that he didn't want to see her anymore. But when she'd gotten pregnant, she'd tried one more time. When he rejected her again, she didn't return until she had Sarah. Offering him something he truly didn't deserve: a place in their daughter's life. A place she hadn't snatched away. Even knowing his dark secret, she had faith in him when he had none in himself.

Danny gritted his teeth. He knew the solution to this problem. He knew it as well as he knew his own last name.

In order to save Grace, he had to let go of his guilt. He had to try again. In earnest.

Or he had to take Sarah back to Grace. For good. No more shared custody.

Halfway to the kitchen to make cocoa, Grace heard a knock on her door and peered at her watch. Who would be visiting after nine at night?

Expecting it to be her parents, who were undoubtedly worried about her because this was her first night without Sarah, she turned and headed for the door. When she looked through the peephole and saw Danny holding sleeping Sarah, she jumped back and yanked open the door.

Reaching for Sarah, she said, "What happened? What's wrong?"

He motioned inside her house. "Can we talk?"

Cradling Sarah on her arm, she looked down and

examined every exposed inch of her sleeping baby. Her gaze shooting to Danny, she said, "She's fine?"

He nodded. "Yeah. It's you and I who have the problem. We need to talk."

Grace's heart stopped. She'd nearly had herself convinced that Robbie was right. Danny had tricked her and he had gotten everything he wanted at Grace's expense. All because she'd fallen in love with him.

But he was back, saying they needed to talk, sounding like a man ready to give, rather than take. Still, this time she had to be strong, careful. She couldn't fall victim to the look in his beautiful dark eyes...or the hope in her heart.

She had to be strong.

"Danny, it's late and our lawyers said everything we needed to say—"

"Not mine. He hardly said anything. And there are a few things I need to say. Put Sarah to bed. In *her* bed."

The gentleness of his voice got to her. If nothing else, Grace knew with absolute certainty that Danny loved Sarah. Knowing her lawyer would probably be angry that she talked to Danny without counsel, Grace stepped aside so Danny could enter.

As she turned to walk up the steps with the baby, she saw Danny hesitate in her small entryway.

Remembering he was always more at ease in her home when she gave him something to do, she said, "I was just about to make cocoa. You could go in the kitchen and get mugs."

"Okay."

When she returned downstairs, Grace saw he had only gotten as far as the stools in front of the breakfast counter. Again noting his hesitation, Grace said, "Don't you want cocoa?"

"I'd love some."

He sounded so quiet and so unsteady that Grace didn't know what to say. She set the pan on the stove and poured in milk and cocoa, waiting for him to talk. When he didn't, she lowered the flame on the gas burner and walked to the breakfast bar.

"Did something happen with Sarah?"

"No. She was fine." He caught her gaze. "Why did you do this? Why are you letting me have her every other week?"

She shrugged. "You're Sarah's dad. She loves you. You love her."

He caught her gaze. "And that's it?"

"What else is there?"

"You didn't give Sarah to me to try to force my hand?"

"Force your hand?" She laughed. "Oh, my God, Danny, when have I ever gotten you to do anything? You didn't believe I slept with you because I liked you. You were sure I had an agenda. You didn't believe I was pregnant when I told you. You kicked me out of your office. You were so suspicious of me when I suggested shared custody that *you* insisted on the agreement. If there's one thing I know not to do it's try to force you to do anything."

"You didn't give me Sarah so that I'd be so grateful I'd fall in love with you?"

After a second to recover from the shock of that accusation, she shook her head sadly. He really did believe that people only did nice things when they wanted something from him. "Oh, Danny, I didn't give you time with Sarah to drag you into a relationship with me."

"Really?"

"Yes. I gave you time with Sarah because you're her dad."

"And you want nothing from me."

Grace debated lying to him. She *wanted* them to be a normal family. She wanted him to be the happy, laughing guy who'd made love to her at the beach house. She wanted him to want her. To welcome her into his life with open arms. She wanted a lot, but she didn't expect anything from him. The way she saw their lives unfolding, she would spend most of the time they had together just happy to see him unwind.

But if there was one thing she'd learned about Danny over the past weeks, it was that he valued honesty. So she took a breath and said, "I want a lot. But I'm also a realist. You won't fall in love again until you're ready. Nobody's going to push you."

He slid onto the stool. "I know." Pointing at the stove, he said, "I think your pot's boiling over."

"Eeek!" She spun away from the breakfast bar and ran to the stove, where hot milk bubbled over the sides of her aluminum pot. "Looks like I'll be starting over."

"I think we should both start over."

Not at all sure what he meant by that, Grace poured

out the burned milk and filled the dirty pot with water, her heart pounding at the possibilities. "And how do you propose we start over?"

"The first step is that I have to tell you everything."

She found a second pot, filled it with milk and poured in cocoa, again refusing to hurry him along or push him. This was his show. She would let him do whatever he wanted. She'd *never* misinterpret him again. "So tell me everything."

While she adjusted the gas burner, he said, "Tonight I really thought through the things that had had happened to me in the past several years, and I realized something I'd refused to see before this."

He paused again. Recognizing he might think she wasn't paying attention, Grace said, "And what was that?"

"My marriage to Lydia was over before Cory's accident."

At that Grace turned to face him. "What?"

"Tonight when I was caring for Sarah in my brand-new nursery and thinking about how sad you probably were here alone, I realized that you are very different from Lydia. She and I spent most of our married life fighting. First she didn't want children, then when we had Cory she wanted him enrolled in a school for gifted children in California. We didn't fight over my pushing him into taking over Carson Services. We fought because she kept pushing him away. She didn't want him around."

"Oh."

"I won't say I didn't love her when I married her, but I can now see that we were so different, especially in what we wanted out of life, that we were heading for divorce long before Cory's accident. Tonight, I finally saw that I needed to separate the two. Cory's accident didn't ruin my marriage. Lydia and I had handled that all by ourselves."

"I'm sorry."

He laughed lightly. "You know what? I knew you would be. And I think that's part of why I like you. Why I was drawn to you at the beach house. You really have a sixth sense about people. I saw how you were with Orlando and listened in sometimes on your conversations, and I knew you were somebody special. More than that, though, you respected the same things I did. Especially family and commitments. You and I had the thing Lydia and I lacked. Common beliefs. Sunday night when we were alone, I realized we also had more than our fair share of chemistry." He paused, then said, "But I panicked."

Since Grace couldn't dispute what he said—or add to it—she stayed silent, letting him talk.

"Tonight, rocking Sarah, thinking about you, hating that you had to give up your child, I was angry that life had forced us into this position, but I suddenly realized it wasn't life that forced us here. It was me because I didn't think I could love you without hurting you."

Too afraid to make a hopeful guess about the end of his conclusions, Grace held her breath.

"I guess thinking about my own marriage and Lydia

and Cory while holding Sarah, I finally saw something that made everything fall into place for me."

Grace whispered, "What's that?"

"That if you and I had been married, we would have weathered Cory's death. You might have honestly acknowledged my mistake in grabbing my cell phone, and even acknowledged that I would feel guilty, but you never would have let me take the blame. You and I would have survived. A marriage between us would have survived."

Grace pressed her hand to her chest. "That's quite a compliment."

"You're a very special person. Or maybe the strength of your love is special." He shook his head. "Or maybe you and I together are special. I don't know. I just know that through all this you'd been very patient. But I'm done running."

She smiled. "Thought you didn't run."

"Well, maybe I wasn't running. Maybe I was holding everybody back. Away. But I can't do that anymore."

She took a breath, her hope building, her heart pounding.

"Because I love you. I love you." He repeated, as if saying it seemed so amazing he needed to say it again. "I couldn't stand the thought of you here alone, and though I don't want to hurt you I finally saw that unless I took this step, I would always be hurting you."

Her voice a mere whisper, Grace said, "What step?"

"I want to love you. I want you to marry me."

She would have been content to hear him say he

wanted to try dating. His proposal was so far beyond what she'd been expecting that her breath stuttered in her chest. "What?"

"I love you and I want you to marry me."

Dumbstruck, Grace only stared at him.

"You could say you love me, too."

"I love you, too."

At that Danny laughed. The sound filled the small kitchen.

"And you want to marry me." He took a breath. "Grace, alone with Sarah I realized I had everything I needed and I could have talked myself into accepting only that. But I want you, too. Will you marry me?"

"And I want to marry you!" She made a move to launch herself into his arms, but remembered her cocoa and turned to flip off the burner. By the time she turned back, he was at her side, arms opened, ready for her to walk into them.

He wrapped his arms around her as his mouth met hers. Without a second of hesitation, Grace returned his kiss, opening her mouth when he nudged her to do so. Her heart pounded in her ears as her pulse began to scramble. He loved her. *He loved her and wanted to marry her.* It almost seemed too good to be true.

He pulled away. "Pot's probably boiling over."

"I thought I turned that off." She whirled away from him and saw the cooling pot. "I did turn that off."

"I have a better idea than cocoa anyway."

He pulled her to him and whispered something in her ear that should have made a new mother blush. But she laughed and countered something equally sexy in his ear and he kissed her deeply, reminding her of her thoughts driving up I-64 the Monday they left Virginia Beach. *She'd found Mr. Right.*

She *had* found Mr. Right, and they were about to live happily ever after.

EPILOGUE

RESTING UNDER the shade of a huge oak, on the bench seat of a weathered wooden picnic table, Grace watched Sarah as she played in the sandbox with the children of Grace's cousins. She could also see Danny standing in left field, participating in the married against the singles softball game at the annual McCartney reunion.

The CEO and chairman of the board of Carson Services didn't look out of place in his khaki shorts and T-shirt, as Grace expected he might. It wasn't even odd to see him punching his fist into the worn leather baseball mitt he found in his attic. Everything about this day seemed perfectly normal.

The batter hunkered down, preparing for a pitch thrown so hard Grace barely saw the ball as it sliced through the air toward the batter's box, but her cousin Mark had seen it. His bat connected at just the right time to send the ball sailing through the air, directly at Danny.

With a groan, she slapped her hands over her eyes, but unable to resist, spread her fingers and peeked through. The ball sped toward Danny like a comet.

He yelled, "No worries. I've got it." Punching his fist into his mitt twice before he held it up and the ball smacked into place with a crack.

Whoops of joy erupted from the married team because Danny had made the final out of the game. For the first time in almost twenty years, the married men had beaten the younger, more energetic singles.

Danny received a round of congratulations and praise. He was new blood. Exactly what the family needed. Grace sat a bit taller on the bench seat, glancing at eighteen-month-old Sarah, who happily shoveled sand into the empty bed of a plastic dump truck.

The married team disbursed to brag to their wives about the softball victory. The singles grumbled that Danny was a ringer. Danny jogged over to Grace looking like a man about to receive Olympic gold.

"Did you see that?"

"Yes. You were great."

"I was, wasn't I?"

Grace laughed. "Men." She took a quiet breath and he sat down on the bench seat beside her.

"Are you okay?"

"I'm fine."

"You're sure?"

"I'm sure."

"It's just that the last time you were pregnant you were sick—"

She put her hand over his mouth to shut him up. "For the one-hundred-and-twenty-seven-thousand-two-hundred-and-eighty-fourth time, all pregnancies are dif-

ferent. Yes, I was sick with Sarah. But I'm only a little
bit queasy this time."

She pulled her hand away and he said, "Maybe you
were sick because—"

She put her hand over his mouth again. "I was not
sick because I went through that pregnancy alone.
We've been over this, Danny." Because he was so funny,
she laughed. "A million times."

"Or at least one-hundred-and-twenty-seven-thou-
sand-two-hundred-and-eighty-four."

She laughed again and he glanced around the
property. "This is a beautiful place."

"That's why we have the picnic here every year.
There are no distractions. Just open space, trees for
shade and a brick grill to make burgers and keep our
side dishes warm. So everybody has time to talk, to
catch up with what the family's been doing all year."

"It's great."

"It is great."

"And your family's very nice."

She smiled. "They like you, too."

He took a satisfied breath. "Do you want me to watch
Sarah for a while?"

"No. It's okay. You keep mingling. We're fine."

"But this is your family."

"And I'm mingling. Women mingle more around the
food and the sandbox. At one point or another I'll see
everybody." She grinned. "Besides, this may be your
last day out with people for a while. You should take advantage of it."

"What are you talking about? I have to go to work tomorrow."

"Right." She rolled her eyes with a chuckle. "Tomorrow you're going to be suffering. Every muscle in your body will be screaming. You'll need a hot shower just to be able to put on your suit jacket."

He straightened on the bench seat. "Hey, I will not be sore."

"Yes, you will."

"I am an athlete."

"You push papers for a living and work out at the gym a few nights a week." She caught his gaze, then pressed a quick kiss to his lips. "You are going to be in bed for days."

The idea seemed to please him because he grinned. "Will you stay in bed with me?"

"And let Sarah alone to fend for herself with Pickleberry?" They'd found Elise to be such a stickler for rules that Danny and Grace had nicknamed her after the governess in the storybook.

"Hey, you're the one who said to keep her."

"Only so we wouldn't be tempted to overuse her."

At that Danny laughed. He laughed long and hard and Grace smiled as she studied him. All traces of his guilt were gone. He remembered his son fondly now. He'd even visited the next-door neighbor who had been driving the SUV and they'd come to terms with the tragedy enough that Mrs. Oliver was a regular visitor at their home.

He'd also hired a new vice president and delegated

at least half of his responsibility to him, so they could spend the majority of their summer at the beach house in Virginia Beach. He loved Sarah. He wanted a big family and Grace was happy to oblige. Not to give him heirs, but because he loved her.

Completely. Honestly. And with a passion that hadn't died. Their intense love for each other seemed to grow every day. He had a home and she had a man who would walk to the ends of the earth for her.

Watching her other family members as they mingled and laughed, weaving around the big oak trees, sharing cobbler recipes and tales about their children, Grace suddenly saw that was the way it was meant to be.

That was the lesson she'd learned growing up among people who didn't hesitate to love.

Somewhere out there, there was somebody for everybody.

* * * * *

FROM EXES TO
EXPECTING

LAUREL GREER

To Rob and our Bear and Mouse. A lot of family juggling took place for this book to get written, and I'm immeasurably grateful for the sacrifices made and support given to have my dream come true.
I love you.

Chapter One

Sneaking out the back door is self-preservation, not bad form, right? Biting her lip, Dr. Lauren Dawson glanced at the clock on the wall of the Sutter Creek Medical Clinic's staff lounge. Five-oh-one. Yup, skedaddle time. After working a series of six-day weeks, her body ached for the cushy lounge chair on her lakeside deck. Getting to start her long weekend while the late-May sun still had heat left in it was worth the faux pas of creeping out without saying goodbye. She threw her leather flats into her messenger bag and slid on her flip-flops.

The door to the lounge creaked behind her. Her stomach sank and she stared into her locker, not wanting to turn around. If it was one of the nurses coming to nab her to treat another patient, she'd—

"Lauren. Glad I caught you before you left. Do you have a minute?"

Damn it. The longer she lingered, the higher the

chance of getting asked to cover drop-ins for an extra hour or two. But no way could she slough off a conversation with the man who held the future of her career in his hand. Squeezing her eyes shut for a second, she forced a smile and faced her boss. "Hi, Frank."

The fluorescent lights of the staff lounge yellowed Frank Martin's gunmetal-gray hair as he took a seat on one of the couches arranged into a conversation pit. "Quitting time?"

Lauren nodded and pulled off her lab coat. "Yeah. Andrew's still very understaffed at work, so I'm picking up some slack for him this weekend. He's got his bachelor party, so he's asked me to cover some zip-line tours, and I'm helping his fiancée with some wedding stuff." As the Director of Safety and Risk Management and the head of summer operations for their family's Montana ski resort, her older brother did more than his fair share of boosting their bottom line. Lauren pitched in where she could despite the clinic's tendency to consume her waking hours. Once her summer holidays started in six weeks, she'd be subbing for her brother, letting him get away on his honeymoon. "Pretty sure I won't get a moment to myself for most of the weekend. Though I'm hoping for a few hours to myself tonight. My dock is calling me."

His mouth curved in understanding. "Well, I won't keep you. But I wanted to make sure you got the partnership papers from your lawyer."

Those cursed papers sat on her kitchen table, mocking her every morning as she ate her oatmeal and berries. Mocking her commitment to follow in her mother's footsteps. Dampness bloomed on her palms. She'd wanted to have a practice in her tiny hometown since she was fourteen. Getting to buy in to the clinic her mother had founded was nothing less than her childhood dream. *So why am I having so much trouble putting my signature on the contract?*

She mentally flicked away the doubt and nodded at her boss. "Yeah, but I've run into a glitch getting the funds released from my grandparents' trust. My lawyer's busy arguing with their lawyers." She gripped the strap of her bag and took a centering breath. Ugh, what she'd do to have her vacation starting today. Both the wedding and working for Wild Life Adventures would be a welcome change of scenery. She would get outside for a few weeks and come back to the clinic refreshed and ready to make her plan a reality.

"Did your lawyer indicate how long it would take to fix the problem?" Concern edged Frank's words.

"She wasn't specific, no. I'm sure it'll be dealt with by the time I'm back from my holidays in July."

"That's two months from now."

Swallowing her nerves, she nodded. "It's not affecting the work I can do, though. So I'm hoping the delay isn't a deal breaker."

"No. Nothing you can do about banking complications." He drummed his fingers on the arm of the couch. "I've been waiting for this for a long time, Lauren. Having a Dawson as a partner again is going to fill a void. You'll be a great permanent addition to the clinic."

Permanent.

Normally a calming concept, but Lauren's heart started to thud as if she were sprinting. She inhaled. Her mother had been proud of her calling. And Lauren was nothing if not a mirror of her mother.

She'd almost given up on their dream once. Never again. She could do this. Was meant for it.

Her heartbeat slowed, but the burn in her stomach refused to subside.

One of the nurses poked her head into the lounge. "Dr. Dawson? Can you take one more patient before you leave? Sutures. Exam room two."

Son of a— Keeping her curse from spilling out, Lauren nodded to the nurse. She returned her satchel to her locker and shrugged back into her lab coat. "Count me there."

Frank touched his brow in a playful salute. "We'll talk later, Lauren. See you Tuesday."

"Have a good Memorial Day." Lauren changed back into her flats, straightened her khaki capris and rushed out of the lounge to her patient. Stupid long weekends and the abrasions and lacerations that came along with them. She picked the clipboard out of the Lucite holder and glanced at the patient file.

Her already complaining gut lurched and the font blurred on the page.

No. N-fricking-O.

Feet frozen two feet from the door, out of view from the patient inside, she stared through the door frame. Only the patient's legs were visible, golden-tan skin over defined calf muscles. Muddy biking footprints marked up the white linoleum. A two-inch-thick black tattoo ringed one ankle. At first glance, it looked like a series of interwoven spirals, but she knew closer study would reveal the second and third stanzas of *Do Not Go Gentle Into That Good Night*. Even marred by a fresh, index-card-size scrape, she'd recognize Tavish Fitzgerald's legs anywhere. Difficult not to, given the nights she'd spent sliding her toes along those hard calves while he'd driven her out of her mind with ecstasy.

She leaned against the hallway wall and swallowed. He must be in town for her brother's bachelor party. So much for him not coming home until a day or two before the wedding. The wedding where Lauren would have to once again stare at Tavish across the aisle. But as the maid of honor this time.

Not the bride.

Lauren's brother was marrying Tavish's sister on the Fourth of July weekend, and Lauren was thrilled to be getting a sister-in-law. She just didn't want to have to see her ex-husband in the process.

Telling herself to get a Godzilla-size grip, she stuck the clipboard between her knees and took the time to redo her ponytail. After a quick wipe under her eyes to check for afternoon mascara remnants, she clutched her clipboard between both hands, threw back her shoulders and marched through the doorway.

A millisecond after she met Tavish's gaze, her bravado tumbled into a heap around her feet. He regarded her with a simmering look as he lounged in the patient's chair next to the examination table. His violet-blue irises pierced through her layers of preservation.

Eyes that color were wasted on a man. Ditto his thick, dark eyelashes and the sun-streaked, tawny hair he never bothered to keep tidy. A navy bandanna, rolled to a handwidth and tied around his forehead, kept the windblown strands from falling in his face. He wore a technical shirt and baggy cargo shorts over black Lycra bike shorts. It was enough to make a woman's heart stop.

But no, Lauren's pulse went into overdrive, thumping loud enough she'd have worried he could hear it except she knew was it impossible. Shrinking under his silent observation, she forced herself to snap into medical mode.

"You did a number on your leg," she said.

Shrugging, he shot her a half smile. "An unruly pine."

Judging by the scrape on his left cheek, the rip in the short sleeve of his shirt and the bandage on his arm, the tree reigned victorious. His chart noted that he needed stitches for a laceration already dressed by one of the mountain first-aid attendants, but her hands were shaking so badly she didn't trust herself to pick up a needle quite yet, no matter how quickly she wanted him out the door.

"Tree, one, you, zero?" She forced out the joke.

"Yeah. Blew a tire. Landed in a snowberry bush, thankfully. Could have been worse. But where are our manners? Afternoon, Dr. Dawson." He bit out her last name.

She flinched at the emphasis. Considering she'd once shared his last name and his bed, the use of her professional title seemed overkill. "Seems silly to bother with the formalities with me."

"You're working. I respect that."

"I don't think it matters where we are. I'll always be just Lauren to you." Her voice came out way softer than she'd intended. Fighting the need to get closer to his hard, muscled body, to offer to kiss him better, she broke her gaze from his and methodically counted the eleven parts of the ear illustrated on the poster over his shoulder.

"You're never *just* anything, Lauren."

The rough sincerity in his voice chafed at her still-raw heart. She froze, not able to look at his face, to see whatever emotion accompanied the sweet words. She grabbed a pair of latex gloves from one of the cabinets and pointed at the examination table. "Up on the bed."

By the quirk of his mouth, the potential double entendre wasn't lost on him. Mercifully, he left it alone and lay down as asked, stretching out his lean frame and propping his head with his good hand.

Pulling her stool alongside him, she positioned his injured forearm for the best access. With tentative fingers, she peeled back the rectangle of gauze and recognized her brother's handiwork in the immaculate row of butterfly strips holding together the finger-length gash. The sterile material of her gloves did nothing to block the effect of touching Tavish. The moment her fingertips brushed his arm, the heat there threatened to melt the glove to her hand.

Ignoring her pathetic physical response, she continued undoing the bandaging. "Your sister's going to smack you for getting scraped up so close to her big day. You should've held off on bodily harm until after the wedding."

Lifting his other hand across his face to touch his abraded cheek, he tilted his lips in a sheepish smile. "I wanted to try a few of the new expert trails in the biking complex. Drew took me."

"You took my brother on the double blacks? You're as bad an influence on him as you were on me." Her chest panged with immediate regret. Way to bring up how he'd made her want to veer so sharply from her life plan. To cover up her folly, she blurted, "At least he wasn't idiotic enough to tackle a tree."

Something crackled behind Tavish's eyes. Probably not the medical tape tugging on the golden hairs of his arm, either.

"You really want to get into this, Laur?" His voice held threads of warning twined with wariness.

No, but probably best to hash things out before the wedding. "We're due."

"I'd rather wait until you aren't in arm's reach of a needle." He glanced at the syringe on the rolling tray, gritting his teeth as she fussed with his laceration.

"Fine with me." She took a breath and shoved the curious blend of shame, wanting and need for escape to the back of her mind. Only in rare situations would she choose suturing over a conversation. Wouldn't be the first time Tavish had her doing something that went against instinct, though. "You're going to need quite a few stitches to make sure this heals properly. The edges are snagged pretty badly."

"Bled like a scalp wound, but doesn't really hurt."

She rolled her eyes and readied the syringe. "You're such a guy."

"You used to like that about me," he said under his breath.

"Used to." She draped the wound and closed her eyes for a second, just long enough to push away the nausea that rippled whenever she had to pierce someone's skin. Frustration flared over the surging acid. She'd learned to control her gag reflex back in the first month of medical school. But the minute her lawyer had given her the partnership papers to sign, it had come back with a vengeance.

Clenching her hands into fists, she breathed until her ears stopped buzzing and she was no longer on the verge of losing the BLT she'd had for lunch. Then she grabbed the needle.

Tavish sucked in a breath and looked away as Lauren worked to numb the area. His brief display of nerves made her hand itch to put down the needle and caress his cheek. She ignored the ridiculous impulse and finished her task.

"Let that set. I'll be back in five."

"Not going to stick around and chat?"

"I have things to do."

His lips twitched with saddened amusement. "Don't let me get in your way."

Half standing, she settled back onto her stool, meeting the challenge in his voice. "You're not in my way."

"That's not the honest Lauren Dawson I know."

She stared at him, trying to make her expression as unreadable as possible. "Fine. It's weird having you in town. And if you're insisting on small talk, where've you been since you were last home? When was that, March?" Not like she'd counted the fifty-seven days. Not purposefully, anyway.

Tavish's expression flattened into impatience. "Here and there. New Orleans for a few weeks. Italy. Brazil."

"You're definitely living your dream." If only he'd been that committed to her. To them.

"Isn't that the point?"

"Obviously. I'm doing the same."

"Sure about that?"

"Even more than when I signed our divorce papers." Though she'd had as much trouble scrawling her signature on that as with the documents for the clinic partnership. "I saw your Peru spread in *Traveler* last week."

"Make you want to go there?"

She shook her head. "Not hardly."

"Right." A visible flicker of defeat made his mouth twitch. "It wouldn't."

"I'm happy here, Tavish." *Damn it.* He'd made her defend her choices one too many times.

"Yeah, now you are. A year ago you were ready to come see the Great Barrier Reef with me."

The truth of that smacked her in the face. Tears welled at the reminder of how her grandparents' accident had turned her family upside down, had forced her to admit how her marriage would never work. Blinking away the moisture, she probed the edges of his wound. "This hurt?"

Not meeting her eyes, he shook his head.

She flushed the gash, biting her lip as saline-thinned blood trickled under the drape. *Hold it together, Lauren.*

"I traveled enough as a kid. I'm good for life." Why couldn't he understand that being rooted in Sutter Creek didn't stifle her as it did him? Besides, she had explored the globe in the past six months—via gorgeous, full-color magazine spreads. Vicarious living courtesy of Tavish himself. She'd bought every issue featuring his work.

The wearied lines in his forehead told her he hadn't changed his opinion about her choices, but he didn't bother arguing further.

"Breathe," she soothed, not liking the strain marking his stubbled jaw. "This won't take long." Thankful for something to focus on aside from the reasons her marriage had failed, she began to suture his wound.

"Getting stitched feels so weird. You probably live for this, though."

Ha, right. She'd be happy if she never saw blood again. A necessary evil, though, in getting where she wanted to be career-wise. "Don't look if it makes you sick."

"I can't not."

"Ah. You're one of those. Common enough."

"Glutton for gore, I guess."

"Checking off all the guy-stereotype boxes today."

Conversation died as she continued her stitches, a neat row of fifteen. Once finished, she dressed the wound and examined his scrapes. "I'm surprised my brother didn't cover up your other abrasions. He's the most anal medic on the mountain."

"I told him not to. I've had road rash so many times, it's second nature."

"It's your face."

He sent her a wry smile. "Worried I'll wreck my good looks?"

More like worried his good looks would wreck her sanity.

She shook her head. "We need to give each other space."

"I'll do my best to stay out of your hair until I leave town. I'm taking off on Sunday—I have jobs lined up until the wedding."

She'd have to learn to pretend ambivalence in his presence by then. She wouldn't let their ruined marriage impact Mackenzie and Andrew's ceremony. "How long are you going to be in town that weekend?"

"Five days." The blank look on Tavish's face gave away nothing. "But, look, Sutter Creek's not that small, right? We won't be in each other's pockets."

Ugh. Sutter Creek was exactly that small. But she appreciated his optimism. "You haven't spent that much time at home since college."

"I know. But I have to, for Mackenzie's sake. You're okay with it, right?"

"It's been a year." Last May, embarrassed by her failure, she'd hidden her short marriage and speedy divorce from her family. The soul-sucking lie of omission ate at her daily. She never wanted to lie to a person she cared about again. And as much as she didn't want to, she more than cared about Tavish.

He stared at her, eyes stark with honesty. His cheek flinched. "This still gets to me."

So not admitting I agree with that one. Lauren brushed a thumb across his jaw, under the abraded skin. She wished she could chalk up the pang of concern to her Hippocratic Oath. But she knew better. "You winced. I'll get you a cold pack for your face."

Giving a one-shoulder shrug, he tossed her a smile. A delicious smile. One he'd used mercilessly when he'd spent hours with his mouth on her breasts. On her stomach. Everywhere. "Don't worry about me, sweetheart."

The careless endearment hung in the air long after he left the room.

She propped her elbows on the table and took the weight of her head in her hands. She could feel the imprint of his words on her skin.

Don't worry about me...

That was the problem with Tavish Fitzgerald. She did worry about him—not for his sake, but for hers.

...sweetheart.

Knowing he'd be in Sutter Creek for the next couple of days, her muscles twitched with a sudden, and long-absent, urge to run away from home.

The last thing Tavish felt like doing after locking horns with the living reminder of his divorce was to go to a bachelor party to celebrate someone else's impending bliss. And offering to pick up the happy groom from the Sutter Mountain base lodge did nothing to help clear his mind of the woman he'd never been able to love like she deserved. The minute he set foot into the rubber-floored hallway next to the ski school, he was thrown back to the summer he'd graduated high school. How many times had he sneaked kisses with Lauren in the staff lounge? He'd worked for Sutter Mountain Resort in his junior and senior years, teaching skiing in the winter and rock climbing in the summer. The work had been awesome. So had finding excuses to flirt with Lauren up at reception.

And if he was going to have even half a chance of enjoying Drew's bachelor party tonight, he needed to get his mind off his high school girlfriend. His wife.

Ex-wife.

Trudging down the hall, he jammed his hands into the

pockets of his jeans. The movement tugged on his bandaged forearm, making him wince. Making him think of Lauren again, of her struggle to stay unresponsive while she'd sutured his cut. Her cheeks had gone all pink and... *Stop it.* She'd been holding back distaste, not desire. He shoved open the door to the ski resort's safety department headquarters. "Greetings."

"Hey." Drew, alone in the room, sat at his desk with his fingers in his dark brown hair. "Get stitched up?"

"Yeah." He rolled his shoulder, hissing at the soreness caused by his dismount into the shrubbery. "Your sister did her level best to chastise me—us—for our stupidity."

"Not surprising. Have a seat."

"Uh, where?" Tavish blinked in surprise at the disastrous state of the office. Outdoor equipment and first-aid supplies covered every surface in the place. During the winter, the office served as the headquarters for Sutter Mountain Resort's safety department. In the summer, it was the nerve center for Wild Life Adventures—or WiLA, as the staff nicknamed it—which offered everything from zip-line tours to rafting adventures. Drew and Mackenzie were damn proud of Sutter Mountain's success. Even though it was one of the smaller resort towns in Montana, they'd been operating at capacity for the last five years. And his friend would be run over by the paraphernalia involved in all that success if he didn't find a minion to organize his crap quick. "Tough to find office lackeys these days?"

"With both Zach and Mackenzie out of the rotation I had to promote my lackeys," Drew grumbled.

"Raw deal. Still, no way should you still be working at seven on a Friday. We should get going. There's a line of shots on the bar at the Loose Moose with your name on it."

"I need another ten minutes."

"All right. It's your party. Guess we'll be fashionably late." Tavish eased his way past a stack of paddles leaning against a shelf and threw himself into the chair behind the other desk. He linked his hands behind his head and leaned back in the cushy leather seat, propping his booted feet on the corner of the desk. The seat springs complained with a metallic squawk.

The complaint from Drew was a hell of a lot more colorful. He yanked off his reading glasses and tossed them onto a stack of invoices. His eyes lit a livid blue. Put Lauren and her brother side by side and he'd barely be able to recognize them as siblings. Lauren, with her blond hair and hazel eyes, resembled their late mother. But temperwise, the Dawson siblings shared a hair trigger.

"Quit it." Drew spat the words out.

"What, this?" He leaned back again, eliciting one more metal-on-metal grind from his chair for emphasis. He shot his friend a cocky grin. "Invest in some WD-40. Problem solved."

"Funny, lubricating the chairs hasn't been a priority." He waved a hand around the office. "We're so short-staffed I barely have time to sleep. I need to find a replacement for Zach or else I'm going to lose it."

"Shouldn't you have replaced him months ago?" Drew's assistant had been injured in a brutal ski accident during spring takedown and had been off since. Add in Tavish's sister being almost seven months pregnant, and Drew was short two of his most experienced guides.

"I *thought* I'd be able to cover for him. Once Mackenzie started showing, she pretty much took over as my assistant in Zach's stead. But he had a setback with his rehab. He won't be back to work until well after the wedding. And without him—or someone to work in his place—Mackenzie and I won't be able to go on our honeymoon." Drew pressed his fingers into his temples.

"Jeez. Getting married makes you overdramatic."

The other man glared before turning back to his computer. "You offering to step in?"

Tavish snorted.

"Then shut it. I'm just emailing a few buddies in Colorado who might be able to help me out. Then we can go."

Him, work in Sutter Creek? *Ha. Right.* Tavish was about as capable of that as his father had been. Even if he didn't have plans to hop on a plane to Alaska on Monday—which he did—there would be no way he could cover for Zach once Andrew and Mackenzie were out of town. Being in Sutter Creek had always made him itchy to leave. Adding his divorce to the mix made that nagging itch intolerable.

But I have a few weeks off after the wedding. And Drew's in quite the bind.

Not wanting to look too closely at the strain lines on his friend's face, he stared at the ceiling and tapped his fingers against the arms of the chair. It would be super crappy if his sister couldn't go on her honeymoon. She'd been talking about the two-week retreat to a nearby spa resort for months. The baby was due to arrive at the end of the summer, meaning it would be a long while before Mackenzie and Drew could get away again.

Tavish couldn't imagine holing up in Sutter Creek with a kid and a wife. When he and Lauren had married last year, it had been because she'd decided to leave Sutter Creek behind, to split time between his assignments and her volunteering internationally. He just wasn't built to stay in one place for long.

Two weeks, though. That would be a heck of a present for Mackenzie. Better than the set of wedding portraits he'd planned on taking for her. Ignoring his conscience as it chomped a hole in his stomach lining, Tavish picked up a pencil to doodle on a piece of scrap paper. "What kind of work?"

"Supervising sites, occasional guiding. Assistant crap."

"Maybe I could help out." He'd have to avoid Lauren, but that wouldn't be hard. She was married to her job at the clinic.

"Uh…you're not the most reliable. No offense."

Tavish bristled. Knowing he was genetically incapable of sticking around Sutter Creek for any length of time was one thing. Having his best friend confirm it was another. "No, man, I think it would work. I'll leave Monday to hang out with the polar bears, then come back for your wedding, hit on the bridesmaids—"

"Hey! My sisters are the bridesmaids."

"Right. Sorry. Scratch that. Still, I'll pitch in here and be gone the minute you're back."

Drew didn't need to worry about his sisters' honor when it came to Tavish. Given Tavish's relationship with Lauren, he'd never seen Cadence, the baby of the family, as eligible. And Lauren? Well, tried and failed there.

Seeing her today had made his brain spin, a clicking whir not unlike the ancient slide projector of his grandmother's that he credited with getting him hooked on photography. Except instead of pictures of his mother being schlepped across the country in her family's old woody station wagon, the images that flashed across his brain starred Lauren's creamy skin against white hotel sheets and the lights of the Las Vegas Strip glinting off the gold band on her left hand. A gold band Drew knew nothing about. Tavish had promised to keep that secret, even though hiding something so monumental from his best friend made him feel like a pile of bear crap.

And when he'd promised secrecy to Lauren, he'd also made a promise to himself—that he'd stop thinking about his ring on that gorgeous hand that somehow knew just the right way to grip him.

More than that—she had a total grip on his heart.

Helping out Mackenzie and Drew ran the risk of having to fight those thoughts from surfacing daily. Hourly. But what kind of brother would he be if he didn't facilitate a final kid-free trip for his sister?

"I can't let Mackenzie give up her honeymoon. She's already had to compromise by rushing the wedding. Thanks to your not having paid attention during tenth-grade sex-ed," Tavish added lightly.

A crumpled-paper ball bounced off his head.

"Asshole. But you're serious about filling in, aren't you?" Drew asked.

He nodded, curving up one side of his mouth in his own disbelief. "It's been a while since I've been able to help Mackenzie."

"It's been a while since you've been willing to help her, you mean."

Ouch. The accusation reverberated in his chest. He rubbed at the resulting ache. "Guess I can't argue with that."

Drew blew out a breath. "Add on the few days you'd be here before the wedding and you'd have to be in town for over two weeks. You sure about that?"

Tavish picked up a hunk of shale that served as a paperweight and passed it back and forth between his hands. "Thanks for the math lesson, but I know what I'm offering."

"Do you still have your EMT cert?"

"Yeah. I'm not stupid enough to enter war zones without knowing what to do in an emergency," he said. "Warning—this offer will self-destruct in five seconds unless you accept it."

Drew tugged at the collar of his polo shirt. "Okay, then. I'll fill Lauren in on the plan tomorrow. She'll be relieved, to say the least."

Every cell in Tavish's body froze. "Huh?"

"Well, you'll be replacing Zach, but Lauren's replacing me. Looking forward to it, or so she says. So you'll be helping her out."

Clenching his fist around the rock, he resisted the impulse to hurl it through the glass pane of the hallway door. Working with Lauren would kill him. She'd consider his involvement the antithesis of help. And he couldn't back out of the commitment now. If he did, Drew would ask questions.

Lauren's inevitable freak-out when her brother informed her would also result in raised eyebrows. Better to avoid any possibility of suspicion. "She and I should start communicating about how I'm going to best support her while you're gone, so let me tell her."

Drew shrugged. "Whatever. I'm just happy that Mackenzie doesn't have to go on our honeymoon without me." His smile turned wicked. "Two weeks of being alone."

"Dude. Sister."

"Dude," his friend mocked. "You have to know what you're facilitating."

"I know you have to shut up about it."

Mackenzie better enjoy her holiday. Because by making the most important woman in his life happy, he'd be making the woman who should have owned that title miserable.

Chapter Two

Lauren woke up on Saturday morning and reveled in not having set an alarm. Clear sky glowed blue through the skylights in her loft bedroom, promising a cloudless morning. And she planned to enjoy her three days of freedom. Freedom from blood, freedom from needles. She wasn't free from her contract, but at least with the financial glitches she could drag her heels a little longer before signing in triplicate. And her 10:00 a.m. date to help Mackenzie make chair decorations and centerpieces all but guaranteed she'd be able to steer clear of Tavish. No way tulle pew bows and glass vase arrangements would capture his interest. He barely stayed still long enough to snap pictures on the ultra-fancy camera habitually slung on his shoulder.

He was happy enough to be still when we were snuggling in bed together.

Swallowing the lump that formed in her throat, she

shot out from the covers. Her plush featherbed and Egyptian cotton sheets felt way too much like the bed they'd shared during their honeymoon in Las Vegas. She needed to clear her Tavish-and-work-filled brain with some fresh air before she headed into town to meet Mackenzie. Throwing on a sports bra, thin jacket and cropped leggings, she jogged downstairs.

Wanting her space to reflect the outdoors, she'd decorated the spacious, cathedral-ceilinged main floor in soft moss and earth tones to complement the green visible through the expansive panes of glass at the front and rear.

She loved it.

Never wanted to leave.

Her gaze landed on the thick manila folder on her reclaimed-barnwood dining table. Damn. *Usually* never wanted to leave. But the house was full of specters this morning. She'd fled the enchanting reminders of nights tangled in Tavish, only to run headlong into her work anxiety. She needed to get away from that contract before it sprouted legs and chased her around the butcher-block island.

Yoga on the dock. Yes. An excuse to leave the house without feeling like a total chicken.

Crisp forest air pricked her sinuses as she opened the glass French doors and toted her yoga mat down the stairs to the long wooden raft. The sun had risen far enough above the lush pines on the opposite bank to lend a hint of warmth to the light breeze. She sat cross-legged on her mat and stared at the ripples marring the surface of the water.

Living out on Moosehorn Lake, a twenty-minute drive from the town center, gave her enough distance not to feel truly pathetic about the double knots keeping her tied to home. She was close enough to take care of her dad and her sister, and to help Mackenzie and Andrew once the baby arrived, but far enough away she wasn't living in their pockets.

She was independent. Owned a stunning, green-roofed log house on a pristine chunk of waterfront. Had a meaningful job that connected her to her mom. So what if she chose to be a homebody, to put her family first? Just because her chosen lifestyle was the polar opposite of Tavish's didn't make it any less valid.

Though it does mean we shouldn't have exchanged rings...

And shouldn't have made promises neither of them was capable of keeping.

She was stretching into downward dog when the roar of a ski boat broke through her meditative breathing. Teenagers, probably. Her nearest neighbor, the quintessential get-off-my-lawn sort, would be pissed off to have boat noise before eight.

A quick glance west corrected her assumption of the age of the perpetrators. She immediately recognized not only the stripe down the side of the sleek vessel barreling in her direction, but the passengers within it.

Not teenagers.

Clearly the groom had escaped any serious abuse at the bachelor party if he was on the lake at this hour. The early-morning sun silhouetted her brother's broad shoulders as he steered from his perch on the top of his seat. Mackenzie's red ponytail blew in the wind from her position in the bow seat, facing backward as the spotter. Cadie snuggled in the passenger seat across from Andrew, the hood of her zippered sweatshirt pulled up.

Lauren didn't need to look to know who they were towing.

Every muscle stood out on Tavish's wetsuit-clad body

as he tore up the water behind the boat, creating an incandescent rooster tail taller than his six-foot frame.

So much for steering clear of him.

All four of them waved as they passed Lauren, seemingly headed for the slalom course a few hundred yards east of her dock.

Giving up on yoga and ready for any entertainment that could distract her from the little voice in her heart that said things she didn't want to hear, she pulled her knees up to her chest.

Her brother aimed his boat through the two white marker balls. She shadowed her eyes and reluctantly admired Tavish as he passed through the course, creating an S pattern as he cut around the balls positioned on alternate sides of the center guides.

She'd have accused him of showing off, but he had perfect right to do so. Tavish Fitzgerald carved up the water like a four-star chef did a Christmas turkey.

Something hot and needy, something she didn't want to acknowledge, pulled at her core and made her skin tingle. She rubbed at the goose bumps on her arms and tried to focus on his skill rather than his amazing body.

After Tavish successfully rounded all six obstacles, Andrew slowed the boat and Tavish sank into the water. Cadie unhooked the tow rope and reattached it at a shorter length, and Andrew kicked the boat up to a roar once again.

Tavish didn't look as competent with less rope to deal with, bailing hard after two passes. Lauren's breath caught in her throat until she heard his laugh echo on the water. Andrew didn't waste any time getting Tavish back up and heading in the direction of her dock.

She cursed her brother's efficiency. Tavish in a wet-suit five hundred yards out had heated her to the point of needing to jump in the chilly lake. Said man, plus said wetsuit, but minus four-hundred and ninety-nine yards might get her on the evening news for proving spontaneous combustion wasn't a myth.

The boat ripped by, and he let go of the rope. He was nice enough not to spray her. As a teenager, he'd been able to drench the entire public dock without getting his hair wet. She imagined he hadn't lost that talent. Then again, had he sprayed her, it might have saved her a load of embarrassment by killing the flush she knew had crept up her cheeks. He knew how to read her. Would know what her pink face meant.

Lauren bent down at the edge of the dock to catch his ski and shook her head in disbelief. "The lake's freezing and the sun is barely up."

"I don't see any ice." With a powerful stroke, he pushed his ski toward her. It skimmed into her waiting hands.

He climbed up the ladder just as she lifted the ski out of the lake, bringing her gaze within inches of the pull of his violet eyes.

She straightened, breaking away from the hypnotizing effect he had on her brain. "You're not supposed to get stitches wet. Plus, the strain could tear them."

"Drew and I made a waterproof dressing."

"And tearing?"

He grinned cockily. "I'm a risk taker."

They were interrupted by the rumbling of the boat as Andrew maneuvered it up to the dock and cut the engine. He turned down the dial on the stereo, lowering the volume on the country song blasting out of the speakers by half.

She smiled at her brother, then shook her head at Tavish. "You're a dumbass."

Tavish laughed and scrubbed the water from his hair. A few chilly droplets landed on Lauren's cheeks. She was surprised they didn't evaporate on contact.

"Nice welcome there, Laur." Andrew raised a teasing eyebrow as he shoved up his sunglasses.

"One of the many services I provide." Lauren grinned. Mackenzie tossed her the bow rope and she fastened the length around one of the cleats.

"We figured you wouldn't be busy," Mackenzie said as Andrew hopped out of the boat and proceeded to offer both his hands to help her to the dock. "We can hold off on the pew bows for an hour or two. Garnet's covering for Andrew this morning."

An hour or two. Doable. Right?

But Lauren had been wrong about Tavish one too many times to believe her own bravado.

Smiling stiffly at her siblings, she tried to ignore her ex-husband as he peeled off his wetsuit.

She failed miserably. There were things a girl could forget in her life. Tavish's ripped abdominals, marred only by a faded appendectomy scar, didn't qualify. But they didn't look exactly the same as they had the last time she'd seen him shirtless—a tattoo wrapped his torso under his left arm, a watercolor nature scene bleeding out of a bold diamond-shaped frame. The bottom of the frame dipped below the waistband of his navy-and-white surfing shorts. The scene looked familiar, but she couldn't place it. She fought the urge to reach out and trace the outline from mountain peak to stream.

Admiring Tavish's taut stomach, another urge built deep in Lauren's belly.

She fought that, too.

Mackenzie tossed him a towel, and he dried the water

droplets clinging to the butterscotch-colored hair sprinkled on his well-formed chest.

Lauren jerked her gaze away. "Cadie, is Ben with Dad?" she asked, referring to her sister's baby son.

Her sister nodded. "They headed off to see some of the new horses at Auntie Georgie's ranch for the day." Doting on Ben became a downright family competition at times. Parenting solo had been that much harder given Cadie had been recently widowed when Ben was born, so everyone pitched in when they could. "We brought chocolate croissants, Laur. Thought we'd have a bite to eat and then do some more skiing."

Accompanied by Tavish's perfectly formed pecs. Great. Drawing from the same well of determination as when she dealt with bodily fluids at the clinic, she forced her lips into a grin and reached for the box of pastries. "I'll take these up to the patio table and go put on a pot of coffee. Want me to boil some water for herbal tea, Kenz?"

"Please," Mackenzie replied, eyes slightly narrowed. She'd glanced between Tavish and Lauren more than once since getting out of the boat.

Lauren beat a hasty retreat to her kitchen. She had to do a better job of hiding her reactions to Tavish over breakfast.

For the next twenty minutes she sipped her coffee, munched on a croissant and participated in small talk. She even did a decent job of keeping her eyes on her food and off the way Tavish's arms bulged under his T-shirt.

Setting down his empty coffee cup with emphasis, Andrew looked at her with a cheeky smile. "You going to try to beat my slalom-course record today, Laur?"

"I just may." She grinned back, feeling in her element for the first time since Tavish showed up for stitches yesterday. Skiing, she could do. She ran into her house to grab her wetsuit and ski, early hour and ex-husbands be damned.

When she returned, Cadie and Mackenzie had taken up residence in the pair of cushioned lounge chairs on the dock. Her brother sat sideways in the driver's seat of his boat, sandals propped on the passenger's dashboard. Tavish straddled the port-side gunwale, one bare foot in the boat and one on the dock. All long limbs and straining T-shirt and way too delicious.

As Lauren strolled down the gangplank with her ski in one hand and her life jacket in the other, she caught him watching her. His throat bobbed. Yeah, she knew she looked good in her wetsuit. The neoprene enhanced each one of her curves. A thrill zipped through her body that he'd noticed.

"I'm up next," she announced. "I want to see what my new ski can do."

"I think it's more the skier than the ski, Laur." Tavish raked a hand through his hair. Sunlight reflected off the twisted gold-and-silver links of a bracelet on his left wrist. "When was the last time you went out?"

"Last weekend." She walked to the end of the dock, watching him with a confident eye as she sprayed lubricant in the bindings and slid her feet in.

"I don't remember you being that into waterskiing," he said, sounding puzzled.

She mimicked the cocky grin he'd sent her way when he'd skied up to the dock. "That's what happens when you stay away—people change. And learn how to trounce you on the slalom course." She sat on the edge of the dock, both feet secure in midcalf-high boots, and held her hand out for the tow rope.

"You want this length?" Tavish's eyes widened. The

rope was still the length he'd last used—one requiring a good deal of skill.

"For now. I'll use it as a warm-up."

He guffawed. "A warm-up. Right."

"Yeah. Right." She left no room for misunderstanding in her voice.

"Okay." He didn't sound at all convinced as he tossed her the rope and sat on the passenger side of the boat with his feet resting on the carpeted engine cover.

Andrew turned to Tavish. "Ten bucks says you eat your words."

Tavish snorted. "Done."

Within a minute they roared away from the dock. Lauren channeled her frustration over Tavish's doubt into cutting back and forth across the wake until they entered the slalom course. Then all thoughts of her ex-husband disappeared as she focused on leaning against the rope, flying back and forth. Releasing her outside arm as she rounded each ball, then pulling the rope in tight to her hip as she turned in the other direction, she did her best to send up a cascade of water twice the size of Tavish's.

As she cut around the third ball of six, she let out a whoop—she'd beaten Tavish's performance. *Ha*. Her competitive streak hadn't kicked in this strong in a while. She'd blame him for that, too. He was already at fault for stealing away the peace of her morning; what was one more charge?

Successfully reaching the end of the course, Lauren held up a palm in a stop signal. Andrew slowed the boat to an idle, and she sank into the water.

"Take the rope in, Tavish," she called.

"Seriously?" His voice lifted in surprise. "Twenty-eight feet off is damn tough."

"And I'm damn good." Satisfaction spread through her

at being able to bring the glow of amazement into Tavish's eyes. "Change the rope. And hurry up. Pretty sure I can feel ice crystals in my capillaries."

"Don't get testy. I just didn't know you were trying to go pro." Tavish unhooked the rope and refastened it, six feet shorter.

"I beat you. Now I need to do the same for Andrew." Lauren took a breath and gripped the rope handle. She'd have to stretch out parallel to the water to get around any of the balls—her five feet and one scant inch worked against her at this point.

"Ready, Lauren?" Andrew called.

"Hit it." Lauren tucked and let the boat pull her out of the water.

She quickly adjusted to the short rope. The heat of temper buzzed in her muscles as she stretched out toward the first ball. Releasing the handle with one hand, she cut around the obstacle. Inches from the surface of the lake, she somehow managed to pull herself up with enough time to repeat the feat on the other side. Her arms and quads screamed at her. She forced her body to submit one last time but that was it. Muscles totally gassed, she ripped back toward the middle of the wake where she stayed instead of trying for the remaining balls. That tied her brother's personal best—she'd beat him by the end of the summer. And surpassing Tavish tasted too sweet to fuss about Andrew's record. Tapping her head with the palm of her hand to signal she wanted to head home, she made lazy passes all the way back to the dock.

Cadie and Mackenzie clapped loudly as she let go of the rope and sank into the water. She shimmied out of her ski and propelled it toward Cadie, who waited for it on the dock. "My turn!" her sister announced, getting ready to enter the water.

Tavish climbed out of the boat, and Mackenzie took his place as spotter, and then Andrew gunned the engine once more.

Lauren busied herself drying off and slipping back into her yoga pants, not happy to be left alone with her ex-husband, who stood by the ladder. With his back to her and his arms crossed, she could only guess that he was feeling the same. But she wasn't in a hurry to find out if she was right on that. The out-in-the-wide-open dock smothered like a musty closet.

By the time she acknowledged him with a quiet "Pretty sure you owe Andrew ten bucks," the boat was at the far end of the lake.

Sitting on one of the lounge chairs, he stretched out his long legs. He linked his fingers behind his head and fixed her with an inquisitive look. "You trying to prove something out there?"

"Maybe." She sat down on the other deck chair and snuggled against the backrest. "Guess I wanted to remind you that just because I'm a homebody doesn't mean I'm boring."

He stared at her for a few seconds, shaking his head. "Pixie, I haven't had a boring moment with you once."

Pixie? Oh, God. He'd started calling her that back in high school once he'd officially surpassed her by a full foot. It had made her laugh then, so she'd put up with it. After she broke up with him—college plus distance did not mix—he'd stopped using the endearment. Until he and Andrew had crashed her friends-only trip to Vegas to celebrate her finishing her residency. He'd confessed to still loving her, to wanting to make it work. And she'd loved him enough to try to compromise. Once they'd exchanged vows, he'd added "Pixie" back into his lexicon.

Usually when he was trying to get her out of her clothes.

Then again, "I love you" had worked like a charm, too. But it had only taken a couple of weeks to learn no compromise was enough to keep that love alive.

He pressed his lips together and looked away. Was he as tortured by the memory as she? He deserved to be, damn it.

"Quite the place you found," he ground out.

Glancing up at the sparkling glass and stained logs, Lauren smiled. "I bought it in the fall."

His eyes turned serious. "I'm surprised you're this far out of town, though. Given how you insisted you wanted to stay close to your dad and Cadie."

"Just because I want to be close to them doesn't mean I need to live next door." Glaring at him, she pressed her water-chilled hands against her too-hot cheeks.

He got a near-apologetic look on his face. "Or maybe they don't need you as much as you claim they do."

The heat in her face spread down her neck, spiraled into her belly and legs. She dropped her hands, clenched her fingers. "I'm less than a half hour away. That's pretty fricking close."

"And if we'd been somewhere else and they'd needed you, you could have—" He sighed. "Never mind. I needed to talk to you about—"

"We've done enough talking."

"I—" He shifted his gaze to the end of the lake, where the boat had turned around. The hum of the engine reached a crescendo as it approached. "I guess it can wait. So, you were pretty impressive to watch out there."

She wanted to insult his own performance to regain a fighting position in their spar, but couldn't, not when any insult would be a lie. "You, too," she admitted.

His expression flickered with amusement. "Was that so hard?"

"No." Some lies were worth the guilt. She pivoted, feeling stronger facing him head-on, and rubbed her hands together to try to increase the blood flow to her ice-cold fingertips. Sometimes she could forget, could go back to when she was seventeen and he was eighteen and they had all summer to flirt and gibe. Other times, the pain of his desertion—and the knowledge she was equally to blame as he was—hurt so badly she expected to spit up blood.

He leaned forward and took her hands in his. The warmth of his touch immediately seeped into her skin. "I didn't think we'd end up like this. I thought we'd move on."

A solid rush of frustration erupted in her chest. "How am I supposed to move on when you keep poking at me, trying to make it sound like it was all my fault we couldn't make this work?"

He sat, mouth open, gripping her hands so she couldn't get away. She pulled, but he hung on.

"Let go, Tavish. We failed at being together. And I've been lying to my family about it for a year. Two transgressions I don't take lightly."

He met her challenge with a gaze that bit straight through to her core. His grip on her fingers changed from a utilitarian warming rub to a more sensual press. "It's not something either of us should take lightly. And had you been willing to tell our families about what happened in Vegas, you might not be so damn stuck."

"I am not stuck." *And he's not going to believe me unless I stop shouting.* She lowered her volume. "What would it say about me if I didn't feel bad for lying to my family?"

"They didn't need to know. That's what you said, anyway." He traced his fingers against the backs of her hands. His touch felt too gentle, too caring, coming from someone incapable of a functional relationship. Lifting one of her hands to his lips, he kissed her fingertips, setting them off like sparklers.

"I don't need you to validate my guilt, Tavish," she snapped. Not only might their siblings be watching from the boat, but his lips plus her skin still equaled electric currents—both problems with potentially disastrous outcomes. Yanking her hands away, she stood. "I'm going to go get more coffee."

By the time she climbed the stairs to her house and entered her kitchen, all her self-preservation had drained from her like a trail of gasoline from the dock to the house, ready to ignite and burn to cinders. She poured herself a fresh mug of coffee but didn't drink, just let the heat from the pottery leach into her hands. It was a safer heat than Tavish's.

Her life felt like an "Oh, God, Dad's coming over in ten minutes and the house is filthy" moment. But she had carefully stuffed her crap into closets so no one would realize how messy she was. She'd been Cadie's sounding board since Sam died, and her father's since her grandparents' fatal car accident last May. Last May when she'd been secretly standing at an altar with Tavish. Goddamn it. Sure, Andrew was a rock, but he had Mackenzie and the baby to worry about, and couldn't always be there for Cadie and their father like Lauren could.

Somehow, she needed to construct a Rocky Mountain-size barricade between herself and her ex-husband. Gripping the kitchen counter, she stared through the window as the boat returned to the dock and everyone piled out. She relaxed at the prospect of no longer being alone with

Tavish. Until realization struck—she'd let him chase her off her own dock. *Shameful.* She stomped back down the stairs.

Cadie flopped onto a lounge chair and snuggled under a towel, and held her hands out to Lauren. "Can I hold your coffee for a few minutes? My fingers are numb."

"Sure." Lauren passed the mug over and sat down in the chair next to her sister's, trying to convince herself that the smell of sandalwood lingering on the cushion hadn't come from Tavish's soft hair. He'd climbed back into the boat and sat in one of the stern seats, concentrating intently on the screen of his cell phone. He'd zipped into a hoodie, but that did nothing to minimize his hotness—just one more article of clothing to strip off him. Getting to undress him in their honeymoon suite while he stood stock-still, eyes burning with need, had been one of the best—

Ugh. What is my problem today?

He stretched, exposing a thin line of tanned, tattooed skin between his hoodie and board shorts.

Thanks for the taunt, universe. That was a hypothetical question. Didn't really need the object lesson.

"Let me know when you're warmed up, Cadie," Andrew said, tugging Mackenzie into the bow seat and pulling her in close next to him. "You can drive and I'll ski back to the boat launch. After this run, I'm going to head into the office for a few hours."

"You were supposed to take the day off," Tavish said in a half-engaged tone, still focused on whatever he was reading on his cell.

"And so were you, but you seem pretty absorbed in your emails," Andrew countered.

"Yeah, just got my itinerary for my Thailand assignment in the fall."

Leaving again. Of course. She steeled herself before disappointment struck, before she wasted any more emotions on Tavish.

Turning off his phone, Tavish jammed it in his pocket. "Sorry. All yours until tomorrow."

Andrew rubbed his hands together and let out an exaggerated cackle. "Better get used to it. In no time it'll be the wedding and I'll own your ass. I think I'll start training you this afternoon so there's less to do in July."

Training? The word skittered down Lauren's spine like an unwelcome insect. She shivered and pinned Tavish with a questioning look.

He paled. "Uh, well—"

"What is going on?" Her heartbeat filled her ears, drowning out the sound of water slapping against the dock.

"Finally found you help for while I'm away," Andrew said, climbing out of the boat with an oblivious grin on his face. "Tavish is going to be your assistant."

Gripping his sandwiched-together flip-flops in one hand, Tavish smacked the rubber against his thigh and huffed out a breath. Ah, hell. That was not how he'd wanted Lauren to find out. He should have told her when he had the chance.

Turning white, she stammered out an excuse of having to have a shower before meeting Mackenzie in town for wedding prep. She sprinted up her multileveled deck as if trying to escape an encroaching forest fire.

And it was up to Tavish to put out the flames. He tilted his chin at Drew, who was sitting on the dock waiting for his turn for a ski. "You know, Lauren and I need to coordinate our best-man/maid-of-honor speeches. I'm going to stick around, throw some ideas by her. I'll catch a ride into town with her."

Drew nodded and zipped up his life jacket. He caught the tow rope from Mackenzie. "See you at the office?"

"Yeah, give me an hour." Provided he made it to town without Lauren dispatching his body on a deserted dirt road.

He hugged his sister and Cadie, ignoring the suspicion written on their faces.

A minute later the roar of the boat retreated into the distance. He stared up at the house, the one Lauren had bought and made into a home without him. Not that he needed a house. Just the opposite.

After Mackenzie had shacked up with Drew, Tavish had taken over her apartment to avoid having to find a new place to stash the few boxes of childhood mementos and photography equipment he'd been keeping in her spare closet. That served as more than enough of a base. No point in owning a chunk of property or some neatly constructed glass and logs if he wasn't ever going to be in town long enough to enjoy them.

He took a deep breath and trudged barefoot up the sets of half stairs. His knock on the glass door went unanswered, so he pulled it open and stepped into the open-concept kitchen and living area. Running a hand along the green-flecked granite counter, he blinked as his eyes adjusted after being in the bright morning sun. "Lauren? You here?"

The dining table sat empty, as did the chocolate-colored leather couches and armchairs curved around a stunning river-rock fireplace that soared all the way to the pine-planked ceiling. He let out a low whistle. Talk about a showpiece. But the house managed to look livable, too.

Touches of Lauren livened the room: clusters of family pictures and splashes of color in throw pillows and an orchid, plum and cream-striped floor rug anchoring the couches. Job hazard, noticing color. Though that didn't stop his friends from giving him grief for knowing the difference between orchid and plum. *Whatever.* The predominant moss-and-tree-bark motif made him think of curling up with a bowl of popcorn under a blanket and listening to spring rain on the tin roof. Thanks to the sudden end of their marriage, they hadn't had the chance to do normal husband-and-wife things, movies on the couch and the like. But they'd been pro snugglers when they'd dated in high school—it took zero effort to remember the comforting shape of her shoulders under his arm.

He wandered over to the mantel, to a pair of photographs in mismatched standing frames. None of him there, not that he expected it.

But he did recognize himself in one sense—he'd taken both the pictures on display. A shot of Drew, Cadie and Mackenzie laughing on a chairlift—he'd been on the chair in front of them and had turned around at the exact right time to capture the women doubled over at one of Drew's jokes. The other one, though—he had to close his eyes for a second before he could fully take in Drew and Lauren on their trip to Vegas, sitting in the center of a small group of Lauren's friends. Lauren wore a tiara, a silly gift from her brother for finishing her residency. Tavish had been working on a magazine spread in LA, so he'd joined them on impulse. And the day everyone else had left, Tavish and Lauren had exchanged rings.

"Why are you still here? Your ride's gone." She threw the accusation out from somewhere behind him.

He turned, held up his hands in mock surrender. "I come in peace."

Gripping the newel post, she shuffled her feet on the

bottom tread of the staircase. Her sleek hair hung in just-showered tendrils around her shoulders, making damp spots on her silk bathrobe. That material would be touchable as hell and, with her soft skin, it would be hard to tell where silk ended and flesh began.

Cool it, Fitzgerald.

He jammed his hands into the front pockets of his hoodie sweatshirt. "Just needed to explain myself."

"Explaining yourself is well and good, but you're getting back to town how?" she demanded.

"Uh, you?"

"Try again, Tavish." Crossing her arms over her chest, she sent him a death stare.

Okay. So his prediction he might end up in a shallow grave wasn't far off. And no way were his fingers getting even close to touching her.

Instead of verbally running in circles, he went for the easy out. He pasted a cheeky smile on his face. "That's a pretty complicated half hitch in your panties, Lauren."

"You can dream about seeing my panties, but it's not going to happen."

He chuckled. She made it so easy. "I don't need to dream, sweetheart. I got my fill in Vegas. You still like lace, or have you moved on to the waist-high, granny kind?"

"Wouldn't you love to know?"

A predictable response, clichéd even, but it pierced the bull's-eye. Discovering white lace under Lauren's wedding dress had killed him. And getting to touch her over the soft material, coaxing sexy moans from her with his fingers? The memory still kept him up at night. He barely held in a groan and ran a hand over his face before she realized just how much he'd love to delve under her robe. To find out what she had hidden beneath. Maybe nothing but her sweet skin.

"Nice house. I recognize the artwork." He jabbed a thumb toward his photography on the mantel.

"Don't read anything into it. You have a way with a camera." Her pink cheeks contrasted with her blanched knuckles, which were clenched in fists at her sides. "And with ruining my summer vacation, apparently."

"You going to give me the chance to explain before you reduce me to ash with that glare?"

"By all means." She stomped into her kitchen and started opening and slamming cabinets before yanking out a coffee canister and grinder and placing them on the granite island. Sure, her anger had grown to the point that he could almost see it shimmering on her skin, but too much white showed around her irises to peg her as solely pissed off. She was covering for something he didn't want to poke too much. Unearthing their feelings could suck him past the point of no return.

He strolled to the island and leaned his forearms on the surface across from where she was shakily scooping beans into the grinder. "Mackenzie and Drew needed help, Lauren. Otherwise they were going to have to cancel their honeymoon."

"Nice to know you're more concerned about your ex-brother-in-law than your ex-wife." She pressed her lips together, brows knitted into a near V-shaped blond line.

Tavish's heart dropped. "That's not… I didn't know I'd be working with you when I offered. And it's about my sister, too, not just Andrew."

Beans whirred in the grinder. She stared at the counter and gripped the machine as it slowed into silence.

"I figured you'd be so busy at the clinic that we'd

barely see each other." He offered the excuse in a gentle voice.

"Whatever." Deserting the coffee, she circled the island and stood close enough to him that she had to tilt her chin to look him in the eye. He had a good foot on her, something she'd always complained about. Why, he didn't know. It had just made it easier for him to pick her up, pin her against a wall and send her into oblivion. Her fresh-from-the-shower scent drifted into his nostrils, a hint of tropical summer and sugary sweetness. His mouth watered for a taste, just one…

And now he was lying to himself and not just his family. Great.

She slumped against the counter. "So, two weeks?"

The urge to touch her, comfort her, licked up his arms. He fisted his hands. "I'm sure if we schedule things right, we can avoid actually being in the office at the same time."

"That's not the problem!" She jabbed him in the chest. Her utilitarian-length nail wasn't sharp enough to dig in, but she put enough force behind it for it to sting. "I can't believe you'd step in with this, but you wouldn't stick around for me!"

He caught her by the wrist before she could poke him again. "You needed more than two weeks, Lauren."

Swiping at her eyes with the back of her other hand, she nodded. "I needed a lifetime."

"And I couldn't give that to you. Still can't." Not if it meant holing up in Sutter Creek. He ran his thumb along the fleshy base of her palm. The tendons in her hand tensed under his touch.

She glanced down at his fingers circled around her wrist, then back up to his face.

Those damp eyes. Holy hell. Through all of his travels,

the countless people he'd captured with his camera lens, he hadn't come across irises that exact blend of amber and spring green. Nor had he ever encountered eyes that could stare right to the core of his soul. A fist clamped around his stomach. He released her arm and tucked a damp wave of hair behind her ear. "That's why we cut and ran. Better for both of us."

"Was it really? Better, that is." Her lips parted and her chest rose and fell faster than normal.

"I'm betting my mom would say it was. My dad jerked her around for almost a decade—did the same to Mackenzie and me—before disappearing. Our decision seems miles more responsible."

Her expression softened, and she touched his face. Skilled physician's fingers drawing down his cheek, leaving behind a trail of aching emptiness. They settled on his left pec. Did she know she owned the organ beating under her palm? That he'd given it to her in high school, and even through long-distance breakups and divorce, he'd never quite gotten it back?

"I'm not putting all this on you, you know," she said. "I changed my mind. Was just as much at fault as you sticking to your need to roam."

He settled his hand over hers and squeezed. "Never thought you were."

"We'll get through working together somehow. Through seeing each other every day."

Anticipation, blended with dread, fused his heart to his lungs. He wanted to see her every day. And knew he'd feel like he was walking on knife blades each day he did.

"Maybe it'll help us find closure," she added.

He snorted.

"What?"

"We've wanted each other for over a decade. I don't

see that ending for me after spending two weeks watching
you trot around the WiLA sites in tight technical gear."

Her cheeks pinked. Her hand still rested on his chest
and her fingertips dug into the muscle a fraction. "Kind
of like you showing up on my dock in a fricking wetsuit?"

"I couldn't exactly turn down the invitation when
Drew extended it. Figured the fewer questions the better." Sending her a pained grin, he brushed the backs of
his fingers along her jawline. "And you can't point fingers about wetsuits."

The corner of her mouth curved as she toyed with
the open zipper on his hoodie, running the tab up and
down the teeth. "Pretty sure Cadie and Mackenzie sus-
pect something's going on between us."

"We'll hide it. Even if you did decide that you were
ready to be honest about our marriage, dropping it on our
families right before Drew and Kenz tie the knot would
be the definition of unfair."

Nodding, she slid her hand under the cotton of his
hoodie. It rested on his waist. What he would give for
her to drop that hand lower, cup his hardening length. He
closed his eyes and shifted his weight, hoping she didn't
notice how much of an effect she was having on him. "I
should probably go."

It would be a long walk back, especially in flip-flops,
but he didn't trust himself to stay in her presence any longer without reaching for the row of tiny buttons holding
the fabric of her robe snug under her breasts.

She stepped into him, until only an inch separated
their bodies. A charged, heated energy thrummed between them, seeped from his skin deep into his bones.
He couldn't be the first to close the space. Couldn't do
that to her.

He didn't have to. Standing on her toes, she pressed a kiss just above the collar of his T-shirt. "I dunno. If we're needing closure... Maybe you should stay."

Chapter Three

Tavish sucked in an embarrassingly shaky breath. "Stay?"

"Yeah." Her lips landed on his collarbone again, along with the smallest flicker of her tongue. A fluttering, resolve-weakening caress. "Stay."

"I shouldn't." He cupped the back of her head with one palm. Taking one of her hands, he twined his fingers with hers. "But when have we ever done what we should?"

She looked at the floor, sucked in a breath and then made fierce, needy eye contact with him. "Never. And we'll be quick."

He chuckled. "I might take my time. It's been a year since I've had my hands on you, and since you're talking about closure, we won't do this again. So I'm going to savor every second."

A faint complaint escaped the back of her throat. Those flushed cheeks, the bare thread of control in her eyes—she'd be the death of him.

Settling his hands on her hips, sliding them over the slick silk, his heart stuttered. Yup, cardiac arrest city. But what a way to go.

Rocking back a step, she plucked open one of the buttons holding her robe closed on the side. The thin strip of material was the only thing keeping him from palming her soft, pretty breasts. Man, he had a backlist of ways he wanted to pleasure Lauren Dawson. Freezing in his cot in Siberia this winter, he'd compiled a mental tally of ways they could have kept warm together. He started to shrug out of his hoodie, but she stopped him with a firm look.

"I'll do that." She frantically shoved the material off his shoulders. It landed on the hardwood with a *swoosh.* "Hurry."

She flicked another one of her buttons open.

His body twitched in agreement with her command for speed. *No, slow down.* "Why so urgent?"

"To make sure we get into town on time."

"They think we're speechwriting. If we're late, they won't question us." His fingers shook as he managed to undo the rest of the delicate placket. One side of her robe fell to the side, baring a hint of supple skin, but another layer of thin material hid the rest of her. Lifting her and settling her on the counter, he groaned. "This robe is keeping me from seeing you, sweetheart. I think you did this on purpose."

"It's buttoned on the side. Inside." A sheen of sweat glimmered on her upper lip. She near to whimpered, forehead creasing with complaint, and scrambled for the bottom of his T-shirt. She tossed the material to the floor and moved on to the Velcro fly of his board shorts.

He placed a hand gently on the side of her neck, kissed the opposite collarbone. "Hold on, Laur. I don't mind speeding this up some, but I don't want to miss the next part."

Shaking, eyes closed, she paused. Clenched her hands around his hips as, with a care he'd only ever felt for Lauren, he popped a few of the hidden buttons holding her robe together. Jade lace peeked out on one side from the parted fabric. He traced a finger along the exposed material.

"Tavish." She kneaded his hips and squirmed under his touch, bucked forward. Pressed her heat into his hardening erection. He let out a loud groan and dispensed with the rest of her buttons. Her robe parted like a jacket, only a few scraps of sheer lingerie covering all the parts he wanted to touch.

Starting with her mouth. "I haven't even kissed you yet." And he'd fix that. He claimed her soft lips with his, nipped and delved and loved her mouth until the faint hint of her chocolate-and-coffee breakfast flooded every part of his tongue.

Reaching again for his shorts, she dipped her fingers under the back of his waistband and cinched her legs around his hips. Her soft center was aligned with his very need. Amazing enough on its own, but then she twisted her hips. He had to lock his knees.

"Tavish, foreplay is nice and all…"

"Nice?" He shot her a look of mock insult and reached a finger down to the lace below her navel, drew a wavy line in and out of the top inch of her panties.

"Really nice." Her chest rose and her thighs tightened around his pelvis.

Tavish's mind cleared of everything but Lauren and how good it was going to feel to bury himself in her body. He flicked open the front clasp of her bra and cupped her breasts with all the reverence she deserved, swirled his thumbs around her beading nipples. "Pixie, you are so gorgeous."

"You, too. But I want more." She framed his face in her hands, took his lips hostage and dueled with his tongue until he could barely breathe. "All of you. Now."

Within seconds of her command, one that came from a place Lauren hadn't known existed, Tavish unwound her legs from his hips. He shucked off his shorts.

Lauren was caught by his beauty. Not unawares. She knew the shape of his muscular chest, the hair that delineated the center of his abs. But having all of Tavish in front of her, having him offer himself to her, made her realize how unprepared she was. Unprepared to deal with the sum of muscles and entrancing tattoo and that sexy happy trail. And every time she tried to speed up the kissing and stroking, he slowed her down.

She didn't want to question having asked him to stay, just wanted to escape into the sensual haze. Shedding her panties, she pulled his hips back into the cradle of her own. A groan escaped from his parted lips. He played with the ends of her half-dry hair, ran his fingers through it. Seemed to savor, soak in the sensual touch.

The trees and water of his tattoo rippled, took on life. She outlined the diamond shape from the top of his rib cage, along the smooth skin of his side until she hit cotton. She nudged down the waist of his boxers, her fingers kissing the tight ridge of muscle that arrowed toward his groin. And something about the movement of his muscle under ink had her straightening. "Oh, my God. You designed your tattoo. It's your river spot."

The waterside nook, accessible only by secluded trail, where they'd last made love...

"Mmm." He licked a path along her neck, leaving behind a shivering trail of skin.

"Tavish, that means something..."

"It means I like trees." Cupping her chin, he stared at her, a wild gleam in his eyes. "Forget about my tattoo and finish taking off my boxers."

I like trees. Utter crap. But now wasn't the time. She hooked both fingers in the elastic at his waist but didn't push the fabric down. "Like this?"

Hissing his agreement, he dropped his head back, exposing tight cords in his neck. And Lord, she craved his taste, the sensation of male skin on her tongue. She nipped and laved above the notch in his collarbone. Moaned as the familiar salt and spice teased her memories.

Wanting to run from the past, she held him tighter, allowed the fever filling her body to translate into agitated strokes and squeezes.

"Come on, Tav. More."

"Shh, Pixie," he soothed.

His hands glided along her skin, like the silkiness of lake water brushing against her limbs while she floated. Every muscle fiber of his body tensed. She sensed him fighting his control, leashing the demanding desire within. Following through on his promise to torment her with slow lovemaking when all she wanted was to speed up. Slow meant feeling. Letting in emotion and eventual heartache. Her pulse jumped, sputtered. *Why, why isn't there a way to enjoy this without thinking about what it means?*

"You deserve better than a quickie on your kitchen counter, Laur," he murmured, trailing his mouth from the tiny mole on her right shoulder to the valley between her breasts. "We should go upstairs, do this right."

Her body throbbed with unspent need. Closure was one thing, but inviting him into her actual bed would only ensure she'd never be free of him. She couldn't sleep there if the memory of Tavish and his tormenting hands and tender words lay beside her. "No. I want you inside me. I want it fast. Raw. Make me stop thinking."

"Lauren." His hands hovered over her breasts, freezing inches away from her aching skin as his irises turned smoky. She closed her eyes against the onslaught of his gaze. How could he see through her so easily?

He palmed the left side of her head and pressed his mouth to just above her right ear. "You're not going to be able to use this to numb you. If that's what you're going for, we need to stop." His chest muscles went rock-solid under her hands, seemed to complain at his statement.

"Stop? As if." Shifting against his rigid, clothed arousal, she coaxed a groan from his lips. *Better.* She had to get him to stop talking. Of course it was going to hurt, but it would hurt whether they got involved or not. Right now, going over the edge with Tavish would soothe some of the tears stinging the backs of her eyes, threatening to well.

His expression, aroused but full of doubt, clouded more. "If this is going to hurt you more than you already are, Lauren…"

"You agreed to this. No crisis of conscience now." Lauren kissed him quiet, tried to erase the darkness from his gaze by brushing her lips across his eyelids. "Don't make me beg, Tavish. Not for real, anyway. I wouldn't be here, doing this, if I didn't want it."

"Okay, then," he rasped, an eagerness riding his scratchy tone. His fevered hands and lips caressed, kneaded, took her down further into the foggy heat. "Wait. We need a condom."

"Yeah. Of course." No need to admit she hadn't actually slept with anyone in the past year. Nor did she want to know if he had.

He scrambled for his wallet in the pocket of his hoodie and pulled out a foil packet.

Taking the protection, she forced his boxers off his hips and rolled it on him, then notched her body against his. She reveled in his hot length as it singed her aroused, aching folds. "Now?"

"Hell, yeah." With an agony-and-pleasure-filled breath, he lifted her, thrust to her core.

Her body spasmed, drew him in deeper. The fluid rhythm of hips and thighs and hands overwhelmed. The intimate lock of his body in hers fit closer than she remembered. How had she walked away from the feeling of being more than herself?

"Faster." She needed the now to wash away the then. Needed pure physical sensation.

No thoughts.

No memories.

And then the ache, the craving, melted into all-encompassing flight and glow. Tavish's groan and release dragged Lauren just that much further into bliss.

She held on to his shoulders, on to the brilliance, for as long as she could. But as his chest heaved up and down, she surfaced from the haze.

She'd never wanted anyone as much as she still wanted him. Yeah, they'd been good last summer.

They were spectacular now.

Her eyes closed and, despite being pressed up against his hot skin, her body chilled far faster than it should have. His head seemed to weigh a thousand pounds against her shoulder. Warning jolts shot up her spine.

Curse the physical-emotional pull still knitting them

together. And though she wished she could somehow unfurl the stitches, they were part of each other's life tapestries. A reality that had made Tavish's propensity for avoiding Sutter Creek so fricking convenient. And made his choice to sub in at WiLA a fatal threat to her heart and sanity.

Doing this hadn't provided closure. If anything, it had torn her heart open that much wider.

Chapter Four

Six weeks later

"Just the usual, Lauren?"

The bubble that had been bumping around her stomach since she woke up lurched at the idea of an iced coffee. Stupid work and wedding stress.

Eight more hours at the clinic. Then you don't have to think about it for a couple of weeks.

A thought that not only failed to calm her unsettled tummy but came with a punch of guilt for wanting to get away from work so badly. But her lawyer had called yesterday to assure her the glitch preventing her from accessing her trust had almost been ironed out. Reality loomed—in two and a half weeks, she'd return from summer holidays a full clinic partner.

Rubbing her twisting abdomen, she shook her head at the barista, Garnet James, who was waiting behind the

Peak Beans' register with a curious smile on her face. "Matcha latte today, please." *And carbs. Like, now.* "And one of the plain scones."

Mackenzie strolled over from the table she'd nabbed, fists pressed into her pregnancy-swayed back. "Make that two scones, please."

Garnet busied herself taking Lauren's payment and dishing pastries onto plates, her red curls bobbing around her face. She and Mackenzie often got mistaken for cousins, given their nearly identical hair color and all the time they spent patrolling together. Garnet worked part-time for the mountain and would soon start working for the new holistic health center that AlpinePeaks, Lauren's family's company, was opening in the fall. The woman knew her way around an acupressure table. Lauren would have asked her about nausea relief, but only someone asking for trouble would bring up morning sick—

Don't even think of calling it morning sickness. *It's nerves.*

She and Tavish had used a condom, dammit.

And she'd gotten her period since.

Two percent failure rate. And your period was really light. Like, say, spotting. And it should have showed up last weekend, too.

Growling at her inner textbook nerd and reminding herself that stress caused periods to fluctuate, she accepted her drink from Garnet.

"Kenz, next time you and Lauren come in for your Wednesday breakfast, you'll be a married lady," Garnet said.

Grinning, Mackenzie danced in a celebratory circle, then winced.

"Ligament pain?" Lauren asked.

"Oh, yeah."

Garnet wrinkled her nose. "I hear that's the worst."

Mackenzie shook her head. "I'll take the third trimester over the first any day. Sore breasts—" *Check.*

"—falling asleep standing up—"

Double check.

"—morning sickness—"

Since Monday... Oh, Jesus.

Her heart raced and spots danced on the edge of her vision.

"So, Garnet," she said in an overly bright tone, "are you excited to quit this place when the health center opens?"

"Couldn't be happier." Garnet eyed Lauren carefully. "You okay, hon? You look pale."

The back of Lauren's throat burned. She wanted to be like Garnet—happy about her new business opportunity. Also key: Garnet wasn't preg—

Don't.

—nant.

Her latte hit the floor. The lid popped off and green, milky liquid splattered her favorite suede flats and the tops of her feet. Pain flared, and holy crap, if her shoes were ruined...

"Ow," she said feebly, staring at the spreading puddle.

"Oh, hon!" Garnet exclaimed. "What happened?"

Tears pricked the corners of her eyes. "I wrecked my shoes..."

"Blakey, bring the mop, will you?" her friend called to the back of the store, hurrying around the counter with a rag.

"I love these shoes."

Mackenzie pressed the back of her hand to Lauren's forehead. "Garnet's right—you're pale. Clammy, too.

You're not getting sick before my wedding, are you? I'm afraid I won't allow that. My day has to be perfect."

Lauren swallowed. "It will be."

As long as your brother doesn't freak out and bolt when he finds out he's going to be a dad.

Fisting her hands to prevent herself from touching her stomach, she glanced between her friends, the puddle, her now-spotted shoes, poor Blake de Haan and his mop—

"I'm so sorry. I'm late." *In more ways than one.*

"Get to work," Garnet said, waving her away. "I've got this."

She croaked out her thanks and hurried for the door before she burst into tears on Mackenzie's shoulder.

Ten minutes later, she leaned against the wall of the single stall in the staff bathroom at work, a used pregnancy test clutched in her hand. It was from a box of samples a pharmaceutical company had left for the lab tech to try out. No one would notice she'd taken one.

The results of the test? Quite the opposite. In another two months or so, maybe three, she'd start showing.

And everyone would notice that.

Bracing her forearm against the cold metal of the stall, she pressed her nose to her skin in a vain attempt to hold back a sob.

A baby.

She brushed her free hand over her lower abdomen, and a swell of sheer joy flooded past the crippling shock gripping her body.

Her baby.

Not just yours. Tavish's, too.

Right. Tavish.

Would he even want to be a father? During their handful of idyllic honeymoon days, kids had come up, and neither of them had been sure if they wanted to be parents.

Awareness, deep and real and so damn right, rushed into her chest. Caring for her patients meant supporting women, no matter what choice they made about pregnancy, but for her... For her, no debate was required. The tiny bundle of cells inside her would eventually grow into a baby. One she planned to love with every inch of her being. She had the resources, support and will to be a great mom, no matter how involved Tavish decided to be.

But holy crap. She was not looking forward to that conversation. And with him returning from his assignment to start fulfilling his best-man duties—and subbing in at WiLA—tomorrow morning, she didn't have long to wait.

"Lauren!" Cadie's sharp elbow landed between two of Lauren's ribs.

Lauren jumped. Yeah, her head had been in the clouds since she took the pregnancy test yesterday morning. A justified state, she figured. However, she wasn't ready to confess the reason for her fog to her younger sister. Especially not while holding a microphone in front of the few hundred Sutter Creek residents who filled the Main Street Square for the Independence Day festival.

Cadie stood at Lauren's side with her sleeping son strapped to her chest in a baby carrier. Strands of dark hair drooped around her face, having been coaxed out of her tidy bun by the heat. Lauren knew her own ponytail wasn't in any better shape. The canopy tent overhead provided shade, but the sun was still making it impossible to look halfway decent in front of the crowd. Or, say, one's ex-husband—the one responsible for guaranteeing Lauren would be the one wearing a baby carrier come next summer.

You were there, too. You can't blame him entirely.

No, no she couldn't. She'd blamed herself almost every

minute since she took the test and went for a quick, confidential follow-up appointment with one of her colleagues yesterday to confirm the pregnancy and review her list of dos and don'ts—stick to low-impact exercise, minimal caffeine, take prenatal vitamins, etc. But she could blame him for looking fresh as a damn daisy in his teal technical shirt and climbing gear. God, had they run out of extra-large shirts or something? The large Cadie had given him was too tight. Indecent, really, snug around his cut biceps and pecs—

Thinking like that got you into this mess.

"You're forgetting to commentate," her sister chided, elbowing her again.

"Right. Sorry." Rubbing her smarting ribs, she focused on the Wild Life Adventures' rock climbing demo in front of her and held the microphone to her lips. "Tavish is getting set to challenge my brother, here. Let's see if he remembers how to do this, ladies and gentlemen…"

Was there really a best time to get life-changing news? Probably not. But this weekend counted as the worst. Tonight she was hosting Mackenzie's bachelorette party, and then tomorrow was the rehearsal, and Saturday, the wedding—

Her gut wobbled and she wiped her sweaty forehead. Unclenching her jaw, she fixed her attention on the crowd. "Holy smokes, everyone! Tavish just bested Andrew's time by a full three seconds. Guess he's managed to do some climbing in between all that picture-taking."

The audience of heat-wearied parents and children wearing star-spangled face paint seemed to like her soft jabs in the direction of their favorite famous son. Tavish might not love Sutter Creek, but Sutter Creek loved him. And given her job today was to entertain with the hope of selling more adventure packages, she'd use his reputation unapologetically.

The sun, out in full glory for the Fourth of July, beat down on the applauding crowd overflowing the grassy square at the center of town. Even after spending more than half her life in the ranching- and tourism-based town, she still loved how the historic Old West buildings blended so well with the newer shale-and-cedar architecture popular in ski towns. Homey and outdoorsy, it felt established. Close-knit. Small. Perfect for raising a child.

For raising a child alone? She gripped the microphone tighter. Sweat beaded along her hairline and made her polo shirt stick to her shoulder blades. But her internal thermostat issues were less a result of the sun and more the fault of the man who'd just raced Andrew to the top of the thirty-five-foot climbing wall. And damn it, she'd happily take the distraction. "If you'll fix your attention on Tavish—" *How could anyone not? His ass. Good Lord...* "—at the top of the wall, the guy who just showed my brother how things are done." She smirked pointedly at the crowd and garnered a laugh. "You'll see he's ready to rappel down."

She explained the technique to the crowd, barely able to focus on her words. The flex-and-spring of Tavish's leg muscles drew all her attention. That, and the fact she was currently growing an embryo he knew nothing about. *Gah.* Maybe waiting a few days to tell him wasn't so bad. It only seemed right that one of them spend the wedding weekend free of thoughts of onesies and coparenting...

The crowd applauded again as Tavish landed on the ground, took a bow.

Show off. She ignored his second bow in her direction. Saliva built up in her throat, made her cheeks tingle, and she shoved the microphone at Cadie. Spinning, she clung to the edge of the table and heaved in a breath, willing herself not to lose her breakfast in public.

"Uh—" Cadie sputtered. "At WiLA, we offer classes from beginner to advanced, for kids and adults…" She continued on with the closing spiel and gave thanks to both the rock-climbing and mountain-biking demonstrators. Lauren owed her sister. Cadie didn't like public speaking.

A minute of slow breathing settled her body.

"What the heck was that?" Dangling the microphone in Lauren's direction, Cadie ran a hand absently over the downy hair on her son's head. Ben's cherubic face was smooshed sideways and his little mouth hung open in his can't-get-more-peaceful-than-this infant way.

That's going to be me soon. Oh, wow.

Straightening, she sent Cadie an apologetic smile. "I guess the heat's getting to me."

Climbing gear clinked, drawing her attention away from her sister. The smile slid from her face as she got sucked in by Tavish lifting his helmet from his head, sweat curling the strands at his nape. He tipped his head back with a laugh at something Andrew said.

She loved seeing him laugh. And damn it, he'd do anything but when she dropped the "dad" bomb on him. *So wait until after the weekend. He'll be happier that way.*

"Lauren!" Cadie squeezed her shoulder and followed her line of sight.

"Sorry, what?"

A dark brow curved up in suspicion. "I was saying you should go home. Take a nap before the party tonight."

"I'll be fine." She yawned. Okay, maybe a nap wasn't a bad idea. Her life was supposed to have calmed down this year. The chaos of last summer, from Cadie moving back to town after her husband's funeral to Grammy and Grandpa's car accident to Lauren's wedding-slash-divorce, had been enough for a decade. Now that she'd gotten her family more settled, this holiday should have been different. But one little word—*stay*—and she was tangled up in Tavish all over again. Would he want to be an involved parent? Or would he take off the same way he had on their marriage?

"You know, if something's on your mind, I'm here to listen," her sister offered.

"Sure. If something comes up, I'll be sure to pull out our sleeping bags and we can stay awake all night giggling about boys."

"I hope we're beyond the crying jags over failed proms and all that. Speaking of guys, though…" Cadie glanced briefly at Tavish, who was packing away climbing ropes. "Have you and Tavish picked up where you left off in high school?"

"Why would you ask that?" Lauren blurted.

"Well, you looked like you were tempted to strip his clothes off while he was climbing."

Her mouth went dry. Oh, damn. So much for covering her reaction to him. "In case you didn't notice, he's kind of ripped. But no, there's nothing going on between us." Her chest clenched. Yet another addition to her stack of lies about Tavish. The guilt grew exponentially every time. But the dishonesty was necessary: Lauren wanted to help her sister heal from her losses, not pile on to Cadie's burdens.

"You guys were good together back in the day."

"Holding on to a high school love is the pinnacle of irrationality."

"You could do with some irrationality." Blue eyes widened on a spot over Lauren's shoulder. "Oh, hey, Tavish."

Wary curiosity crossed his face as he set a stack of

plastic tubs down in the back corner of the tent. "What's that about high school loves?"

Oh, crap. He'd heard them. At least in part. "Cadie's is over there." Lauren threw out the excuse, pointing to the raised wooden sidewalk that lined the stores on the south end of the square. "Remember Brad Gillis? She broke his heart when she went to college and met Sa—"

Her sister's eyes dampened, no doubt from the reference to her husband.

Lauren mouthed a quick *Sorry*.

"We were champion heartbreakers after high school, eh, Lauren?" Cadie wrapped her arms around Ben, who was still sleeping securely in his baby carrier. She made a big show of greeting a family perusing the pamphlets at the information table.

Acid singed the back of Lauren's throat. She wanted to slough off the accusation, to assert that she hadn't broken Tavish's heart when she dumped him during her freshman year of college, but the careful mask he wore made her wonder otherwise. Her chest tightened. Swallowing her nausea and her protest, she grabbed a bottle of water from a cooler with a shaky hand and sat on a folding chair.

Tavish tracked her movements with a studied eye. Worry tweaked his already uneasy expression. His strong hand landed between her shoulder blades as he crouched on his toes next to her chair. "You okay, sweetheart?"

"Um, did you not see Cadie when I mentioned Sam? Not my finest moment."

"She's not going to fall apart because you brought up her husband." His calm, low tone only made her insides hollow out more. He took her wrist and notched two fingertips against her pulse. "Drink that water. Gotta watch for heat exhaustion in this weather."

She snatched her arm away from his grasp. "I'm a fricking doctor, Tavish. I know how to avoid heat-related illness." She didn't, however, know how to tell him the truth. And for the sake of the wedding, she wasn't going to breathe the word "baby" until she figured it out.

Chapter Five

Tavish took a swig from his bottle of local wheat beer as he watched women flock to Drew's Search and Rescue buddies on the crowded dance floor.

Built in the basement of the Sutter Creek Hotel, the Loose Moose had to be the only establishment owned by the Dawsons' company that didn't pride itself on five-star, swanky service. It earned its fifteen-year Best Bar in Sutter Creek title by serving up cheap drinks, free pool and a loud mix of country and rock music. Nothing about its decor, especially not the moth-eaten, one-eyed moose head mounted over the archway to the washrooms, deserved reward. But it had an air so familiar it remained one of the only parts of Sutter Creek that Tavish missed when he was away. And given the girls were planning some sort of classy affair for Mackenzie's bachelorette party, the bar served as a guaranteed escape from Lauren.

At the festival this morning, she'd made it exceedingly

clear she wanted nothing to do with him. And he wasn't going to force things, not when the attention should be on Mackenzie and Drew. Until the wedding couple departed for their honeymoon, he'd make sure none of the tension between him and Lauren spilled out from behind closed doors.

"You not going to take advantage of your proverbial second-to-last night of freedom?" He nudged his friend and pointed at the debauchery on the dance floor.

Drew rubbed his hand under the collar of his striped dress shirt. "Uh, no."

"Good. I'd flatten you if you so much as looked at a woman aside from my sister," he said cheerfully. "But you passed the test."

"Lucky me."

"Yes, you are. Don't forget that."

"Don't plan to."

He clinked the neck of his bottle against Drew's gin and tonic. What Drew had with Mackenzie was nowhere near the kind of relationship Tavish was capable of having. Neither he nor Lauren had been able to compromise enough to make their marriage work, screwing over any chance they'd had to stay together. And if that was love, it wasn't worth it. Wasn't much different from his father chasing rodeo fame and forgetting he had a family at home. How his father's wanderer gene had skipped his sister, he didn't know. But she was like their small-town-loving mom all the way. Not so, him. Which was a damn boon for nurturing a career that had him exploring the world's nooks and crannies, but not so much for maintaining a relationship with a woman only interested in one particular hidey-hole.

A flurry of movement from the doorway caught Tavish's eye. His sister shimmied into the bar, decked out in a crown and an abomination of an '80s prom dress. That shade of bubble-gum pink was like a nuclear weapon against her auburn hair. A flood of glitter-decked women followed in her wake.

"What are they doing here?"

"Who?" Drew swiveled to look. A grin split his lips. "Looks like I can dance, after all." It didn't take him more than a second to shoot off in Mackenzie's direction and only about ten more to get her onto the dance floor.

Leaving Tavish with nothing to do but stare at his ex-wife. Lauren's outfit was the opposite of abominable. Dark jeans sucked tight to her toned thighs. Fastened high on her neck, a sheaf of cotton candy-colored fabric hugged her hourglass figure from her breasts to her hipbones. And then she turned.

Backless.

Un-goddamn-believable. How was he going to keep his eyes to himself when Lauren's sweet skin was exposed and begging to be stared at?

He shifted, trying to adjust to the sudden discomfort in his jeans. He'd have to face Lauren from the front tonight. Not that looking at her face and curves from that angle turned him on any less.

The women scanned the room, must have figured out there were no empty tables because they zeroed in on him in his vacated booth and sauntered over, Lauren and Cadie in the lead.

"Can we toss our stuff here?" Cadie asked, rustling for something in her purse and perching on a chair.

"By all means." He motioned to the empty booth seating and the handful of chairs he'd appropriated hours ago. Most of the women dropped their things on the vinyl bench and traipsed away to join the gyrating mass in the sunken dance floor.

Twisting her hands, Lauren glanced around as if to decide where to sit.

Jesus, no need for that. If she didn't get a hold on how awkward she got around him, the entire bar, not just their siblings, was going to start wondering what their problem was. He grabbed the wooden back of the one closest to him and pulled it out from the table. "Here. Sit."

"I— Fine." Clutching a shoulder-wrap thing in her hands, she settled on the edge of the chair.

A delicious waft of pineapple upside-down cake—perfume? Body cream?—hit his nose and he almost groaned as his groin twitched again. "Defeats the purpose of a bachelor party to bring the bride."

"Hard to say no to said bride when she starts pouting," Lauren retorted. Way too many emotions were written on her face for him to decipher. Annoyance for sure. Heartache, maybe. And a sliver of fear. His gut clenched on that last one. Didn't sit right, Lauren being scared.

"Up for a game of pool?" He tried to smile his way into her good graces.

Lauren peered at Tavish, declining with a shake of her head.

"How about a drink, then?"

"I'm the DD," she said in a rush, then seemed to check herself. "But if you're insisting, I'll have a sparkling water."

If she was going to make him work for her company, he'd play along. "Nah, I'll get you something nicer."

"Fine." Though her flat lips said otherwise.

"You want something, Cadie?"

"Just a beer, please."

"Light lager, right?"

A smile brightened Cadie's light blue eyes. "Yeah. Good memory."

Lauren's cheeks stretched in surprise. Did she not think Tavish was decent enough to remember basic facts about his friends? Ouch. He missed her faith in him, no matter how ill-deserved it had been.

And for the sake of tomorrow's rehearsal and the dinner to follow, he needed to talk her out of her jitters. "You know, I was supposed to get another drink for Drew, and I'm not going to be able to carry all that. Could you give me a hand, Laur?" Shooting her an innocent look, he cocked his head.

She opened her mouth as if to protest but rose and followed him without complaint. Careful to touch only the paltry strip of her blouse at her lower back, he guided her toward the mirror-backed bar curving against the rear corner of the room like the hip and shoulder of a guitar. No small feat. The place was packed for the holiday. A large crowd of scantily clad college girls clustered up to the bar, taking their chances on the infamous Wheel-of-Shot-Fortune. The skirts were short. The laughs were tipsy. The smiles screamed "available." He wanted none of it.

Ouch. I'm getting old.

Or, despite the impossibilities, he still wanted the woman weaving through the crowd at his side.

They lined up behind a cluster of people. Lauren nudged his hand with hers, forcing him to drop it from her back.

"It's crowded, Pixie, and you're not exactly tall. I don't want some drunken fool to elbow you in the head or something."

She rolled her eyes. "Exactly. It's crowded. Full of people I have to live around on a daily basis. So it's better I watch for flying elbows myself."

Not the hill to die on. "Whatever suits. But you could

do with dialing down the tension. Given it's crowded with, as you said, people you have to live around."

Her petite frame deflated.

"Tell me what you want from me this weekend." Never mind that he knew what she really wanted from him. And it was something he'd never be able to give.

She grimaced. "Sleeping together last month—well, it didn't exactly turn out how I expected."

"Closure was a pipe dream?"

The dim, recessed lights overhead shone in her damp eyes. *Damn.* "You could say that."

"So, like I said, tell me what you want."

"I want to *not* have this conversation in the middle of a packed, scuzzy bar, Tavish."

Fine. If waiting would make her less anxious, he'd extend her that courtesy. "No insulting the Moose, now. Pretty sure it adds to your family's bottom line more than the ski hill does."

A genuine smile, the first he'd seen on her face all day, spread across her lips. "You're probably right. Meet me for a paddle around the lake tomorrow morning. Nine, at the East Moosehorn boat ramp?"

"Done."

They managed to hold on to the bit of levity while collecting their drinks and returning to the table. But the minute they rejoined Cadie, she tensed up again.

He sighed. Her own worst enemy, his ex-wife.

She reached for her drink and popped the cherry between plump, glossy lips.

Visions of those lips wrapped around him made him hard as the goddamn table leg.

Hell. Maybe he should bow out politely, join the crowd on the dance floor. Better than being in the vicinity of

Lauren's pouty mouth. Better than wanting to kiss that pout away. "I should go give Drew his drink."

Cadie caught his forearm. "He's too busy feeling up Mackenzie to hold a drink. Stay. Chat. I'll get the next round."

Having spent their teens staring at each other, communicating without words, Tavish figured Lauren would correctly interpret the I-can't-exactly-say-no-to-your-sister look he tossed her way.

She nodded and pursed her lips around the straw of her cocktail.

And so began the longest ten minutes of Tavish's life. He managed to smile, talk with Cadie about her son and her job, tell her about Russia and Peru and his next contract—a job in Phuket starting in September. He'd been lined up to go to Nunavut in northern Canada—a follow-up to his Alaska trip—immediately after finishing his stint at WiLA, but that had fallen through.

"You're not working for the rest of the summer?" Disbelief edged Lauren's voice. "I thought you couldn't live without your job. Direct quote, in fact."

Her jab landed, blunt and heavy, on his rib cage. Some of the last words he'd spoken to her before they'd decided to separate came back to him. *Lauren, I want this marriage. Really. I've wanted you since I was fifteen and now that I have you I don't want to let you go. But I can't take pictures of Montana forever.* And could remember her reply, too. He'd just buried it deep enough that it didn't surface. Ever.

"Even I can take a break, Lauren."

"Since when?" The question hovered on a screech.

"Since I realized I needed to go somewhere without seeing it through the viewfinder of my Nikon."

Cadie's gaze shot between them, as if she was trying

to follow the conversation but knew well and good she was missing something. "Are you going to hang around here, Tavish?"

He laughed. "Yeah, no. I'll be gone the minute the happy couple gets back from their honeymoon. If I can't get another job to pass the time, I think I'll head to Australia and get some skiing in."

A shadow passed across Cadie's face and it was his turn to cringe about bringing up a subject that reminded her of her husband's death. "Right," she said in a shaky voice. "Skiing. Fun." Her attention fixed on a point across the room. She narrowed her eyes. "Good grief. Zach should not be dancing. Not even with his crutches. Excuse me."

She left, melting into the crowd on the dance floor. Tavish kept his gaze on the clusters of people dancing under the swirling lights and pulled from his beer. "Is Zach one of her rehab clients or something?" Drew's assistant had moved to town last summer, so Tavish didn't really know the guy.

"No, just a good friend. He was close to Sam." Lauren's words came out irregular, chopped with strain.

And when he looked at her, her face twitched with obvious effort to stay blank. What was she trying to hide from him? He couldn't see it having anything to do with Zach. Maybe she didn't like to see her sister upset? What had they been talking about before that…? Ben. Cadie's work. His end-of-summer travel—*Oh*. His gut hollowed.

Their stay-versus-go argument, yet again. The last time they'd hashed out their relationship, they'd ended up with their clothes strewed over Lauren's kitchen. And though he didn't expect another trip down memory lane—or being presented with an itemized list of his failings—to lead to more naked shenanigans, he didn't see the point of dwelling on their miles-apart needs.

The desire to tell her what she wanted to hear ripped through him—that he'd be happy to stay in Montana for the summer, see if they could work things out. But that smacked way too hard of his dad's broken promises. Tavish refused to lie to a woman about what he could be for her.

Offering up a cheerless smile, she said, "You look serious."

"You, too."

Her quiet laugh held a good portion of *Yeah, you think?*

"All things considered, I think we're holding it together pretty well. Being in a wedding party is a special kind of torture on a good day."

She laughed again. A sad one, but he'd take a laugh over tears.

"Really," he continued, "we should get an award for this. Fate's really rubbing our faces in it, making us watch our siblings get married." Gripping his bottle in both hands—yeah, it would warm the beer inside, but he didn't want Lauren to see him fidget, or worse, give in to the temptation to pull her into his lap and kiss her until the turned-down corners of her mouth curved up—he peered down at said siblings. Drew was an island of navy and white in the middle of a hot-pink sea.

A fast country song blasted on the speakers. Mackenzie was shaking her groove thing as best she could with seven and a half months of baby belly out in front—that had to be throwing off her center of gravity by now.

"How did you find a maternity prom dress just that ugly?" he asked Lauren.

"One of the other bridesmaids is a wunderkind with a needle. She altered it. Raised the skirt to an empire line and—" She cut herself off with a knowing look. "And you don't care."

"Not about the details, no. Wish I had my camera, though. Kenz's smile is pretty terrific picture fodder." He pulled out his phone and did his best to capture his sister's joy with his limited technology.

Mackenzie must have felt her ears burning because she looked up and wagged a no-paparazzi finger at him. The gesture turned to a clear *You and you. Get your asses on the dance floor.*

Lauren's hand landed on his knee. Her fingers dug in. "Tavish, we can't dance. The last time…"

"Yeah, I remember. You were the bride."

You were the bride.

Yup, she had been. And, once again, his strong hand gripped hers and was pulling her onto a dance floor. The energy in the club at their Vegas hotel had been similar to tonight. Her fingers dug into Tavish's shoulders as uncontrollable flashes of affixing a veil over her up-do and sliding a garter into place dominated her mind. Then, they'd only lasted ten minutes on the floor before escaping up to their room to avoid public indecency charges. Not happening tonight. Tonight was about this weekend's bride and groom. She had to make sure the night ended with no one being the wiser to veils and garters and honeymoon dances.

And with him remaining clueless about the baby. That plus sign had changed Lauren's mind—in an instant she'd known motherhood was the right choice for her. But she couldn't make that choice for Tavish. And when she'd given him an out last year, he'd taken it all too easily… God forbid he get spooked and leave before Andrew and Mackenzie had the chance to tie the knot.

The beginnings of a headache throbbed behind her eyes. Dropped her forehead to his hard chest, she inhaled the warm, woodsy scent lingering on the cotton hugging his delicious muscles. The fragrance soothed like pain medication, unraveling some of the tension pulling at her facial muscles.

He lowered his head close to her ear. "It's just one dance, Lauren. For Mackenzie's sake."

"Can't disappoint the bride."

"We should probably get used to it. Don't the best man and maid of honor have to dance at the reception?"

She tilted her chin to meet his gaze and made a face.

He matched her scrunched expression, then grabbed her hand and spun her in an awkward circle before bringing her close again. She bit her lip to hide her amusement. Tavish wasn't much of a dancer, though he tried. They'd spent most of his prom wrapped in each other.

She hadn't bothered to go to hers. He'd been in Europe on a college exchange, and she hadn't wanted to torture herself, so she'd studied for her advanced placement biology final instead.

"What are you thinking about?" he asked, voice as low as it could be given the throbbing, slow beat.

"How I aced my AP biology final."

"Huh?"

She sighed. "Prom. You missed my prom."

His hands tensed in their loose loop around her back. "Thought I apologized for that before, during and after the event itself."

"Yeah, you did."

"And I'm pretty sure you got back at me for it by dumping my ass."

"I didn't dump you because you missed my prom."

She'd dumped him because she'd known he'd miss

every other important event in their lives. Her med school aspirations and his dream of being on the cover of *National Geographic* had misaligned worse than the cock-eyed, neon beer signs adorning the scarred black walls of the Moose. There had been no point to waiting for the inevitable collapse. And their ring-exchange experiment had proved she'd been way smarter at nineteen than at twenty-nine.

Pink bled into Lauren's peripheral vision as Mackenzie sidled up, hands over her head and hips shaking. Andrew stood behind her with his hands on her waist—or lack thereof. A disgruntled wrinkle formed on Mackenzie's forehead. "Are you guys arguing again?" She shouted to be heard over the raucous beer-and-whiskey song currently entertaining the crowd.

Tavish flattened a *Who, me?* palm to his chest.

Better to let him deal with his sister. She had Andrew to handle. Her brother was eyeing her as if he finally had all the pieces of a jigsaw puzzle laid out and was about to start assembling them. She huffed out a dry laugh. No way could he guess the past she shared with Tavish.

Or the future, for that matter.

She yelled, "We're fine," at her brother and mirrored Mackenzie's arms-up, hips-boogying shuffle. Exhaustion settled in her joints, made it hard to keep her body loose and in time with the beat. If she could predict the future, maybe she could get her nerves to settle, could muster the guts to haul Tavish off the dance floor, find a quiet bench outside and be honest with him. She fought the urge to touch her stomach. She wanted the connection, but wasn't ready to broadcast the baby to the world—to Tavish.

The song's tempo picked up for the final chorus and the movement of the people around them lost the rhythm, turned a little frantic. Eyes wide, Mackenzie nestled into Andrew's tall frame.

"Come closer, sweetheart." Tavish tugged at Lauren's hand, raised an eyebrow when she glared at him.

Sweetheart? Shut up, she mouthed, glancing at Mackenzie and Andrew to make sure they hadn't heard Tavish's slip.

Before she could get a good read on their faces, an arm flailed out from the group next to them, smacking her on the side of the head. She let out a yelp and ducked.

Concern flashed across Tavish's face and he threw up a hand, shielding her from further jostling. And he must not have been anticipating the DJ leaving dead air between songs—must have lost his fricking mind, to boot—because his bellow rang clear across the bar. "Watch yourself around my wife, you prick."

Chapter Six

Colored lights imprinted on Lauren's retinas and the skin of her cheeks numbed as her brain stuttered to a halt. Her knees shook. Tavish hadn't just called her his wife in front of two hundred Sutter Creek residents, had he? He couldn't have. In front of her brother? And Mackenzie? Probably Cadie, too…

"Wife?"

"What the hell?"

Andrew and Mackenzie's shocked responses blended together, answering the question Lauren really hadn't wanted answered.

Oh, God. Her mind whirred. This called for major damage control. Maybe they could keep the news in the family for the weekend, just until the wedding was done. But splashes of pink clothing surrounded her. Fascination blazed on the other bachelorette party attendees' faces. Tavish's holler had reached their ears, all right.

All wrong, more like.

"Tavish?" Mackenzie's shrill tone stabbed Lauren between the ribs.

"I—uh—" Didn't seem like his brain was functioning any faster than Lauren's. But someone had to say something.

"Ex-wife," she offered weakly.

"As if that's better. Why did we not know?" Mackenzie let out a loud curse and looked like she couldn't decide who best deserved her stabby glare. "And you had to announce this *now*? Stellar timing."

"Mackenzie—" Tavish started.

She held up a hand. "No. No excuses. I'm going home." Pushing her way off the dance floor, she was out the door with Andrew on her heels before Lauren could get her legs to move.

Her feet were stuck to the floor, muscles immobile from shame. Heart hammering hard enough it threatened to break a rib, she sent her big-mouthed ex-husband a disbelieving glare. *"Tavish."*

"What's going on?" Cadie materialized at Lauren's side. "Why did Mackenzie leave? And did you just say 'wife'?"

"Ex-wife," she repeated, snapping out the word. "I'm sure Tavish would love to explain given he's the one who announced it to the entire bar."

Anger darkened Cadie's eyes. "Well, someone had better fill me in."

Tavish's hand landed on Lauren's shoulder. "Lauren, I'm sorry, I—"

"Sorry? You're *sorry*? Too late!" Snatching the martini glass from Cadie's hand, she sloshed the blue drink into Tavish's face.

Eyes closed, he slowly ran his tongue over his lips—

oh, how dare he look smoking hot after what he did tonight—and wiped the sleeve of his no-longer-white dress shirt over his cheeks. "Seriously?"

Regret immediately crawled into her stomach. So much for keeping a low profile. "I owe you a drink, Cadie."

"No, you owe me an explanation! You were *married*?"

"Yeah, well—"

"And you're not now?"

"No, we—"

A single sob interrupted Lauren's attempt to explain. Cadie's shoulders jerked and her chest visibly shuddered.

Lauren would have been able to handle anger or any of its by-products. But the tears streaking down Cadie's blotched face made the backs of Lauren's eyes sting. She followed her sister to their table. She sensed Tavish close behind but couldn't bring herself to look at him. Anger churned through her belly. At him, yeah. But more at herself.

"Cadie, I should have told you. But you had Sam's death to deal with, and then Ben arrived, and it never seemed important."

Her sister's jaw dropped. "You don't think you're important to me?"

"Of course I do, I just didn't think—"

"You're more than my sister, Laur. You're my best friend. Or I thought you were. But friends don't lie to each other, and you did *this morning*. Said you weren't involved."

She wasn't going to insult her sister by pulling out a "Technically, we're not involved anymore." She'd be connected to Tavish for the rest of her life, though in a far different way than they'd hoped for when they'd promised each other a life of love and respect. Forever in the marriage sense had lasted all of twelve days. Forever in the parenting sense would be starting in around mid-February, give or take.

She should just blurt that out, too. A cherry on tonight's fricking drama cake.

But no. There was a sacredness to telling a man he was going to be a father. No matter her ire, she wouldn't take away what would hopefully be a poignant moment for him.

Unless he deserts you again...

She shoved the thought from her mind. She'd worry about that after the wedding. First, she had to fix things with her sister. Mackenzie and Andrew, too. She sent Cadie a pleading look. "You have enough to worry about without taking on my problems."

"I'm not fragile. I would have been there for you, just like you have for me." Cadie started to back up.

"I know. I screwed up—"

"Yeah, you did. I naively thought I meant as much to you, that you'd rely on me if you needed me. Obviously not. Relationships need to go two ways, Lauren. It can't just be you giving all the time." Cadie grabbed her jacket from the booth. "I need to make sure Mackenzie's okay."

Lauren sucked in a breath as her sister spun and retreated. With each of Cadie's steps, all Lauren's attempts to shore up her family slowly drained away. Her closeness with her sister, gone. And as soon as her dad found out, he'd probably react the same as Cadie. Protecting her family from more pain—the purpose of having kept the secret—was supposed to have helped them stay together, not push them apart.

Tavish held a clean dishcloth under the faucet in Mackenzie and Drew's kitchen. Cleaning the blue cocktail off his face was child's play compared to cleaning up the mess he'd made by letting his temper get the best of him. He'd spent a good hour trying to convince his sister that the secret coming to light actually meant he and Lauren *wouldn't* be sniping at each other for the rest of the weekend. A bald-faced lie, obviously—thirty seconds after Cadie had left the bar, Lauren had stormed out, still looking like she'd have preferred to crack a beer bottle over his head instead of throwing that drink in his face. But the dishonesty was necessary to get Mackenzie to believe that tomorrow's rehearsal and Saturday's wedding would go off without a hitch.

Footsteps on the tiled kitchen floor announced Drew's return from tucking Mackenzie in. Arms crossed over his chest, he hitched a hip on the counter and fixed an impressive serious-ski-patroller look on his face. "When I suggested we start the weekend off with a bang, that's not what I had in mind."

Tavish flinched. He'd earned the thinly veiled disgust. Keeping his marriage a secret had been easy enough to do when he never saw Lauren. A change in proximity shouldn't have altered the parameters *that* much. "I don't even know where to start."

"Start by telling me Lauren got home safe tonight."

Damn it, he couldn't even guarantee that. Wringing out the cloth, he bought himself a few seconds by hanging it over the kitchen faucet and ambling over to one of the bar stools tucked under the kitchen counter. He spun the stool around, straddled it and rested his arms on the wooden back. "She took off before I could talk to her."

Drew yanked his phone from his pocket and typed out a rapid message. "And Vegas, Fitz? How did you get married without me noticing? I mean, we were drunk a good chunk of the time, but not *that* drunk."

No, but on what should have been their last morning, Tavish had left Drew sawing logs in their hotel room to meet Lauren for brunch.

The minute she had smiled with her lips pursed around the rim of her coffee cup, Tavish had known in every particle of his being that he wanted to stare at that smile over the breakfast table for the rest of his life. They hadn't dated for a decade. But his heart had clung to her, no matter how far he'd traveled.

"Marry me, Pixie," he'd blurted.

"That's Dr. Pixie to you," she'd joked. All the gold had faded from her eyes, leaving them a deep, shocked green. "You're serious. Tav. *Oh.*"

He'd counted. *One. Two. Three. Four.*

On *five*, she'd crawled onto his lap right in the middle of the hotel restaurant. Her hungry, hands-to-the-face kiss had said "yes" for her.

"Tonight?" he'd asked.

She'd nodded, then disappeared for the rest of the day. And when he'd seen her in the chapel… Holy hell. Straight hair curled into submission and piled on her head. Sky-high stilettos that hadn't brought her close to his height, though he'd grinned at the effort. And her dress. That scrap of silk still taunted him in his dreams.

As did their promises. *For richer, for poorer, to have and to hold.*

And her fingers had snapped in his face.

Wait, that's not right.

Fingers *were* snapping in his face. Drew's.

"Dude, what?" Blood pounded in his head. He filled a glass of water and drained half of it.

"Lost you for a minute. Focus. You. My sister. Married."

"Yeah. You left. We didn't. We'd intended to come

home from our honeymoon and make the announcement
in person. But then we got the call about your grandparents' car accident. After that, everyone was grieving."
She'd floored him with an ultimatum—stay in town or
file for divorce—right after the funeral. "Seemed easier
to keep it between the two of us."

Drew's brow knitted. "So it was just a random Vegas
thing?"

"No. No way. We honestly thought we could make a
go of it. But neither of us wanted a part-time marriage,
with me gone most of the year."

"How did you not think of that beforehand?"

Being condescended to like a kindergarten student
was the opposite of awesome, but Drew deserved answers. Finally releasing the valve on his secrets was a
welcome relief, too.

"We'd agreed to switch up who was working at any
given time. Me taking contracts in between her working
stints in overseas areas." Tavish shook his head. "When
your grandparents died, she backpedaled from buying
plane tickets and researching humanitarian missions to
calling Frank Martin about committing to a future partnership. I told her I couldn't give up my job. And she
gave her ring back."

Tavish rubbed that same ring, twisted and disguised as
one of the links on his bracelet. Entwined with his own
band. A constant reminder he couldn't be trusted with
someone else's heart.

Drew's gaze flattened. "You both should have compro-
mised. Especially you. Marriage surpasses everything."

Easy for Drew to say. Tavish agreed that most of the
time, marriage ranked above all else. But he didn't believe it was right for either him or Lauren to change the
utter fabric of their personalities for the sake of stay-

ing together. "With my assignments, I can't settle in one place."

The other man drummed his fingers on the table. "Selfish."

"Documenting refugee crises is selfish?"

"It is if you're putting your job before my sister."

Tavish took a breath. He rubbed at his breastbone. *No. Our split was for the best.* As a kid, he'd lain awake for too many nights listening to his mother sobbing in the kitchen after one of his father's few-and-far-between phone calls. He had loved Lauren too much to want to subject her to an equally miserable marriage.

Had loved. Right. Try "still loved."

And probably always would.

Crack. Plop.
Thwoop. Crack.
Plop.

Oh, *no, no, no*. Lauren hated waking up to the sounds of club hitting ball, had purposely not bought a house near the golf course to avoid the torture. She'd cursed her childhood-bedroom view of the eighth tee of the Sutter Creek Golf Club many a time as a teenager. Unless she'd fallen asleep at her dad's...

Rolling over, she blinked. Nope, the sunlight streaming in through the skylight placed her firmly in her lakeside house.

And threatened to split her head. How the hell did she feel hungover without having had anything to drink? Oh, wait. A scant two hours of sleep would do it.

And the neighbor currently preventing her from sleeping away last night's humiliation was lucky she was the one person in Montana who didn't own a hunting rifle.

Thwoop. Crack.

Dragging herself over to her open window—it sounded like she was almost on top of the noise—she spotted the perpetrator.

Tavish oozed a weekend-sexy "Exercise is nice and all, but I'm better made for putting down this driver and sliding between your sheets" aura. He stood on the middle level of her tiered deck with a driver grasped in both hands. His gray athletic shorts sat low on his hips, right below that delectable, lick-worthy ridge of muscle that arrowed toward his groin. An ancient University of Montana ball cap sat backward over his tawny hair. His T-shirt hung out of the back of his waistband. With each swing the balls easily hit the middle of the six-hundred-yard-wide lake.

Squinting against the bright sunshine and the resulting jab to her retinas, she didn't call the knee-jerk "You're breaking the law, idiot!" out the open window, instead taking a moment to lean on the sill and stare at the view. He'd woken her up, so it was only fair she steal the opportunity to appreciate that admirable expanse of sexy torso. His tattoo rippled as he aimed and knocked a ball far enough into Moosehorn Lake to make a pro green.

Her stomach flipped, ending the pleasure.

Morning sickness? Fury?

Both.

At least fifty percent of her wanted him to follow his golf balls to the murky lake bottom and not return.

The other half was going to relish looking at him. A blessed distraction from the mammoth task of convincing her family to forgive her. And as much as Tavish's announcement had been the catalyst for last night's fiasco, she was at fault. She'd lied by omission to protect her family, not to hurt them. Talk about backfiring. Why hadn't she been honest? Not the day after her grandpar-

ents' funeral, but some point in the past year. At least
then she would have been able to control the way they
found out.

After brushing her teeth and scrounging a preg-
nancy-safe painkiller from her bathroom cabinet, she
pulled sweatpants and a dilapidated Colorado Avalanche
T-shirt from her closet and headed out to confront Tavish. He'd make an excellent patsy on whom to pawn her
self-loathing.

She pulled her sliding door open. The metallic scrape
made her head pound with fresh enthusiasm. She held
her hand against her forehead to combat the dizziness.

Tavish turned, but stayed on the deck a level below
her, arms loose at his sides, golf club in his right hand.
Dropping the driver to the planking, he quickly pulled
his shirt out of his shorts and over his head.

The sun made her orbital bones ache. The decking
chilled her bare feet. And the look of utter misery on
Tavish's face dulled the temptation to project any self-
directed anger toward him.

Why, why, why did she become such a sucker whenever undiluted emotion crossed the absurdly beautiful
planes of his face? Only one way to protect herself from
her own weakness—evasion.

"Shh," she pleaded. "Pretty sure my headache just got
classified as category five."

"Sorry, sweetheart." His lips twisted in regret. He
picked his club back up and spun it like a top, catching
the shaft before it could clatter to the deck. "Did you
drink last night?"

"No."

"So why the headache?"

She winced at the stiffness in her neck as she sat on

the top of the three-stair set between decks and curled her bare toes around the middle step. "Barely slept."

"That why you bailed on me for our morning paddle?"

"Oh, crap…" She screwed up her face in apology. "Our plans slipped my mind when the night got eventful."

The guilty flush in his cheeks deepened from pink to crimson. "If I could rewind, I would, Laur."

"I know." She tried to dig out a sympathetic expression. Wasn't sure if she managed one, but he smiled back, at least. "This is going to affect you as much as it does me. It's too bad…" The first positive thought of the day struck, warmed her. "No. It was bound to come out at some point. I guess now was better than five, ten years in the future. Our families would have been even angrier had we kept the secret longer. So why not yesterday?"

Tavish's mouth gaped for a few seconds. "Oh, the wedding. Us working together. Take your pick."

"Good points. And don't get me wrong—I'm upset. My sister is beyond pissed at me. A good chunk of the town witnessed the likely candidate for the most embarrassing moment of my life. But at the same time, I feel—" she surprised herself with the word that came to mind "—free."

Tavish palmed the top of his frayed-around-the-edges maroon ball cap. "Free? How?"

"My slate's clean. No more lies. No more secrets." Her conscience poked at her. Okay, one. Maybe it was wrong to wait, even for two more days… "So…my deck. Golfing. Interesting—and illegal—choice."

His fist pulsed a few times around the grip of his club. "When you didn't show up for our paddle, I figured you were avoiding me. I needed to be able to pretend I was here for some other reason than to beg your forgiveness."

Lauren's mouth turned sandy. "Beg?"

"On figurative knees." He shifted his feet. "Real ones, if it'll make the difference."

A replay of what Tavish had done to her the last time he'd been in front of her on his knees cut through the throbbing in her head. Heat blasted her cheeks. "Not necessary. I believe you."

"Huh. I wasn't expecting you to be so agreeable."

"I've spent a lot of time—" she sighed "—the whole year, really, feeling sorry for myself, feeling you gave up on me. I assumed my family would do the same if they learned the truth. And because of my dishonesty, well, I wouldn't blame them if they did."

He opened his mouth, protest written in his eyes.

She held up a hand. "But feeling sorry for myself isn't going to fix anything. I need to earn their forgiveness. Try to put things back to normal so that Andrew and Mackenzie can have a stellar wedding."

He cocked an eyebrow, too playful for comfort. "You sure you don't want me to beg?"

She bit her lip. "Nothing good happens when you beg me for things, Tavish."

"Yeah?" He reached forward with the driver, dragged the cool metal head along the top of her bare foot.

"Yeah. It usually ends up with me losing my dignity."

"Your clothes, maybe. But not your dignity."

His sensual tone dragged along her skin, delved into the needy parts of her core. A strangled gurgle escaped her. "Okay, if I'm going to forgive you and we're going to make sense of this, that has to stop. No innuendos, no remembering the past, no pretending anything about our relationship worked. You're leaving."

He gave a nod, blanked the hints of sexual promise from his face. "That is what I do."

"I'm staying." She had to adhere to that decision more than ever. Her child—their child—would need stability.

"That is what you do." He spoke church-quiet. Church-serious.

"And because we both have to live with whatever happens here—" she waved a finger back and forth between her chest and Tavish's "—we need to recognize there's no way we can go back to any part of what we had."

"Oh, I recognize that but good." His sardonic tone spread to his eyes, darkening the violet to thunderstorm gray. The identical shade his irises turned post-sex.

Her brain surged with discomfiting flashes of sneaking kisses down hidden trails the summer he'd graduated, of lounging in their king-sized honeymoon bed, of the weight of her wedding ring on her finger.

She rubbed her temples for a few seconds, then pressed her fingers to her eyelids, but failed to clear her head.

He stared at her, spun his golf club again. "Now what?"

"Now I wait four hours until I can take another Tylenol."

The sound of a vial of pills being shaken prompted her to open her eyes.

Tavish held out a travel-size container of generic acetaminophen.

She shook her head. "I've already had my limit. Uh, you always carry around painkillers?"

"No. Your brother and I had a long talk last night, after which I reacquainted myself with Johnnie Walker."

"We make quite the pair."

"Yeah, we do." Tavish's eyes shone just enough to betray his vulnerability.

Unbearable. She threw up her hands. "What did I just say?"

"You said no more lies."

Her headache stopped her from shaking her head. "No, I said we can't go back."

"Sure. Doesn't mean I don't wish we could."

"Don't wish. *Don't.*" She'd wasted a heap of good wishes on Tavish Fitzgerald. Birthday candles. The first star to appear on countless clear summer evenings. Coins thrown backward over her shoulder into the grizzly-bear-shaped fountain in the town square.

Wishes only resulted in a lighter change purse and a whole lot of shame. She'd almost given up her dream of the clinic for him. She'd convinced herself that her mother would have been okay with the change in plans for the sake of Lauren finding love with the man she'd wanted almost as long as she'd wanted to be a doctor. She could at least thank Tavish for his timing. At least he'd showed his true inability-to-stick colors before she'd burned bridges with Frank Martin.

He let his club clatter to the ground and shoved his hands into his pockets. "You can't tell me you never wonder, Lauren."

"No, I can't." Pulse racing, she twisted her hands. She didn't need to wonder. She knew. Knew his lips could coax a moan from her mouth and his hands could drive her body into a frenzy. The craving to let him swirled in her belly.

Ignore it, ignore it.

But how?

With a blur of limbs and lips and lust, Lauren stood and pressed herself into him, trying to kiss him out of her system. She melted into his magnetic heat. And he wasn't resisting. His lips caressed hers with a fervent thirst. His fingers grasped her hips with enough force to leave marks.

Her hands roamed his back. Took in the texture of cotton and tight muscle. Creeping her fingers up the warm skin of his neck, she wove them into the short waves at his nape, knocking off his ball cap.

She stretched onto her toes and he held her secure. Physically secure, anyway. Emotionally, she was slipping from her stable footing.

His fingers slid under the elastic of her sweats, teased her lower back at the edge of her panties.

Common sense, Lauren. Do not set yourself up for another broken heart.

She tore her reluctant-to-be-torn-away lips from his and backed up. What was she thinking? If they were going to have any chance at a functioning coparent relationship, she needed to keep her hands to herself.

And more than that, she needed to tell him. For him to understand just how stupid it would be for them to have sex again, he needed to know all the variables.

"Tavish…" She swallowed.

"Yeah?" He smiled, a feral flash of straight white teeth. His chest rose and fell rapidly.

Taking a step backward, she settled on a stair edge. "Come sit for a second."

His face screwed up in confusion. "Huh?"

Nausea panged in her stomach. *Ack, not now.* "I need to tell you something."

"Okay…" He eased down next to her on the stair and reached for her knee, but dropped his hand to his side before making contact.

She swallowed the saliva flooding her mouth. "I— Oh, crap." Running for the deck railing, she hung over the edge and heaved what little was left of her dinner from last night into the huckleberry and Oregon grape plants covering the ground below.

"You sure you didn't drink last night?" Tavish was at her side in a second, gripping her shoulders with unyielding hands as she crossed her arms on the railing and buried her face in her elbow.

"Positive. I can't drink. I'm pregnant."

Chapter Seven

"That's a lot of blue lines," Tavish croaked as he took in the four positive pregnancy tests arranged into a military-precise row on Lauren's bathroom vanity. She'd been kind, humoring him by running to the drugstore to pick up the tests. He'd believed her when she'd told him. But at the same time, he'd wanted to see the proof.

Hello, proof.

His knees wobbled and he sat down on the edge of the fancy-ass marble bathtub before he completely humiliated himself by collapsing on the floor. The grout pattern between the shiny, white tiles swam in his vision as he clenched the side of the tub and blinked. Cold seeped into his palms and a chill spread through his limbs. He shivered and drew in a too-shallow breath.

Lauren plunked down next to him and held out a small, plastic trash can. "Just in case."

The numbness gripping his body shattered. One loud

ha turned into two and then a cascade of near manic laughter.

And she let him have his moment to completely lose it. She set a gentle palm on his back, murmured, "I know," but left it at that.

He managed to catch himself before his harsh guffaws turned into sobs. He hadn't cried in years. Decades. But if he let down a child like his father let down their family? Son of a bitch, his tear ducts stung. "How did the condom break without us knowing it?"

"Who knows? Microscopic tear? They're not fail-safe."

He let out an ear-blistering curse.

"Look," she murmured, "you don't have to decide anything today. I know neither of us was sure about having kids before…"

"Irrelevant now."

"No, it's not. No one's forcing me to have this baby—I know my options. But I have the resources to be a single parent. And we can figure out how much or how little you are going to be involved—"

"You're not going to be a single parent, Lauren. I watched my mom burn the candle at both ends and sacrifice too damn much to *ever* let you go through the same. I'm going to be involved."

She startled and her hand moved to his shoulder in what seemed like an attempt to steady herself.

The ferocity of his vow surprised him, too. Did he believe he had it in him to be a reliable father? No. For the sake of the child—his child, their child—cutting and running might be best. Deserting her, though, deserting a baby… Acid bit his throat and he almost had to take her up on the offer of the garbage can to puke in.

Swallowing, he let out a dry laugh. "And here I thought screwing up yesterday was as eventful as it could get."

Her mouth quirked. "This news we should definitely keep to ourselves. We have time, Tav. Let's settle in to this a bit before we commit to anything."

He recognized her words for what they were—an out. Checks and balances to make sure they didn't race head-long into an arrangement that crashed and burned like their marriage had. And he respected her caution.

Had he earned her doubt? Hell, yeah. Did he wish it could be different? Yeah, just as much as—no, more than—he had for the last year when it came to their failed marriage.

"Look, I have an appointment to get to. And we both have the rehearsal to deal with." She put a hand to her stomach, that ubiquitous pregnant-woman gesture he'd never before felt connected to. But now… His palm grew restless with the urge to slide over her hand. He resisted temptation.

"I guess I'll see you later, then," he said.

"It's probably best." Her face, pale since she'd been sick on the balcony, shifted into a forced smile.

And as he strode from the room he cursed how he always managed to be the one leaving, always managed to prove himself his father's son.

A few minutes later he sat in his SUV, frozen with his hands on the steering wheel. He needed to get into town, to go to Mackenzie's and apologize again. But if he went to talk to his sister without decompressing some, she'd sniff out that something was wrong.

No, wrong wasn't the word. But right didn't fit, either. He shook his head. He needed time to think.

We have time, Tav.

Huh. He hadn't noticed it at the time, but Lauren had

shortened his name. For the first time in a year, to his memory. Warmth eased some of the chill from his insides. He didn't like admitting how good her familiarity made him feel. How desperate he was for scraps of what they'd had.

Yet another thing to contemplate. Turning the key in the ignition, his internal autopilot kicked in, pointing the car away from town. Driving down a gravel road, he cranked his stereo, let some old-school Bruce Springsteen force out thoughts of his wife. *Pregnant wife. Ex. Ex-wife. Either way, though, pregnant.*

He parked in a turnout five hundred yards from his thinking spot. Back in high school he'd found a nook of sandy riverbank that had become his refuge when he was yearning to escape but couldn't. He'd taken his first award-winning picture at sixteen there, had figured out photography was his ticket out of Sutter Creek.

Pulling his sketch pad and beat-up wooden pencil case—filled to bursting with charcoals, chalk pastels and graphite and watercolor pencils—from under the passenger seat, he headed for the grass-lined trail. He trudged down the uneven path and reached the little clearing, a patch of sand just big enough for two people to sit with their feet in the water. He'd come here with Lauren. Would he be coming here with their kid in a few years? Before filing for divorce, she'd made it very clear she wouldn't want a half-time husband. But he wanted some sort of regular visitation. What that would look like, well, they'd have to work on that.

Sighing, he kicked at the sand with a toe. The river ran a muted, glacial jade, opaque in the center fading to clear green on the edges. The scent of baking pines and sweet grass hovered between cloying and refreshing as it eddied in the breeze. Settling against his log, Tavish took off his sandals. He breathed in Montana wilderness and put pencil to paper. He could have easily taken a series of stunning photos to capture nature's majesty. But his work was commercial. Sketching was personal, something he did for himself. And this place mattered enough that he'd had it inked on his side last winter.

He set about recreating what he'd captured in a photograph back at sixteen. Juniper-green pencil blended into walnut brown and warm gray. Smudging his strokes with a fingertip and water, he managed a passable interpretation of the river rushing over a rock a few feet away from his submerged heels. He stared at his creation. Knew that color.

Remembered making the comparison to Lauren's eyes the last time he'd been here with her.

Right after the funeral, she'd been frantic. He'd calmed her down with words and hands and pleasure. If only they'd stopped there. The minute they'd started talking, she'd shocked him with her sudden change from wanting to travel the world with him to never wanting to go five miles past home again. She needed to be with her family, needed to follow through on the clinic. And when he'd pointed out that those desires might fade as she worked through her grief for her grandparents, she'd vowed she'd never change her mind.

Somehow, that train wreck of a day hadn't tainted this place for good.

He turned and smoothed the page. Pencils flew. Green to brown again, then cream and medium flesh tone for skin, the occasional raw sienna freckle, a mix of ocher and cadmium yellows for hair… Maybe the act of physically putting Lauren on paper would free his mind.

It certainly couldn't make him want her more. He was

already teetering precariously on the edge of that cliff again.

And he hated how much it would hurt when he landed. Because he wouldn't be landing anywhere good. This pregnancy had struck any more casual sex between them right off the table.

A baby was the one tie they couldn't undo. A little being that might have eyes as hazel as Lauren's, or maybe the shock of blond curls he'd had as a kid...

Sketching and smudging, he lost track of time. His feet went numb from being in the rushing water.

A vibration in his pocket jarred him from his artistic zone. He checked his cell display. Mackenzie. *Crap.*

He decided to head her off at the proverbial pass. "Hey, Kenz. Sorry, I was going to come by this morning, but I got caught up—"

"With your tuxedo fitting?" she cut in.

Tuxedo fitting. Double crap. "What time is it?"

"Noon." She sounded singularly unimpressed. "You missed your appointment."

"I— No. I went over to talk to Lauren and then had... other stuff that came up. I'll go do it right now." He snapped his sketch pad shut and squeezed his phone between his shoulder and his ear to allow him both hands to pack up his pencil case and do up the toggles on his sandals.

"Okay. I have my final appointment in a few minutes, too. Come see me when you're done with yours. Penance, big brother. You owe me."

"I do." He started jogging down the trail. "Give me fifteen minutes."

A few winding roads and one stoplight later, he was back in Sutter Creek and in Dreamy & Dapper's parking lot.

After confirming that he wasn't a total moron and the measurements he'd emailed the store were indeed correct, he readjusted his ball cap on his head and strolled to the women's side of the store. By the glare the sales associate directed at his feet, he guessed there was some rule about wearing shoes around the overpriced, overspangled merchandise, so he slid out of his Keens and padded over to a plush pink chair. Sat among the sparkly stilettos and the poufy gowns and the pervasive memory of standing up at the altar with Lauren, her curves enhanced by a fussy little dress. *Penance, indeed.* He groaned inwardly and shoved the vision away, but the general surroundings of white and frill didn't give him much of a reprieve.

"Hey." Lauren's quiet voice broke into his thoughts, saving him from certain death by overexposure to taffeta. She stood a few feet away from him, wearing what had to be her maid-of-honor dress. The sweep of turquoise silk nipped and tucked at all the right places, highlighting all his favorite parts of her petite frame. His mouth went dry. "Hey. You look…"

"Ill? I've been sick three more times this morning."

She did still look pale. And he hadn't even asked her how she was feeling. He was such an ass. "Try incredible."

A tiny smile tugged at one side of her mouth. "Didn't expect to see you here."

"I—"

"Tav! You're here." His sister rushed into the room. Well, rushed as much as she was able, given she was waddling more than walking these days.

He stood and tried to look like he was enjoying himself.

"You're so forgiven for having forgotten your appointment." Mackenzie gave him a quick kiss on his cheek, sent him a look that they'd talk later and headed for the back of the store.

White. Frills. And *alone with my ex-wife.* A few choice curses rattled around in his head in time with the lingering Johnnie Walker throb. He rubbed his eyes.

Lauren looked from his decade-old hat to the ratty Yale T-shirt he'd put on this morning when he thought they were going kayaking. "Decided not to dress up for the occasion?"

"I haven't been back to the apartment. I went out to the river—" He cut himself off. The admission seemed too intimate.

"Figured you would," she said in a low voice.

And then all the focus shifted to Mackenzie as she emerged from the dressing room. Tavish stood back, separated from the oohs and aahs and tears. Tomorrow was going to be a cryfest if this was the reaction everyone had to a swath of white fabric.

He smiled at his sister, who looked like a chic Roman fertility goddess. "You look beautiful, Kenz."

"Thanks." His sister glowed—with love, with pleasure, with the flush of motherhood.

A notion of Lauren, belly all big with his baby, cheeks pink with that same glow, popped into his head.

Um, brain? Give me a break, here. That's a ways off yet.

Though not all that far off. Time would pass. Lauren's stomach, currently flat and taut under her fancy dress, would soon curve out, no doubt making her sexier than she already was. And then they'd feel precious kicks. And she'd complain about looking like a house and would demand ice cream...

And unless he made some major changes, he'd miss all that magic.

Damn it.

* * *

Lauren didn't know what to expect from the rehearsal dinner beyond the obvious: Tavish and Mackenzie's mom, Gwen, had gone to great expense to host an upscale affair. Crystal and linens fancy enough for an actual wedding graced the round tables on the stone patio.

Shaking her head, trying to prevent her spiky slingback heels from sinking into the lawn, she knew tomorrow's mountaintop ceremony and casual cocktail party in the midstation lounge would suit her brother and his fiancée far more than tonight's swanky atmosphere. But if Mackenzie was okay with the country-clubbish feel of the yard, Lauren wouldn't make a fuss about how ridiculous it was to host a party that didn't suit the honorees. She had enough to worry about having to pretend she wasn't getting the silent treatment from the other bridesmaid. Not to mention having the best man watch her like he couldn't decide whether to wrap her in protective bubble wrap or book a flight to Tasmania. But the rehearsal had gone off without a hitch, so she'd count that as a win. Apparently no one had noticed the family drama simmering under the surface. Or if they had, they hadn't mentioned it.

And they'd better keep on not mentioning it. It sucked enough that her sister wasn't talking to her on a weekend that should have been about having a wonderful time as a family. She didn't need their second cousins from New England questioning why Cadie wouldn't look her in the face. Didn't want to explain herself one more time.

Telling her dad this morning about the divorce had been plenty. He didn't seem to be as angry as Cadie. He'd been more quiet than anything, agreeing the wedding was the priority. That had all been over the phone, though, and she wanted to confirm his forgiveness in person. She spotted him over by the linen-bedecked bar and headed his way. She felt a little calmer when she was able to wrap her arms around him and rest her cheek on his summer suit jacket. "Hi, Dad."

"Just the girl I wanted to see." He took her under his left arm and accepted a drink on the rocks from the bartender with his right. "Need a drink?"

The offer caught her off-kilter. She'd been so busy worrying about Tavish that she hadn't come up with a good excuse not to be drinking. When she'd filled her dad in about the divorce, she'd kept silent about the baby. Nor did she feel guilty about that secrecy like she had with her marriage. The pregnancy was something for her and Tavish to coddle for a while before telling anyone else. But if she wasn't careful, her not having any alcohol would get noticed.

"I'm going to hold off until dinner, I think," she explained to her dad before addressing the bartender. "Could you make me a virgin mojito?"

The bartender nodded and took out a martini shaker.

She turned her attention back to her dad. With his mirrored sunglasses stuck in his hair and his good-humored grin, he looked more ski instructor than resort owner. His years of hard work showed in the sprinkling of gray in his brown-black hair, but the crinkle lines in his forehead were from smiling, not stress. Edward Dawson lived for his family, not his company. She wanted to follow in his footsteps in that. Lucky that her family and her job were intricately woven.

A niggle of doubt teased her consciousness at the word *lucky*. She pushed it aside and returned her dad's smile.

"You look like you got some sun, Cookie. About time."

"After my vacation, my clinic hours won't be so crazy." She hoped. She'd have to talk to Frank sooner

rather than later about her workload once the baby arrived.

"So you got your paperwork in?"

Lauren flashed to the stack of papers still on her table, still being ignored. "I—I will." She bit her lip. Should she tell her dad about the almost panic attacks she'd been having when she tried to scribble her signature on her contract? About the way her heart lunged into her throat whenever she pictured her name inked on the line?

"You know," her father's mouth tightened, "you don't have to sign on with the clinic. Any time I've brought it up lately, you've ended up with a frown on your face."

She closed her eyes for a few seconds. *Honesty. I said honesty.* "I…"

"You…?" he prodded.

Medicine doesn't… She stopped the gut-churning thought from finishing, took the mocktail the bartender held out and sipped away her conscience. "I'm happy, Dad. I'm going to deliver the agreement to Frank on my first day back from holidays. But I'm glad I took the time to ensure it's the right decision."

"Of course it's the right decision. You've been aiming to work in Sutter Creek since you were in high school. And your sister needs you here. As do I."

"I know." And a clinic partnership met every vocational goal she'd set. The Dawson name deserved to be on a plaque on one of the doors at the clinic again. So her trouble committing made no sense. Unless it meant… *No.*

"Your mom would be so proud of you, following in her footsteps." He laid a broad hand on the side of her head, stroked her hair. "She was a firecracker, right up to her last day. So are you."

Obligation pressed down on her chest. He had to bring out the big guns, didn't he? She wanted to be like her mom. And she didn't need the reminder that she'd been away on a stupid trip to summer camp when her mother had died of unexpected complications after a routine tumorectomy. *Stop it, Lauren.* She tried to inhale some courage. "I won't let either of you down. I've done that enough already this week."

With a slight eyebrow lift, he said, "I thought we were going to leave that alone for now."

"I still feel awful," she murmured.

"Look, I love Tavish like a son, but you'd make each other miserable. You fixed your mistake. That's what matters."

"Thanks for understanding." And for reminding her why she needed to stop scanning the property for a certain pair of violet-blue eyes.

He released her from his embrace and pressed at his sternum.

Worry shot up her spine. Hands on breastbones were rarely good signs. "You okay, Dad?"

"Eh, just reflux. Frank's got me on acid reducers."

She relaxed a tad at that admission, but not entirely. "Da-*ad*. Small symptoms can mask big problems."

"No nagging, Cookie. I'm exercising, eating right." He glanced to the side, eyes darting everywhere but her face. "Crud, I just remembered. The Creekside catering manager needed something confirmed with Mackenzie, and asked me to pass on the message. Excuse me for a bit."

He gave her one last squeeze and walked over to where her brother leaned up against the gazebo, snuggling with Mackenzie. The couple was deep in conversation with crutches-bound Zach Cardenas.

Had Lauren been in the market for a retired Olympian with rumpled hair and a cocky grin, she might have been interested in Zach. She had dated in the past year. Sut-

ter Creek was full of eligible men during ski season, and Zach was single, well-employed, charming. But Lauren had already tested the rumpled, cockily grinning waters, and found them to be life-threatening. And Zach's green irises didn't merit a second look compared to the purple-blue light show of Tavish's eyes. A light show walking toward her right now. *Crap.*

She pivoted ninety degrees, doing her best lawn-ornament impression and poking at the mint in her drink with the straw. Had he noticed her noticing him?

She watched him from the corner of her eye. The linen-and-twinkle-light atmosphere didn't suit him any more than it did Mackenzie and Andrew. He'd put on a pleated tuxedo shirt, probably to avoid confrontation with his mother, but the top two buttons were undone and his French cuffs were open and rolled up his muscular forearms. His jeans, faded in all the right places—all the places Lauren wanted to reacquaint herself with—completed the picture of a man so comfortable in his own skin that he'd wear leather flip-flops to a fancy party and look spectacularly hot doing it. She couldn't have been more opposite from him if she'd tried. Her own feet pinched in her heels, but being maid-of-honor at a glitzy rehearsal dinner required stilettos.

From halfway across the lawn, each step he took echoed low in her belly, pulsing aches of needy curiosity. Adjusting the flared skirt of her dress, she gave in to temptation and eyed the soft, blue-white denim covering his strong thighs.

He came to a halt six inches too close to her, close enough to feel the heat of his body. If he wanted to, he could lean in and kiss her. He wouldn't, especially not in public. And she shouldn't have been disappointed by that. But she was.

Physical intimacy was so far off the table now that they were going to be parents. But an undeniable magnetic want pulled them together. Arousal tugged between her thighs. The instinct to fit her body against his tempted rather than screaming *Danger*.

You do not want that. You can't.

"People watching?" he asked, turning to face the same direction as her.

"Um, Cadie and Ben." She pointed across the lawn, to where her sister, both hands holding Ben's, bounced the baby on his chubby legs. The pair crept along. Cadie looked to be showing off for Zach, who sat on the grass. Zach had been Cadie's husband's closest friend. But by the look on Zach's face, he didn't think of her like a guy did his buddy's widow. *Hmm. Must ask Cadie about that.* If Cadie ever started talking to her again.

She sipped at her drink and racked her brain for something to fill the silence. No small talk came to mind. Only massive, life-changing topics. The baby. Her uncertainty about her job. Wanting him back in her bed. Wishing they could find a way to be in each other's lives.

To create a life together.

Though I guess we already did that...

Glancing at him, she started at his wide eyes and pale skin. "Uh, why the shell shock?"

"Ben looks like you." His words came out jagged, like he had scar tissue in his throat.

"Kind of. Except for his eyes." Her nephew's cornflower-blue irises were all Cadie. Other than that, Tavish had a point. Ben had Lauren's blond hair, different from his dark-haired mother.

"I wonder if... I mean, our, uh... Well, she or he might—"

"Yeah," she said quietly. And unless Tavish did a massive lifestyle about-face, he wouldn't be around to see the miracle of watching a child grow. He'd miss seeing fragments of his own expressions flashed back at him. God, she couldn't imagine choosing that. Preferring instability and floating on the wind over providing a firm foundation for a child.

Tavish put a hand on her lower back and rubbed tiny circles with his fingertips.

The painful truth of his choices didn't take away the pleasure of his touch. The protective, masculine, guide-her-around-the-floor weight that made her so damn hot. She filled her lungs, tried to control the hurricane whipping along her limbs. "I remember watching you teach ski school. You were great with kids."

"Sure. But growing up, it didn't matter how many times my dad would tell me he loved me over the phone, I still doubted his sincerity when he missed my birthday." He pressed his lips together, stayed quiet for a few moments. "I might have been three, four, five, but I remember it like it was yesterday."

"So how are you going to be different?" There was no need to point out he'd already abandoned her, just like his father had done.

"I'm trying to figure that out." He drew his free hand down her cheek.

Too much. Too. Much. Her insides crumbled at the light caress, a rockslide of emotion pummeling her gut. He could be so sweet. So loving. But his habit of leaving before anyone could leave him? She didn't know how she was going to live with that. It was no longer just her she needed to worry about. Her eyes stung. She opened them wide, then blinked to prevent any tears from forming. Time to change the subject. "You shouldn't touch me. Everyone's looking at us."

He traced one more tender circle before withdrawing his hand and rubbing his neck. "I came over here for a reason. We need to figure out our speeches for tomorrow, make sure our stories aren't overlapping or anything."

"Speechwriting? Wasn't that the excuse you gave for staying at my house after waterskiing? We both know how that ended."

A dry bark of laughter shook his shoulders. "This won't, I promise. Work only."

"Fine." Lauren sucked the dregs of her drink through her straw before handing the empty glass back to the bartender. "One more, please."

Tavish shot her a questioning look.

"God, Tavish, it's nonalcoholic. And if I can make it through a family wedding without anyone noticing I'm not drinking pinot grigio, I'll call it a win," she said.

Once she had a full glass in her hand and Tavish had a beer in his, he returned his hand right to that same drive-her-crazy place and guided her toward the house. "We'll have privacy in my mom's office."

Great. Just what she needed—privacy and Tavish Fitzgerald.

Chapter Eight

Tavish steered Lauren into his mother's office, an expansive, rectangular room with a solidly built mahogany desk in front of the draped window and a sitting area to one side. The walls held his mother's multitude of books: legal texts related to her work as an attorney, historical biographies, mystery novels. He might have gained his father's need to flee, but he'd also inherited his mother's adoration for the written word. He definitely preferred the latter trait.

What would he pass on to his child? Hopefully more than an eye for composition and a tendency for transience.

His heart panged as Lauren slid away from his hand and took a seat on one of the wide armchairs flanking a granite coffee table. Mile-high barriers erected with one cross of her gorgeous legs and a mask of a smile. She took her teeny purse from her shoulder and slipped a piece of paper from it. "So. Speeches."

He nodded, pulled a sheet of loose leaf from his back pocket and slung himself into the chair opposite her. "Hey. We're away from the crowd here. Away from our families. Relax."

"Okay." The word came out uncertain, but her shoulders sank against the back of the chair.

They haggled over who got to tell which embarrassing story, and remembered way too many good memories from growing up, from back when they'd first fallen in love with each other. For a half hour, things ceased to be about the present.

Mesmerized, Tavish took in Lauren as she scribbled edits onto her closing paragraph. She held her pen cap between her lips.

He really wanted to be that chunk of plastic.

A flash of the inevitable struck. "Screw it."

"Screw what?" The words came out garbled around the pen cap.

He leaned toward her, placed damp palms on the cool, rock tabletop. "If I were being crude, I'd suggest each other."

Green-gold eyes widened. Her lips fell open and the pen cap clattered to the table. "No. We can't. Terrible idea."

By the flush in her cheeks, and the temptation glistening in her eyes, she looked damn convincible.

He lowered his voice to a near whisper. "Terrible? Really?"

She nodded fervently, sending her ponytail swaying.

"I wouldn't say terrible. Ill-advised, yeah. But we've never been less than spectacular in bed."

"That would complicate things even more."

His ex-wife wasn't just a pretty face. He'd always found her intelligence one of her more compelling traits.

And he was about to prove himself way less smart than she was. But she'd wanted honesty.

He could at least give her that.

"I love you, Lauren."

Mouth gaping, she stared at a point over his shoulder for a good minute. Finally, after he thought his heart would beat straight from his chest and out the door, disbelief lit her eyes. Her fingers loosened on the chair arms and the tips of her fingers turned pink again. "You mean you *did* love me."

"No, I mean I do love you. And now, with you carrying our child..." If he wasn't careful, what he felt for her would metamorphose right back into him being insanely *in* love with her. He moved to her side of the table, sat on the edge of the granite with his elbows on his knees. He captured her gaze with his. "We both know all the impossibilities, but for some God-only-knows reason, my feelings for you haven't, aren't and probably won't go away."

"That was grammatically incorrect," she breathed, sinking as far back as she could. "You could get your master's revoked for that."

"It got my point across. And stop trying to change the subject." Pinching one of the ruffles of her skirt, he teased the material between his fingertips.

Her teeth tugged her lip. The gauzy fabric on her tempting-as-sin breasts stretched as her breathing rate increased.

"All I'm saying is loving you is part of the equation for me," he said.

She leaned toward him, took his face between her palms. "We're crazy."

He groaned. That talented mouth, millimeters away from his skin. So close to touching. His tongue moistened his dry lips.

Crack. The door flew open and hit the wall.

Tavish jolted as his sister materialized in the doorway. Lauren's head jerked to look behind her. Her nails dug into his cheeks.

"Brother of mine! I've been looking for you everywhere." Mackenzie put a hand on her hip as she entered the room. Her eyes fixed on Lauren's hands, still cupping his face. "Oh. Jeez. Didn't mean to interrupt."

Lauren released him from her grip and stood up, turning so fast she wobbled on her heels. "You're not."

His sister crossed her arms. "Have you kissed and made up?" Pink bloomed on her cheeks. "Well, maybe not kissed. But made up."

"Yeah, we're good," he said, lying through his teeth but not seeing any other option.

The sigh Mackenzie released was loud enough he was surprised it didn't ruffle his hair from halfway across the room.

"Good enough," he clarified.

She crossed her arms and slid her gaze between Lauren and him. "Are you sure this is all in the past for you?"

"Our lifestyles are as incompatible now as they were last summer," he ground out. His seat on the coffee table put Lauren's right hand directly in his line of sight. She clenched it into a fist and the blood drained from her knuckles.

"That's not an exact answer to my question," Mackenzie said doggedly.

"It's the only answer you're getting."

It was all he could do not to reach for Lauren's tense fingers. To try to work them back to relaxation.

"I don't know why you think you can't grow roots, but I believe you can," his sister said.

His gut bottomed out. Her faith in him made no sense,

given how little he'd been around for the last decade. "Why? I've never proved that. Just like Dad couldn't."

"You're here now, aren't you? And you're staying to help after the wedding."

He shook his head. It was a nice thought, but he didn't share the same confidence in himself. Knew too intimately the skin-crawling feeling that prompted him to leave. That he ignored even now. "Do we seriously have to have this conversation?"

Her eyes narrowed in a you-owe-me glare. "Maybe you've changed."

Not unless he could alter his genetic code. "I don't think so."

Lauren let out a squeak. "I'm going to go find my brother."

"Lauren, wait." He reached out a hand to stop her but she evaded his attempt and swept from the room.

Mackenzie watched her friend leave and then glared daggers at him. "I think it was something you said."

"Gee, you think?"

"Yeah. And I think you're selling yourself short."

"No," he snapped. "We're just going to try to get through the weekend without stealing any more of the attention you and Drew rightly deserve."

"And then?" She sounded appreciative but suspicious.

"Then we're going to keep WiLA running. And when you're back, I'm gone." But not for as long as last time. He wanted to support Lauren where he could during her pregnancy. That would mean more frequent trips home. Even if he was suppressing his restlessness every second he was in town.

Mackenzie closed the space between them and sank into the seat Lauren had vacated. "I wish you'd stay." Her words spurted out like an arterial bleed.

"I'll come back."

"When? Two, four, six months from now?" Her voice took on a helpless tone. "You've only been home thirteen days of the last year."

Her arithmetic wormed its way under his skin, made him stiffen. "I didn't know you kept track."

She shot him a look of womanly scorn. "Of course I do."

He placed his palms on her knees and gave a squeeze. "I'll come back the minute you call me to say you're in labor. I'm going to take my uncle duties seriously. Someone's going to have to take some decent newborn portraits." And maybe by then he and Lauren would have a plan for their own child.

"I see." Mackenzie groaned as she eased back into the chair and toed out of her flats.

Concern panged at the sound of his sister's discomfort. "Are you okay?"

"Physically? Yeah."

"You're sure?" He examined her belly.

It twitched.

So did he. "How is that 'okay'?" Jesus, he had a lot to learn. With Lauren's medical background, she would know it all. And he'd probably end up feeling as incompetent supporting her through pregnancy as he did at the idea of becoming a father.

Mackenzie laughed. "That's normal. I'm pregnant with an active kid, is all." Her voice saddened. "I don't want a professional set of family photos taken on a brief visit home. I want you living in the same zip code as me."

"Kenz—"

"It's just… My old apartment's so close to my new house. You could live there for good. I could see you every day."

His throat tightened. Maybe he'd start using her place more often—he'd need some sort of home base if he was coming for visits with the baby—but it becoming his full-time residence? *Yikes.* Saying *I love you* was one thing. Living it was something he'd never quite managed to do. And he had just over seven months to learn.

The next morning Lauren dressed in her turquoise maid-of-honor gown. It felt tighter than yesterday. Had to be her imagination, or maybe discomfort from morning sickness. She was weeks away from showing. Ugh, if only she wasn't so pale against the vibrant shantung silk. She'd applied as much blush as she could without looking like a clown, but somehow last night had sucked all the color from her cheeks.

It was still only seven forty and Mackenzie had wanted to sleep until eight, but Lauren hadn't been able to follow her friend's lead. She'd been awake, staring at the ceiling for hours. Because the wedding dress code was reasonably casual, they'd decided to do their own hair and makeup. Lauren had pulled her hair back into a French twist. Pinned in tight. Just like her willpower to get through the next sixteen hours without falling apart.

Step one: avoid all thoughts of the words *I* and *love* and *you* being uttered by her fricking ex-husband.

Step two: well, no need to get carried away. Step one was going to take enough of her energy.

She brushed her hands over the below-the-knee hemline and took stock of her situation. Still pregnant. Her sister still hadn't spoken to her.

And Tavish still loved her.

Which was part of his *equation.*

But so was the fact he didn't think he'd changed. Seriously, how could someone hear they were going to become a parent and not change in some way?

She swallowed, trying to make the tension in her throat spread to her heart, provide some firm support for the day. If she managed to crawl into bed tonight retaining any semblance of emotional wholeness, she'd head straight for the convenience store and buy a Powerball ticket.

She glanced in Gwen Fitzgerald's main bathroom mirror one last time to make sure her all-day lip gloss hadn't adhered itself to her teeth, then made her way to the kitchen. Cadie, Mackenzie and she had stayed overnight after the rehearsal dinner. Mackenzie had slept in her old bedroom and Cadie and Ben had stayed in the main guest room, leaving Lauren lucky—*ha! There's that joke of a word again*—enough to spend the night in Tavish's old room. The collection of memories he'd taped over his bed—tickets from the Garth Brooks concert he'd taken her to in Missoula, his acceptance letter to Yale, a roll of camera film he'd refused to develop or tell her what was on it—had long disappeared. But the memory of him had spooned up against her, keeping her awake until the wee morning hours.

Hoping the bags under her eyes were disguised by the careful application of concealer, she sat down at the kitchen table with her sister, who was busy feeding a sleeper-clad Ben yogurt and applesauce. Cadie wore her bridesmaid's dress, identical to Lauren's, but had buttoned a men's Oxford shirt over the satin.

One of Sam's? Couldn't be. Her sister hadn't brought more than a box of her late husband's belongings when she'd moved home from Colorado. She swam in the garment, still way too thin even a year and a bit after being widowed. Jeez, on the summit of the mountain, where the ceremony was to take place, she'd blow over if a gust hit her.

"Sexy shirt," Lauren teased.

Cadie glanced down at her front, then back up at Lauren. Her lips pressed into a line and indecision flashed across her face before she cleared her throat. "Perfect for the ceremony, right? I know the light blue isn't quite the same as the turquoise, but it's close enough. I found it in Gwen's guest closet."

"It'll work awesome for pictures." She drummed her fingers against the table. "Can we talk, Cades?"

Her sister's smile stretched her skin across her jaw, cast hollows in her cheeks. "You didn't need me—didn't want to—and that hurts. But we shouldn't think about it today."

Lauren drew back. "But I do need your help."

"Don't force the issue just to make up."

"I'm not." It wasn't about finding something random to confess in order to make up with her sister. She needed Cadie as a confidante, damn it. There was no one else to talk to about Tavish.

"Yeah?" Cadie spooned another tiny heap of applesauce into Ben's surprisingly clean mouth, sounding cautiously hopeful. "Ready to stop treating me like I'm going to fall apart?"

"Yeah. I just didn't think you needed to worry about me. Didn't want to be your tipping point."

"Ah." Cadie switched containers and scooped yogurt onto the spoon. She let out a frustrated breath. "I'm not helpless, Lauren. And I don't get why you became the mama bear."

"Someone needed to be."

Her sister studied the floor. "You're not Mom, Lauren."

"I know that."

"Do you?" Cadie looked up, stared straight into all of Lauren's dark, ugly corners.

"Uh-huh." She couldn't get the sound out with the convincingness she wanted. "No one could be like Mom."

"No one *needs* to be like Mom."

Her chest tightened. She couldn't quite bring herself to agree.

Letting out a long breath, Cadie fed Ben the last scrapings from the bowl of applesauce. "It's too much effort to stay mad at family. I'll probably be hurt for a while, but it's impossible not to forgive you, Laur. But tell me something. When did you start sleeping with Tavish again?"

Lauren's jaw hit her lap. She reflexively touched her stomach—obviously still flat, so Cadie hadn't figured out about her failed attempt at closure that way. "I— What do you mean?"

"Come on," her sister scoffed. "The way he was looking at you last night? The way you were looking at him? No way has it been a year since you've done the dirty deed."

"Uh…" She wasn't going to lie to her sister again, but she couldn't make her voice work to admit the truth.

Cadie wiped Ben's face with a wet cloth and took her babbling son out of the old high chair Gwen had unearthed from the attic. Bouncing Ben on her lap, she pierced Lauren with a saberlike gaze. "You're not the only person who's worried about her sister. It's not exactly easy to mend a broken heart."

"My heart's already broken, Cadie. It can't get worse."

Cadie's look of disbelief was clear, and echoed the warnings in Lauren's gut. "Falling in love with someone twice isn't worse than doing it once?"

Not when you'd never stopped loving the person. But

loving Tavish wasn't enough. Hadn't been then, wouldn't be now. The day of her grandparents' funeral, he'd sat in his thinking place, a pleading look stretching his handsome face. *I can't take pictures of Montana forever.* And then the clincher: *Please. Love me enough to come with me.*

She'd said no.

And now her pregnancy made following him doubly impossible.

But living with the look of devastation she'd put on his face was no easier a year after the fact. Words tumbled out before she could stop it. "Memorial Day weekend. When he was home, we…"

"Made love—"

"Had sex."

"Semantics." Cadie waved a hand. "I think you love him, so it's making love."

It so had been. "I'm not going to disagree."

Ben tugged at one of Cadie's loose curls. Cadie untangled his fingers from her hair and kissed his fingertips. And Lauren flashed forward a year or two, to having her own baby. Alone, like her sister.

Her stomach rolled and she wrapped her arms around her midsection. "You want me to confide in you? Here goes—I'm pregnant."

Cadie froze, the only movement in her body the long, slow blink of her eyelids. Even Ben's tiny palm smacking her on the nose didn't get her moving.

"It's not that big a deal," Lauren joked, though the poor attempt at humor came out way too wobbly to be worthy of a laugh.

"You're pregnant."

"Yeah. I have a bone to pick with a certain prophylactic company."

Cadie shook her head. "Does he know?"

"Yeah."

"What are you going to do?"

"We haven't gotten that far." Lauren's heart clamored, made her want to rip the traitorous thing right out of her chest. Beyond its physiological necessity, the organ had been way too much trouble as of late. "He says he wants to be involved. But he also insists he can't settle in town." She scrubbed her fingers over her mouth, then stopped. Stupid nervous reaction, making her smear her lip gloss.

"That's a bit contradictory," Cadie said carefully, plunking Ben's diaper-cushioned bottom on the table in front of her.

"Just a little." Lauren fisted an abandoned paper napkin and began to worry the edges. "Get this—he says he loves me."

"He probably does," Cadie ventured. "But the way he loves and the way you need to be loved don't line up."

A wave of anxiety knocked Lauren off kilter. Were they too misaligned to even function as parents? "So what do I do?"

"It's not about what you do, Laur. It's about what he does. If he's going to say he loves you and wants to be involved, then he needs to prove that to you."

And that would be great and all, provided he was able to prove himself. But if he tried and failed, she didn't know if she could put herself back together again. Or if she talked to him about it and he refused to even try—for her, or their child—what would she do then?

Before Lauren could reply, Mackenzie entered the kitchen wearing a thin, knee-length bathrobe tied over her bump. "This looks like way too serious a conversation for my wedding morning." She grinned and placed her hands on the sides of her stomach. "You both look great. And I'm about to, as soon as I feed the poppy seed."

Cadie looked at Mackenzie's stomach and then pointedly at Lauren, but didn't say anything to break her confidence. "Kenz, don't get me wrong. You're stunning and gorgeous and every synonym for beautiful in the entire world. But that baby you're carrying is way too big to be referred to as a poppy seed anymore."

For the rest of the morning they fought with Mackenzie and Cadie's curls, got their fingers stuck together with false eyelash glue and interspersed the curses that followed with a whole lot of laughs. Plenty to occupy Lauren's attention. But keeping her mind on wedding prep involved more effort than she was capable of. The possibility of Tavish proving he loved her and wanting to be involved in raising their baby consumed her, refused to go away.

A wildflower carpet ringed the grassy area where, framed by summer-bare peaks, Drew and Mackenzie kissed at the end of their wedding ceremony. Tavish watched with stinging eyes, but hadn't heard a word. The script from his own vows, long since memorized, played on a loop in his head.

Love. Honor. Cherish.

Funny how fulfilling those vows had meant breaking off his marriage.

But the baby meant reconnecting in some way. It wasn't going to be as lovers or partners in the true sense of the word—nothing like having your *I love you* replied to with *We're crazy*—but there was still an intimacy involved in being parents.

The recessional music started and he pressed pause on the mental tape before it drove him totally insane.

Making eye contact with his ex-wife, he met her in the center of the altar and took her hand in the crook of his arm. They followed the bride and groom down the aisle.

It was utterly impossible to retreat from an altar with Lauren without envisioning her face when the organist at the little chapel on the Strip had struck up the beginning notes of "Can't Help Falling in Love with You." Lauren's hair still smelled sultry, tropical, like swimming under a Hawaiian waterfall. The scent wafted at him on the mountain breeze. Then, he'd wrecked her fussy up-do not five minutes after they'd left the chapel. That limousine ride...

He interrupted his memories with a string of silent swearing. Nine hours to go. Sure, they'd be working together for the next couple of weeks, but at least they wouldn't be thinking about weddings the whole time.

No, we'll be thinking about babies.

An incongruent blend of excitement and terror climbed into his throat as they approached the end of the aisle.

"Everyone's looking at us," Lauren whispered.

He slowed his pace to accommodate her. Her stupidly impractical—but atrociously sexy—shoes looked to be getting stuck in the ground.

"Well, you're starting to get that rosy pregnant glow," he replied, voice just as quiet as hers.

She flushed, hissed out a shush.

He cleared his throat, which had clogged as soon as he'd connected Lauren and pregnant and glow. "You're too easy to tease, sweetheart."

"I'm not in the mood." She dug her fingers into his arm. "I'm already having a hard time thinking about anything but embryos this morning without you bringing it up."

Blinding him with science. She was so damn sexy.

"Hey. Put it aside for the moment. Enjoy Mackenzie and Drew's day."

"You sound calm." She didn't. Confused, sure. Panicky, definitely.

"Mission accomplished," he muttered.

They headed for the location Mackenzie and Drew had chosen for their pictures, a wooden-railed viewpoint with a stunning vista of Sutter Creek and Moosehorn Lake. Teetering on her high heels as she followed the tree-lined path, Lauren linked her hands around his forearm. "These pictures will be beautiful, but I might break my ankle in the process."

He untangled his arm from her grasp and gripped her around her shoulders. "I could carry you."

She stopped walking, jaw hanging open as if he'd lost his mind.

Not far from the truth, really. "What? Drew picked up Mackenzie fifty yards back." The happy couple were the only ones ahead of them. The wedding guests were heading for the chairlift that would take them down to the cocktail party at the mid-station Creekview Lodge, and his mother and Edward Dawson trailed behind with Cadie, Ben and the slow-moving, injured Zach Cardenas.

"They just got married, Tavish. He's supposed to carry her around. If you did the same for me, people would talk. They already are, I'm sure."

"No one cares what we do, Lauren." He figured if he said the words with enough force, they'd become true. "Did you enjoy the ceremony?"

She gripped his arm tighter and started walking again, gaze affixed to the ground. "You wrecked it for me."

"Huh?" He figured between holding her up on their walk down the aisle, and helping her along now, all he'd done was stop her from falling over.

"I kept getting distracted by the mental picture of looking like Mackenzie come winter."

Tavish's gut tensed. "My thoughts might have drifted in that direction over the past forty-eight hours."

They walked silently for twenty more yards or so until they caught up to Mackenzie and Drew and the wedding photographer. Having their pictures taken prevented them from having any more private conversations. As much as he would have loved to, with being in the wedding party Tavish wasn't able to do all the photography for the wedding, but he did take the portraits of Mackenzie and Drew by themselves. As he snapped frame after frame, he recognized the looks of bliss on their faces as the same one he'd worn for the first five days of his own marriage. But they would manage to make those looks stick. Wouldn't fail like Tavish had.

Chapter Nine

In the corner of the turquoise-spritzed lounge of the Creekview Lodge, a pair of musicians played an acoustic guitar rendition of "Bewitched, Bothered and Bewildered." Lauren decided it was her theme song. She fit the definitions of all three of those words, and was closing in on bedraggled, beleaguered and besieged. Her hair had wilted during the speeches, and she was tired of talking to people who were being overly polite and obviously not asking her about Tavish. All the while their eyes glinted with curiosity.

Lauren sneaked out one of the sliding doors onto the balcony. She didn't begrudge her brother his lot in life, swaying to the music with his new wife. He deserved to fall in love and be happy about fatherhood and marriage and having a job he loved. But everything about today reminded her about how she had the opposite.

There was no point in falling in love with Tavish

again. Parenthood would be mostly on her shoulders—
he'd float in between trips to maintain a connection with
their child, but not with her. Cadie was right: Tavish saying he loved her wasn't enough. The words needed actions to mean anything.

The night air, still warm despite the setting sun, provided no relief from the sweat trickling under her strap-
less bra. She skirted behind the cluster of chairs arranged
for the post-dusk fireworks and headed to one of the
wooden staircases. Diamond-patterned metal grates
lined the steps. Necessary to stop skiers from slipping,
but treacherous for summer heels. Clinging to the cedar
railing, she minced her way from the deck to the ground
below. She didn't want to miss the fireworks, but wanted
to watch them alone. She squinted in the dim light and
found her way around to the picnic tables on the west
side of the building. Climbing onto the nearest table of
the group, she hiked her dress up enough to allow her
to sit cross-legged. She tugged off her shoes and rubbed
the balls of her feet.

As perfect as things were going to get. Removing articles of clothing couldn't alleviate the ache in her chest.

The sunset blended peach into pink into mauve, a gift
for the eyes. Tavish could do wonders with this display
of color. How could someone so capable of capturing
beauty not be willing to create the wonder of a marriage or a united family? But deep down she knew why.
It wasn't that he didn't want to. It was that he didn't believe he could. If time travel were possible, going back
a few decades and tearing a strip off Tavish's father for
having jerked his family around would be one of her first
stops. But fantasizing wouldn't actually result in Tavish
dealing with his issues. In him being an equal, committed partner.

Her eyes welled. Pulling her legs to her chest, she dropped her forehead onto her knees. The silk hem of her dress substituted for a tissue, absorbing her tears. She gently dabbed at her eyes with her fingertips. Her waterproof mascara would hold out, but the soft, brown eyeshadow was a goner. She gave up trying to look good and wiped with her thumbs until no trace of tears remained on her face.

The crunch of dress shoes on dirt approached from around the corner of the lodge.

She didn't need to ask who it was. Struggling to control her jagged breathing, she raised her voice to make sure it carried. "You followed me?"

"Yeah," Tavish called, voice low. He finally appeared—all half-disassembled tuxedo, rangy body and chiding expression. "You shouldn't be out here by yourself. You might run into a bear. And no one has any reason to come to this side of the building."

"That was the point. And I'd rather take on a bear than wedding guests."

"Me, too." Hands jammed into his pants' pockets, he stopped in front of the table. He'd lost his jacket after the speeches, and had removed his tie and rolled up his shirtsleeves since she'd last seen him dancing with his mother.

Too freaking sexy. She cleared her throat. "You weren't bamboozled into getting the show preserved in pictures?"

"Bamboozled?" A grin spilled light into his eyes. He climbed up on the table and settled behind her. His bent legs cradled her own. "No, my camera's retired for the night. The other photographer is competent enough."

She stayed tilted forward—though tempting, leaning back was a display of affection that would lead into dangerous territory. He rested his hands on her shoulders, massaging them with capable fingers.

Her flesh heated, went pliable. She stifled the moan threatening to erupt.

He pressed a thumb into a tender knot.

"Ahh," she groaned.

"Sorry. You're tight."

Yup, her muscles were wound to match her brain. "And I came out here to get some time away from everyone. Including you." *Especially you.* "No offense. But I'm hitting my limit for the day."

His hands stilled, solid and warm on her bare shoulders. "Guess I didn't help matters last night."

Her disbelieving snort echoed across the picnic area.

Dropping his forehead between her shoulder blades, he exhaled. "Hopefully, I won't make as much of a mess of helping out with your family's business as I have of our personal lives. Not that I'm taking *all* the credit here. It's unfortunate we can't find middle ground. But that's not new."

His words lacked true inflection, sounded over-rehearsed. As speeches went, she'd preferred his first of the evening, when he'd sweetly toasted his sister. She reached back with a hand, wove her fingers into his wavy mess of hair. "It's not about middle ground anymore. It's about creating security for our child."

"I know," he murmured. His hand slid from her shoulders to settle low on her belly.

Oh, that felt too good. Not in a tearing-clothes-off kind of way. No, Tavish's palm caressing her stomach felt like Sunday mornings in cozy pajama pants with animal-shaped pancakes and a sippy cup of apple juice alongside their mugs of coffee.

So a lie, then. It feels like a lie.

The brief spate of pleasure drained from her body. Losing the energy to keep herself upright, she leaned against his hard chest. His arms encircled her. Fingers finding purchase on his wrists, she teased the light dusting of hair and warm skin. The links of his bracelet were warm from the heat of his body.

She studied the piece closely. White and yellow-gold strips, bent and fused together in an irregular design, made a series of modern, Celtic-like knots. Only two twisted links, one thinner than the other, were identical in pattern. A pattern etched into her memory as she'd worn it on her own finger for a short-but-unforgettable spell.

"Tavish." Her voice echoed hollow from her chest. "These are our wedding rings."

"Yep," he murmured. His lips came to rest on the back of her hairline at the base of her French twist.

"You're still wearing your wedding band?" *And mine?*

"Not exactly. I took it off my finger." He traced the backs of his fingers down her shock-frozen cheek. "But somehow I couldn't let go of it."

Don't ask. You don't want to know. You don't *want to know.* "Why?"

Damn it.

"I couldn't let go of the last thing I had of you." He nuzzled her ear, buried his brow in the curve of her neck.

The need to reiterate her position, more to remind herself of her commitments rather than to remind Tavish, built up until it spilled out of her mouth in a torrent. "Love's not just feeling, it's doing, too. I'm not saying you need to be here every second of every day to be a good father, but you need to figure out some sort of regular visitation. Something concrete, dependable.

"I'm not going anywhere—I've got my job and my family. I have to mend the rift I've caused, prove I'm there for them. Re-establish my equilibrium well before the baby arrives. Their support will be critical as my pregnancy progresses and after the birth. But if you can figure out a way for us to have your support, too…"

"So stop thinking and start acting?" Tavish said, tone thoughtful. He splayed one big hand across her abdomen and slid the other up to cup one of her breasts. Languid heat ambled down her limbs, saturated her fingers and toes until they felt like lead weights. "Works for me."

She groaned. "We can't…"

"I'm not suggesting we make love, Lauren." One of his fingers circled her nipple and even through her dress and her bra it sent shockwaves of pleasure through her body. "But keeping my hands entirely to myself seems a shame."

"We're in a pretty public place…"

The first few bursts of fireworks thundered above them. "No one's coming around here. Terrible view of the show." Sliding out from behind her, he laid her down gently and climbed off the table. Excitement bordering on frenzied need tore through her as he stood at the end of the table and stroked callused fingertips along the insides of her thighs. "Awesome view for me, though."

Rising up on her elbows, she stared at him as the heat of a flush spread from her thighs to her belly to her breasts. "What are you doing?"

Tavish braced a hand next to her body and brushed his other thumb along her cheekbone, pulling her in to share a kiss that melted her insides. "You wanted actions over words."

"This isn't the kind of action I meant."

"I'll try what you meant. But I want this, too." His words weighed her down, and she sank against the hard wooden tabletop, destroyed by the powerless hunger in his gaze. "You… I can't…"

"You can, sweetheart. Open for me."

Whimpering, she let her legs fall to the sides. A thrill swirled in her core at seeing him on his knees. Eyes shuttered, he held her gaze as he sneaked her panties to the side. His thumb dipped into her center, and she bit her lip as her needy flesh throbbed around the sweet abrasion, then spasmed in complaint when he withdrew.

He settled his palms on the very tops of her thighs. "What do you want, Pixie?"

Her pleasure dulled at his words. She wanted all of him. Every day, every minute. She couldn't have that. But she could have him for a moment. And what a moment it would be. "I want your mouth."

The tawny curls on his head, lit with flecks of red and blue and green from the fireworks overhead, lowered to her most sensitive place. Hot breath panted against her skin. "Here?"

"Close."

She could feel him smile against her sex as he pressed the barest of kisses to her aching want. "Here?"

"Closer."

"Here, then." Spreading her with his thumbs, he ran his tongue along her slick flesh.

Raw currents of pleasure poured through her as she went tense and boneless all at the same time. She wanted completion, but this was too good to rush. Nothing mattered more than the aching press of his mouth against her center, of his tender hands loving her as if she were the best gift he could ever be given. Her body didn't care about the impossibilities, only registered the perfection of having his tongue curving around her sensitive, wet bud. Her muscles strained and her back arched. "Tavish!"

"Let go, Pixie." And his skilled fingers and mouth wouldn't let her do anything but.

She forgot about everything, a blessed gift, as he tormented and touched her until she dissolved under a sheet of white light. Booming fireworks covered the sound of her release.

"I love making you gasp my name," he mumbled. His breath came out in rushed gusts as he rested his cheek on her stomach.

"Mmm."

He righted her panties and tugged her skirt back into place. Utterly sated, she sent him a wobbly smile.

"Love making you smile, too." His expression faltered. The satisfaction dimmed in his eyes. And in that moment, she could almost read his mind.

If only it was always this easy.

By the end of Monday, after spending the morning at the outdoor rock-climbing facility and the afternoon polishing up winter brochures for the ski school, Tavish's mind hummed. It might not be the same as facing off with a polar bear with only his camera as a buffer, but working for WiLA had kept him engaged all day long. So much so he'd gone out after his shift and taken a series of pictures better than any of the work he'd done in Russia over the winter.

Inspired, and shocked by how much he wasn't hating life in Sutter Creek, he picked up the office phone and dialed the department head of Media and Theatre Arts at Montana State. *Nothing serious. Just putting feelers out.* Lauren wanted proof that his relationship with their baby would have some stability to it. And the thought of his child growing up with any of the doubt he himself had borne crushed his chest like a boulder. He couldn't always be around. But he could work on making his schedule more predictable. And maybe pick up some work closer to home for part of the year.

Dropping his name ranked as one of the more obnoxious ways to start a conversation, but it did get him the department head's direct line PDQ.

As soon as the receptionist put him on hold, he started doubting his decision. *Hang up. Hang up.*

His hand refused the command.

"Bob Davenport speaking."

Tavish vaguely recalled the man's name from somewhere, but the people he'd met over the course of his career were too numerous to always put a face to. "Good afternoon, Dr. Davenport. This is Tavish Fitzgerald. Thanks for taking my call."

"I know your work well. And call me Bob. What can I do for you?"

Hang up. Hang up. "I'm wondering if you have any positions coming up on your faculty in the near future."

That was the opposite of hanging up. *Argh.*

"Well." Bob Davenport sounded flabbergasted. "We don't have any specific positions… Were you looking for full-time?"

"No. Not at all. Maybe two courses a year, max. Preferably to do with environmental photography. Getting the message of a cause, an emergency, across in a few frames."

"No political causes?"

"I could teach it. But I'm not going to accept any more of those assignments." Tavish used to get a rush from war zones and unstable regions. But getting killed by an IED while on assignment was no longer an option. He couldn't promise to always be in Sutter Creek, but he could at least do his best to stay alive.

Davenport hummed thoughtfully. "Do you have a master's degree?"

"Yes, from Yale."

"Good, good. Send me something on paper, but you're plenty qualified with that degree."

"I figured. And I'm interested in settling semipermanently into the area now." The words were coming out of their own volition. They had to be.

"I have to say, I'd scrounge up some money to make room for you. I can't offer you a permanent position, but you could come in as an artist-in-residence. It would involve teaching seminars, supervising some student projects, and would give you some time to continue with your own work. The salary is by no means substantial…"

Ah, academics. Tavish had a feeling the hiring process wasn't as simple as Bob Davenport made it sound. Then again, it didn't matter if it didn't turn out. This was an exploratory call, not a commitment. "I'm not worried about the money. I'll keep doing location work."

"When would you want to start?"

"My schedule's clear come November. I could be yours for the winter session."

Holy hell. He blinked, floored by his own statement. The winter session? Talk about a way bigger step than he'd been intending on taking today. *How's that for action, Lauren?*

"I don't want to get ahead of myself, but I feel good about it," the other man said.

The receiver vibrated against Tavish's ear as his hand started to shake.

"I'm going to make this happen," Davenport continued. "We can't pass up someone of your caliber."

Sweat beaded on Tavish's forehead and dampened his T-shirt despite the air-conditioning. "Thank you for the compliment," he choked out.

"I'll call you back as soon as I figure out logistics. Give me a few days."

They exchanged cordial goodbyes, then hung up.

Tavish stared at the phone. That had been too damn easy.

He'd completed his masters to get more credibility behind his name, but maybe it would come in handy, provide him with a challenging and productive job in Montana. One that would still allow him to work abroad. Hope blossomed in his chest. He could experiment with how many assignments he had to take in a year in order not to feel like he was crawling out of his skin in Sutter Creek. Half the year here, half away, maybe.

He closed his eyes. Defeat erased his desperate attempts to be positive. The urge to leave would come. Maybe not as often as in previous years. But enough to be a wall between him and Lauren. Half a year. How could that possibly be enough?

But how could he not at least try?

Chapter Ten

Lauren trudged toward the base lodge early Monday evening, giving mental kudos to her brother. Running WiLA was a pile of fun, but that fun came with a fair degree of challenge. So far today she'd juggled staff scheduling requests, put out fires with a bookings glitch and called in a maintenance crew when a fuel injector had crapped out on the Peak Chair's prime mover. However, it was better than suturing wounds.

No. Dealing with a fricking diesel engine is not better than medicine. She shoved the door of her brother's office in the basement of the main lodge and held back a groan as it swung open.

Tavish sat at Zach Cardenas's desk, studying a sketchbook. She'd been hoping for some time to herself to end the day, but no, no reprieve for her.

Probably a good thing given they needed to talk about what had happened at the reception, though knowing a conversation was necessary didn't mean she actually *wanted* to have it. Maybe he expected quid pro quo for how well he'd pleasured her on that picnic table. It would only be fair. That table, or maybe his tongue, merited being bronzed. But though they'd walked back to the lodge hand in hand—separating before they'd run into any guests, mind you—she hadn't seen him yesterday. This morning, he'd kept things super light between them, greeting her with an exaggerated, sexy grin and a comment about getting to play secretary to the boss. Did he intend to end the day in the same vein?

Slumped in his chair, he lacked his customary, just-shy-of-arrogant confidence. He greeted her with a bare nod. No more teasing, then. Whatever was on his page was demanding his full attention.

She straightened her hiking shorts and perched herself on the corner of his desk. "Where's my end-of-the-day innuendo? It perked me up better than a coffee this morning," she teased.

He lifted a shoulder and traced her knee with the pencil in his hand. "Just tired."

Based on the color in his cheeks and the lack of smudges under his eyes, she doubted it. "You sure?"

"Yeah." He ran his hand through his hair. "I just got off the phone with…work stuff. Got me a little edgy, I guess." Dropping his pencil on the desk, he traced her knee with the tip of his finger instead.

Her breathing kicked up a notch. She linked her fingers with his to prevent him from traveling closer to the hem of her shorts. Hyperventilating would not project an I-can-take-you-or-leave-you image.

Leaning forward, she caught a better view of his creation, which looked like his thinking place. She'd last been there with him after her grandparents' funeral.

She'd been distraught and he'd used his skillful hands and mouth to get her mind off her grief. Then they'd argued.

And he'd left.

Just like he'll leave in a few weeks. She forced the thought to linger, let the full weight of it settle on her shoulders. "Can I see?"

His guarded eyes studied her for a moment before he passed the book to her with a flick of his wrist. "I guess."

Lauren rotated the pad. The flowing water was indelibly and precisely etched. Alive on the page. "Tavish," she breathed. "This is incredible."

He shrugged. "Fine arts electives came in handy. I can create something decent with most art materials."

"This is beyond decent. You could sell this. I feel like I could put my hand through the page and bring it out dripping."

"Thanks for the compliment, but I couldn't sell my sketches."

"But drawings and photography are both art. And you're gifted in both media."

"I'm not above selling my art. Obviously. But that—" he pointed at his sketchbook with the unsharpened end of his pencil "—that's me. I don't sell myself."

"I can see your heart in this, definitely. I think I get what you mean." She flipped the page.

And was staring into a mirror.

Her breath caught in her throat. "Oh, my God."

She tried to breathe evenly. He'd rendered her face with such detail, such reverence. If his art was a part of him, then did he consider her a part of him still?

"Tavish." She traced a finger along the two-dimensional replica of her nose.

He kept his gaze on his tented fingers in his lap. "Your eyes are the same color as the river as it changes from

shallow to deep. I was at that spot, and remembered..."
Turning red, he looked around the room with a panicked
jerk to his motions. He stood and grabbed a clipboard. "I
have to go debrief with the rafting folks."

He bolted through the door faster than the river at
spring melt, leaving Lauren holding a mirror-image picture of herself but no longer knowing who she was beneath the surface.

Straggling into the WiLA office two days later, Lauren collapsed into the office chair. Hump day number one
was over, and she was pleased with how she'd done so
far. Andrew's job was mainly supervisory, but like her
brother, she couldn't help but get involved in operations.
She'd have preferred to actually do some of the guiding,
but being pregnant precluded buckling on a climbing har-
ness. Tavish had filled in the gaps where necessary—they
made a good team. On the job, at least.

A single daisy, stuck in a water glass next to her key-
board, drew her attention to a sticky note attached to the
flat-screen computer monitor.

Meet me at my place at 7.

My place.
Huh. Up until now, Tavish had always called the pretty
apartment just off Main Street "Mackenzie's place." Lauren sank farther into the chair. Why did he have to tease
her with little steps toward growing roots? It didn't matter how many little steps he took—he wouldn't be able
to make the big leaps.

Don't forget that. If they were going to function together as parents, they had to resist their emotions—and
their physical pull. So what if he still kinda-sorta wore

their wedding rings? She still hadn't convinced him to stay put in Sutter Creek.

But...my place...?

No. She couldn't count on him.

Stay firm.

She recited the words to herself as she closed up and headed home. As she changed into a T-shirt and a stretchy skirt that skimmed her knees. As she drove to Tavish's, and especially when she read the Post-it note on his door, written in the same bold print as before.

Come on in, sweetheart.

Her internal stay-firm mantra wavered in the face of his words, the confidence of his penmanship. And when she cautiously opened the door, walked through the entryway into the high-ceilinged living and dining area, the chant shriveled and died.

All of Mackenzie's old furniture—gone. She stroked her hand along the back of the polished leather couch. He'd decorated with raw-wood coffee and end tables and a Peruvian rug. A square dining table filled the other end of the rectangular room. Some late-nineties rock played quietly from the docking station on a tall, wide bookshelf next to the unlit fireplace. An assortment of hardcovers and paperbacks stood on the half-filled shelves.

And the art—a fist of emotion gripped her throat when she realized he'd personalized the walls. An eclectic blend of his photography—the sharp angles of New York City architecture, the twirling spires of Eastern Europe, the towering ice of Antarctica—mixed in with internationally flavored prints. Every single item a piece of Tavish.

Her eye was drawn to the mantel. Oh, sweet Lord. Two

framed pictures were nestled with a collection of colored rocks. One of Andrew and him hanging off a rock face, and one of Mackenzie, their mom and him at Mackenzie's wedding that he'd clearly had printed in the last few days. She said silent thanks for the fact he hadn't put up a picture of her—that would have reduced her to a helpless puddle of skin and bones and need.

"Lauren?"

She spun. "Hey."

He stood in the doorway to the little galley kitchen with a tomato-splattered dish towel tucked into the waist of his jeans. One muscle-roped arm braced against the door frame. Good God. The human body was a marvel, and Tavish's, with all its long lines and hard definition, never disappointed. Desire curled in her belly, stirring against her fascination with every part of him. Her confusion rolled into a great, brewing, uncontainable churn.

His eyes gleamed. "Hungry?"

"Sure." For more than food. She cleared her throat. "I like what you've done with the place."

"Thanks. I'll need to have a home base for the sake of the baby, and this works. I thought I could put a crib and stuff in the spare room."

Unsettling reality encroached on the happiness from seeing his personal mark on the apartment. Why hadn't she considered the separation involved in coparenting—him having his time with the baby, her having her time? Dealing with custody and deciding who got what weekend and arguing over holidays? Her stomach rolled worse than from morning sickness.

His brow wrinkled. "Isn't this what you wanted, Lauren? Me, showing some consistency?"

"Well, yeah, but—" She bit her lip.

"But...?"

But what she said she wanted and what she really wanted were two different things. Him making changes to support her and to love their baby checked boxes but didn't actually fill her soul.

"I love you," she blurted. Holding herself up under his startled, steaming gaze, she balled her fingers into fists and fought the hot moisture pricking the corners of her eyes.

"I love you, too." Tavish took two long strides and gathered her into his strong arms. Kept her upright as her legs turned to gelatin. She gripped handfuls of the back of his soft T-shirt and lost her grip on her tears.

"Hey, shh." He stroked a gentle hand through her loose-hanging hair. "We'll figure something out."

His shirt muffled her "How?"

"We'd intended to compromise before—we can do it again. Maybe you and the baby can travel with me sometimes. Your family isn't asking as much of you as they did last year—"

"No." She leaned back and wiped her eyes before staring into his. The hope glinting there shattered her heart. "It's not about what they expect from me. It's about what I expect of myself. And I want to be here for them. Nor will I be able to leave the clinic for long stretches of time."

Music from the docking station filled the hollow silence of the room. Failed to fill the hollowness of her heart.

Tavish didn't say anything, just pressed his fingertips into the base of her spine.

"We might be able to manage if you only left for two or three months a year."

Dropping his hands from her body, he jammed his fingers into his hair, squeezed at the messy strands. "I was thinking more half and half. But I'm trying, Lauren. I even called about taking a part-time position at Montana State—"

"You did?" Losing control over her jaw, she stared at him, hands hanging limply at her sides. Staying resolute was so much easier when it was all his fault. But now— the apartment, the job...

Tavish's forehead wrinkled. "Yeah, I did. I can't put our child through what I was put through. I know you're not willing to come with me when I work—can we come up with a different solution?"

She could barely look at him, so sweet and hot and staring at her with challenge flashing in his eyes. "You left me last time. You will again."

Was that her voice, that desperate, shrill noise?

Anytime she'd heard that tone come from anyone else, she'd viewed it as a sign of stubborn irrationality. That couldn't be the truth in her case—her devotion to her family and the clinic wasn't irrational. Tavish changing his life only affected Tavish. A compromise by her had the potential to hurt the baby, her dad, Cadie... They needed her to be here, to support them. And she had to follow through on her promise to her mom, follow through with the clinic. She pressed both hands over her heart in an attempt to quell the ache in her chest.

Tavish let out a gust of air. With a slight nod of his head, he said, "You're right. I'll eventually leave. But this time, I'll come back."

"And a part-time relationship between us is no less plausible now than it was last year."

"Not unless you're willing to sever the umbilical cord between you and your dad—"

"Enough." She cut him off before he could hammer any further dents into her reasoning. The professional in her started to nag that she was nearing the definition of phobic, but she ignored it. Wanting her family happy and safe was not a phobia. It wasn't. She'd seen what happened when she acted selfishly. "Do you remember where I was when my mom's surgery went sideways? At summer camp, having a grand old time. And when my grandfather was dead on the side of the road, my grandmother in a coma, I was off marrying you. Pretending that it was okay for me to have given up the plans I'd made with my mom before she died." She rambled on, desperate for him to understand. "I won't put myself before my family again. My dad and Cadie need me here. And the baby will need that stability, too."

"And what if I need you?"

His pleading whisper pushed her over the edge. "I have to go." She crossed her arms, tried to hold in the blood from the verbal knife he'd just shoved between her ribs. He needed to stop looking at her like he was tearing into pieces. She couldn't handle it. Because he was compromising. He was trying.

Which only made it obvious how much she wasn't able to do the same.

Backing toward the front door, she said the only thing she knew would make him shut up, make him close off. "Call me if you decide you love me enough to put me ahead of your job."

Chapter Eleven

"Lauren Dawson? Come in, Lauren Dawson." Tavish had arrived at work today intending to press her more after she'd bolted from his apartment last night. They'd made eye contact at a morning staff debriefing but she'd run off the second the meeting ended and had ignored his text messages. Much like she was ignoring his end-of-shift radio pages.

Maybe she was avoiding him because she was afraid he'd be angry over her sharp parting shot. Maybe it was a measure of self-preservation. Either way, he wasn't mad—she had a right to call him out on his flaws, and he got her need to protect herself. It only left him more determined to prove that he loved her and wanted to try for a solution. They both needed to figure out how to have a balanced perspective on their hometown. He wasn't the only one who had a messed-up tie to the town. Lauren wanting to help her family was one thing. Being petrified to leave home was another. And her eyes had snapped with real fear yesterday.

Pressing the push-to-talk button, he repeated his page. She was scheduled to be doing safety checks at the river-rafting base camp, well within transmission range. He leaned back in his seat, picking up the list Lauren had left taped to Zach's computer screen. Back when they were married he might have called it a honey-do list, but they hadn't been married long enough to get into the habit of her making him lists and him pretending to complain about it.

The domestic picture made him smile, even though they weren't even close to finding that together. His efforts to chip away at his issues with Sutter Creek hadn't been enough for her so far—her rejection last night had made that more than clear. Had left him feeling emptier than he knew possible. The desolate look on her face had been enough to make him want to start digging a trench in her front yard. Prove he wasn't going anywhere, even if he couldn't believe he had that in him. Of course, she would have made it easier to tell her all of this had she picked up her phone one of the ten times he'd called her since she fled, leaving him with a pot full of spaghetti sauce and a heart full of regret.

About thirty seconds passed by before his radio crackled. "Lauren Dawson here. Is that you, Tavish?"

"Yeah. Uh, this is an open channel, but your cell seems to be off. Would you meet me for dinner at the hotel lounge?" Time to step up further. If she could show him a little patience, he'd be willing to go for a longer trial period.

The radio sat silent for way too long. After she'd given him enough time to knit a sweater, she replied, "I'll see you at six."

He heard every second tick by on his watch until it finally read six o'clock. He arrived at the lounge early, having gone home to shower and change into a pair of dark jeans and a checked dress shirt. Settling into one of the wing-backed chairs at a table for two, he studied one of the deer-horn-chic chandeliers.

The minute Lauren walked into the room wearing a casual, swirly, hot-sauce-red dress, his heart stopped.

"Look what you're missing," the dress screamed.

Message received, Dr. Dawson.

Heads turned as she traveled through the room. He stood and pulled out her chair.

"Tavish." She sat and crossed her legs. "Thought we covered everything we needed to last night."

"We covered it. But we didn't make any decisions. You ran off after making some awfully hypocritical claims." He tried to look her in the eye but she kept her gaze on her water glass as he sat. "As if I'm the only one who's committed to my job at the expense of our relationship."

Squaring her shoulders, her eyes snapped. "You have five minutes to convince me I want to order something for dinner."

No guarantee she'd stay even if he managed an argument worthy of one of his mother's closing statements. Better to make his point in the limited time she was giving him rather than wait and hope she'd let him buy her dinner. Unraveling the thick cloth napkin from his cutlery, he laid it over his lap. "You know, I never really think about it, but I guess you own part of this place, don't you?"

"Yes. Ten percent. Twenty-five of the new holistic health center that's opening next month." She glanced at her thin gold watch. "Four minutes, thirty-two seconds."

"And you're sure you enjoy being a doctor more than working for AlpinePeaks?"

Her eyes flashed. Not anger, though. Fear. "Medicine is me. And you're down to four minutes," she snapped, a poor attempt to cover up her obvious discomfort. She sank into her chair as if trying to blend with the navy-striped upholstery.

Impossible in that dress. Not that she needed to be wearing anything specific to stand out to him.

"The baby's the most important priority, and I fully intend to make my work schedule predictable," he said. "I'm willing to do a test run before the baby arrives, too. See how long I can stay in town before getting the urge to hop on a plane. I'll stay in town until I head for Phuket in the fall, and will come back when my contract is finished. We'll see where we stand. But I can't be the only one who gives, who sacrifices. You have to consider your choices, too."

Lauren blinked her mossy-gold eyes, the moisture in them almost forcing him to slide off the chair and fall to his knees. Her brow lowered and her lips pressed together. She sat there for a few seconds, staring at him hard enough to etch a laser dent in his forehead.

"And which of my choices would those be?" she bit out.

He pressed his lips together. She hadn't been willing to listen when he'd tried to argue that her dad and Cadie were grieving less than last year, so a different tack might be best. "I remember your mom being a compassionate woman, Laur. Had she lived, do you really think she'd have expected you to stick to a teenage dream?"

"It was her dream, too."

"Was it? Or was she just humoring what she likely thought was an in-the-moment passion?"

She covered her mouth, one hand crossed over the other, and let out a muffled, tearless sob.

The noise cut right through him. He was too far away to reach her, didn't know if she'd want him to anyway. "What do you need, Pixie?"

Squeezing her eyes shut, she fisted folds of the red fabric of her skirt. "I need to give those papers to my lawyer."

Wow. He'd gotten more than five minutes, but the answers he'd hoped she'd give eluded him. He'd hoped some more compromise on his part would prompt her to take even a tiny step toward him. Seemed he was out of luck there. What was it going to take to loosen the grip that Sutter Creek had on her?

Friday morning, Lauren got to the WiLA office early. She hadn't been able to sleep more than a sweaty patchwork of dreams and haze. Add in her pregnancy-induced craving for naps, and she was dragging her feet as she entered the office.

Yawning, she settled at her brother's desk and shifted papers around, staring at a few columns of numbers before recognizing her sleep-deprived uselessness. She'd screw up all her efforts to organize the winter first-aid inventory if she tried to do anything number-related. Instead, she opened a web browser on her brother's computer. Spending ten minutes getting caught up on royal family gossip was completely justified.

At 8:22 a.m., Tavish strolled in with his camera bag slung over a muscular shoulder. A pair of mirrored aviators managed to keep his hair sticking up only four, instead of six, ways to Sunday. Dark charcoal water splotches marked the gray cotton of his T-shirt and his khaki shorts looked to be completely soaked through.

Only his flip-flops looked dry. His smile was so wide it sucked all the administrative boring out of the room. She wished she could keep that level of energy in a jar for the days when life stole the grin from her face.

"Felt like a swim?" she asked.

He met her cocked brow with a sheepish smile. "I slipped on the edge of a bridge and ended up waist high in the creek."

"On which trail?" Clients taking headers into creeks wouldn't be the best for business.

"Summit."

She narrowed her eyes, no longer worried about people slipping and falling. "All the bridges on Summit have rails. And they were all intact yesterday."

"I might have been sitting on the railing." The corner of his mouth turned up. "It was the only way to get the right angle of a pair of dragonflies hovering over a rock in the middle of the creek."

"Did you wreck your camera?"

"I'm like a cat. I always land on my feet with my camera hand in the air." He demonstrated with an exaggerated pose.

"You are kind of catlike."

"Graceful?"

"Elusive."

A faint shadow crossed his face. "Ouch."

Heat splashed Lauren's cheeks and the back of her neck. "Sorry. Not what I meant."

"What did you mean?" Caution edged his tone.

"I was referring to your wanderlust, not your personality."

His earlier demeanor that had shone 120 watts of vibrancy into the room dimmed. "Right. Anyway, I need to ask a favor of you."

"Of course." Anything to make up for insulting him, for accusing him of being something he wasn't.

"I scratched myself. I was hoping you'd clean it up for me."

"Okay." Did her voice shake? *Please, no.*

Tavish looked at her funny.

Gah, her *okay* had for sure vibrated.

"You don't have to, Laur. I can go to the clinic."

She shook her head. "Of course I can do it."

"You sounded—"

"I'll do it," she insisted.

She led the way to the red-cross-labeled door at the end of the hall. Flicking on the light, she motioned him in. "Lie facedown on the cot."

The room suffocated her like a mouse hole. A stainless-steel counter and supply cabinets lined one wall; the cot, the other. Tavish settled himself along the length. Lauren glimpsed blood-soaked gauze and her stomach turned. She would love to blame morning sickness, but nope.

On his stomach, Tavish propped himself up on his elbows, straining the shoulders of his T-shirt. She snapped on a pair of gloves, would have preferred reacting to his hard muscles rather than his cut calf.

"I hope this habit of me being attacked by errant branches and you having to patch me up stops after today," he said.

"Me, too. Wouldn't want any more scars on you." Would prefer to never see his blood again, was more like it. She really hated...

No. You're fine. Swallowing, she slid a thick pad of sterile dressings under Tavish's calf to absorb the saline she planned to use to clean out whatever lay under his bandage.

She peeled back his makeshift dressing. Objectively, his cut wasn't bad. Through the lens of her nerves, though, she had to resist the impulse to dart from the room. "God, you're a bleeder."

"Yeah. Always makes it look worse than it is."

Whenever a real emergency hit, adrenaline kicked in, masked her fear. Times like this were what killed her—plenty bloody but lacking the life-or-death chemical surge.

Metallic saliva flooded her mouth. She clicked into automaton mode: clean, dry, dress. A bead of sweat trickled from her temple along her jaw.

"All done," she whispered. She grabbed his old dressing and the dirty under-padding. And she had no time to do anything except spin, aim for the sink and lose her breakfast.

Head hanging over the basin, forehead pressing against the cool metal tap, she turned on the water to wash away the evidence. She hadn't been uncontrollably sick from handling a wound since the first weeks of medical school. She'd trained herself not to react. Why had it changed?

Don't ask a question you don't want the answer to.

She glanced at Tavish and rested her forearms on the counter edge.

He sat straight-backed against the wall with mile-wide eyes. "Morning sickness?"

"Yeah."

His expression flattened. "You're lying."

"I'm not." She bit the edge off the *not.*

"Try again."

Lying required too much effort. "Blood makes me sick." She let that hang in the silence as she rinsed her mouth with water from the tap.

He stood and took her in a tight embrace. Her clammy forehead rested against the skin of his neck. His river-dampened clothing cooled the heat of embarrassment from her body.

"Does this usually happen when you're working?"

"No. I learned to control it. It's just come back over the last month or so."

"Because of the baby?"

She'd love to blame being pregnant, but couldn't bring herself to do it. "No. It's the stress of the partnership."

He exhaled through pursed lips. A faint whistle rode the stream of air. "Lauren."

The warning tone singed her pride. "I'm dealing with it."

"How?"

"I find the closest toilet." She smiled out her humiliation, pressed dry lips to his cotton-covered clavicle. "It's funny, you know…"

"I don't see you laughing," he murmured.

"Not funny ha-ha, funny hmm." Tracing her fingers through his hair, she said, "I've had thousands of good days in my life, yet it's the bad ones that have defined who I am."

"That's not unusual. I wouldn't be who I am today without my father having bolted." His words came out so matter-of-factly, she'd have missed his decades-old pain had she not been peering at his face.

"Exactly. And my mother's death clarified so much for me. Everyone started to say how much I was like her, and how tragic it had been that she'd died so young without really having been able to put her mark on the medical field…"

He sat down on the cot and pulled her onto his lap,

rubbing her bare knee with one rough hand. "Those two things aren't connected."

"Sure they are. That's what pushed me to become who I am."

"But it doesn't mean you can't change. If medicine doesn't make you happy, then you should try something else. You were going to give up the clinic to work internationally. Maybe you need to change fields entirely."

Her spine drew up. She met the encouragement in his gaze with what she hoped was confidence. "I can't just find a new career. Yeah, I was going to give up the clinic for the sake of our marriage. I'd convinced myself my mom would have been okay with that. But I was wrong."

"How can you be so sure?" His voice was so low she could barely hear it.

"I make a mark for her, Tavish." Working at the clinic, holding their family together—filling in the cracks that had formed when her mom had died.

He stroked a calming hand up to her shoulder blades. "You need to make a mark for you, not for everyone else."

"It's the same thing."

"There you go, lying again."

The murmured accusation sneaked under her skin. She squeezed her eyes shut, but not before moisture gathered at the corners. "I can't let my family down any more than I already have."

He wiped at her cheeks with the pad of his thumb. "Letting yourself down is the bigger crime."

He was making way too much sense. She hugged her rib cage. The vain attempt at shoring up her throbbing middle fell short. A cavernous ache spread from her chest into her limbs. "I can't be that selfish."

His arms stayed firm around her, as if he could sense how close she was to stumbling backward and curling into a ball on the cot. "Are you going to expect our child to be a doctor?"

"No." She pressed the pads of her thumbs against her eyes. "Of course not."

"So why would your mom—"

"I told you yesterday!" Her heartbeat raced. "It's about my expectations for me."

"Can't those adjust, Lauren? Parenthood's kinda the ultimate game changer."

"Are you finding it that way?" she retorted.

"Yeah, I am." Awe brightened his beautiful face. Acceptance and happiness she'd never expected from him. He'd made the commitment to stay for the summer and didn't seem to be regretting his decision at all. He'd proved he could change. So why couldn't she do the same?

She clamped down the thought. Tavish changing meant him trying to be a good father, a good partner. But the changes he was suggesting she make would be the opposite. Following him around the world would mean less stability for their child and would make it impossible for her to support her family. Scrunching up her face, she sighed, but it came out more like a wheeze.

He blanched and dropped his hand to her belly. "You feeling okay?"

"Baby-wise, yeah."

His obvious relief came out with a long breath. But he didn't take his hand away. Spreading his fingers low on her stomach, he kissed her forehead. "Never thought I'd hear myself saying this, but I'm so damn impatient for when I can feel our baby move inside you. To have you get so big that your bump gets in the way when I sneak a kiss."

Petals of pleasure—from the naked vulnerability he

showed, from the rush of joy of the intimate touch—
bloomed through her body. She settled her hand over
his, wanting to savor every second of having him connect with their child.

With her.

Her opportunities would be limited. And that sucked.
Only having him with her for six months of the year, dealing with weeks, months maybe, of Skyping and sleeping
next to an empty pillow, sounded miserable. But less miserable than having him sleeping in a separate apartment
when he was in town to visit their child. She didn't know
how to deal with him being away from her. Arranging
visitation, though, dropping off the baby at his apartment and going back to her big house alone... So much
worse. She couldn't meet him halfway when it came to
the clinic, to her family. So to compromise at all, she'd
have to learn to deal with missing him. To give him a
chance to leave and, like he'd said, trust him to return.
She made sure her smile tinted her tone when she said, "I
thought we'd agreed you weren't going to sneak kisses."

"No way can I stick by that promise," he growled.
With his hands on her waist, he spun her until she straddled his lap, groaning as she rolled her soft center against
his hardening length.

"No way would I want you to keep it." She cursed the
barrier of their shorts, layers of fabric keeping her from
blissful fulfillment. Bracing her hands on his rock-solid
shoulders, she closed her eyes and rolled her hips, welcoming the heat from the tantalizing friction of their
bodies.

Curving a hand under her ass, he dug his fingers into
the hair at her nape. His mouth singed the flesh over her
pulse as he laved the tender place. "This has gotta be for
more than a day, Lauren. I can't do more back-and-forth."

"Neither can I."

A deep groan rumbled from his lungs, vibrated against her ribs. "There'd better be a lock on this door. Wrap your legs around me."

She did. And he lifted her effortlessly, took a step forward. The snick of the dead bolt sounded, and then they were back on the cot and his fingers were scrabbling at the hem of her work polo. "I like you in teal," he said. "It brings out the green in your eyes. Makes me want to grab my camera." He lifted the shirt over her head and dropped it on the foot of the cot. Her bra followed suit. "But I like you better like this."

Cupping her breasts, he drew his tongue around one peaking nipple and then the other.

"Tease," she complained, pressing her fingertips into his upper arms as tantalizing pressure built at her core.

"Patience, please." He grazed his teeth on her nipple. Her breasts tightened under greedy pulls and sucks from his slick mouth. The rough-but-tender caresses of his hands coaxed a flood of desire through her body. It pooled in her veins, weighed down her limbs. But she had to touch him, too.

Two seconds of effort on her part had his shirt joining hers on the cot. "Lie down."

He stilled with his mouth over her breast. "Sorry?"

A gust of breath carried the word, cooling her wet nipple and sending shivers along her spine. "On your back. Lie down."

A raw flare lit his eyes and he obeyed, ripping off his sandals and sliding out of his shorts as he went. He was all hers, gold-shot, tousled hair on the white pillowcase, long body stretched out on the gray wool blanket. Beautiful, lean muscle and taut skin that she got to use for her own purposes. *For his pleasure.* He had thrown her off by kneeling in front of that picnic table the last time they were intimate. And she wasn't going to kneel—not today, anyway—but she was going to play.

Her shorts and shoes hit the floor, but she left her panties on. Her heart raced at the thought of him discovering how wet they'd become from having him kiss her breasts. Climbing on top of him, she lined up her swollen flesh over the ridge of his sex. Way fewer clothes between them without their shorts on, but even her panties and his boxers were too much.

Resting her hands on his abdomen, she played slow, silent piano over the cut ridges. "You took unapologetic advantage of my emotional state the other night. Had me like putty in your hands." She smirked at him to make sure he knew any advantage was freely given. "Question is, can I torture you into a similar state?"

"You can, Pixie. Anytime you want. Except…" He took her hands off his belly and brought them to his mouth, worshiping her palms with his lips. "I want to love you right this time."

He tugged on her arms, and she collapsed on his chest. Inhaling deeply, she filled her nose with his sultry, masculine scent. Bliss. "I don't remember complaining. If anything, I got the better deal."

"I disagree." She heard his smile. "Making you fall apart is about the best thing I get to do in life."

So why on earth was he so insistent that being around her all the time was such a problem? She checked the thought. It wasn't being around her; it was being around home. Hopefully his staying for half the year would be enough for both of them.

Rucking a hand into her hair, he flipped her gently onto her back, hovering over her with all his delicious bulk, his eyes smoky with need. "This is more what I had in mind."

"You on top?"

"No, you in my arms."

She melted at that, at his tender kiss. Their mouths fused, nipping and licking and tasting. He had both her panties and his underwear off in less than a blink of an eye.

With his weight on one arm and that hand tangled in her hair, he slid his other palm down the center of her torso until his fingers dipped over the bud of her arousal. "How'd you get so wet?"

It was probably pregnancy hormones in part, but mostly him. "You're good at this." She tilted one side of her mouth and reached to stroke his erection.

He released a groan so loud she shushed him—they were at work, after all—but she kept moving her hand, savoring velvet skin over rigid shaft.

He froze in place, his hand cupping her mound. She ached for the smallest movement. She twisted against his hand as she continued a slow rhythm with her own.

"I—Lauren. *Please*."

"Please stop? Please more?"

"Please *you*." He shuddered back to life and slipped his fingers down farther, into her. Her center clenched, begging him for more. "This."

She nudged him, guiding his body over hers, and his hips between her thighs until he was fully seated and they were both panting.

It was too much. Too good.

Too good to be true?

Wrapping her legs around his powerful hips, she silenced the thought and rode the ecstasy until her mind was blank.

Chapter Twelve

Satisfaction ebbed and flowed in Lauren's limbs. Tavish's chest warranted the award for best pillow in Montana. But responsibility tugged her out of the hazy wonder of the smell of their pleasure lingering in the air and the warmth of their bare skin where it touched. They could only hide in the first-aid room for so long before someone came looking for them. "We need to get back to work."

"Right. We're at work." He made a self-deprecating noise. "Classy."

"Oh, as if we're the only people who ended up using this cot for...personal shenanigans."

"Not sure if that makes it better," he murmured into her hair. "We're off tomorrow. We could spend the whole day somewhere way more romantic."

"We should take my canoe out."

He winced melodramatically and bent his leg, laying

a hand over the bandage. "Too wounded. The only cure's rest. Naked rest. Write me a prescription."

She pressed her lips to his delicious chest to muffle her giggle. "Take two orgasms and call me in the morning?"

"If I'm lucky." His tone turned reluctant, and he peeled himself away from her to get dressed.

She followed suit, wondering if he was as saddened to see her fasten her shorts as she was by him pulling his shirt over his head, covering up the delightful six-pack she almost had mapped with her fingers. She'd need to work on committing it fully to memory later. "Is your leg bothering you?"

"Stings, but nothing serious. I had a pretty thorough doctor."

She chewed on the inside of her lip. "I should make sure you're not under my care anymore, though. Not if we're together again. Ethics and all that."

"Ethics?" He blinked as if his thoughts were coming too quickly to process. "What about ethics and your other patients? Not in the sense of relationships," he said in a rush. "But when it comes to your fear of blood."

Looking up, she caught something in his expression that shot fear to her core. She crossed her legs on the cot and toyed with the clips on her hiking sandals. "I'm sorry?"

He settled next to her and laid a hand on her crossed ankles. "Will you always be able to guarantee that your duty to your job is going to be enough to make you a dedicated doctor? What if you stick with it for the sake of obligation, and then get to a point where your phobia impedes your ability to care for your patients?"

"My *phobia*?" Coming from him, the label felt like a wrecking ball crashing through the tower of reasons she'd created to stick with her job. Her hands started to shake and she grabbed handfuls of the scratchy gray blanket to steady them.

"Lauren. You get physically sick at the sight of blood. I'm not the medical professional here, but how is that not the definition of a phobia?"

Her lips parted but she couldn't get any sound out.

She'd been so focused on herself and on her belief she *wouldn't* fail, she hadn't truly processed the consequences of what would happen if she *did*. And he was right: given her recent inability to control her phobia—she had to be factual and start calling it that—it might at some point stop her from doing her best job. Might put a patient in harm's way, or prevent her from providing the best care possible. Prioritizing her desire to be like her mother over patient health went against everything she'd sworn upon completion of her medical degree. Her patients had to take precedence.

She gripped his hand with both of hers and let the truth sink from her brain to her heart to each cell of her body. It wasn't just the partnership that was the problem, it was medicine entirely. "Maybe I could go talk to someone about it. Get some therapy."

He traced a small circle on the back of her hand with his thumb. "Do you want to do that?"

"No." She looked into his eyes and repeated the realization with more emphasis. "No. I—I love having a career that helps people. That's something I'm always going to want. But being a doctor was never about me. And you're right, I can't risk harming a patient."

He stared at her with enough love to fill the inside of Sutter Mountain. "If you're worried about losing your mom in some way if you quit…you won't. The fact you and Drew and Cadie exist is enough of a legacy." He cleared his throat. "*Our* baby is a legacy."

Toying with the sprinkle of golden hair at his wrist, she said, "You're getting rather psychoanalytical there, but you're right." Holy crap, was she doing this? "I have to quit."

Disbelief cascaded through her. *Yup, doing this.*

He enveloped her, a perfect sum of strong muscles, fresh, air-scented cotton and genuine support. "Proud of you, Pixie."

Nice to know, but would her dad feel the same? Also, Frank was a good family friend and was going to be shocked as anything. And changing careers while pregnant... *Oh, my God.* She pressed a palm to her shaky stomach. "I need a minute. Alone."

"Sure." With tender lips, he brushed her cheek. Brought warmth back to her goose-bumped skin. Unlocking the door and swinging it open, he disappeared into the hallway.

Resisting the temptation to bury her face in the thin, medical-issue pillow on the cot, she stood and remade the bed with fresh sheets and blankets from the supply cupboard. Then she attacked the sink and counter with disinfectant. Trying to scrub her worries onto the stainless steel didn't work worth a damn.

With nothing else to clean, she headed for the office, numb and in a daze. Who would she be if not a doctor? What the hell would she do with herself?

"Lauren!"

She jumped at the blur of sunshine-yellow movement across the room.

Zach Cardenas sat at his desk, crutches leaning next to him. The color of his moisture-wicking T-shirt was almost as cheery as his expression. Lauren's pile of order forms fluttered in his hand. "These look good. You're a natural."

Not enough that she saw herself working for her brother as a career... Her gut clenched, and she hid her uncertainty behind a forced smile. "Zach. What are you doing here? Andrew told me you weren't back for weeks."

"Yeah, that was his opinion. Wanted me to focus entirely on my rehab. But I'm bored as hell at home. No reason I can't come do paperwork."

She collapsed into her brother's chair. Having the extra help for the next week would be nice if it wouldn't set back Zach's recovery. And having Zach's problems fall in her lap as a distraction from calling her dad counted as the best timing of the day. "Did you talk to Andrew about it, or are you using him being on holidays to sneak in unnoticed?"

He cringed, emphasizing the squareness of his handsome jaw. "More column B."

Lauren tsked. "And your therapist gave you the okay? Andrew said something about you being on skis this winter being more important than you working during the summer."

"As long as I limit my hours, I'm okay to put some work in." His face fell. "I can't stand sitting on my butt with nothing to do. I'll be able to work a half day and put in enough hours of physio and swimming and stationary biking to be healthy by October. I know it."

Tavish appeared in the doorway. "Zach. G'morning."

Zach gave him a cursory nod. His gaze lingered on Tavish's shirt. *Oh, crap.* He'd put it on inside out.

"I think if you can take more time off, you should take it," Lauren said, trying to distract Andrew's assistant from deciphering what she'd been doing with her ex-husband while technically on the clock. "I have things under control."

Zach smacked his palm against his desk. Lauren

jumped, along with Tavish. "I've been living off your dad's generosity for long enough."

Tavish started to sift through a tangle of carabiners on a far shelf. "Drew's going to be pissed if you come back early. I'm not going anywhere. I can keep filling in for you."

Yet another confirmation that Tavish intended to stick to his promise of staying around for the summer... It soothed like aloe vera on a sunburn. More solid, more real, more a guarantee rather than a desperate wish.

Zach grimaced. "Yeah, tell you what. Don't tell Dawson I'm back, and I'll take all the flack when he inevitably loses it. So fill me in. What've you guys been up to for the last week?"

Lauren and Tavish spent a full half hour answering Zach's multitude of questions concerning work.

"Have you guys taken any time to breathe since the wedding?" Zach asked.

"No," she said in sync with Tavish's, "Nope."

Zach glanced between them. "You should take the rest of today, then. I'll hold down the office, and I'll get Garnet to stand in as field supervisor."

"But we already have the weekend off," Lauren protested. "I like being busy."

It gave her an excuse not to quit her job or to call her dad right away.

"Don't listen to her," Tavish said. "We'd love the extra time. We could get out of town for a couple of nights. Go for a canoe in Yellowstone, maybe."

"Yellowstone," she croaked, a fist slowly clamping around her windpipe.

Tavish glanced at her, gaze evaluating. "Never mind. We'll stay local."

Zach looked at them funny. "What's the excitement in that?"

"Well, you might need us," she fudged.

Reaching over, Tavish covered her clasped hands. "And Moosehorn's good enough."

She let out a shaky breath. Yellowstone wasn't that far. But still. She hadn't been farther than Bozeman since she returned from Vegas. The idea of crossing state lines, the possibility that something could happen to her family while she was gone, made it feel like the marrow was shrinking in her bones.

"No one will need us if we take off for an overnight," Tavish promised. "But we can hold off on that."

"Or go. We'll be fine without you," Zach agreed, no doubt assuming Tavish meant something at work.

He didn't. She got the message, loud as a cracking avalanche. But for some reason he was giving her a pass, even though he thought she was irrational for being afraid to leave her family. Respecting the need for baby steps, maybe?

Baby. Right. She closed her eyes. She didn't have time to dawdle. She needed to address the paranoia she'd developed when her mom died. She'd challenged it once. Had completed her residency in Billings, then headed for Las Vegas. And her grandparents had been in their car accident. Not being able to say goodbye to Grammy, or to stand at her dad's side when he'd decided to have the ventilator unplugged had been unbearable. She didn't think she was responsible for any of her family members' deaths. But she'd always considered herself responsible for not having been able to support her dad and her siblings.

And she could no longer pretend she was acting like a healthy person.

Her breath hitched as her heart started to gallop. Only one way to move forward. After hitting the water with Tavish, she'd assemble the dregs of her courage, talk to her dad and go quit her job.

The only thing quieter than being out on the lake was being out on the lake with Lauren. Tavish was happy to enjoy the rustle of the wind in the trees and the slap of water against the canoe and their paddles without conversation. But he'd been staring at her back for over an hour and her shoulders looked tight enough to use as a springboard. Made him feel guilty for appreciating the stretchy mauve fabric shifting across her upper back as she paddled in the front seat. One of those built-in-bra, yoga situations that were invented to torture people who made a study of the female form. The shirt exposed tantalizing triangles of skin. The streamlined lifejacket she wore did little to cover up her sexy shoulders. He'd spent a good portion of their expedition plotting a route of the freckles he planned to kiss.

As much as his groin loved the view, the coffee and toast he'd had for breakfast churned in his stomach whenever his mind drifted to their earlier conversation. She'd made some major decisions today. And, yeah, he truly believed her quitting would make her happier. But would their compromises, their attempts to cobble together a life, make her happy, too? Being home this time felt different, for sure. Almost…right.

An aftershock of disbelief rolled through him, and he exhaled into a firm paddle stroke. Home had never *been* right, but he liked that it was starting to feel that way. Hope glimmered, a promise he'd be able to be the man Lauren and the baby deserved.

The midday sun glinted off her blond ponytail. Had

he been able to reach it he'd have tugged it to get her attention. "Keep it down up there. You're drowning out the birds."

She laid her paddle across her lap and scratched the back of her head with her middle finger.

"Aw. The romance is overwhelming, sweetheart."

Her other middle finger joined the first, the pair of profane gestures framing her ponytail.

He adjusted the angle of his paddle to make sure they didn't veer off course with her taking a break from her steady strokes. "Want to talk about it?"

"It's more a matter of doing it, Tav." Her brief over-the-shoulder glance gave him a glimpse of her pale skin and stress-widened eyes.

"*It* meaning...?"

"Going in and talking to Frank. And my dad. I should do it this afternoon. But I think I might need to give myself a day." With a wide grip, she clutched her paddle.

He flicked a small spray of water at her right arm. "You're going to break that shaft if you don't ease up."

Shaking the droplets of lake water from her forearm, she pivoted on her seat, bringing her feet around and facing him. She slid her paddle under the bow thwart and let go. It landed in the bottom of the canoe with a *thunk*. Twisting her hands in her lap for a few seconds, she made a face and then held on to the gunwales, tapping her fingers against the fiberglass hull. "One could say I'm having a hard time relaxing."

"Noticed that." He stilled his strokes and let the boat glide. Wanting to get a smile on her face, or at least earn a protest, he positioned the blade of his paddle over the water in an obvious I'm-going-to-spray-you angle.

"Peril awaits down that trail, Fitzgerald."

He raised a teasing eyebrow. "Peril?"

"Of the worst sort."

Resuming his stroke rhythm, he grinned. "Then I'll have to behave. I need a replay of our morning mischief." She smiled back, dipped her cupped hand in the water and showered him in the face, chilling his skin. "You need to cool off."

He dragged the back of his hand across the rivulets dripping from his jaw to his T-shirt. "Good aim." Though she'd thrown a lot more at him lately than just a palmful of lake water. "Would you rather head for shore and go deal with it? Then we'd have the rest of the weekend to relax."

The shake of her head sent her ponytail swaying. "I'll talk to Frank tomorrow morning. He usually does paperwork for a few hours on Saturday before he heads off golfing."

"What about your family?"

She blinked long, as if her indecision was weighing down her eyelids. "Soon."

Soon. Talk about a word that defined his life. Soon he'd be spending the winter in Sutter Creek. Soon Lauren would start to show.

Soon they'd be a family of three.

If living together for half the year counted as being a family. Tension gripped his chest. After they'd tried him being home for a few months, he could reassess. Rubbing his palm against his aching sternum, he sent her a lopsided smile. "Uh, speaking of telling people things—when are we going to make our sprout public knowledge?"

The birds on the shore had enough time to sing a symphony as she chewed on her lip. "Three months is pretty usual, and I'm eight weeks along by medical standards. Though Cadie already knows."

He tried not to narrow his eyes, but alarm bells rang in his skull. "I'd like to at least tell our parents."

"I'd like to wait."

"Why?"

"It's still early." Her voice went achingly quiet. "I could miscarry."

Miscarry. His throat closed over and he had to cough. "Yeah, but… Would it be so bad if our families knew about a miscarriage?"

By the way she stared at the tree line, pine boughs must have become the most fascinating view on the planet. When she finally looked at him, the green in her irises had swallowed any golden light. "If I miscarried, would you still stay?"

"I—" Would he? The baby had been the push to get him to commit to living at home half time, but… "Lauren. I'm staying for you just as much as the baby."

"Right." She dropped her gaze to her knees.

Which was a relief because the lack of trust on her face made him feel like he was hanging from the Peak Chair by his fingernails.

Time. Time would convince her. And could maybe help her see that he was stepping out on an emotional limb, too. "You know, you aren't the only person who's been hurt in this relationship. The first time we broke up, you were the one who cut and ran."

She made a dismissive noise. "A high school break-up is on a different continent from a divorce."

"Tell that to my nineteen-year-old self. I was devastated."

His words came out soft, but by the way her face crumbled, she hadn't missed a syllable. "Maybe there's too much bad history between us to make this work."

"Not if we decide to move beyond our past." The six or

so feet separating them was too much to handle. Leaving his paddle next to Lauren's, he crouched low. He held on to the sides of the canoe and maneuvered forward, then sat on the metal bow thwart and braced his knees against the fiberglass sides. He took her hands in his. Jesus, they were cold. And not just the one she'd dipped in the lake.

Her gaze dipped to his makeshift seat. "You're too heavy to sit there. You'll break the canoe."

"I'm more worried about making sure I don't break your heart."

By the next morning Lauren wished she'd taken Tavish up on his advice to talk to Frank and her dad yesterday. As she walked into the clinic and waved at the receptionist, she smothered a yawn. She'd be in a better head space had she not spent the night fretfully tossing and turning.

She headed for Frank's office before she turned on a heel and went back to her car. Three deep breaths in the corridor filled her with just enough courage to step over the threshold.

Her boss, in his usual work outfit of a lab coat over a plaid dress shirt, removed his reading glasses and slid them into the breast pocket of his white coat. He tilted his head. "You don't look rested for someone who's been on holidays for two weeks."

"Yeah. I didn't sleep well." Declining his nodded invitation to sit, she handed him the envelope stuffed with unsigned contract papers. "I need to give you the contract back."

"Finally." With an outstretched hand, he took the document and shot her a satisfied smile.

All the blood in her body rushed to her head, thundering like a summer storm. "I didn't sign it."

He froze, but for his open, no-longer-smiling mouth and one raised, gray-speckled eyebrow. "What?"

Hands sweaty, she fiddled with the embroidered hem of her cap-sleeve blouse. "No. I'm afraid I'm going to have to give my notice. I need to…to pursue other options."

He laid the packet on his desk blotter and sat back, linking his fingers behind his head. "I'm confused, Lauren."

"I'll bet. I am, too, really. But I've come to realize medicine isn't as fulfilling as I'd hoped it would be. And it's too important to only commit to halfheartedly. Which precludes me from becoming a partner, or from working here in a different capacity."

He blew out a short burst of air. "Wow. I didn't expect this."

"I hope it won't be overly difficult to replace me."

"It's less about struggling to find someone and more about not wanting to have to."

She winced.

"I expect you'll be able to work for the four weeks' notice in your existing contract?"

"Yes, of course. Though I've been dealing with some, uh, queasiness lately. Might I ask to steer clear of suturing?"

"We can arrange that." He paused, calculation whirring on his face. "And if any other health or family issues are playing into your decision, know that we can adjust for that, too."

She shook her head. "To be blunt, I can't keep trying to bring my mom back by trying to be her, Frank. I need to live for me." And saying that out loud to someone other than Tavish released a buildup of pressure in her chest. Her body tingled as a sense of rightness filled her. After an awkward goodbye, Lauren headed for her car. Come mid-August, she would be free. Free to… Who knew?

Panic flooded her veins. Her polite-society vocabulary dissolved, leaving behind a selection of expletives more suited to a hockey locker room. Crawling behind the wheel, she let a few of them fly.

Her single-minded focus on medicine left her with a minimal grasp on what her other career-oriented aptitudes were. Money wasn't an issue—her savings and her AlpinePeaks profit share would provide for her and the baby for a long while. But she wasn't satisfied with the idea of doing nothing. Maybe she could explore a position at the new holistic health center. She could pitch in more with the opening, see if there was some sort of health management position she'd be suited to.

The possibility of working for one of the family businesses, working with Cadie, no less, took away some of the sting of quitting. Plus, long-term commitments elsewhere would be tricky with her going on maternity leave in eight months.

Holy crap. I'm actually changing careers. Something her dad should find out from her, not the Sutter Creek grapevine.

Going to see him in person would be the right thing to do, but after facing Frank, she was out of backbone. Shame rolled in her stomach as she pulled up her dad's number on her cell, but her lungs loosened, finally allowing a full breath. She wouldn't have to look at him when she let him down.

Giving her notice and admitting to Frank that she'd entered medicine for the wrong reasons had been easy compared to this. She itched to press the disconnect button.

He answered after two rings. "Hey, Cookie. What's shaking?"

"Oh, I dunno, Dad." *My voice, for one.* She drew in air, tried to bring her pitch down a half octave. "Got a minute?"

"I'm all ears." Alarm erased his previously cheerful tone.

"I've quit my job."

Silence.

A load of it.

"You what?" he said.

She clicked over to her hands-free device and took her time explaining her phobia, the expectations she'd always felt from him and her family, and how she'd felt she needed to make up for her mom's shortened life.

More silence.

A lump filled her throat. She barely forced out her question. "You still there, Dad?"

"I'm here." He coughed. "Just give me a few seconds to process."

The few seconds clicked by slower than a year. "Um, want to tell me what you're thinking?" She didn't really want to know, but might as well rip off the proverbial Band-Aid.

"I'm…shocked. Confused about what you'll do with yourself. Not to mention feeling guilty for so often having compared you to your mother. Why didn't you tell me how much pressure that put on you?"

"I was scared," she whispered. She could picture him sitting palm to forehead, elbow on the edge of his desk, as he often did when thinking.

"I'm sorry, Lauren." The rough regret in his voice scraped against her skin.

"Don't be sorry. For as much as I don't want to be a doctor, I—I liked being close to Mom."

Slow breathing filled the speaker. "I'm feeling pretty thrown here, Cookie. Can you do something for me?"

"Sure, Dad. Anything."

"Get some space, some time away by yourself—you need to think about what you'll do next, and you're too busy when you're at home."

He wanted her to leave? Her stomach twisted. Before her morning sickness could take over, she cut their call short and dropped her forehead to the steering wheel. After a minute or so, her nausea settled. She started driving down streets she'd traveled thousands of times, didn't really need to see to safely pilot the vehicle. The familiarity left her brain with way too much freedom to stew over her conversation with her father. Did he want her to get away from town? From Tavish? From their family?

Gah.

Maybe her dad was right. And Tavish, too, about her family not falling apart if she went away for a weekend. Her brain threatened to overflow; clearing it sounded like a brilliant plan.

A few minutes later she knocked on Tavish's apartment door.

A moment passed before it swung open. And wow, that moment had been worth the wait. A pair of green-striped boxers hugged his hips, right below the V of hard muscle that pointed straight to a tempting, cotton-covered bulge. Most of him was on display. Delineated biceps and powerful thighs and a drowsy grin. "Hey, Pixie."

Her heart warmed at the endearment. "Hey, yourself, sleepyhead."

She walked into his embrace. He smelled like clean sheets and warm man. The anchor of his rock-hard arm muscles around her adrenaline-wearied body was everything she'd needed since she'd walked into Frank Martin's office. Her mouth met his, kissed away the trace of chap on his lower lip. "Let's go somewhere. Together."

His eyes opened wider, lost some of their just-wakened cloud. "Where?"

"Yellowstone." She tugged on one of the buttons of her blouse and threaded the fingers of her other hand into the crispy hair above the waist of his boxers. "But first, I'm taking you back to bed."

Hours later, body sated, she snuggled under the thin feather duvet. A clatter rang through the open bedroom door, followed by a soft curse from Tavish.

"Whatcha doing?" she called.

He came back into the room, holding a flat, brown-paper-wrapped package under his left arm. He looked ready to attack the wilderness in beige nylon cargo shorts, a threadbare Sutter Creek Canoe and Kayak Club T-shirt and a pair of hiking sandals. Her heart fluttered—part anxiety, part anticipation—at the possibilities.

"Unwrap this." His shoulders slumped a fraction and he ran a hand through his hair.

She sat up with the sheet tucked under her armpits and took the gift, tearing off the paper.

Framed with matting colors of sage and cream, his river drawing looked even more real than when she'd last seen it in the office. Choking on the tears clogging her throat, she whispered, "Your sketch…"

"It'll match your living room. If you want it in there, of course. No obligation."

"It's perfect."

He brushed his fingers along her arm. "I was thinking of you when I drew it. It just seemed right to give it to you."

"It was a big place in our life."

"Yeah. Beginnings." He sighed. "Endings. Uh, the tattoo on my side is all about you, too."

Oh. *Oh.* She'd wondered about the connection. God, if she was looking for proof of how deeply his feelings ran, she couldn't get much more than him permanently inking the memory of their love on his skin. She kissed him softly. "Thank you."

After drawing her further in, turning the kiss long and hot and nerve-jarring, he said, "Let's go find more big places."

"Right. Gear all packed?"

"Let's get gone."

She pressed a hand to her chest. Could she do this? Fully face her fears? Yes or no, she was going to try.

Chapter Thirteen

Tavish's mouth watered as his feet crunched on the rock-strewn path. Nothing on the Grebe Lake trail could hold a candle to watching Lauren's hamstrings tense and release. Every once in a while she'd turn to smile at him, her metallic-green, oversize sunglasses making her look like a June bug. And the activity had brought the color back into her cheeks. About time. When he'd driven across the Montana-Wyoming border, she'd gone sheet-white.

Curiosity ate at him to find out what had happened when she'd spoken with Frank Martin and her dad, but she hadn't wanted to talk about it when he'd prodded.

He'd wait.

And would watch her legs in the meantime.

When they got to the lake's edge, she shed her socks and shoes and immediately headed for the water. Knee-deep, she turned around and grinned. Her obvious delight filled his chest to bursting, making him feel like he'd won a Pulitzer. And when she lifted the bottom edge of her athletic tank to drag the sheen off her face, his tongue begged him to drop to his knees, to lick the exposed inches of her pale stomach. Was he crazy, or was there a little fullness around her waist that hadn't been there a week ago?

"You look hungry, Fitzgerald." A smile played on her lips.

"I am."

"Well, I'm not on the menu. Yet." Her smile turned to a full-on grin. "Make me lunch. Your kid needs to be fed."

My kid. Wow. But he was getting used to the phrase. Damn attached to it, really.

They settled in on a sandy, secluded stretch of lakefront and unpacked their hastily gathered picnic from his day pack.

Lauren reclined against a log, shoes off and knees bent. Her tanned calves matched the golden-brown sand that caked her feet after her wade in the lake.

A palm-size cluster of condensation-frosted grapes dangled between her forefinger and thumb. She sucked the juicy buds of fruit from the stem. Plump lips enveloped a grape and then, with a pop, disappeared, along with Tavish's hold on his lust. He wanted her to suck his skin in that same methodical way.

Not in the mood for exhibitionism, he reached for food instead. There was no guarantee they wouldn't be interrupted by other hikers.

She shot him a sly, sexy smile.

Then sucked.

Grape. Grape. Fingertip.

Lust burned his skin and he swallowed. "You prepared to follow up on that smile, Dr. Dawson?"

Her mouth gaped, playful mood vanishing from her face and posture. "I won't be a practicing doctor for much longer. Weird."

Way to go, Fitzgerald. He'd been so careful not to mention work. "Weird in a good way?"

"Yeah, I think so."

"We don't have to talk about it."

"I'm ready."

He listened intently to her explanation of her resignation and talking to her dad. She'd done swift work, untangling herself from her job. And with no longer being attached to the clinic, would she change her mind about traveling with him when he worked? Something else to find out when the time was right.

He shifted to sit next to her and ringed his arms around her shoulders. Dropping a kiss on her head, he said, "That can't have been easy."

"It wasn't."

"I have something to tell you, too. I haven't signed off on anything, but that job at Montana State I called about? I've been offered an artist-in-residence position for January. I can't start until then because of the few contracts I have for the fall, but I thought I'd give it a shot."

She gripped one of his knees and looked at him, solemn, doubtful. "You sure you want to do that?"

"I'm sure I want you, Lauren. I'll do my best."

"I don't want you to make yourself miserable for me. Or the baby."

Tavish nuzzled her neck. An outdoor lake-and-flora smell, the one fabric softener manufacturers spent millions trying to reproduce but never came close to, clung to her skin. "I've been pretty miserable without you. And no way do I want to miss out on watching you growing our baby this winter." He didn't know when the urge to leave would kick in. Given he was his father's son, it would hit him eventually. Because of that, he wasn't going to promise forever. But he could promise his best. He'd *always* give his child—and the woman he'd created that child with—his best. Hopefully it would be good enough.

He spread his fingers across her stomach. Incredible that the beginnings of a human dwelled safe inside her. "I love you, Lauren. And I figure it's worth doing what I can to see if that love can survive. I want to be connected to you beyond parenting together. And we're both closer to finding middle ground. You're here with me today. Maybe you'd travel with me again before the baby's born. Phuket has some nice resorts. We could stay on a few weeks after I'm done my assignment in the fall. Chill out on a pair of beach chairs—what do people call it, a babymoon?"

"Tavish." The ache in her voice pulled at any sense of hope he was attempting to generate. She shook her head. "Being willing to go on an overnight camping trip a few hours from home is a heck of a lot different than going to Thailand for a month. I *just* quit, for God's sake. I won't be able to take a vacation if I'm figuring out a new job."

He sighed. "You'll get vacation time, Lauren, so be honest—it's the home part that's holding you back. And given the world didn't fall down around your ears when we crossed into Yellowstone Park boundaries, you could probably safely get on a plane, too."

"Traveling halfway around the world is different from pitching a tent a couple of hours from home. This is too fast, too much pushing." She emphasized the last few words, making them echo across the lake.

He forced himself to suck in a calming breath. "We'll take it slow, then."

Her eyes shuttered and she let out a slow breath

through pursed lips. "We'll take a pause, you mean. This is enough for me for now."

A pause? Fine. Or so he'd convince himself.

Lauren woke up to the twitter of early-morning birds and insects. She squinted at the tent walls, lit cobalt in the shadows of the trees around their campsite. That dim, just-after-dawn light. Tavish's arm lay heavy across her rib cage, his breathing steady against her back.

Why was she awake?

A buzz sounded from inside her backpack. Ah, her phone was the culprit. Stupid social media alerts, going off at all hours even out in the wilderness.

All hours. Hours from home. An anxious tingle crawled through her abdomen. The scent of vinyl started to unsettle her stomach and she reached for her water bottle just as another buzz interrupted the silence, from the pocket of Tavish's hoodie this time.

Coincidence? Her heart started pounding as she rooted around for her cell. As she closed her hand around it, it went off again. She reared up from the mattress and looked at the screen.

"What's wrong, sweetheart?" Tavish murmured, voice raspy.

"Cadie's calling." Fear ripped through her as she answered. "Cadie? What's the matter?"

"I'm at th-the h-hospital in Bozeman…" Cadie stuttered, and not from bad phone reception. "Dad. A heart attack."

"No!" She fell back against Tavish, who swore under his breath and caught her in his embrace. Cadie's words blurred together. Something about surgery and wanting Lauren home.

"But I'm hours away!"

"Dad will be in surgery for a while anyway. Just come as fast as you can."

Guilt squeezed Lauren until the phone fell out of her hand. She curled into a ball in Tavish's arms. *This is my fault.* She'd left her family, and yet again something had gone wrong... She wasn't home for Cadie or her dad when they needed her. *Again.*

In a fog, she shook as Tavish picked up the phone and promised Cadie they'd be there as soon as they could.

"I shouldn't have come."

"Shh."

"They need me and I'm not there." Tears pricked her eyes. "What if he was stressed out about me quitting?"

"Hey." He squeezed her tight, but the comforting support only made her feel worse for not being at home, hugging her sister. "You didn't cause this in any way. Grab your backpack. I can have everything taken down in ten minutes."

Muscles weak, she dressed, stuffed her belongings into her pack and threw it in the vehicle. He yanked on yesterday night's sweats and long-sleeved T-shirt, grabbed his own bag, and let down the food he'd strung up in a tree. He had the fire out and the tent stowed away before she'd even managed to deal with their sleeping bags.

She tried to help further, but her fingers fumbled her tasks. Fear curdled her stomach, souring the back of her throat. She gave up and sat in the passenger seat, letting the tears come.

By the time Tavish shut the hatch and climbed into the driver's seat, her breath was coming in gasps and her diaphragm was starting to ache.

"Pixie. You need to get your breathing under control." He ran his thumb across one of her tear-slicked cheeks.

His eyes were a stormy violet-gray. "In and out, Laur. You can do this."

Pretending it was yoga class, she followed his instructions and managed to slow her sobs to irregular hiccups. "Start the car, Tavish."

"I want you to be calm first."

"I'll be calm when I see my dad alive and complaining in post-op."

Exhaling in clear frustration, he shook his head but started the vehicle. Her regret over giving in to selfishness, for having left town, haunted her for the first two hours of their drive.

A half hour from the hospital, Tavish, who'd—bless him—stayed mostly silent since leaving the campsite, gripped her hand and cleared his throat. "It's just a coincidence."

She pulled her fingers from his grasp. Crossing her arms around her already constricted ribs, she couldn't hold in her self-directed vitriol any longer. "Well, I'm sick of my coincidences hurting the people I love."

Tavish guided Lauren into the hospital waiting room, hand at the base of her palpably knotted neck. The pastel green walls matched her complexion. Her morning sickness had kicked in the minute they'd passed through the sliding doors into the lobby. She'd sprinted to a garbage can and puked up the granola bar he'd made her eat as they'd passed through West Yellowstone.

Cadie sat in one of the banks of institutional fabric chairs, clasping a sobbing Ben to her chest like a life preserver. A wet splotch marked the front of her gray hoodie.

Lauren fell into the chair next to Cadie. She hugged her sister and her nephew at the same time. "Here, let me take Ben." Lifting the baby, she kissed his tear-streaked cheeks. "Hey there, buddy. How 'bout you calm down for Auntie Lauren?"

The shudders gripping Ben's tiny body lessened then stopped.

Tavish sat next to Lauren and stared at her, awe spreading through him. Man, she was going to be a good mom. With any luck, she'd make up for his inevitable screw-ups. He'd spent some time around children on the job, but his learning curve would be mighty steep.

Relief softened the exhaustion lining Cadie's eyes. "Thanks. When I'm wound up, he won't settle."

"Any time." Lauren smoothed a hand over Ben's fine hair. "What's going on? Angioplasty? Bypass?"

"Angioplasty. Dad's in recovery—everything went fine. The surgeon said we should expect to be able to see him around nine."

"Oh, thank God. I don't know what I would have done…" Lauren shook her head and let out a huge breath in spurts. "Have you had breakfast?"

"No." Cadie looked apologetic. "I fed Ben, but not me. I don't think I could eat."

"Me neither," Lauren said.

Tavish reached around her and stroked the backs of two fingers along Ben's soft cheek. Soon it would be Lauren having, holding, soothing *their* baby. A thrill of possession shot up his spine. He could get used to the weight of her against his chest, her arms full of little boy. But the resurgence of her I-need-to-be-no-more-than-three-feet-away-from-my-family-at-all-times routine made him wary. Hopefully, once the initial panic over her father subsided, they'd be able to get back to her talking about travel. "Cadie, did you get a hold of Drew? We tried in the car but he wasn't answering."

Cadie nodded. "He and Mackenzie should be here soon."

"Andrew called me ten minutes ago," Zach Cardenas said as he arrived in the doorless archway. He leaned on his crutches. "They're almost here." His throat bobbed. "I'm so sorry, Cadence. I came to see if I can help in any way."

Cadie's face crumpled at the same time her eyes brightened. She jumped up and rushed to Zach, who leaned to his left and put his weight on his nonbraced leg. He wrapped her in his arms. One of his crutches fell to the floor. And as his eyes closed, his heart cracked clear across his face.

Tavish knew that look, knew that feeling. Knew his face was probably as obvious as Zach's.

"What do you need?" Zach asked.

"I don't know. Aunt Georgie's going to come as soon as she finishes all the morning chores out at the ranch, and I can't really ask her to babysit. But I want to take Ben home."

"I can do that," Zach said.

Cadie shook her tousled curls. "You're using crutches. Ben's too active for you."

"You have a stroller and a baby carrier. I won't have to lug him around all that much." Zach tipped Cadie's chin up. "I can handle Ben for a few hours. Garnet's got everything under control at the office."

"Okay. You can follow me home, then." She freed herself from Zach's arms and busied herself with taking a now-sleeping Ben from Lauren and transferring him to his stroller.

Lauren, shooting her sister an "I see what you did there, looking at that guy in that way" brow arch, slipped off her shoes, rested her heels on the edge of the chair and sank against Tavish. He absorbed her weight into his side and kissed her hair, which looked rather like she'd been standing in a windstorm. He wasn't about to point that out. "You should both eat something."

"I can't," Lauren said. "I won't keep it down."

"Your dad's going to be fine. And you need to think of yourself," Tavish emphasized. He lowered his voice to a whisper. "Think of the—"

"Fine." Her jaw jutted out. "But I'm not eating cafeteria crap."

"I can bring us something healthy from home," Cadie said. "Though that'll be well over an hour with driving."

"I'll survive," Lauren said.

As Cadie and Zach's footsteps—or crutch squeaks, in Zach's case—faded down the hallway, Lauren slid away from Tavish and dropped her head against the back of the chair. "Don't be so obvious. I'm not ready to announce my pregnancy to the world."

"But Cadie knows."

"And Zach doesn't."

"Sorry. I tried to whisper." Tavish's stomach gurgled. "I can't wait for breakfast—what can I get you from the cafeteria?"

Lauren nodded. "Tea, please. Green."

He headed for the elevator.

Alone in the waiting room, Lauren inhaled, gagging at the hospital smell. She didn't have much longer to deal with the smells of medicine—disinfectant, latex, bodily fluids. But her flash of happiness over that vanished when she remembered why she was in the hospital in the first place. Worry made the base of her throat tingle. *Dad will be okay.* Angioplasty rarely resulted in complications. She wasn't a cardiologist or a surgeon, but she knew enough.

Even so, her knowledge didn't stop the stress from corroding her stomach lining.

Tavish returned after ten minutes, holding a disposable tray, replete with cups and two muffins, in one hand.

"I brought you a muffin just in case." He sat next to her and kissed her softly. "Any news?"

He was being so attentive. But that didn't bring ease. In her under-slept, stressed state, her whole body buzzed, waiting for the rug pull. Waiting for him to bolt after her freak-out this morning. "No, no word yet."

"Come here." He welcomed her with arms she'd grown too used to over the last couple of weeks.

Sliding her legs over his lap, she clung to him, dug her fingers into the tense muscles of his shoulders. Even if her father's cardiac event meant she wouldn't be able to take any more steps forward, she needed Tavish's support. But if he kept pushing her like he had yesterday, their relationship wasn't going to go far. Were they better off giving up now, focusing on coparenting? No way was Lauren setting foot outside Gallatin County after she gave birth. Her baby needed a stable home. Safe. One where parents didn't get sick or die when their children weren't home.

Out on the trail yesterday, he'd smiled bright enough to give the sun a run for its money. Even the short distance had brought him joy. How much happier would he be had she been able to go farther? And she wouldn't be able to live with herself if she was the reason for that smile dimming again.

Unpleasant and unwanted, the truth hardened into a ball in her throat. She swallowed and made herself spit the words out before she convinced herself it was okay to keep holding him back. "You're not going to be happy in a relationship with someone like me, Tavish. Even part-time."

He jerked and a strange, still energy overtook his body. "We'll manage, Lauren."

No. Managing wasn't good enough. Wasn't fair for anyone. She couldn't expect Tavish to stay if she wasn't going to be able to compromise. "You should go."

"What?" He wove his fingers into her hair, held her head to his chest. His heart thudded against her ear. The physical comfort was the most unfair of teases. "I want to be here for you."

"I know you do. But you have needs, too. You deserve an equal partnership, someone who can meet you halfway. I thought I could do it, but I can't." She had to protect her heart as best she could. They had seven months to talk about sharing responsibility. She couldn't do seven more minutes with Tavish at her side, knowing she couldn't go with him when he left, couldn't be what he needed. Shifting her legs from his lap, she settled her feet on the floor. She gripped the edge of her seat and tried to muster strength. Alone.

"Lauren." His voice rasped, pain slicing into the sounds. "Give yourself some time. You've had a big shock—no need to make decisions right now. I think between me working at the college part-time and taking shorter assignments—"

"No. Part-time won't work."

"But…" The tendons and muscles of his hand slackened on her back. Then the comforting weight was gone. "You can't mean that."

Oh, she could. Yeah, she was hurting him, and she hated herself for it. But hanging on to something flawed and hurting him even more, keeping him in a relationship that would slowly make him miserable? She loved him too much to do that to him.

Shooting to his feet, he paced in a circle in front of her. He stuck his hands behind his head. The naked anguish in his eyes shredded her insides.

Tears welled, dripped onto her sweatshirt. "I love you. I can't ask you to compromise further, knowing it will make you unhappy."

"You want to talk about unhappy? *This* is making me unhappy, sweetheart. It's not right. I need you. And I want to be the man you need." His arms fell to his sides and he lingered in front of her for a minute or so, lips parted, silently begging.

"Just leave. Please." When she broke eye contact, unable to handle the violet bruise of his eyes any longer, he spun around. His footsteps receded.

Jarred by each reverberation of rubber against linoleum, Lauren's heart shattered.

Chapter Fourteen

Tavish stormed away from the waiting room. He'd done what Lauren had asked, but he didn't like it. The craving to stay with her, to hold her and wipe away her tears, overrode everything he'd ever wanted. That, he didn't know how to deal with. His instincts were all wonky. She was trying to leave him. He should be cutting and running first, saving himself the inevitable arterial bleed of having her break things off for good. Of her limiting their relationship to cold shoulders and stilted conversations on his visitation days. But his muscles resisted every step he took away from her. *I love you. I can't ask you...*

Alarm bells sounded in his mind. He stopped short, sandals screeching on the floor. She was pulling the exact same crap on him as he'd pulled on her when he'd left her sitting on the banks of the river. The classic "I love you so I'm going to push you away" garbage that had been his MO since he was a kid. Since his dad had left him.

Blinking away the moisture in his eyes, he clenched his hands into fists and straightened. *Try again, Pixie.* No way would he let her make the same mistakes he'd been making for most of his life. But who was he to show her how to love? He didn't even trust himself to commit to more than half a year with her and the baby.

Loving her—at least right now, while she was dealing with her dad's trauma—would require meeting her more than halfway. Sweat broke out on his palms and he slumped against one of the hallway walls. Could he do more than half a year? She clearly didn't trust him to, with her talking about him being unhappy. But he'd told her the absolute truth—leaving her was not right. Walking away while she sat alone in that uncomfortable hospital chair made him unhappier than staying in Sutter Creek ever had.

The mammoth task of convincing her to trust him weighed him down as if he were stuck under six feet of packed snow. Because before he could convince her to trust him, he had to learn how to trust himself.

And he didn't know where to start.

Weariness flooded into his muscles. More caffeine would jolt him back to reality. Having left his coffee behind, he needed to get another before he began the stake-out he intended to hold in the lobby on the main floor. He'd damn well sit there until he figured out how to show her that pushing him away was a stupid-ass way to express love.

He peeled himself off the wall and strode into the elevator. The smell of antiseptic and illness permeated the space and seeped into his pores. A shower would be nice, but he couldn't risk heading home and having her think he'd left. With a ding, the doors opened on the ground floor. Before he could exit, a couple rushed in, leaving him no room to squeeze out.

"Tavish!" His sister flung herself at him. Her freckles competed for space with the mottled blotches on her face. She'd always turned bright red when she cried.

"Kenz. Hey." He gripped her tighter. She felt rounder than she had a week ago. "You grew."

"Thanks for the reminder, jerk."

"It's a good thing," he assured her.

She snorted, obviously unconvinced. But he meant it. And excitement nudged away some of his irritation over Lauren's you-should-go nonsense. Pretty soon her body would start changing. He wanted it all, from feeling the baby kick to dealing with inevitable hormone swings. "You're not leaving, are you?" His shirt muffled Mackenzie's voice.

"No, I was going to get myself a coffee."

"How's my dad?" Drew's haggard expression broadcast his level of distress.

Tavish wished he had a father he could feel that depth of emotion for. "Recovering well. I'll take you to the waiting room."

As they rode back up to the cardiac floor, he filled the couple in on what he knew. The waiting room was empty—Lauren no longer sat where he'd left her. At the nurses' station, a guy in blue scrubs told them where to find Edward Dawson.

Drew held Mackenzie's hand as they hurried to the designated room. A nurse stopped them before they entered. "Sorry, you're going to have to limit it to one more visitor. He already has two."

"I should leave. Lauren doesn't want to see me anyway." Tavish backed up.

Mackenzie shot him a questioning look before stand-

ing on her toes to kiss her husband. "You go in, honey.
I'll take a walk with my brother."

Drew's brow wrinkled. He clutched Mackenzie close.
"If you're sure."

"We've been sitting for long enough. A stroll will do
me good. Text me if you need me."

Nodding, Drew ducked into his father's room.

"Let's go somewhere happier," Mackenzie said.

Lauren sat at her father's bedside, her attempts to reg-
ulate her breathing a fricking failure. Illness came with
the territory of her job. But her dad, pale and swathed in
blue hospital linens and monitor cables was completely
different. She could have lost him. God, she'd almost
missed getting to tell him he was going to be a grandfather again. Her final memory of his voice could have
been that quiet, shocked tone as he'd processed her having quit. Her eyes went hot.

Her aunt Georgie stood with Andrew against the wall.
The two were talking quietly about the arrangements
that needed to be made to get Edward some help at home
and work for the next while. Lauren planned to ask Dr.
Martin if she could take some family time, or at least cut
her schedule down until her contract expired, to allow
her to give her dad a hand.

"Laur, we're going to go make a few phone calls. We'll
be quick," Andrew said.

"Sure," she murmured as her brother and her aunt
left the room.

She traced her fingers along her father's wrist. Her
father stirred.

"Daddy?"

He grimaced and then opened his eyes. "Cookie. Hey."

Her lower lip started to wobble. "Oh, Dad."

"Love you."

"I love you, too." Lauren squeezed his anesthesia-chilled hand. Hers wasn't much warmer, really. "Don't move, Dad. You're in the hospital. Do you remember what happened?"

"Yeah. Woke up. Four-thirty?" Swallowing, he glanced around the room without moving his head. He'd want water to moisten what had to be a surgery-munged mouth, but she couldn't let go of his hand just yet. "Crushing pain. Surgery."

Relief swamped Lauren at the sound of his voice, releasing the tears welling in her ducts. "I was so worried about you. But the surgeon said everything went fine."

"It's all pretty foggy."

She sniffled. "This is my fault. I stressed you out too much by quitting my job."

Her father's gaze sharpened. "Try again. I worked too hard and pretended I ate well. My blood pressure was through the roof. I kept that from you."

She wasn't going to let him distract her with his own puny sins. "You needed me. And then I left. Just like I did with Mom. And Grammy and Gramps."

"Lauren." His voice quieted. His fingers clenched hers. "When you were fourteen, did you know how to cure post-surgical infections?"

"No. Of course not," she admitted.

"And would you have stopped your grandparents from driving to Billings that day?"

"No. It's not about controlling what happens…"

"Then what is it about?"

"It's about making sure I'm here for you and Cadie and Andrew if something goes wrong."

"Cookie, you came home as fast as you could. We've

had some hard times as a family, but we've gotten through them together."

His assurance boosted her conviction. "Exactly. I need to stay so that we can keep facing stuff together."

"Lauren. That's not what I meant. We don't have to live in each other's pockets."

She shook her head, pulling her chair closer to the bed. Resting her head on his hand, she tried to believe him. And couldn't.

Her father, eyes tired, stroked her hair. "Would you expect me to cancel all my business trips or my annual Dublin vacation just in case you or Cadie or Andrew needed me?"

Agh, that makes sense. But it's different. She'd been the one to support her father, her sister, over the past year. If they didn't need her support, and if she didn't need to be a doctor for her mother's sake, then who was she, really?

"I'm afraid," she admitted.

"Of what?"

Dark spots formed behind her eyelids as she shut them hard enough to make her cheeks hurt. "Losing you. Mackenzie, Andrew, Cadie. Everyone."

"Tavish?" her dad asked quietly.

"Yeah." But she'd already lost him. Instead of working through her fears and taking the risk of compromising with him, her instinct had been to run away. Protecting them both. Except she hadn't protected him at all. She'd hurt him. And her clinical side shone a beacon into the hidden parts of her psyche, the ones she didn't want to look at. If a patient sat down in her office and told her a phobia was standing in the way of the person fully living life, Lauren would refer them to a counselor immediately. *Physician, heal thyself.*

"I don't know how to be with him. But we're not going to be able to completely sever ties." The alluding words came out before she thought about the fact her dad was hooked up to a half-dozen beeping machines. *Frick.* Getting big news hours after heart surgery wasn't in his best interest. She threw out a cover. "Because I love him."

Pain edged his smile. "You always have, Cookie."

"And it's never been enough, Dad."

"It's going to have to be, isn't it?" He glanced at the ceiling, then back at her. "I promised myself I wasn't going to compare you to your mother anymore. But I can't, not when it comes to this—she always got sick early in her first trimester."

"And…" she said, one last desperate attempt to evade the subject.

"Lauren—" his wan smile turned chiding "—you can't be retching in the bathroom all week at work without people noticing. Rumors made their way up the chain to me. I was going to wait for you to say something, but this morning reminded me that sometimes we shouldn't waste time."

Truth. She and Tavish had wasted so much time. A decade, really. Definitely the last year. "I'm pregnant, Dad."

"I know, Cookie. Which thrills me, truly. But how are you feeling about it?"

"About the baby? Fantastic." *The baby needs me.*

And Tavish said he needed her, too. But her meeting the baby's needs would mean not meeting Tavish's. Her inability to properly love the two people who were entitled to all she could give pinched her rib cage tight enough to steal her oxygen.

And she couldn't see a way to love them both without risking too much.

* * *

Mackenzie's "somewhere happier" involved navigating a warren of hospital hallways. Tavish strode behind her, surprised at her speed. She moved at a good clip for someone with a serious waddle. They emerged through a set of glass doors into a well-tended prayer garden. "Hopefully we won't have to be in a hospital again until I'm giving birth to this little one." She rubbed her belly and then her back. "Today's been pretty awful. Andrew's in shock."

"I could tell."

"And as much as I feel bad complaining when I'm not the one who just had a heart attack, my back is killing me. Being away, having time to ourselves was nice, but I'm so ready to have this baby."

"You got this, kiddo. Only four more weeks."

"Shh, don't tell Mackenzie," she joked in a theatrically quiet voice.

"You'll make it." He coughed. "Can't wait to meet him or her. I'm going to need the practice."

His sister reached for his arm and dug her short nails into his skin. "Practice?"

"Lauren's pregnant."

Mackenzie's eyebrows hit the sky. "No."

He cringed. "Crap. She didn't want to tell anyone yet."

She gave him a rib-cracking hug. "This is amazing! Your kid will be so close in age to mine! Cousin buddies. When did this happen? How?"

"When I was in town for the bachelor party. And the usual way." A smirk sneaked past the solemnity of the day.

"You're going to be a *daddy*. Holy jeez." Her smile faltered. "You must be crapping yourself."

He lifted a shoulder. "I'm feeling surprisingly calm about fatherhood, but pretty pessimistic about Lauren and me. She…she pushed me away today. Said she loved me too much to ask me to compromise any more than I already have."

"Sounds familiar," Mackenzie said grimly.

"Nothing like having your own horse crap flung back in your face."

A thoughtful hum passed through her closed lips. "You don't have to stay away."

"I know. I don't want to."

She startled. "You don't?"

Tavish paused, letting the scent of a nearby honeysuckle bush drift over him. He'd smelled the same fragrance yesterday on their hike, found it calming. Not so, today. If only he could go back twenty-four hours… *No.* Going backward never helped. He and Lauren needed to move forward. Together. It meant trying something entirely different on his part. For Lauren's sake, for the baby's, he'd stick. "I want to stay."

She nudged him with an elbow. "Have you told her how you feel?"

He bristled. "Yeah. She doesn't trust me. But a child? It's all-consuming, Kenz. I can't imagine wanting to go anywhere."

"I understand." Mackenzie's surprise softened into acceptance and sympathy. "It has a way of superseding everything."

The thought that had been lurking on the edges of his brain for a couple of weeks made it to his tongue. "So how could Dad have deserted us?"

A frown crossed his sister's face. "Immaturity. Selfishness. Bad choices. Take your pick."

"It was his nature." And Tavish was going to have to fight his own nature. He wouldn't give in like his father had.

"No, it was his choice. Just like it's yours. And you seem to be choosing the opposite."

"I'm trying to. But I've acted like him way too many times not to think that I inherited his tendencies."

She poked him in the chest. "You are not like Dad. He never wanted to be a parent. You do."

His mouth fell open. "He didn't want kids?"

Mackenzie served him a look of disbelief. "You thought he had? Why else would he have completely cut ties with us?"

"I'd never thought about it that closely." A lie. He had. He'd just ignored the answer, hadn't wanted to admit that his father didn't want him at all.

Acknowledging it now was no less of a shiv to the gut at thirty than at thirteen. The scenario he'd drawn for himself, of his dad being torn between wanting to be at home and wanting to get away, started to vanish into the ether of his childhood, replaced by the hard reality of complete rejection.

But the pain of analyzing his father's true feelings was followed by a flash of relief. If he was so different from his father on wanting children, he might be different on raising them, as well. The brick of genetics started to crumble inside him. He put a hand to his lightening chest. His stomach throbbed like he'd taken a gut shot. But it didn't itch with the need to flee.

Mackenzie stared at him with wide, compassionate eyes. "You'll be a great dad. And there's no reason you can't be with Lauren."

Oh, to be that confident. Despite the shift in his own

perspective, Lauren still stood in their way. "I can work on our trust problems, will stay in town for most of the year. But if she's still so ruled by fear and can't believe me, it'll hurt us over time. She pushed me away today. She said it was because she loved me and couldn't be what I needed, but I've said that way too many times myself to believe it."

Every time he'd spouted crap like that, it had been because he was afraid of something. Lauren claimed to be afraid of leaving her family. He didn't buy that anymore. She was afraid of people leaving her. And why wouldn't she be? Her mom, her grandparents—

Him.

Damn. Well, he'd prove her fears wrong this time. He wiped a hand down his face. His breath, thrashed by his nerves, came out jagged. He'd spent his whole life believing himself to be his father's replicate. Shifting away from that belief turned his self-image a hundred and eighty degrees. And if the arguments that had convinced him didn't convince Lauren...

He swore under his breath.

Mackenzie kicked him in the ankle.

"Ow. No one's in earshot."

"You're in a prayer garden. It's the principle of the thing." His sister's voice vibrated and her facial muscles twitched with what looked like pain. She swayed and her hands went to her belly.

He grabbed her around the waist and had to tense his arms to keep her upright. She was slowly becoming deadweight. Her knees must have given out. He shored her up against his side. "What's wrong?"

She hissed out a breath. "I think I'm having contractions."

He swore again. This time she didn't give him trouble over it. "You sure?"

Nodding so hard her whole upper body shook, she squeezed her eyes shut. "Yup. My water just broke."

Chapter Fifteen

Lauren clutched her dad's hand and watched him breathe long after he fell asleep again. She knew what he'd been trying to tell her. But even if he and Cadie and Andrew could live without her, the baby couldn't. Her little sprout—her heart panged at the memory of Tavish using the term—needed stability. Needed not to go through the agony that Lauren had experienced one too many times.

The door opened and Tavish stalled before entering the room, bracing his hand on the frame above his head. Concern stretched his skin tight to his jaw. "I need you, Pixie."

Her lip wobbled. "You said that. And I'm sorry, I can't—"

"Shh. That's not what I meant," he said, keeping his voice low. "Mackenzie's gone into labor. She's been having contractions all day, mistook it for a sore back. And she's begging for you. She's really worried about delivering early."

"Oh, God." Lauren shot to her feet. Grabbing his hand, she yanked him toward the nearest flight of stairs.

She'd been present for about twenty births—some as an intern, some as an attending—and she'd always found the delivery process sharpened her brain, making every part of the births clear in her mind.

Not so with Mackenzie's. The lack of official responsibility in the delivery took away the distinct sense of time. The hours blurred. Keeping Mackenzie calm. Keeping Andrew calm. Holding hands. Counting minutes between contractions.

For a first birth, and a premature one at that, Mackenzie's labor went fast. Intense, sure—she turned the air blue a few times—but no complications.

At three sixteen in the afternoon, Lauren breathed a sigh of relief. Her nephew's Apgar score was a nine out of ten, his lungs were developed, and aside from being a little small, there were no aftereffects of being born premature.

Her nugget of a nephew nestled against his mama under Andrew's watchful eye. Holy crap, Lauren was so the third wheel all of a sudden. Well, fourth.

"They're going to want to move you to a recovery room now, Kenz. I should go," she said.

Hair lank against her flushed face, Mackenzie sent Lauren an exhausted smile. "Thank you for being here."

"Thank you for letting me." She traced a finger down the cheek of her dad's new namesake. "You cooperate for your mama, okay, Teddy?"

She walked around to give Andrew a hug. "Congratulations, Daddy."

Despite the under-eye circles betraying his need for

sleep, her brother still managed to grip her with grizzly bear strength. "I didn't understand until I saw him, Laur, but wow. I'm going to give my boy the world. Just like Dad did for us."

Just like Dad. Give my boy the world.

Like every parent should do. She held on to her brother as shame weakened her knees. If she sheltered her child as she'd been doing herself, she'd be depriving the sprout in the worst way. Her brother glowed with devotion after all of fifteen minutes of parenthood. She'd feel the same way about her baby, would travel to Mongolia if it meant making him or her happy. And chances were, with half of Tavish's chromosomes, the kid would crave adventure.

Straightening, she stepped away from Andrew and took a centering breath. She would have to find a balance between settling and soaring. Doing so would mean a hell of a readjustment between her and the man lying two floors up in a hospital bed. Years of habitual guilt tried to rise, bubbling in her stomach.

Enough. Dad will be fine.

Her instincts didn't want to believe it, but she'd find a counselor who could give her strategies to deal with her fears. Untying herself from the burdens of her mother's and grandparents' deaths wasn't going to cause her to lose her good memories of them. And her family wasn't going to desert her if she wasn't there for them every moment. Her priorities needed to fully shift to creating a well-rounded life with the tiny being she was going to bring into the world, and to the man with whom she wanted to share each moment of parenthood.

Of everything.

"You'll be a fabulous father," she told her brother.

"And you'll be a fabulous mother," Mackenzie cut in.

Lauren stilled. Knowing smiles stretched both Mackenzie's and Andrew's faces. "You knew?"

"Tavish spilled the beans," Mackenzie explained. "But I got a little busy here, forgot to bring it up."

"I— Yeah. I'm seven weeks along."

"Amazing," Mackenzie said. Her expression went serious. "You'll be great together."

Lauren's stomach tumbled somewhere near the foot pedals of the adjustable bed. "I— Maybe. Instead of fighting for him, I told him to leave. I shouldn't have," she said in a rush when Andrew's eyebrows rose and Mackenzie's mouth firmed into a line. She took a deep breath. "And if he's headed for the airport again because of me being an idiot, I'll never forgive myself."

"Go find him. Talk to him. You'll figure it out." Laying a protective hand on her baby as he started to snuffle against her chest, Mackenzie shot Lauren a look hovering between cautious and hopeful. "Promise you'll listen to him."

Her friend's plea buoyed her. She would do more than listen to Tavish. She'd finally say the right thing.

Squinting against the bright primary colors of the maternity waiting room, Tavish pressed dial on his phone for the third time. Lauren had disappeared after their nephew had made his way into the world. He thought she'd returned to her dad's bedside, but nope. Nor was she answering her cell.

He hung up and gritted his teeth. Since when was she the one who took off? She'd started to apologize to him before he'd interrupted her with the news about Mackenzie—had he totally misread the situation? He'd assumed she'd meant *I'm sorry, I was wrong.* Maybe she'd still meant *I'm sorry, I can't do this*. The tendons in his neck tensed.

Where are you? he texted.

Her answer came quickly. I needed some fresh air.

His heart sank. Alone?

No. Come find me.

A picture of water rushing over her feet followed the invitation. Their river spot.

He sprinted for his car and broke a good dozen traffic laws while tearing down the highway to the trail that would lead him to the woman he needed more than the oxygen filling his lungs. By the time he emerged from the path into the clearing, his chest heaved from exertion.

Lauren sat on the log, swaying a little.

He rushed forward and braced his hands at her hips, supporting her slender frame. "Hey, there. Am I going to have to nag you to eat again?"

Settling against his arms, she shook her head. "I had a few energy bars. I'm just tired. Your sister, though. I've got nothing on her. What a heroine."

"You will be, too."

He straddled the log with her in between his knees. She drew her legs to her chest, leaned into him and hummed happily. Some of his tension seeped from his limbs. She wasn't proclaiming her undying love, but she definitely wasn't acting like someone who didn't want to be with him anymore. "You disappeared on me. I thought you'd gone to visit your dad, but he didn't have a clue where you were."

"He was fine. Aunt Georgie was there. And, like I said, I needed the fresh air."

Desperate that her willingness to leave her father's bedside meant she'd be willing to address the roots of what tied her so strongly to home, he flattened a palm against her belly. "I have a few things I need to tell you."

She shook her head. "Me first."

Being in Tavish's arms, soaking up his protection and possession, had to be the best feeling in the world. Loving him had never been the question. And now, she'd finally be able to compromise like he deserved.

Tipping and turning her head, she brushed a kiss along the underside of his jaw. The muscles clenched and released under her lips.

The shadows in his cheeks wavered between a smile and a grimace. God, she needed to erase all that uncertainty from the handsome features she intended to look at for the rest of her life. But where to start? Maybe with the simpler stuff. Ease in slowly.

"I'm starting to feel like a pretty big failure for not knowing what I want to do for a career," she admitted, letting the words betray the ache in her chest.

He stroked her back. "You'll find out a way to turn one of your hobbies into a job."

"I was thinking about how much I loved helping out the Canoe and Kayak Club with their athletic training back when I was in college. Had I not been so freaked of surgery, I would have probably gone into orthopedics. Maybe I can look into going back to school, get some more education and work at the new holistic health center like Cadie..."

"Just focus on finding something you find fulfilling," he said. "No one will think less of you if you take a few months to decide."

"I'll be showing by then. That'll limit my options."

Holding her head to his chest with a palm, he stayed silent.

Aching to fill the silence—to prevent her brain from churning itself into butter—she said, "Helping Mackenzie deliver made me think about my pregnancy a lot."

"I imagine it would," he murmured. "It's definitely been on my mind today."

Speaking of "on my mind..."

"Andrew said you never left the hospital. Even after I told you to go."

His eyes darkened. "I went for a walk. I wasn't going to desert you."

Right. Well. Staring at the water, she took a deep breath. The river faded from evergreen in the center to rusty rock on the edges. It teased the boulders in the middle, bubbling and gurgling in a calming way that completely belied her nerves. "I wanted to come here for a reason. I screwed up the last time we were here. And I need to make it right."

"Okay..."

After a deep breath, she found her courage. "When I was in the delivery room and saw Andrew holding Teddy like the little guy was one of Mom's Venetian glass Christmas ornaments—" Taking one of his hands, she toyed with his callused fingers. "And I mean, I've seen that infinite-parental-love look before, many times in the delivery room, but this time, it was different. So different. That'll be me soon. Us. And when Andrew said he'd give his son the world... I want to be that, do that, for our baby. With you."

A breeze brushed across her skin, threatened to topple the emotional house of cards on which she teetered. She forced her fingers to still and stared at him straight-on. "Ask me. Ask me what you asked me the last time we were here."

His fingers twisted around hers. "I don't want to ask that anymore."

A vise clamped around her chest, turned one notch. "You have to. Please. Believe me. I'll give the right answer."

His slow blink, his rapid lip lick, turned the vise once more. "Lauren... I already believe you. It's all over your face. But I don't need that answer from you anymore. I don't need to know you'll come with me."

"But..." Disappointment clawed back the hope that had started to fill the cracks in her heart. She swallowed. "I thought that's what you wanted."

"It was." He slowly caressed her cheek with his palm. "But as much as you've changed, so have I. I need to know that if I tell you I intend to stay here—for good, with you, with our baby—that you'll trust me. That the issue of my job, or my past tendency to get gone, won't keep coming back. We couldn't live with that haunting us for the rest of our lives."

She owed him not to placate, not to give him the knee-jerk *Of course I trust you* that wanted to rip from her lungs.

"What changed?" she asked.

"The same thing that changed you. I want to give our baby every opportunity possible." His voice was so low, so gravel-filled and raw, she could barely hear him. Picking up a flat, river-polished stone and rolling it between the flattened fingers of both his hands, he flicked it at the water. It skipped once, twice, three times before sinking. Inhaling deeply, he continued.

"The last time we were here...we'd just made love. You wanted to stay. And all I wanted was to get the hell out—not away from you, or away from our relationship, but out of Sutter Creek."

She remembered that. His tense jaw, so handsome but so wrecked. His fraught plea. *Love me enough to come with me.*

Now, she loved him enough to go anywhere.

But more than that, she loved herself enough to allow her to go. Loved her family enough to know they'd support her in that decision.

And the contrast between Tavish's face today and his face the last time they'd been here was as clear as the water rushing past their feet. All panic, gone. All skittishness, gone.

And, most importantly, he wasn't gone.

"You want to stay," she breathed.

"Damn right, I do. I'm not my father. And I promise you I'll never become him." The gravity in his expression, not sad-serious, but one that acknowledged the profundity of the situation while still sparkling with anticipation, solidified her shaky foundation.

She knew Tavish. And he was telling God's honest truth. Every molecule in his body projected a singular message: he wasn't going anywhere.

Not now, not ever.

"I trust you." The dregs of fear melted into the log and down into the sand at her feet as she burrowed into his embrace. "And I'll be happy with one child, so that we can stay more portable."

He shook his head. "I want a big family. We can work on turning that house of yours into a home of ours. I spent my twenties running all over the world. My thirties will be about creating my own—our own—world. You. Me. Kids. Our parents and siblings and nieces and nephews." He reached into his back pocket and pulled out his passport. "I've always carried this on me. Take it. Safeguard it. Our children are going to need stability."

She took it from his hand and slipped it back into his pocket. "No. You hang on to it. Yeah, kids need stability, Tav. But they need wonder, too."

"Then let's give them both. Starting with parents who love and are committed to each other." He shifted her out of his lap and knelt in the sand, looking up at her in earnest. "Will you marry me, Lauren? Again?"

"Yes." A wave of unstoppable joy erupted, shimmering perfection throughout every pore of her skin. "Yes!"

He unfastened his bracelet and linked it onto her wrist, threading the toggle through a middle link to make it fit. The loose end dragged against the back of her hand. She stroked the center links, the rings they'd exchanged last summer. "We can have these reshaped into bands."

Surprise lit his features. He rose, sat and pulled her onto his lap again. "You don't want to start fresh?"

"No." Letting the warmth of the sun, and of Tavish's love, sink in, she pressed her lips to the corner of his mouth, then tilted over and took his mouth in a full, sensuous kiss. "Our past has made us just as much as our present and our future. I want to be rid of the barriers that have kept us apart, but I still want to hang on to the love I had for you then. It's just a matter of building on it. Of creating our home together."

"Home's wherever you are, sweetheart. And I've never wanted to have it so much."

Epilogue

Fourteen months later

Lauren smoothed a hand up her infant daughter's straining back. Points to her sister for swearing Ben sensed his mommy's anxiety. It sure seemed to be the same for Charlotte. All the misery in the world was screwed into her tiny, teary face. Lauren's heart ached with guilt at the same time it jittered with nerves.

"I'm sorry, sweetheart," she whispered, bobbing around the kitchen island. "Shh."

"I'll get her calm. And you, too." Hips resting against the counter, Tavish tugged at Lauren's upper arm until both she and Charlotte were encircled by strong muscles. His wide palm rested on Charlotte's back, working its magic as usual. The baby's snuffles turned happy, and she nuzzled into Lauren's chest.

"I shouldn't be going back to school so soon," she

squeaked, melting into her husband's embrace. "Charlotte's barely six months old—what if she gets hungry, or starts crying or..."

Tavish's lips curved against Lauren's cheek. "If she gets hungry, I'll feed her. If she cries, I'll find a way to make her stop. And in three hours, when your classes are over, you can come back and make sure I've done a good job."

His words slowed her pulse from a sprint to a jog. "You're so fricking good at being a daddy. And a husband," she added in a rush.

He toyed with her finger, rubbed his thumb against the gold band he'd put there last New Year's Eve. Nine months later and it felt like the ring was a part of her. If only it didn't feel like she was sawing off a limb by leaving her daughter to upgrade her health education coursework, and everything would be back to normal. But she needed to take this step. She'd worked at the holistic health center from when it opened last fall until Charlotte's birth, and she wanted to take the exam to become a Community Health Education Specialist, which meant upgrading her degrees with some sociology credits.

"How about I play chauffeur?" he offered. "I'll take Charlie and she can nap in my office."

Tavish had gone from artist-in-residence at Montana State to sessional instructor within two semesters. His classes had filled up quicker than any other photography course. Lauren had been tempted to take one herself, but it didn't quite fit in with her program. Plus, she could get private lessons from the most in-demand instructor on campus any time she wanted.

"Okay," she said sheepishly. "I'll drive myself on Friday, I promise. These are just first-day jitters."

"Pixie, I'll drive you anywhere, anytime. In fact, how

does bypassing school, driving on to New York City sound?" he said, clearly teasing.

"That would completely waste the tickets we have booked for our anniversary," she scolded.

"I can't wait to take you up Rockefeller Center." His eyes lit as they started to get the diaper bag ready for their daughter. "But promise me we'll come right back home?"

"If you want."

Utter seriousness, blended with utter contentment, set his eyes a deep violet. "I have everything I want right here. No place in the world could ever compare."

* * * * *

LET'S TALK
Romance

For exclusive extracts, competitions
and special offers, find us online:

JOIN US ON SOCIAL MEDIA!

Stay up to date with our latest releases, author news and gossip, special offers and discounts, and all the behind-the-scenes action from Mills & Boon...

 millsandboon

 millsandboonuk

 millsandboon

It might just be true love...

MILLS & BOON

MODERN

Power and Passion

Prepare to be swept off your feet by sophisticated, sexy and seductive heroes, in some of the world's most glamourous and romantic locations, where power and passion collide.

MILLS & BOON
MEDICAL
Pulse-Racing Passion

Set your pulse racing with dedicated, delectable doctors in the high-pressure world of medicine, where emotions run high and passion, comfort and love are the best medicine.